Quebec, C
May 28, 1...

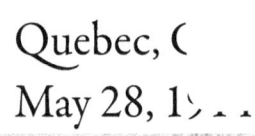

S.S. Empress of Ireland

The Empress of Ireland

Juliet Rosetti

Published by Moonbow Books, 2025.

This is a work of fiction. Similarities to real people, places, or events are entirely coincidental.

THE EMPRESS OF IRELAND

First edition. January 20, 2025.

Copyright © 2025 Juliet Rosetti.

ISBN: 979-8230097600

Written by Juliet Rosetti.

To my mother, who made readers of us.

Chapter One

St. Lawrence River docks, Quebec
    4:27 p.m.

The cat was a ginger: tiger-striped and golden-eyed. Unusual for a ginger, it was female, its sides bulging with unborn kittens.

She'd been the ship's cat on the great liner for four years, ever since she'd been a kitten herself. The thrum of engines vibrating up through the deck was familiar to her; sometimes she purred in response.

The cat's sensitive ears picked up the chunk of shovels, the rattle of coal, the hiss of water heating to steam from the boiler rooms below. Whistles shrilled; men shouted; bells clanged. She knew what it meant: the ship would soon be moving.

A vibration tickled her paws: the slop of waves against the ship's bow, far below. The pulsations weren't right: she could *feel* the wrongness through the pads of her paws.

Something...

Her whiskers quivered; her ruff hair spiked.

Fog.

Nervously, she paced the space that was her refuge—a storage locker on the forward deck, a place safe from the trampling feet of passengers, the marauding hands of children.

Her refuge no longer felt safe. It felt like a trap.

A man flung open the locker door and poked his head in—the man who brought food and dried her with a warm towel when ocean spray drenched her fur. "Ow's my Tabby, then?" he cooed, hunkering down, holding out a plate of fish still warm from the frying pan, the smell so delicious it made her drool; she could almost feel the tiny bones crunching between her teeth.

Yet the urge to flee was stronger than her hunger. It was a sickness now, a desperation to be away from this place. She shot between the surprised man's legs, bounded up a hatchway, dashed along the deck, veered toward the gangplank, thronged with boarding passengers.

"Oi! Grab that cat!" called the man, now much too close behind. The cat put on a burst of speed. Weaving between legs—a splash of marmalade against the burned-toast blacks and browns of passengers' trousers and skirts— she made her way to the bottom, leaped onto the quay.

Someone's suitcase bumped her. She skittered away, streaked along the quayside toward the buildings lining the docks: freight depots, storage sheds, boathouses . . . *There!* A shed whose low-slung porch hid spider-webbed hidey holes. She darted into its shadows.

The man kept shouting for her, burling through the crowd, earning himself curses from the tired, irritable people waiting in line. She watched from her hiding place as he clumped past, still shouting, "Anyone seen a cat?"

The cat's nose led it to the chunk of rotting fish in a corner. Setting a paw on it, she'd just settled down to nibble when a boy's face appeared in a jagged opening. He thrust a groping hand toward her. Growling deep in her throat, she squirmed farther back into the dark space, waited until he went away.

There was an enormous, bellowing *blaaattt*, a ground-shaking noise that set up a tremor in the shed's floor. The noise hurt her ears, but didn't frighten her; she'd heard it hundreds of times. The stink of coal came to her nostrils as smoke from the ship's giant stacks boiled out, turning the air gray all around, spraying clinkers. For a dizzying moment it seemed as though the massive ocean liner stood still while the land moved away.

Then the ship was gone, the coal stench whipped away by the sea breeze. Gulls flapped down onto the posts of the pier, squabbling over scraps of garbage. Watching them through half-closed eyes, the cat wondered whether the gulls were good to eat.

Chapter 2

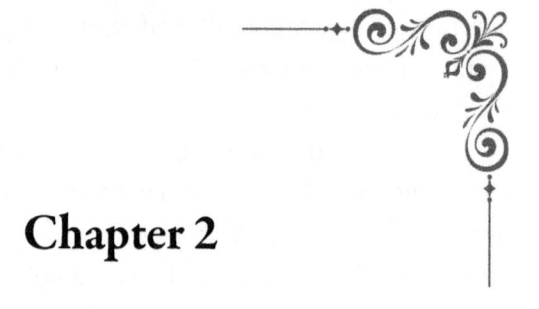

4:40 PM
St. Lawrence River, off Ile d'Orleans

Chief Steward Hazlitt glared at the man slouched before him, mouth set in a mutinous line, hands jammed in pockets.

His name was Reggie Ludsnap. *Of course it was Ludsnap.* Who else had ever given him so much aggravation?

"You were supposed to be up on deck toting luggage, showing passengers to their staterooms, checking passports," Hazlitt snarled. "Instead, you go chasing after some damned stray cat—"

"It weren't no stray. It were *my* cat. My own personal cat, like."

"You were running all over the blasted ship, shoving aside the *first class* passengers, acting like a jackass—I've already had two complaints and we've only been underway twenty minutes. Gad, man—we're loaded to the scuppers with nabobs and bigwigs. Lord and Lady Montgrief, the mayor of Toronto, Duchess Something or Other, the chief of some god-forsaken Pacific island—"

Ludsnap bristled. "Not one of 'em is worth a whisker off my Tabby's chin."

"Consider yourself on report, pending disciplinary action," snarled Hazlitt, "on charges of failing to perform your duties in a *'good and seamanlike order'* as specified in the ship's code of conduct. If I wasn't so short on crew, I'd have you thrown overboard."

THE EMPRESS OF IRELAND

A flicker of fear crossed Ludsnap's face. "Can't ruddy swim, can I?"

"That's your lookout, ain't it? Now get the hell out before I decide to toss you over the side myself."

Wouldn't be all that tough a job, Hazlitt mused. Ludsnap was a scrawny Liverpool wharf rat—all gristle, bones, and mouth. Popular with passengers, though, he grudgingly admitted. The cabinet minister and his wife who made the voyage to England yearly had specifically asked that he be assigned to their stateroom.

Soon's they landed in Liverpool, though, he'd give Ludsnap the bum's rush, Hazlitt vowed. That particular piece of Scouse garbage might be fit for a tramp steamer, but he had no place here, aboard the pride of the Canadian Trans-Global Line—the elegant *Empress of Ireland*.

⁕

"Give us a cuppa, Marie," Reggie Ludsnap begged, letting himself into the kitchen through the *Staff Only* door. "Hazlitt just gave me a royal bollocking — I'm in need of your strongest stuff."

"You think I ain't got better things to do than wait on you, Snapper?" Marie growled. "I got a thousand meals to get out, in case you didn't notice." But she didn't mind, not really; she had a soft spot for Snapper, who took shameless advantage, though he was the only one who could get round her. As Head Cook on the huge ocean liner, she oversaw a staff of thirty. She'd been told she scared people; in fact some of the staff believed she could put the evil eye on them. Her size alone was enough to intimidate people.

She was tall, as women in her tribe tended to be, big-shouldered and broad in the stern— Snapper's teasing term for her big bottom. She was Ojibwe, from the *Aan'aawenh*—the Pintail Duck clan. Her eyes were large and dark, her cheekbones wide, her hair crow-black, its wiry curls a curse from some distant voyageur who'd had a taste for native women.

"What'd you do *this* time?" asked Marie, snatching the tea kettle off the burner and pouring steaming water over Earl Grey leaves. "Why's Hazlitt puttin' the hooks in you?"

"I were only trying to catch my Tabby." Snapper's voice wobbled. "She run away, Marie! I brung her a nice plump herring, cooked just how she likes it, but when I try to hand it over, she up and takes off. Runs clear off the ship! Now why she gone and done that, ey? I treated 'er good, didn't I? From the time she were a kit no bigger'n a scone. When we got to Liverpool I was gonna take her to me mum's, see that she had a nice safe place on account of her being in the family way—Tabby, I mean—not Mum. I could feel them kits right through her belly. Mum's mad for cats—she would of loved Tabby, but now Tabby's took off—and when I chased her she went and hid. She ain't never acted that way before."

"I donno, Snapper." Marie passed Snapper the sugar bowl, knowing his sweet tooth. "Cats just act strange sometimes. They can see spirits, you know."

"Ahh, that's a lot o' scutter."

"Don't you scutter *me*! Ain't you never seen a cat staring at something in a room you can't see, but the cat's eyeballs is tracking something?"

"Yeh, I guess. Tabby done that sometimes."

"Cats *know* things that humans don't, I'm telling you." Marie slid a yeast roll over to Snapper. "You know about the Titanic cat, don't you? Mouser, her name was—belonged to one of the ship's stokers. Ten minutes before the ship upped anchor, Mouser carried her kittens off the ship, one by one, clamped in her mouth, and no matter how anyone coaxed her, she wouldn't go back on that ship. Somehow that cat *knew* the ship was doomed."

"Ahh, come on, pull me other leg, lass." Snapper crammed the roll into his mouth. No matter how much he ate, he never gained an ounce. He was rake-skinny but ropy with muscle beneath his steward's uniform. He was blue-eyed, with sandy, cow-licked hair and ears that stuck out like signal flags. He claimed to be thirty, but Marie guessed twenty-four was closer to the mark. "You think my Tabby got the heebie-jeebies cuz she felt the ship was cursed or something?"

"Animals *know* things!" Marie picked up an onion, set it on a wooden block, and began chopping, the knife chunking in a rapid rat-a-tat. "They can feel stuff that humans can't."

"Ehh, get on with ya! This ship is safe as houses. Lloyds o' London went over her with a fine tooth comb, bilges to bridge, before they'd give 'er the old thumbs-up— and Lloyds don't sign off unless everything's all shipshape and Bristol fashion. This is the sixth crossing I been on with the Empress and the worst ever happened was that time everyone got sick off those bad fish. I was cleaning up puke for days."

"No bad fish ever came out of *my* kitchen," Marie flared.

"Nah, nah, it were that Typhoid Mary what filled in that time you was off trying to get your kiddos back." He slurped the last of his tea, stood up, patting his pockets. "I'm out. Borrow me some bifters, old girl?"

Marie reached into her apron, pulled out a crumpled pack of cigarettes, slapped it into his palm. "This what you're looking for? Half the time I don't know what you're talking about."

"That accent's purest Liverpool, me girl. Called *Scouse.*" He leaned into the stove flame to light his cigarette. "Gotta go. Ta for the scran, Memengwa."

Marie flapped a dishtowel at him, shooing him out, laughing. *Memengwa* was her Ojibwe name. *Butterfly*, it meant—a name gift from her grandmother. Snapper was the only one she'd told, and he liked calling her by it.

She turned back to the stove. She had two hundred Parker House rolls to bake and the third class tea to have on the table by five o'clock. Third class always ate early, unlike first and second, whose dinners were set at the more fashionable eight-thirty.

Glancing out through a porthole, Marie caught a glimpse of the river. The St. Lawrence was wide as a lake here, vibrant blue, speckled with chunks of thawing ice. Even though it was the end of May, this *was* Canada, after all, and Spring came along as slow as a boy on his way to the dentist. But today's departure had come amid clear, sunny weather. Everyone had seemed in high spirits; there had been no complaints of lost luggage, no ill omens. Except for Snapper's cat.

Nothing could explain why a small ginger cat had been so desperate to flee the ship.

Chapter 3: Bridey Collins

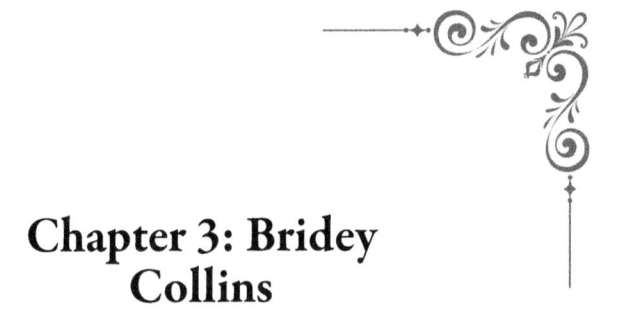

It took all of Bridey's self-control not to roll her eyes as her employer, Lavinia Wilberforce, dithered over which outfit to wear, having dragged every single gown out of her steamer trunk. She was holding them up one by one, striking poses in front of the floor-length mirror, turning this way and that, eyeing the results with a critical eye.

"It is absolutely *vital* that I make a good show this evening," Lavinia prattled. "My first appearance in the dining salon will set the tone for the entire voyage. I need to *establish* myself, d'you understand?"

She flung down the bat-winged, beaded Schiaparelli and peevishly kicked aside the burgundy crepe Dior crumpled on the floor.

Eleven thousand dollars worth of clothing there, Bridey thought—and not one of those gowns would accomplish the impossible: make Lavinia slim and beautiful.

And who'd be up all night ironing knife edges into the fussy little pleats or pressing around the beads without melting them? Why, *herself of course!*

"I need to look polished," Lavinia said, inspecting a pair of pointy-toed satin pumps. "I won't have those women with their fancy English pedigrees snobbing it over me because I'm from the provinces! I intend to establish the pecking order immediately."

Pecking order was right, Bridey thought, smothering a snicker. Lavinia's feathers ruffled easily; she puffed up like an angry hen when she was angry; her turkey wattle neck quivered, and her beady dark eyes, beneath hard-edged crescents she drew on with a black pencil, were always on the lookout for a tasty scrap of gossip.

She was in her late fifties, Bridey estimated, and none of her expensive creams were disguising her age any more than the chin strap she wore at night was defeating her jowls.

As for the dye job she'd had done just before the voyage, in an attempt to achieve Mary Pickford's fetching blonde curls—it had turned her hair an unflattering brass.

She insisted that Bridey call her *Madame*—as though she'd married into royalty rather than to a man who'd made his fortune selling shoe polish door to door in Moosejaw, Saskatchewan.

"Don't just stand there, you dozy twit," Madame snapped. "My hair needs doing. Get out the curler."

Groaning inwardly—because Madame's hair took *hours,* Bridey rummaged through the jumble of luggage, cosmetics, shoes, and the rest of the mess Madame had made of her stateroom in just an hour. At last she found the thing——a metal contraption with a hollow barrel.

Bridey, who'd never even been on a rowboat, had pictured the ocean liner like the illustrations in books—masts and billowing sails and sailors climbing the rigging. To her surprise, the liner was a modern-looking vessel, all sharp lines and angles, with two enormous copper-colored smoke funnels. It was steam-powered, like a locomotive. And it was *electrified!*

Every stateroom had a chandelier with light bulbs and an electric kettle. You just plugged the kettle in and five minutes later you had water hot enough for a cup of tea—or in this case, hot enough to fill the barrel of the curling device. Pouring in the boiling water, Bridey was extra cautious, because the thing was like a big metal insect, likely to sting if you weren't careful.

Madame plunked down on the bed—another surprise for Bridey, who'd pictured rows of crude cots, not this feather bed with a padded headboard and a satin coverlet. It was like a room in a grand hotel, Bridey thought—not that she'd ever actually been in a hotel; she was from Charlesbourg, a working class suburb of Quebec—elegance of any kind was hard to come by.

Bridey set to work, first sectioning off a strand of Madame's hair with a comb, setting a tissue-thin paper over it, then twirling it around the barrel of the curling iron, fastening it in place with a bobby pin. Madame's hair was limp and fine, unlike Bridey's own thick, wavy auburn hair—hair that was the envy of her friends, but was a nuisance—it took forever to dry, and however tightly pinned, would spring loose whenever it damn well pleased. She disliked her eyebrows, too—dark wings totally out of style in a world where Lillian Russell's plucked brows and cupid bow lips set the standards for female beauty. She *did* like her eyes, though—Mum's eyes—wide and blue-green.

Bridey's arms soon ached from the strain of setting Madame's curls. Her back hurt, too, from bending over at an awkward angle, and her stomach—well, her stomach had been tetchy ever since she'd set foot on the ship.

Only it wasn't seasickness, Bridey thought, fear quickening her heartbeat; she'd thrown up that morning, back in the Wilberforce mansion on Rue St. Germaine, then had hastily brushed her teeth and spritzed on cologne before Madame could notice the sick smell on her breath.

Lavinia was not an intelligent woman. She had no interests beyond fashion and the doings of the British royal family. When she read, her lips slowly sounded out the words—but even the dullest-witted woman could twig that a girl who was sick in the morning might be pregnant.

And if she *did* find out? The thought made Bridey's hands shake, and she botched a curl. No doubt about it, Madame would throw her out. Perhaps literally. Bridey could picture Walson, the butler, kicking her down the front steps of the Wilberforce mansion while Lavinia screeched "I'll have no filthy sluts in *my* house!"

"Look what you've done, you clumsy cow!" Madame suddenly shrieked. "You've frizzled the right side!" Face crimson with temper, Madame snatched up the curling iron and struck Bridey with it, the barrel clunking her skull and burning the side of her neck, making her cry out in pain and shock.

"This is the most important night of the voyage and you have *ruined* it for me!" Lavinia's face was so contorted that Bridey stumbled backwards, frightened. When Madame was in a temper, there was no predicting what she might do.

"I'm s- sorry!" Tears sprang to Bridey's eyes. It was so unfair—she'd curled Madame hair the same way as always—but the dye must have had chemicals or some such in it that made her hair unusually dry and brittle.

"If we weren't on board this ship I'd sack you this second!" Madame raged. "Oh, *do* stop that sniveling! Go fetch ice water!"

For a stunned moment, Bridey thought Madame was concerned about the burn on her neck, which throbbed painfully and was starting to blister, but in the next instant that foolish notion was dispelled as Madame, scrutinizing her own mottled face in the mirror, snarled, "I can't go to dinner all flushed! I'll need ice water to soothe my face—a quart at least. *Mineral* water!"

"But I don't know where—"

"Ask a steward, you ignorant Irish guttersnipe!"

Chapter 4

The ship was vast and confusing, and Bridey was soon lost in the maze of gangways, stairs and companionways. When they'd arrived aboard a few hours ago, Elmer Wilberforce had led the way; he was familiar with the ship because he and Madame made the voyage on this ship once a year, supposedly due to Elmer's business affairs in England—but Bridey suspected the trip was just an excuse for Madame to parade around showing off her gowns. And this year they'd decided to bring along Bridey to take care of all the irksome tasks that a woman of Lavinia's social standing couldn't be expected to bother with; all of *her* time would be spent socializing, seeing and being seen.

Bridey realized she'd taken a wrong turn several corridors back. She didn't even know which deck she was on. To her relief, she saw a steward ahead—at least she thought he must be a steward; he wore a high-collared dark jacket and the kind of stiff-brimmed hat she thought of as a captain's cap. "Excuse me," Bridey said, hurrying up to him. "Where could I get some ice?"

"*Ice*, ma'am?" The man, who had pouchy eyes and a bushy mustache, grimaced. "No notion a'tall, sorry. I myself am in search of a porthole through which I can divest the contents of my stomach—excuse my crudeness, Miss."

"Oh—but I thought you were—"

"A steward? Second time I've been mistook for one—I suppose it's my uniform. "I'm Ralph Holmes of Toronto, First Sergeant in the

Salvation Army—the army that marches in the service of the Lord. We're a hundred seventy strong aboard this ship— men, women, and children, all of us heading for the world convocation in London." He smiled, his mustache twitching. "Do you like music, Miss? Because our band is performing in the third class general room this evening. All are invited, believers or non-believers. And a thumpin' grand band they is! Be sure you come."

"Yes, I will, I'll try—I've got to—"

She broke away from him and began making her way down a corridor, conscious of time ticking away, of Madame growing angrier and angrier as she waited for her ice water. The ship's kitchen must be nearby, because cooking odors wafted through a ventilation duct—a whiff of frying pork chops that made her stomach lurch. *Oh, please, don't let me be sick—not now!* They'd have ice in the kitchen, though, wouldn't they? She'd find the back door, sneak in and ask someone for ice.

Bridey was concentrating on how she'd manage to carry the ice back without it melting when an arm suddenly shot out from a recessed doorway, seized her and pulled her into a dark alcove between racks of life preservers.

"Hey babycakes," a voice whispered in her ear.

Bridey whipped around to face him. "*Sean!* You scared the daylights out of me!"

"I been looking for you all over the ship."

"Where'd you *think* I was? Trapped in that tiny room waiting on the old hag hand and foot, unpacking her stuff—she's made a pig's eye of that room, trying on and taking off about a million gowns! She'll have me up till midnight, ironing out all the wrinkles!"

"What're you bellyachin' about?" Sean growled. "You're swannin' around in first class with the nobs while I'm down in the bottom, next to the boilers, sweatin' like Paddy's pig!"

THE EMPRESS OF IRELAND

You wouldn't be on this ship at all if I hadn't given you the money for the ticket! It was on the tip of Bridey's tongue, but she bit it back. Sean got surly when reminded that he wasn't earning a penny on his own, him having trouble keeping jobs—but it wasn't Sean's fault that factory jobs, with their brain-numbing repetition—weren't challenging enough for him, or that he was too restless to sit at a desk all day in a clerk's job—that was how he explained it, anyway. His was a body made for action, Sean bragged—he was a warrior, not some pettifoggin' clerk! It *was* a fine body, as Bridey well knew—wide-shouldered and long-legged, and he had the face to go with it, his eyes a startling pale blue beneath black brows, his hair dark and wavy. What spoiled Sean Corkoran's good looks, what stopped him just short of being matinee idol handsome—was his mouth, set in a perpetual pout that proclaimed *I've been robbed of something I'm owed.*

"Sean, let go," Bridey hissed. "If I don't get back soon she'll—"

"What's the hurry? Ain't you got a kiss for your sweetie?" He leaned in and kissed her—hard, biting her lip. She'd told him she hated the biting, but he kept on doing it.

"Hey, you two—get a room!"

It was Gorcey, leering from a nearby doorway. And if Gorcey was here, it meant—*oh Lord, yes, there they were*— the rest of Sean's pack: Murf, Suds, and Moose, as scummy a crew as you could scrape off a saloon floor, mock-punching each other, cackling with laughter, and making crude comments, as though they were eighth grade boys out at recess instead of men in their twenties. Unfortunately, Sean had needed them along to pull off *The Plan.*

"Don't forget, you're part of this, too, Bridey-bird," Sean whispered, pulling her more tightly against him. "You promised you'd help."

"I already *did* help!!" she protested, shoving him away. "Gave you every cent I had!" Leaving herself short—she couldn't even buy herself a packet of hair pins until the tight-fisted Madame finally paid her.

"That ain't the kind of help I mean," Sean said, lowering his voice. "I'm talkin about you being the key player in this whole thing—haha—*key* player, get it? You're our secret weapon, Birdy Brain—you oughter be flattered you got the biggest part."

She hated it when Sean, thinking it was terribly clever, twisted *Bridey* around into *Birdy*. "Oh, leave me be!" she tried to pull away, but Sean clamped her jaw, his hands stinking of cigarettes and greasy food, bringing her face close to his. "I went over all this with you a week ago," he snarled. "Did it fall outa that bird brain of yours? Like I told you, we hafta get into the strong-room—the which has got a padlock the size of a hub cap, all solid iron. It takes *two* keys to open the stinkin' thing, because when you've got two million in bullion sittin' in a room you don't want bums like us breaking in. So the ship's Chief Officer keeps one key, the hired guard keeps the other, and when they get to Liverpool they both got to stick the keys in to unlock the thing."

"Sean, I've *got* to get back—"

"Shuddup and listen." He grabbed her hair, twisting it in his fist until she cried out in pain, his knuckles rubbing the raw burn on her neck. Using her hair as a leash, Sean pulled her into a closet—a storeroom for the kitchen, Bridey assumed from the bins and boxes and the strong smell of coffee beans.

"We already *have* the Chief Officer's key," Sean said, "because I bribed someone on the inside. Flash enough cash and they'd stab their own granny." He gave her a little shake. "Pay attention now, Birdbrain. The key you need to get your hands on will look like this." He pulled a key out of his pocket, about four inches long, new and shiny, its tabs intricately cut.

"What am I supposed to do— just go up to this fella and ask if I can borrow his key?" Bridey asked.

"Don't be stupider than you already are. You play up to him—you know how youse girls do. '*Oh, Mister, let me feel your big muscles! Hey, fella, get a load of these bazooms!*"

He gave her a scathing top-to-bottom once-over. "Fix yourself up, will ya? Put on some powder or something." Scowling, he ran his eyes over Bridey's gray broadcloth uniform, black stockings and sensible shoes. "Don't you got something brighter, maybe low cut to show off your boobs?"

"It's my *uniform*, Sean—she makes me wear it."

"Well, swipe something brighter from the old lady. Red, maybe. Yeah, guys like red. You put your mind to it, you can reel in this sucker like a fish on a line. Play up to him, and while he's distracted you fish the key—"

"You want me to act like a *floozy?*"

"You'll do what it takes for the cause." Sean's mouth tightened into a hard line. "You got to toughen up—you're a soldier of Eire do' Fein now."

"*Eire do 'Fein!* I'm sick to death of hearing about 'em! All those blatherskites ever do is talk big! Far as I'm concerned, they can all go to hell!"

It was a mistake, she realized too late, insulting the cause Sean was so passionately attached to. "*Shut up shut up shut up!*" he ranted, landing a slap with each word—her nose, cheek, eye—and then, temper still on the boil, he punched her in the stomach.

"*Sean—stop it!*" Bridey shrieked. "The *baby!* You'll hurt the baby!" Her heart was beating so wildly she thought it might explode

"*Baby?*" His gaze darted to her belly. "You got a bun in the oven?"

She nodded, using her sleeve to mop the blood drizzling from her nose, knowing she'd have a devil of a time getting the bloodstain out.

"Who put it there then?" He demanded, fixing her with an icy stare. "You been screwing around behind my back? You think I'm too stupid to notice how that Pierre Labeau been sniffing after you? Or don't you even know? Maybe you been letting anyone in pants have a go—"

"How can you *say* that!" croaked Bridey, "You know it's yours. From that time —the day your cousin had her First Communion and you—" she broke into sobs, unable to continue. Bridey had always imagined her first time as a kind of honeymoon, she and Sean in a hotel room, flowers on a table, Sean whispering sweet words, assuring her he'd be gentle because he didn't want to hurt her—

But it hadn't been like that at all. The day of his cousin Rosalie's First Communion—it had been a dreary winter day—while his relatives were down in the kitchen having cake and ice cream, Sean had taken her up to his uncle's garage attic, thrown her down onto a moldy couch with squeaky springs and heaved himself on top of her, his breath sour with the whiskey he'd been swigging all afternoon.

What he'd done to her had made her cry out in pain. That had made him angry; he'd called her a whiny baby and went storming out, leaving her there alone to clean herself up, pressing her rosary's crucifix against her belly, muttering Hail Marys , praying that the horrible thing he'd just done to her wouldn't make her pregnant. That couldn't happen on someone's first Communion, could it—all that holiness floating around ought to provide some sort of protection, oughtn't it?

It hadn't. Praying hadn't helped either. Six weeks later Bridey had realized she was pregnant. She'd been planning to tell Sean about it on the voyage, maybe some night when they were arm in arm, watching the moon rise over the river. Not like this, not with him in such a rage he might harm the baby.

"I can't be tied down with a kid!" Sean began pacing in the narrow, coffee-smelling space. "It'll ruin all my plans. They need me in the movement! Big things are happening and Sean Corkoran is going to be part of them." His lower lip thrust out. "And now you have to go and ruin everything for me, getting yourself knocked up, you dumb bitch!"

He punched the wall, and a burlap sack fell over, spilling navy beans off a shelf; they made a *pip-pip-pip* noise as they bounced on the floor.

" I d-didn't do it on purpose, Sean," Bridey pleaded.

"Yeah, I bet. I got it as a fact from Cubby Reardon that a woman can make a baby *take* inside if she wants—so's she can trap a guy into marrying her, ruinin' the dumb sap's life.'

"But we love each other, Sean! We-we're getting married."

His eyes narrowed. "Don't count on it. You think I want to marry someone who won't even do what she's told? I need you to help with this key business, and all you do is whine about it."

"I'm sorry, Sean, but playing up to some man, I-I-just can't—"

"Look, it ain't like you're some innocent little virgin. I took care o' that, dint I? So you just walk past the guy, waggling your sweet little fanny, then you act like you twisted your ankle or something and he's a gent, so he stops and helps the poor little frail girly—"

He fluttered his eyelashes and pooched his lips. "You turn on the charm, use some of those waterworks on him. Get him alone somewheres, maybe you let him get to first base, maybe you reach in his pants, play a little yank the handle, while he'd distracted you fish out the key—"

"I won't!" Bridey suddenly exploded, her burst of anger surprising even herself. "I won't act the whore for you, Sean Corkoran—it's crude and disgusting and I—oh, God, I wish I was dead!" She wrenched open the closet door and staggered out, feeling as though she'd aged a hundred years in the past ten minutes.

"Come on, Birdbrain, get back here!" Sean burst out of the closet behind her, but Bridey wheeled away from him, wanting only to be away from him, alone, like a wounded animal. *Sean didn't want to get married! And he didn't want the baby!* She'd known he wouldn't be thrilled—after all, he barely had money to support himself, let alone a child, but she'd imagined that he would be at least a *little* glad.

Blinded by tears, not knowing where she was going, Bridey reeled along corridors, tripped up stairways, and at last heaved open a heavy sliding door, finding herself out on an open deck. Wind cooled her burning face, whipped her hair. In front of her was a railing and beyond that was nothing but water and sky.

Lurching to the railing, she gazed down at the sea—well, a river, really, but it looked like an ocean —a wide expanse of seething blue-gray water, glinting with a million points of light so brilliant they hurt her eyes.

What would it feel like to plunge deep, deep, into that water?

What was there to live for, after all? She hated her life. She hated being a servant to her bullying employer, being paid such a measly wage she'd never be able to save up enough to get away. Marriage to Sean was to have been her escape—it was the dream that had sustained her since she'd been a girl.

Sean was four years older than her and had chummed around with her brother Billy. She'd had a crush on Sean for as long as she could remember, spying on him secretly when he came over to play cards or sneak cigarettes with Billy. Sean being so good-looking, he had lots of girlfriends, and Bridey had made up stories in her head about how it would be if *she* were his girlfriend, not just his pal's snot-nosed little sister.

Then came that night at her cousin Ed's wedding. She'd been seventeen; she'd worn her hair up; her face had been pink and flushed from dancing. Sean had seen her from across the room, ditched his steady girlfriend, Lucy Horner, and asked Bridey to dance. As he'd held her in his arms, Bridey had realized that she was in love with him. In just a few years, she told herself, it would be herself and Sean, in this same hall, having their first dance as a married couple.

But that had been five years ago, when she'd still believed all that June-moon-spoon stuff. Now she was twenty-two—too old for silly romantic fantasies. She had to face the ugly truth: Sean didn't want to marry her. By the time they arrived in England, the baby would be showing, and Madame would fire her, and she'd be left on her own in a strange country, not knowing anyone, with no money and no husband, not even knowing how to find a doctor. Probably no respectable doctor would treat an unmarried girl anyway. She had become a *fallen woman. A woman of loose morals.* Without a husband she'd have no way to support herself; she'd have to beg for bread on street corners—

It was all too much. Her life was nothing but pain, guilt, self-loathing. Even the glorious sunset only seemed to mock her misery. Gazing out over the water, though, it occurred to Bridey how quickly she could put an end to all her troubles. Two minutes—that was how long it took to drown, she'd once read.

But if she committed suicide, she'd go to Hell. And the baby she carried—would that innocent little being also go to Hell? From somewhere close by, she could hear Sean yelling for her. Why was he coming after her? Not because he was worried about her; not because he loved her, Bridey now realized; he only wanted her so he could use her for his scheme—a plan that was going to get him and his whole rat pack thrown in jail—and probably herself too.

She climbed a step higher on the railing. She couldn't face a life without the man she loved. She couldn't go back to her hometown, either, because her pregnancy would disgrace her family; Pop would die of shame.

Do it now—before someone tries to stop you!

Trembling all over, her heart thudding so hard it was painful, Bridey hitched herself higher and swiveled around until she was facing out toward the river. She couldn't swim a stroke; she'd sink straight to the bottom. It would be fast.

"*Bridey!* Where are you, Birdbrain?" Sean's voice, close by. Too close.

I'm sorry, little one, she whispered, and tensed herself to jump.

Chapter 5

Snapper

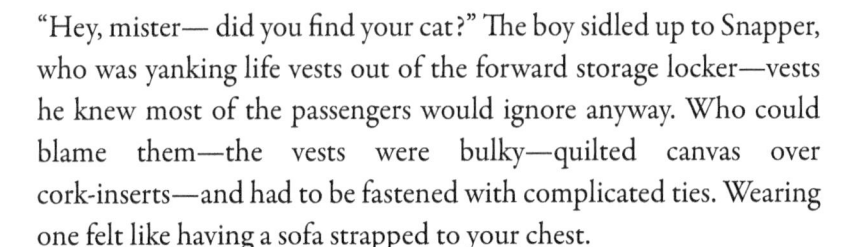

"Hey, mister— did you find your cat?" The boy sidled up to Snapper, who was yanking life vests out of the forward storage locker—vests he knew most of the passengers would ignore anyway. Who could blame them—the vests were bulky—quilted canvas over cork-inserts—and had to be fastened with complicated ties. Wearing one felt like having a sofa strapped to your chest.

Snapper studied the boy, a Black kid around ten years old, curiosity and mischief alight in his eyes. He wore patched pants, a jacket with frayed cuffs and a too-large cap over neatly-trimmed hair.

"Nope," Snapper replied. "Didn't find it. A cat don't want to be found, you ain't gonna find it."

"I seen him! I seen him run off the boat and go hide under this green building that said *Ships Outfitters*. I got down on my belly and reached under and tried to grab him, but I think he was too scared."

"He's a *she,* mate. Name of *Tabby*. And stubborn as most females."

"How come she ran away?"

"Donno why cats do anything, do I? Maybe she got mad at me. Who're *you,* anyway?"

"Charles Barrows. You can call me Charlie."

"Reggie Ludsnap. But everyone calls me Snapper." Reggie extended a hand, which the boy solemnly shook.

"Where's your folks, Charlie—I know you ain't here on your own." Snapper stifled a grin, because he'd already twigged that the kid was a stowaway.

"My folks? They're over there, by that big horn thing." Charlie pointed vaguely toward a cluster of well-dressed people, all of them white as whipped cream, standing beneath a cowl vent on the forward deck. "Uh-huh, that's them, all right!" He waved, cupped his hands, shouted, "Hi, Mum!"

Hi, Mum, indeed! It was that bit of flim-flammery that won Snapper's heart. One of his duties was to roust unticketed passengers exactly like this boy, but he couldn't bring himself to do it; he'd already taken a shine to the kid. Charlie reminded him of himself at that age—poaching rides off trolleys, scrumping apples off push carts, and at twelve, stowing aboard a canal boat that'd dumped him, penniless and starving, in Leeds. "Are you the captain of this boat?" asked Charlie, obviously impressed by Snapper's natty uniform.

Snapper chuckled. "Nah, just a steward, lower than the captain's spittoon. And it's called a *ship*, not a *boat*, got it? C'mon, I'll give you the ten cent tour, turn you into an able-rated seaman. You, young salty sea dog, are standing on the finest ocean liner currently sailing the seas, *the Empress of Ireland*. She runs fourteen thousand tons with a twin screw propeller powered by triple expansion engines. She's five hundred feet long, sixty-five feet in the beam—that's the widest part of the boat, measured port to starboard."

Gripping Charlie's shoulders, he swung him around. "Okay, now we're facing the front of the ship—only us old salts say the *bow*, not the front, got it? And the back of the ship is the *stern*. Now stick out your hands. Go on, hold 'em out." He tapped Charlie's left hand. "Put your thumb and finger together until it makes a *P*."

Charlie did. "It looks like the *Okay* sign."

"Well, it ain't. It's a P. For *Port*. Only landlubbers say left side. Us sailors say *port*."

"Aye, sir." Charlie's mouth quirked in a grin.

The kid was a bit of a wise guy, Snapper noted approvingly. "Awright, now spread out the fingers on your right hand. Wide, so they look like a star. *Star*board, got it? Facing the bow, on your right, that's *starboard*."

He had Charlie repeat it a couple times. He got the lingo fast—bright kid.

"Another thing," Snapper said. "When you're talking about the part of the ship near the stern, you say *aft*. If you're going toward the bow, you say *forward*."

"Forward and aft," Charlie repeated. "Hey, how fast can this ship go?"

"We run her at a speed of twenty knots. That's about twenty-three miles an hour to lubbers. Course we can go faster once we're out on the open ocean, but here on the St. Lawrence we have to run her slower."

"Because we might bump into something?"

"Damn right. We're still two hundred miles upstream from the mouth of the river, where it pours into the Atlantic, so we ain't far from the banks on either side. No guff, Charlie, I won't sleep nights until we're out of this gor-blasted river. Got a evil reputation. Treacherous, see? A fog comes down you can be real close to the shore and never know it until you run aground and find yourself in the middle of a herd of cows. And it's *always* foggy, this time of year. You got all these ice chunks in the water from the snow melting, and then the warm spring air meets the chilled river air and —*wham*—a fog comes out of nowhere, a fog so thick you can take bites out of it like ice cream."

"Ahh, you're fooling."

"I ain't, neither. Now look up there—" Snapper pointed toward the upper deck. 'What do you think that part is called?"

"The top of the boat?"

"That, sailor, is the *bridge*. Where the captain and the officers operate the boat, where the navigational equipment is kept."

"Can we go up and see it?"

"Do you enjoy getting a kick in the arse?"

"What? *No*!" Charlie stared at him.

"Yeah, well that's what the both of us would get if we asked for a sightseeing tour up there while the brass was doing their jobs." Snapper checked his watch. He was supposed to be on duty down in second class, checking that the passengers were in the correct cabins, hauling stray luggage down to the hold, taking a head count so Marie knew how many would be showing up for meals, passing out seasick pills, cleaning up the mess seasick passengers had already spewed —instead he was playing hooky, showing off his sea lore for the kid, who was soaking everything up like a sponge. *But what the hell*—Hazlitt was probably going to fire him anyway. Might as well have a lark before they gave him the heave-ho. They'd reached the mid-ship boat deck now, and Charlie stopped in front of the number five boat. "Hey— a lifeboat!"

"Nah, we use those for bathtubs."

Charlie gave a snort of laughter. "You're fooling."

"You win, mate—that is indeed a lifeboat. Ever heard of the Titanic?"

"Sure! It crashed into an iceberg and a thousand people drowned."

"Weren't the iceberg that killed those poor sods—it were the penny-pinching bastards as didn't put enough lifeboats on that liner." Snapper ran a hand over the gripes on the boat's davits, checking for tautness. "Well, that ain't going to happen on the *Empress*. She's got so many boats we got 'em stacked up on the decks like yesterday's newspapers. Thirty boats in all and each of 'em can hold two dozen people—that's in addition to the collapsibles, which are sort of like rafts—wood and canvas."

"Oh, man, this thing is hard as steel!" Charlie rapped his knuckles against the boat's hull, enjoying the clang it produced.

"Righto—it *is* steel. Solid as houses. Weighs two tons. I'd like to see the wave that could overturn this thing!"

"I want to see where they keep the bullion!" Charlie said, losing interest in the lifeboats.

Snapper shot him a sidelong look. "Now how'd you know about that?"

"The silver *bullion*?" Charlie snickered. "Everybody in Quebec knows about the bullion! The mines out west ship their silver ore downriver to Quebec every spring. My pa told me about it—before he . . . before . . . . while he was still around. He worked at this factory where they strained the bad stuff out of the ore—the impurities, he called 'em, and what's left is pure silver they make into bricks—they're called ingots, I think. And they load two million dollars worth onto this ship when it takes its spring voyage downriver and it goes to—where's it go, anyways?"

Snapper rubbed his jaw, flabbergasted that the cargo of silver bullion was such an open secret. "I donno. London, I s'pose, Paris, Germany—-they don't tell *me*."

"What if someone tried to steal it?"

Snapper elbowed him in the side. "Eh, pull me other leg, boy! That silver is locked up tight in the ship's strong room, the which is plated in two inch thick steel. Double locks on the door, what's also solid steel. You could jackhammer them walls and never make a dent. Plus they got an armed guard—they hires 'im special from the U.S.—sitting outside the strong room day and night. Anyhows, even if you could get in there, how'd you walk off with the bullion? Stick it in your pockets?"

"I still want to see it."

"Awright, only watch your step. Remember what I said about getting a kick in the arse? You get on the wrong side of that Bakersfield guard, you'll have a *bullet* in your arse! Those fellas do not call out a second warning."

Charlie's eyebrows shot up. Probably picturing a rough bloke with a knife clenched between his teeth and bullet bandoliers across his chest, Snapper thought as they clacked down a companionway to E deck, which was crowded with jostling passengers heading for the dining room, among them dozens of Salvation Army members in uniform jackets, toting musical instruments, one of them carrying a tuba so large it was blocking the way of the grumbling passengers behind.

"Let's get out of this dogfight." Snapper led the way down a narrow set of stairs, turned left at the Men's head, and halted in front of a steel door with an enormous padlock and a sign warning *Restricted Area, No Admittance.*

"Where's the guard?" Charlie asked. "I wanted to see his guns."

"He's—" *He wasn't there!* Snapper stared at the empty chair opposite the door. *Where the hell was the guy?* He'd been sitting there every time Snapper happened to pass—a surly Yank with a cig stuck in the corner of his mouth and his piece across his lap. He'd probably gone off to the jakes—but something about his absence felt *off* to Snapper. "Never mind about that," Snapper said. "I'll take you to the wireless room. Loads more interesting."

It was on the top deck, situated as closely as possible to the fifty foot high antennae attached to the ship's mast—it was this which transmitted the radio signals, Snapper explained. As he slid open the wireless room's door, the two wireless operators, Ferguson and Bamford, looked up.

"Oo's this then?" Joe Ferguson asked, giving Charlie a friendly grin. "They's signing up sailors out o'grammar school these days?"

He was twenty-three, with a round, youthful face and a rooster crest of red hair. Alf Bamford was the same age; both had just graduated from the Marconi wireless training program. They wore high-collared white shirts and suit jackets; the Marconi Company liked its employees to look spiffy. Like Snapper, they were Scousers.

"Nah, this is Charlie," Snapper said. "I'm teaching him the finer points of seamanship." This got a bark of laughter from both operators. Charlie stared around, fascinated by the room's complicated equipment, including an apparatus that shot an electrical spark between two knobs. "How's it work?" he asked.

"Look." Alf bent over a gadget on his desk that looked to Charlie a bit like an oversized mousetrap. "When I press down here on my transmitter? If I press real quick, it sends out a dot, and that electric signal goes up the wire to the antennae on the ship's mast, the which is up so high it can send out a radio signal to another antennae—in this case the one on Father Point, just up the river—and they hear the dot there through their headphones. If I hold the key down longer it makes a dash—"

"*Morse code*!" Charlie said excitedly. "I learned it in Boy Scouts!"

A bell jangled in Joe's gadget and the receiver started clicking as though ghostly fingers were pressing on it. He put on a headset and began scribbling a message. "Strictly by the book," Alf told Snapper. "You ain't s'posed to be here, awright?"

"Twenty-two skiddoo, then—we'll bog off." They left the dark room, emerging into light and wind and a horizon ablaze with color, as though enormous vats of rose and purple paint had been splashed across the sky.

"Wow!" Charlie breathed. "It's amazing!"

Leaning on the railing, Snapper fumbled out a cigarette. "Make me choose between a sunset and a pint o' beer, I'll take the sunset."

"Are you allowed to *sit* on the railing?" Charlie asked.

"Yeh, go ahead. Once your stupid self falls in the river, the crabs'll nip off your toes for their tea."

"How come *she's* sitting on the railing then?" Charlie asked, pointing aft, at a slight, gray-clothed form nearly lost in the overhanging shadow of the top deck.

"*Oh, Holy Christ!*" Cigarette still clamped in lips, Snapper erupted into action, thundering down the narrow length of deck, yelling at the top of his lungs, *"Don't do it, don't do it, don't do it!"*

It was a girl, realized Charlie, pounding along in Snapper's wake—and she was about to jump.

But Snapper, putting on a burst of speed, lunged at her, flinging an arm around her middle, pulling her up and backwards all in one motion. Charlie—whose after-school sport was wrestling—would have called it a *full body bind*. Snapper plunked her firmly down onto the deck, her heels clunking on the wood.

Charlie edged up to the girl, who was really pretty, even though she looked kind of beat up. "Were you going to jump?" he asked.

She stared at Charlie out of wild, unfocused eyes, opened her mouth to say something... and collapsed in a dead faint.

Chapter 6

Bridey

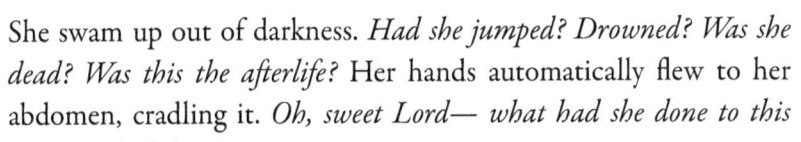

She swam up out of darkness. *Had she jumped? Drowned? Was she dead? Was this the afterlife?* Her hands automatically flew to her abdomen, cradling it. *Oh, sweet Lord— what had she done to this innocent little being?*

The aroma of frying onions drifted to her nostrils. How odd that devils—or angels—would be cooking something so mundane! Bridey's eyes flickered open.

A woman was leaning over her, sloshing a warm, wet washcloth over her face and numb hands. It felt lovely on her chilled body—this *must* be heaven—although the woman, who was large and bosomy, with a mass of black hair and wearing a grease-speckled apron, didn't resemble the angels on church windows.

"Feeling better, honey?" She spoke in a husky voice, a voice that sounded like brown sugar and cinnamon in warm milk. "You think you could tell me your name?"

"Bridget Marie Collins," Bridey rasped. "Everyone calls me Bridey."

"Bridey Marie—that's pretty. My name's Marie too. Marie Lavallier. I'm the head cook.

"How... where *am* I?"

It was a stupid question, Bridey realized. The clamor of banging pots and scraping spoons, the aromas of brewing coffee, melting butter, and baking bread—she was in the ship's kitchen, or close to it, lying on a cot, propped up on a pillow that smelled like Lux soap, in a narrow alcove —a sick bay, she guessed, where the kitchen staff got treated for cuts and burns and suchlike. She could just glimpse the enormous ship's kitchen, where white-uniformed men and women were scurrying around, stirring the contents of large kettles, thumping pans of bread into giant ovens, rolling out pie crusts, chopping vegetables at reckless speed...

Memory returned with a sickening jolt; Bridey sat upright. *"Ice!"* she moaned. "Oh, Lord—I was supposed to get ice for Madame! She'll have my hide!"

"She the one give you this?" Marie put a finger on Bridey's bruised eye. As delicate as the touch was, it still hurt.

"No," Bridey whispered. "It was my boyfriend—he got mad when I—"

Everything swarmed back: Sean wanting her to act like a tart to get the key off the guard. Their quarrel, his cruel words, his punching her. The memory brought hot tears; she brushed them away, ashamed of being such a weakling.

"This boyfriend—he the one who gave you this too?" Marie asked, lightly patting Bridey's stomach.

Bridey gasped. "You *know?* How did you—do I look fat, do I *show?*"

"No, sweetie." Marie gently raked Bridey's hair out of her eyes. "When you came to just now, first thing you did was set your hand over your belly —it's a thing pregnant women do, like an instinct, I guess. But it ain't just that. I can tell when a woman has a baby inside. It's like the baby is—I don't know how to explain, but it's like the baby is trying to tell me it exists, that there's a little soul in there. I know that sounds cockamamie—don't ask me to explain it. I've just always had it. Sometimes I know before the woman knows herself."

Marie dabbed a wet cloth on Bridey's cut lip. "Maybe it's because I'm from a long line of medicine women. My grandmother always knew when a person was going to die. But it passed down to me the opposite direction. I can tell when a little human first begins to *exist*. And your baby's a *girl*, by the way."

Marie heaved herself to her feet, left the alcove, and came back a minute later with a cup of tea on a saucer. "You drink this now," she ordered. "I put in extra sugar because it helps when you're recovering from a —well, let's call it a *shock*."

"I tried to do away with myself, " whispered Bridey, taking the cup, which jiggled in her trembling hands.

"Lucky for you, Snapper grabbed you before you could go through with it. Then you fainted and he brought you in here, scared you'd try for a round two."

"But I *wanted* to end it!" Bridey wailed, slopping tea. "I don't want to go on!"

Marie patted her shoulder. Bridey held her breath, expecting a sermon. Instead Marie said, "Who's this *Madame* you're scared of?

"Mrs. Wilberforce. She's—"

"*Her!* No wonder you tried to kill yourself! I would too if I worked for that she-devil."

"You k-know her?"

Marie laughed. "Everyone on the staff knows that nasty old witch! Always demanding special treatment, nothing's ever good enough for her, she goes around claiming she's a cousin of Nathan Bickerstaff, the muckety-muck who owns this ship, and whatever you serve her, she'll find something wrong and send it back."

"That's exactly what she's like! She got mad at me for botching her hair!"

Marie winked. "I always make a point of spittin' in her soup."

Bridey surprised herself by laughing out loud, delighted at the image of Lavinia's spat-in soup.

"How long you worked for that grizzly-in-a-girdle?" asked Marie.

"Just a few months. Before that I worked as a general maid for another family— scrubbing, laundry, lots of heavy work. Then I heard that Madame—that's what I have to call Mrs. Wilberforce—was looking for a lady's maid. Running errands, washing her dainties, doing her hair, that kind of thing—it sounded so cushy! But then when I didn't do things right, like ironing her blouses, she'd throw a fit. One time she beat me with a clothes hanger!"

Unaware that she was doing it, Bridey rubbed the burn on her neck. "She made me go along to England with her and Mister, made it sound like it would be a jolly holiday, said they were paying my ticket in place of my wages— but it's not been a holiday at all—I'm still working around the clock, and I don't have a moment's privacy—and I'm scared of what will happen when she finds out I'm going to have a baby. She'll fire me for sure, and I'll be stuck in a foreign country, not knowing anyone."

"What about your folks, your family?" Marie asked.

Bridey slurped tea from the saucer, knowing it was uncouth, but somehow tea tasted better that way. "My ma died when I was sixteen. There's just my older brother and my pops—who'll likely die of shame when he finds out what I went and did."

"Got pregnant, you mean?"

The blunt words made Bridey wince.

"Listen, now—did you do this to yourself?" Marie's black brows drew together in a scowl. "No gal gets herself pregnant. There's always a man—and they don't always ask before they do the nasty."

"I—I didn't want to, but if I didn't let him, I thought he'd—"

"Stop loving you if you didn't give in?" Marie gave a bark of laughter. "Sweetie, every rotter in the world pulls that one."

"We were planning to get married—but now he won't."

"Count yourself lucky."

"What am I going to do?" Bridey moaned.

"First thing? You're going to eat." Marie set an ice cube wrapped in gauze against the burn on Bridey's neck. "Hold that there till I come back."

Marie hurried out and returned a minute later holding a bowl of something golden and savory-smelling. "It's chicken broth, with a bit of carrot and potato and onion. It's been simmering all afternoon—it's intended for first class—only for them its *soupe au poulet.*" She handed Bridey a spoon. "Go on, *eat!* You need to get your strength back. You're eating for your baby now, too."

Bridey took a sip. Then another. Finally abandoning restraint, she slurped an enormous spoonful. "O*hhh.... so good,*" she breathed, and proceeded to spoon up every drop, scraping the bowl and ending with a resounding burp.

"Good girl," Marie said, chuckling. "All right, next problem—getting you back to your room and bringing the old harpy her stinkin' ice."

"I've been gone so long—she'll be furious!"

"I'll take care of that. And as for your other little problem..." She gave Bridey a long, level look. "There are things I could give you, herbs and the like . . . ."

"To get rid of the baby, you mean?"

"Do you *want* to get rid of it?"

"I ...d- don't know."

"You have enough time to think it over. I'd say you're only three months along. You been sick?"

"Sometimes. Mostly the mornings."

Marie nodded. "Right on schedule then. Now as for your *last* problem . . . wait, I'll be right back."

She returned a few minutes later with a man in tow. He was large, dark-haired and grimy-skinned, with white teeth against a dense black beard. He carried a plate of food and was raising a forkful to his mouth, evidently having been conscripted by Marie in the middle of eating his supper.

"This is Louis," Marie said. "Works in the boiler room, when he ain't up here scrounging food. Louis Perrault, meet Bridey Collins. She works for that gorgon Lavinia Wilberforce, and she needs escorting back to her room."

"Enchanté de vous renconter," Louis said, scanning Bridey in a swift once-over. Bridey was used to men staring at her—she always had the feeling that Sean's lowlife mates were picturing her without her clothes on, but there was nothing lewd in the way Louis was studying her—as though she were a beautiful, exotic bird that had just landed on his finger.

"He barely speaks English," Marie said. "But if he don't do what you tell him, clonk him on the head. He understands *that*. Now hold still—I'm going to bandage you."

"I don't need a—"

"Sure you do. Don't you remember how you took a header while you were running around fetching ice for the spoiled old bat?" Marie pulled a roll of bandages from a drawer and, using sticking plasters, pasted a bandage across Bridey's forehead, being careful not to snag her hair. "Try standing up."

Bridey stood, feeling slightly dizzy, listening as Marie and Louis spoke in rapid Quebecois—Canadian French, only some of which Bridey caught—you couldn't live in Quebec without picking up enough French to scrape by on.

Marie whacked Louis on the back. "This ox needs to do something more useful than take up space for three at my table and gobble food meant for paying passengers. So he's going to walk you back to your stateroom and explain to that *vache moche*—ugly cow—how you met with an accident on your way to fetch her ice, and that you might have cracked your skull and need to lay down for the rest of the day."

"Here." She thrust a small bowl of ice cubes swimming in water into Bridey's hands.

"Thank you, Marie," Bridey whispered. "*Merci. Vous êtes un ange.*"

"Naw, I ain't no angel." Marie kissed Bridey on both cheeks. "Listen, that *putaine* gives you trouble tell me—I'll throw *her* over the side!"

Louis took Bridey's arm and gently escorted her out of the room, keeping her arm tucked into the crook of his elbow, as though he were a top-hatted gentleman escorting her to a cotillion, rather than a grimy giant with coal dust ground into his knuckles. Bridey tried to keep track of the corridors, gangways and stairs as they walked, in case she needed to find the kitchen again.

"*Quel travail êtes-vous?*" she asked, trying to make conversation, wincing as she realized she'd said, "What job are you?"

But he understood. Deep lines at the sides of his eyes fanned out as he turned to her, smiling. "*Trimmer,* mademoiselle. Shovel coal into furnace. Too much, she burn too hot, too small, she lose steam. *c'est un art.* And what work do you have, Mademoiselle?

"I'm a domestic, " she said dully. Not really understanding why she was confiding in this stranger, she added, "But I don't intend to be a servant the rest of my life! Some day I want to go to Teachers' College."

" *C'est admirable,*" Louis said, smiling.

Admirable? Sean didn't think so. He hadn't even understood why she'd bothered finishing high school, and he thought her idea of becoming a teacher was foolish—what would other men think of him if he had a wife bringing home a paycheck?

Of course that had been when Sean still wanted to marry her. Now she wasn't even sure they were still engaged.

"Ah, *Voici la pièce, n'est-ce pas ?*" Louis said.

Bridey was surprised to see that they'd reached the Wilberforce stateroom. Louis banged on the door. Lavinia yanked the door open, gasping in shock as she saw the big man standing there. "Madame," he said, making an elegant bow. "I am bring Bridey. *Blessée lors d'une chute, pauvre fille*—she falls and hurts."

"*What?*" Lavinia's eyes darted to Bridey's bandaged forehead. Before she could ask more questions, Louis thrust the bowl of water into her hands. "For you, Madame. Bridey head bad, *je dois me reposer beaucoup.* She need much rest."

He turned to go, but frowned as he spotted the room's porthole, which Lavinia had opened for a breeze. He strode across the room and slammed it shut. "*Ceci n'est pas autorisé,*" he said sternly, shaking a forefinger at her.

Madame scarcely waited until he was out of the room before exploding. "The nerve of that *filthy man!* He looked like a common laborer! Standards have fallen shamefully on this ship. I will be making a personal report to my cousin, Nathan Bickerstaff—he's the ship's owner, you know— on this appalling state of affairs." She whipped around to face Bridey. "And if you think for one moment that you can lounge about coddling yourself you are mistaken!"

Chapter 7

Bridey
   8:14 p.m.

———⁂———

"Get out my corset, lace me up!" Lavinia ordered.

There was to be no *reposer* for Bridey, who was once again at Madame's bleat and call. *The corset! Where had Lavinia packed it?* Pawing through the jumble in the steamer trunk, she finally found the complicated contraption of rubber, elastic, and whale bone.

Whale was the apt word, Bridey thought, biting her lip to suppress a grin as she pushed and pulled Madame's blubbery flesh; by the time she'd laced Lavinia to the point where she couldn't draw a deep breath, Bridey was panting from the effort.

""I've decided I'll wear my hobble," Madame announced "I doubt there'll be a single woman aboard who's been able to get her hands on one yet—they'll all be sick with envy!"

The dress, a shade between acid yellow and gold, lent Lavinia's complexion an unflattering sallow tinge. It had a draped bodice and a narrow waist from which a triangular pouf of fabric fanned out at the hips, resembling drooping saddle bags. A velvet band at the knees narrowed the remaining skirt into a slinky, movement-hampering sheath—a *hobble.*

Like the hobbles on horses—you couldn't take a stride in the blasted things; the restriction at the knee forced the hobble skirt wearer to move like a prisoner in a chain gang, Bridey thought scornfully; if a madman with a knife was chasing you and you had to run for your life, you'd be mowed down before you took two steps.

Hobble skirts were the most ludicrous fashion Bridey had ever seen, and yet, the style was taking the world by storm. Every girl she knew wanted one; her best friend Florence was saving up her lunch money, going without eating, starving herself in order to afford a hobble. *Why did women do that,* Bridey wondered. *Why did they want to lose their ability to move freely for the sake of a ludicrous fad?* Was it because the appearance of helplessness made one seem more frail, more feminine, more attractive to men?

Bridey didn't dare voice these opinions to her employer, who was slowly rotating in front of the stateroom's full-length mirror, studying the effect from all directions and looking quite smug. Bridey couldn't halt the laugh that bellied up, unstoppable as a sneeze—and had to turn away, pretending a coughing fit—because Madame looked like a large, bad-tempered, half-peeled banana.

"Stop that infernal hacking!" Madame barked. "Fetch my gloves."

The gloves went up nearly to the armpits and took five minutes to put on. They would have to be peeled off when Madame was served her food, and then put back on, finger by finger, when the meal was finished.

Bridey would have preferred staying alone in the stateroom, but it was part of her job to accompany Madame wherever she went in public; Lavinia loved having other women see how she could afford her own personal ladies' maid—a kind of fashion accessory, like a handbag. In a way Bridey was grateful to be dragged along; it gave her an excuse to avoid the odious task Sean had given her: finagling the key from that security guard. But her dereliction niggled her conscience. True, Sean had been horrid to her, but if she truly loved him, she would have done what he'd asked. Doing something she found loathsome would be a test of her love for him. The fact that it was difficult and repugnant made it all the more valuable—a shining, pure gift of her love—a sacrifice. Oh, why did she have to be afflicted with this cursed Catholic sense of guilt?

Eventually she and Madame found the dining salon, where a small crowd was gathered, waiting to be seated. The women were all exquisitely dressed, most of them in beaded and sequinned gowns in vivid shades: royal blue, violet, crimson. Wearing her plain broadcloth uniform, Bridey felt like a sparrow amid peacocks.

A steward named Ross led them to a table at the center of the room, but Lavinia sulked as her chair was pulled out because she hadn't been invited to sit at the captain's table. Bridey had caught a glimpse of the ship's captain earlier as they'd boarded the ship. Tall and square-jawed, his icy blue eyes set in a hard, level gaze, Captain Henry Kendall looked every inch the British officer. Ross explained that the captain's duties required him to be on the bridge just now rather than dining with the passengers, but Madame nevertheless felt she had been slighted. Recklessly flinging around the Bickerstaff name, she tried to wheedle another steward into seating her at the table of the next most prestigious man present—the ship's doctor, a handsome young man named James Grayson. That gambit failed, and they ended up at a table with Mrs. Hiram Endicott, a *grande dame* in Quebec society.

As Madame deemed proper, Bridey was relegated to a chair behind her own, where she could hand Lavinia her shawl or fan or whatever else she demanded, thus demonstrating to the other wealthy snobs what an obedient little servant she possessed. At least the servant was getting a good meal out of it, Bridey reflected—beef tips in a mushroom wine sauce, served with tiny, roasted potatoes and asparagus, and even though Bridey had to balance her plate on her knees, she savored every bite.

Dessert was strawberries over little baked meringues, topped with swirls of whipped cream. Coffee and chocolate mints followed, and as the women at the table began to rise, Bridey realized the meal was over. She shrank from the prospect of returning to the stateroom, being trapped with Madame for the next eight hours. She'd have to beg an iron from a steward, and set to work ironing piles and piles of wrinkled gowns while Madame blissfully snored.

Lavinia pinched her arm. "Pay attention, you little goose! I *said*, Go find my husband. He'll be in the smoking room with the other gentlemen. Tell him I am waiting to be escorted back to my room."

Bridey scowled. She hated playing messenger between husband and wife. Half the time they were furious with each other and it was Bridey who got the brunt of their misplaced rage

"*Go!*" Madame whacked Bridey's shoulder with her fan, giving Mrs. Endicott a sideways glance to see whether the old snob was impressed by how sternly she'd dealt with a lollygagging servant.

As Bridey wove her way between tables, she heard Madame complaining to Mrs. Endicott, "Honestly, one simply cannot find reliable help these days. I used to have a lovely Swedish girl, Ingrid, but she got too above herself and I had to let her go. Nothing for it—I was forced to settle for Irish servants—barely literate, most of them, hardly know how to use the indoor toilet!"

Bridey skidded to a halt. *Illiterate, was she*? She'd graduated at the top of her high school class! She ought to go back and give those two gossip mongers a dose of the truth: Ingrid had quit because Elmer Wilberforce, the old goat, couldn't keep his paws off her! But of course she wouldn't do that—Madame would accuse her of telling lies and fire her on the spot, and she couldn't afford to lose her job, not with this baby growing in her.

Choking down her anger, Bridey hurried out and found the smoking room, just down from the dining salon—she could have found it just by sticking her nose in the air and sniffing the foul odors of cigar and pipe smoke it gave off.

Intimidated at the prospect of entering that all-male preserve, Bridey slipped into the room, trying to avoid notice. It was like the inside of a chimney in here, a heavy fug of smoke permeating the room, making her cough. Fanning aside the smoke, she stood on tiptoes, trying to spot Elmer Wilberforce—a needle in a haystack task in this room full of black dinner jackets, Prince Albert beards, big bellies, and loud voices, each man trying to outshout the others, as arguments raged over whether there'd be a war in Europe.

She found Elmer Wilberforce, who was bellowing his opinion, treating bystanders to a shower of spittle. "Of course we'll have a war! Why do you think the emperor of Austria is complaining that all his military-age men are fleeing Austria for Canada?"

As another man began shouting a rebuttal; Bridey slipped up to Elmer Wilberforce. "Sir?"

He turned to her with a scowl that made her quail.

"Mrs. Wilberforce says to tell you she's waiting to be escorted back to her room."

"Not now, " he snapped "I'm in the middle of important things here. Run along, tell the old gal I said she can go to hell. *You* take her back, that's a good girl." He patted her back, his hand straying too close to her bum. *Oh, he was vile!* Jerking away, she wove her way through the room, squeezing through clusters of men whose faces leered, whose hands groped. It was as though her maid's uniform gave these wealthy, self-important men the right to pinch and paw as they pleased. She was a servant, a paid underling—a thing to use and discard.

A stout, red-faced man sidled up to her, his veiny hand fumbling toward her breast. She elbowed him in the ribs before scurrying out of the room.

She wished she'd kicked him in the bawbags.

Chapter 8

10:18 p.m.
Sean

He shouldn't have belted Bridey that hard, Sean privately admitted. But sometimes a slap was the only way you could learn women to respect you, that's what Pa always said. And now—funny thought—he might be a pa himself before long.

The notion of having a kid was growing on him—a boy who'd look up to his old man, the hero who they'd soon be writing songs about. *Corkoran the Brave, the Patriot of Ireland;* they might even put up a statue of him on O'Connell Street in Dublin. They'd be talking about it for years, how Sean Corkoran had pulled off the *Heist of the Century:* he could already see the headlines.

It hadn't been easy; he'd had to make sacrifices; he'd had to take a job as a feckin' janitor on board this very ship during her run downriver last fall. Filthy job, it was, too. Swabbing decks, cleaning up puke, washing umpteen million windows on this tub, taking orders from that arrogant prick Hazlitt.

Never any respect from the other crewmen, either. The trimmers and firemen from the boiler room were the roughest of the crew—biceps like cannon balls, dark as devils from the coal dust, swaggering around like their balls clanked. And he could tell they considered him, with his ever-present mop and bucket, the lowest of the low—wouldn't give him the time of day. But he'd stuck with the job, he'd endured the abuse, miserable as any prisoner in a Brit jail—for the sake of the Cause. He'd had to take a lot of shit, but he'd learned what he needed to: he knew every inch of every deck, he knew the crew; he knew where the strong room keys were kept; he knew exactly how the bullion would be guarded as the ship moved downriver on its spring voyage.

The sticking point had always been how he was going to get the bullion out of the strong room without being noticed. He'd gnawed away on the problem for months, coming up with one scheme after another, but always snagging up against the stumper: how did you transfer a ton of bullion off the ship undetected?

The solution had come about by a stroke of luck—a sign, Sean thought, that God was on his side. It had happened the day an April snowstorm had dumped a foot of snow on the city. Having quit his janitor job by then, Sean had spent the day at a saloon in the Sainte Roch quarter of Quebec. Feckin' bartender had refused him another drink until he'd paid his tab, so he'd punched the bastard. The barman's mates had clobbered Sean, given him the bum's rush into the street. He'd collapsed on the curb, head in hands, nursing his bruises and his hangover—and then a god-awful noise blasted his eardrums.

A horn of some kind, its high, brassy notes sending spears of pain into his head—and then—oh, *God's bloody, weeping wounds*—drums started pounding! Bleary-eyed, he'd watched as a uniformed troupe—the men in Mountie-style hats, the women in bonnets—marched down the street, blowing into instruments and banging on drums—some sort of parade.

Finally the noise stopped and a man with gold braid on his sleeves set down a crate, stood up on it, and started shouting at Sean and the bums in the gutter, his voice harsh on Sean's beleaguered ears.

"My friends, I see many of you out there who have reached the depths of depravity. I see hungry, cold men, sleeping on the street, feeling the effects of demon liquor, men who believe themselves to be damned, men who believe that no one in this world cares if they live or die. But your brothers and sisters in the Salvation Army care about you. Pick yourselves up, put yourself into the Lord's hands, begin to believe that God has a plan for you. Come along, march with us! It's only a short distance—to a place where you will be offered a hot meal, a wash, a clean, warm bed—"

"They got beer there?" called out a fellow hunched over a nearby steam grating, his stink clogging Sean's nostrils. Then he leaned over and puked all over Sean's shoes.

Anything was better than this.

Lurching to his feet, Sean staggered along in the wake of the band, wincing every time the cymbals clashed, until they came to a rambling building on Beaucage Street. They hadn't lied about the scran; one of the bonneted ladies handed him a mug of hot, sweet tea as soon as Sean walked through the door. They had food set out on a sideboard: cold cuts, cheese, rye bread, pea soup—plain but filling grub, and you could have as much as you could eat. Sean fell onto a bench at a table and dug in, ignoring the Sallies, who kept peppering him with questions, intent on saving his soul. He responded to their badgering with a shrug. Eventually all the Hallelujah Hollerers lost interest in Sean and started jawing among themselves about some big shindig they were all excited about—it seemed every Salvation Army person in the world was going to this rally in England at the end of May. A hundred seventy strong from Quebec Province, they were all sailing aboard the *Empress of Ireland*.

Sean's ears pricked up. That preacher had been right—he *was* seeing the light! Heaven was being revealed to him! These God-botherers were going to play into his hands and they didn't even know it!

11:45 PM

Now, on the deck of the great ocean liner—as a paying passenger this time, not as a lowly puke-mopper, Sean checked his watch, dismayed to see that his hands were shaking. What he wouldn't give for a shot of whiskey right now, a nip to steady his nerves.

He made his way down to E Deck and hurried along the corridor until he found the closet—the one he'd used to stash his gear in as a janitor. He rapped out *Shave and a Haircut*—the agreed signal, and Gorcey yanked the door open from inside, looking relieved to see Sean.

"Should of waited to see who it was before you opened the door," Sean growled. "I coulda been anyone."

One slip-up and they'd all be in the brig. Sean bent to examine the man sprawled on the cramped closet floor, his head squished against a wet mop, his hands tied with ship's line. His name was Harris—one more detail Sean had taken care to find out. He worked for Bakersfield, the U.S. security company who had the contract to deliver the bullion to Liverpool. H*e looked* like a Bakersfield—short, slicked-back hair, spotless shirt and jacket, shined shoes—only at the moment the guy wasn't looking too great because Moose McGill, who wasn't called *Moose* for nothing—had come up behind when Harris emerged from the john and sapped him with a twelve inch blackjack—leaving the guy out cold, with a lump the size of a corned beef sandwich growing out of his head.

"I got his gun!" Gorcey boasted, fishing a shiny black pistol out of his pocket and twirling it, gunslinger style. If the moron accidentally pulled the trigger, they'd have every crewman on the ship down on 'em, Sean realized, once again regretting ever inviting Gorcey in on the job. "Forget the damn gun," he snapped. "Did you get the key?"

"You bet." Gorcey fished a key out of his pocket and slapped it into Sean's hand. Hard to tell in this dim light, but it appeared to be a perfect match for the key Sean already had in his possession. He'd had to quick change the plan after Bridey had gone running off in a huff. Her feminine wiles hadn't been needed after all; one blackjack could do the job faster than a dozen eyelash-batting females. Harris would likely be out for hours—blackjacks packed such a wallop they were considered lethal weapons, same as guns or knives. Sooner or later, though, someone was going to start wondering where Harris was and get up a search for him. There wasn't a second to waste.

Moose, Suds Finnegan, and Murphy were waiting where he'd told them, out on B deck, smoking and trying to blend in with the passengers taking the air. Sean was surprised to see how dark it had gotten. The sun had set, there was a chill in the air, and the ship blazed with lights.

"Shuck your coats," he told the others in a low voice.

There was a lot of awkward shuffling, but at last they'd all stripped off their overcoats, revealing the high collared maroon jackets beneath.

Gorcey's strained across his sloppy beer gut, and Moose's was too tight in the shoulders. Murf had filched the jackets from the marching band's storage closet at St. Mary's High School, which he'd once attended—uniforms made for skinny teenaged boys, not a bunch of out-of-shape mugs who lived mainly on beer. But it was unlikely anybody would give 'em a second look, Sean reassured himself—one Holy Roller looked pretty much like another.

He motioned, and the others fell in behind him, trying to look like a marching band, but mostly stumble-bumming along; Suds stomped on Murf's heel and Murf whipped around and smacked him in the gob; then Suds retaliated with a punch toMurf's kidneys.

"Knock it off," Sean growled, and was gratified when they followed orders; he'd always thought he had the makings of a commander. *Eire do 'Fein* would probably give him his own division to run when this was all over. *Captain Corkoran—that* had a ring to it!

It had been Pa's brother, Uncle Pat, who'd introduced Sean to *Eire do 'Fein*. Patrick Corkoran, who lived in Galway, had come over for a visit with the Canadian Corkorans, bringing all the news from Ireland. Sometimes him and Pa invited Sean along when they went to McCleary's Pub—it was where the Irish of Quebec gathered to sing old songs, tell old stories, rail at England's historic mistreatment of Ireland, and get soused. And that was where Sean had first heard about *Eire do 'Fein* —an Irish word that sounded like *Ire d' Fayne* and translated to *Ireland for Itself*—meaning an Ireland free from the tyranny of British rule. The stories of Irish martyrs, men who had stood up against British guns, who'd fought for a free Ireland—had fired Sean's imagination. In *Eire do 'Fein* , a nobody like Sean—just another stiff with no job, shite at hockey, a school dropout—could find a place, could maybe even become a hero. The men at McCleary's, the ones who told the stories and belted out the songs—they treated Sean as though he were already one of them. They respected him, he felt sure of it. They bought him pints; they clapped him on the back and told him he was a fine young fellow; they told him Bridey was a sweet thing but he could maybe do better; they invited him to come to meetings, which were held in the basement of *Sacre Couer* Church under the pretense of it being a prayer group but was actually where the real work of Eire do`Fein got done. So far his mates and him had raised enough money to buy two hundred Lee-Enfield rifles from a Toronto arms manufacturer and have them shipped to Eire do`Fein contacts in Galway.

Things were happened in Ireland, Uncle Pat promised: plans were afoot; preparations were being made; arms were being hidden; recruitment was going on. There's be an uprising —a lot sooner than the British expected, maybe as early as 1916, and centered in Dublin. The Irish day of liberation was coming.

And Sean Corkoran was going to be a big part of it: he'd donate the bullion money for weapons toward that day of liberation—why, his initials were practically carved into the bullets!

Somehow his group of clodhoppers bumbled down three sets of stairs, emerging into the third class general meeting room, which was crowded with the chumps who couldn't afford first or second—mostly men and women who'd made a good life in Canada and were now going back to visit relatives in the old country: Poles going back to Poland, Bohunks to Bohemia; Micks heading to Liverpool, which had more Irish than Dublin.

The Sallies were in full swing, up on a low stage at the front of the room, tootling out tunes; Sean thought he recognized *Onward Christian Soldiers*. He made a quick reconnoiter of the room, feeling conspicuous in his dark red uniform—the Salvation Army band was in navy blue. If anyone asked, him and the others would claim they were from the Saskatoon Sallies, who would naturally have different uniforms. It only took him a minute to find what he was looking for: the band's instrument cases, piled higgledy-piggledy in a storage area behind the stage; it was concealed from the audience by a high folding screen.

With everyone's attention on the musicians, it was a simple matter for Sean's crew to skulk back behind the screen and begin snatching up cases—all black leather, in various sizes and shapes. The long, narrow one that looked like a carrying case for a shotgun was for a slide trombone, according to Murf. Didn't matter what shape though; the important thing was how much weight they could carry.

"Split up—go out in different directions," Sean hissed.

The band swung into "*There is Power in the Blood*" to great applause, unaware that their instrument cases were being made off with under their noses by a troupe of red-clad imposters.

Chapter 9

10: 39 p.m.
Charlie

Snapper fixed it for Charlie to get fed in the second class dining room— a glass of milk and a plate of *poutine*—fried potatoes and cheese curds in a rich brown gravy. Charlie gobbled it down like the starving boy he was, and Snapper swiped a plate for himself. You never saw this kind of goulash back home, but he'd developed a taste for it since he'd been in Canada.

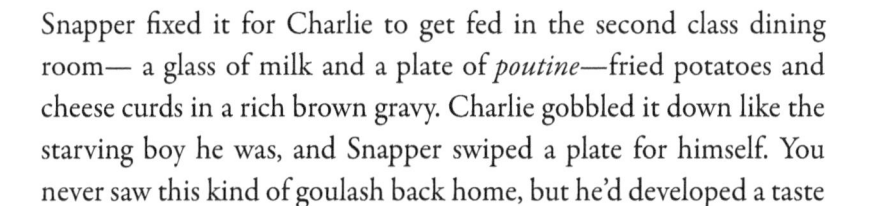

"Time for you to get bunked down," Snapper told Charlie as they headed onto the promenade deck after supper. "Where's your ma and pa at?"

Charlie shrugged, a deep flush stealing from his neck to his hairline.

"Come on, mate—you don't have to stick with your gobshite story about the family that don't exist. Breathe easy, lad—I ain't gonna turn you in. S'long as you give me the straight poop—how come you snuck onto this ship?"

"Wanna get to Liverpool," Charlie muttered.

"Yeh? Well, who don't, huh? Liverpool's got it all—the River Mersey, wall to wall pubs, and the finest slums in Europe."

"My pa went there," Charlie mumbled.

"That what this is about? Your pa took off and you're trying to find him?"

Charlie nodded. "He was supposed to have this good job waiting for him in Liverpool. He said he'd send his wages back, but he never did. And my baby brother got sick, then Ma got sick, and we can't pay our rent—so that's why I got to find Pa, so he'll come back home."

"Your mum know where you are?"

Charlie stared at his shoes. "Nah. She wouldn't have let me go if I'd told her—I had to sneak off. But I knew this ship was going to Liverpool and that's where Pop is. I'm going to find him and we'll go back home together."

Wasn't going to happen. Snapper had known too many shiftless buggers who got fed up with the responsibility of supporting the kids they'd brought into this world, who lit out on their own, forgetting the hungry kids left behind. And Charlie's pa sounded exactly like that kind of punter.

"I might be able to help you sniff out your pa once we get to Scousetown," said Snapper, "For now, though, you gotta get your forty winks. I'll take you down to third class—they got spare bunks."

Charlie looked considerably more light-hearted as they made their way down, now that he knew Snapper wasn't going to turn him in. They were on the port side of C deck, when Charlie pointed and cried, "Look—a ship!"

Approaching from downriver, sailing close to the western bank, was a massive ocean liner, its lights all ablaze, "It looks like a whole city out there!" Charlie cried.

"That's the *Alsatian*, heading for Quebec," Snapper said. It was built along the same lines as the *Empress,* only her stacks were red instead of gold.

Charlie watched, leaning on the rail, as she swept past. "How do they keep from running into each other when it's this dark?"

"Same reason as streetcars don't run into each other on the streets of Quebec," Snapper said. "All the ships got to follow the same rules. Look up there on our bridge, What do you see on the port side?"

"That red light, you mean?"

"Yeh. Now you can't see it from where we are, but on the starboard side of the bridge there's a green light. A ship that's dead ahead will see both lights—which tells 'em the ship is coming straight at 'em. But if a ship alters its course, only one of the lights will be visible and the oncoming ship will know which side of her bow is coming at 'em."

Charlie frowned, trying to make sense of it.

"But that ain't all. There's also mast lights—otherwise known as range lights—white lights high up on the mast. The aft one is fifteen feet higher than t' forward one. See, that way a ship ten miles up the river can see you long before your red and greens come into view, and can work out how far away you are."

Charlie yawned widely.

Snapper laughed. "Awright, Mr. Salty Sea-dog, let's get you bunked in."

The third class compartments were on the deck closest to the waterline, just aft of the boiler rooms. Charlie followed Snapper into a large room that smelled of dirty socks. "Boy's cabin," Snapper said. "They keep the kiddos what ain't with their families off to theirselves here, so the adults don't got to put up with their monkeyshines."

The real reason, which Snapper kept mum about, was that there had been too many instances of lowlifes luring young kids into dark corners, doing nasty things to 'em that ought to have gotten the culprits hung, far as Snapper was concerned. So dormitories had been set up down here, supervised by matrons. The boys' dorm was bare-bones plain: four rows of bunks, with foot lockers for storage. It was noisy, filled with shouting boys. One boy—he looked to be about eleven, with floppy blonde hair, wearing checkered pajamas—was bounding from top bunk to top bunk, in a game that apparently required him to make an entire circuit of the room without touching the floor. He misjudged on his last jump, fell, and thumped to the floor at Snapper's feet. He grinned sheepishly up at the steward.

"Mighta known it'd be you, Reilly," Snapper said, hauling him to his feet. "You ever tried stayin' out of trouble?"

"Eh, come on, Snapper, don't be a killjoy."

"Charlie Barrows, meet Tom Reilly." He gave the blonde boy a hard-eyed stare. "Who is going to find you a bunk and show you the jakes, ain't you, Tom?"

Charlie had been in situations like this before, where one boy had to show the newcomer who was boss right off. This usually involved picking a fight, but Tom Reilly just stuck out a hand. "Nice to meetcha," he said, grinning. "Where you from?"

"Quebec."

"I'm from Vermont. In the USA."

"*Vermont?*" Charlie, who'd never met an American, was surprised.

"Yup. We took a train across the Canada border that took us all the way to this boat."

"It's a ship," Charlie corrected him.

"A *big* boat. Same thing. My ma and sisters got this dinky room in second class, but I'd rather die than be in with my sisters, so Snapper said I could come down here and sleep in the dorm."

"Yeh, I said you could *sleep* down here," Snapper said. "Which you are going to do, starting now, instead of bouncing around like a kangaroo with a burr up its butt."

Reilly waited until he was sure Snapper was gone, then turned to Charlie, his eyes shining with mischief. "Forget about goin' to bed, Charlie. Wanna see something that'll make your eyes pop?"

Chapter 10

Captain Henry Kendall
   12:48 A.M.
   Off Riviere Trois Pistoles

Kendall poured himself another mug of coffee. His eyes felt sandpapered; he was tired to the bone, having been up since four that morning, overseeing all the complicated preparations required for a great liner's departure. Hadn't been any use trying to sleep, anyway, because it was one of the nights the nightmare came.

Always the same—he was back on the square-rigger *Iolanthe*, and Aasheesh, the insane Trinidadian, had materialized out of the dark, clamped a wiry arm around Henry's neck, and dug his dagger point against his mouth. *"Aasheesh don't like boys that blab,"* he hissed. *"He cuts out tongues of boys who tell lies on poor Aasheesh."* The knife sliced excruciatingly into the corner of Henry's mouth, jabbed at his tongue. Footsteps rang on a ladder as the third mate came off his watch—and Aasheesh hastily released his grip and melted away into the shadows, leaving Henry retching on the blood trickling down his throat.

Two days earlier, Aasheesh and another crewman had been throwing dice, when Aasheesh, screaming that the man was cheating, had suddenly plunged his dagger into the man's heart, knelt on his chest and shrieked that he was going to rip out the man's guts and use them for shark bait. Henry and a Welsh topman named Owens had hauled Aasheesh off the dying crewman—a hell of a job, Aasheesh fighting with the ferocity of the deranged, until a burly waister had clonked him with a belaying pin and dragged him off to the brig.

They'd been off the north coast of Australia, and the ship's captain—a Nova Scotia bluenose named McCaig—planned to keep Aasheesh locked up until they reached the port of Darwin, where he'd be turned over to the civil authorities and tried for murder, with Owens and Kendall testifying as witnesses.

But just two days later, Owens had been found dead in his bunk, his throat slit so brutally his head had nearly been severed. Aasheesh's cell was empty; he'd contrived an escape and a murder, all in the middle in the night. A manhunt for him was launched on the ship, stem to stern, but while the crew had been searching for Aasheesh, the wily Trinidadian had been hunting Henry Kendall—and had come up behind him out of the dark, intent on murder—would have succeeded, too if that Third Mate hadn't come along in time.

Aasheesh had been locked up again, but Kendall had no faith in those bars. He'd decided that his best chance of surviving was to jump ship. He'd made it to Darwin, then had headed inland, through the Northern Territory, then into Western Australia, eventually finding himself in the middle of a gold rush. In three months of digging he'd not found a single gold nugget—although he had pried out, quite by accident, a chunk of black opal the size of a man's foot—said to be worth a fortune.

Henry had bounced around Australia for a year, until one day, in Carnarvon on the west coast, he'd been coshed by a press gang and forced to serve aboard a Dutch hauler that was short of hands—a tub carrying three hundred reeking tons of guano. Henry soon discovered that she was an unlucky barque; she leaked like a sieve; she lost her mizzen in a gale off New Zealand and her topgallant off Cape Horn. For two hundred days the exhausted crew manned the pumps to keep the vessel from sinking, until finally, the ship and its stinking, starving crew limped into Falmouth Harbor in England.

If he'd had any sense, Kendell reflected, he would have stayed on land, sold his black opal and used the money to buy a house. But he still hadn't gotten the sea out of his blood; instead he'd signed up for a stint on the Mersey, a freighter out of Liverpool, and had ended up as its first mate.

The days of sail were drawing to a close, though—everything was steam these days. He'd gotten a job on one of the *Canadian Trans-Global's* ships plying the Atlantic trade, spent eleven years learning the ropes and gradually working himself up—until at last, bypassing more senior officers, he'd been appointed master of the *Empress of Ireland*, the most prestigious ship on the trans-Atlantic route.

Although he'd made frequent voyages as one of the ship's junior officers, this was the first time he'd been given total command of the *Empress*. She was a beautiful ship with a first rate crew—French Canadians, English, and Irish mostly: well-trained, hard-working, no slackers or troublemakers that he'd noticed.

The river, though. He hated the St. Lawrence. Give him open ocean, give him an Atlantic gale any day over this wild, treacherous river. It was still skimmed over with ice in some spots— and he'd been warned about the fogs. Probably so much bunkum—tales put about by old salts, trying to put the wind up him—the nautical version of a snipe hunt. The fogs couldn't actually be *that* bad.

As though to illustrate his point, fog wisped across the bow just now. The company had standing orders for a captain to reduce speed in the event of fog; Kendall reached for the engine room phone, debating whether to call down. It would be a shame to reduce speed just when they'd built up a decent momentum. Excessive caution would make his officers lose respect for him, Kendall thought.

A breeze came up; the fog floated away.

JULIET ROSETTI

So much for the fearsome St. Lawrence fog.

Chapter 11

Marie
    12: 30 a.m.

In the course of one day Marie had overseen the preparation of meals for one thousand passengers, plus six hundred crew. For first class: *Beef Tenderloin Tips, Cream of onion soup, Potatoes Florentine, lobster salad, Creme brulee, and Strawberry Schaum torte*. And wine, of course. Lots and lots of wine; however they prinked their fingers when they drank their tea, the snobs could swill down wine like any rummy in the gutter.

Second class's dinner had been nearly identical to that of first class, but without the lobster salad. If the nobs found out their meals were coming out of the same kitchen that cooked for third class; if they realized that their *creme brulee* was the same vanilla pudding third class was getting, they'd have choked on their *Moet et Chandon*.

Marie preferred third class. Those passengers didn't get a full dinner on the first night—just a tea served at five-thirty in the afternoon, but it was simple to set up: cold sliced sausage, cheese, three kinds of bread, potato-leek soup, cabbage slaw, and vanilla pudding. And they were grateful for it! For some of them, it was the only decent food they'd had in weeks. Third class passengers never complained.

Now, close to midnight, all the diners were gone, the dishes were cleared, and the dirty tablecloths had been bundled down to the laundry. The kitchen staff's duties weren't finished, though—now they had to set up for breakfast. Puffy-eyed and slump-shouldered, they sleep-walked around setting out the breakfast plates and cutlery, squeezing oranges for juice, or assembling the enormous percolator, which would produce the hundreds of cups of coffee required in the morning. Eggs had to be set out to warm up for the morning's omelets—because eggs straight out of the ice box didn't whip.

Marie was so exhausted she didn't think she could even make it to her cabin.

But her exhaustion, Marie realized, was composed more of anxiety than sheer tiredness—the weight of her own guilt. If Steede, the Chief Officer, discovered that the key was missing, all hell would be unleashed. Losing that key wasn't like losing a pocket watch or a wallet; it was the strong room key. The key to two million dollars.

She'd managed to filch the key when she'd taken dinner to the officers' mess. All of them removed their jackets and slung them over the backs of their chairs when they sat down to eat. Marie had been around men long enough to know where they automatically stuck their handkerchiefs, cash, and papers—or their wedding rings when they had devilry on their minds—into their jacket's left hand breast pocket.

Nobody had been watching her; all eyes were on the warm apple pie Rose and Sally, her kitchen assistants, had been setting out on the table, to the officers' enthusiastic response. Meanwhile Marie had sidled up behind Steede's chair, reached into his jacket—carelessly flung over the back of his chair—fished out the key, and slid it into her apron pocket. Nobody—not even the sharp-eyed Chief Steward Hazlitt—had caught it.

An hour later, as she was boiling chicken bones for stock, that shifty chancer Sean Corkoran had sidled up to her. "You got it?" he'd asked, talking out of the side of his mouth as though he were some hard-boiled con planning to bust out of prison.

She shot him her spooky-medicine-woman look, wishing she could whack him with her soup ladle until his skull rang like a bell. She hadn't liked him last year, when he'd been a janitor, and she didn't like the little *zhingo*—weasel—now. Beneath his swagger, he was a weakling—the kind who when questioned by the police would give her up in a second. She'd made sure he handed over the money before she'd handed over the key, because she didn't trust him any more than she'd trust a fox with a leg of lamb.

Marie had hated stealing that key. She was honest by nature; she never told lies; she had never in her life taken a penny that wasn't hers; she'd never skimped on her shipboard duties. But when you were in desperate need, you did what you had to do. For two hundred dollars she would have flown her under-drawers from the mast pole. She'd told herself she didn't know what the stolen key was going to be used for, but knew she was lying to herself: she had a pretty fair idea that the weasel was after the silver bullion.

Marie yanked open the spice cabinet above her cutting board. Two yellowing photos were thumb-tacked to the door: her two beautiful sons. The photos had been taken by a travelling photographer who'd come to her village some years ago. She'd watched, fascinated, as he'd gone about his task, and it had seemed almost magical, the way he disappeared under a black cloth while his strange-looking apparatus pointed its snout toward its subjects, and then the man squeezed a bulb and a sulphur-smelling powder ignited with a bright flash, capturing a person in that moment. Most of the older tribe members refused to let their portraits be taken, believing the camera stole one's spirit. But Memengwa didn't believe it—she desperately *wanted* a picture of her two boys, her *Nimki* and *Noodin*. *Thunder* and *Storm i*n the Ojibwe language.

The boys were twins, born within an hour of each other on a spring night of wind and lightning. They had grown into their names: small whirlwinds of energy and mischief, Nimki fat-cheeked as a chipmunk, with the same bright black eyes; Noodin with solemn eyes—the eyes of an old warrior whose soul had been born back into the world—and a thatch of black hair like a ramble-shamble bird's nest; Memengwa could always tell when a storm was brewing because Noodin's hair stood out in a feathery ruff around his head and sparks flew if you tried to touch it.

Their *deydey*—father—was Marie's husband, *Giiwedin,* who'd been pleased to have two sons at once, considering it a tribute to his potency; the way he strutted around you would have thought he had pushed out those babies himself. Giiwedin had worked for a lumber company in a camp on the Sagueneay River; he was a driver—a raftsman who steered giant flotillas of logs downriver to the mills, a job requiring incredible balance and coordination. Memengwa had worked for the same lumber company as a camp cook—it was where she'd learned how to cook food quickly and in huge quantities.

She took down the photos of her boys, handling them carefully because the oils on hands ruined the shiny paper. The boys' hair had been long then, Nimki's neatly braided; Noodin's fluffy as a wolf's tail. She had dressed them both in traditional clothes for the sitting: vests she'd needle-pointed in colorful designs, headbands, moccasins beaded in the pintail duck clan style. At the last second Nimki had plucked a blue jay feather off the ground and stuck it rakishly in his hair, insisting on wearing it for the photo despite her objections.

Why had she scolded him? That small feather, sticking out above his left eyebrow, was so endearingly silly it made her laugh and cry every time she looked at his photo.

Giiwidin had been killed when the boys were only five. She'd always thought it would be the river that killed him—log-driving was madly dangerous—there were rapids to negotiate, rogue trunks that suddenly reared up on rocks and came smashing down, treacherous logs that spun beneath your feet and tumbled you into the water—and once you were down underneath the vast raft of logs it might be impossible to find a way back up against that log ceiling; drowning was a common fate for lumbermen.

But it hadn't been a rogue log or rapids that had killed Giiwidin. It'd been whiskey. He and his crew had been playing cards one night in a temporary camp, all of them drinking, but the bottle Giiwidin had drunk from had been cut with something—maybe rat poison, one of Giiwidin's mates later told her, Whatever it was, it had sent Giiwidin into convulsions that had killed him.

She hadn't wanted the boys to know the truth; instead she had told them their father had died bravely, defending his friends from a *mukwah*—a bear. Let the boys grow up thinking their father had died a warrior.

Without Giiwidin, there was only her to support her boys. To make ends meet, Memengwa had taken the cook's job aboard the ocean liner. Compared to a logger's camp, the ocean liner was utter luxury. Food didn't have to be kept in a snowbank to stay cold; she didn't have to build a fire to cook the food, and she had a staff of thirty to assist her.

Her brother, Migitzi, as was traditional, took over a father's role for her boys; he and his wife Okwi cared for them while Memengwa was on the ship. It was a regular run: Quebec to Liverpool, and took four and a half weeks to get there and back. She was content with the way things were going: she was earning enough money to pay her brother and his wife to keep her sons, and when she came home, she climbed into bed with the twins, cuddling one on each side; no longer Marie the ship's cook; she was the mother of Nimki and Noodin, their *Nimaamaa*

And then she came home one weekend and the boys were not there. Her beating heart, her soul, the very blood that surged through her veins—stolen at the whim of officialdom.

It was the new law, passed by politicians in Ottawa. Native people, they had decreed, must be forced to give up their ways and assimilate into Canadian culture. Children must learn to speak in English; must learn the Christian faith; must leave all things native behind. Including their families. Nimki and Noodin, along with thirty other children from Memengwa's village, had been torn away, loaded onto a train, and sent away to institutions and orphanages whose job it was to take the Ojibwe out of them—by whatever means were deemed necessary.

Memengwa herself had been ripped away from her family when she'd been only eight years old, but in that case it had been the Catholic Church which had instigated it. Memengwa and her siblings had been raised Catholic; like most other members of her tribe, they'd gone to St. John's, a little log building with a bell steeple in her village. She'd liked the services: the permeating scent of incense, the chanting, the joyous thunder of the organ, the mumbo-jumbo of Latin, the candy handouts at Christmas and Easter.

But the Church higher-ups had decided that the only way to save the souls of Ojibwe children was by separating them from the pagan influence of their families and isolating them in boarding schools run by nuns and priests.

Memengwa had been taken to a town fifty miles from Ashquasing, her village, and forced into a Catholic boarding school. The first thing the nuns did was rename her. *Memengwa* became *Marie*. She had to wear uncomfortable, scratchy white people clothes and tight shoes.

THE EMPRESS OF IRELAND

She was forced to speak English. Not one syllable of Ojibwe was to be uttered. Nor was French, which was strange, thought Memengwa; French was very close to Latin, the holy language of the church. Ojibwe children caught speaking French or Ojibwe were punished by having cayenne powder ground into their tongues and being forced to wear a sign around their necks reading: *I am a stupid Indian.*

Marie struggled in school. Sister Hubertus spoke English with a strong Irish accent that Marie found difficult to understand; thus, the nun believed Marie to be mentally defective. She seemed to take particular joy in tormenting Marie, ridiculing her deep, husky voice, calling Marie *Man-girl*. But despite the scorn heaped on her, Marie learned quickly; within a few months she was at the top of her class. One day—it was about a week after a heavy snowfall, and everyone's feet were wet, icy water dribbling along the floorboards—Marie could not sit still on the hard wooden fold-down seat of her desk. She had a burning sensation, a maddening itch, in her pee-pee area. The grown Marie, looking back on that small girl, realized that it must have been a urinary tract infection, probably caused by the poor sanitation in the girls' dorm. It itched and itched, and the only relief Marie could get was by scratching. She worked on the arithmetic problems she'd copied off the chalkboard using her right hand and reached stealthily under her skirt with her left to scratch the horrid itch.

"Marie Lavalierre!" Sister Hubertus's voice rang out, startling her so that her hand jerked a jagged line across her paper. "What are you doing?" The nun swooped down on her like a great black bat. "What are you doing with your hand, filthy child?"

"S-scratching, Sister."

"I *know* what you were doing. I *saw* you!" The nun's eyes bulged behind the thick lens of her spectacles. She was breathing hard, standing so close that Marie could see the toast crumbs caught in the scraggle of mustache above her lip. "I am going to stamp out this abomination for once and all. Why do you think we tie your hands to the bedstead at night?"

"So we can't escape?" Marie quavered.

Rosary beads cracked across her face. *Wrong answer!* Her hand flew to her cheek, gouged by the sharp edge of the rosary's crucifix. Abruptly she felt herself being lifted up by her hair, shoved and prodded and marched up the aisle between the rows of desks, the children on both sides, as they had been taught to do when someone committed an offense, pointing their forefingers at her, scraping the other index finger along the pointer in the *Shame, shame, shame on you* gesture.

Marie's stomach twisted; she knew what was coming. The nuns had done it to Joe LaGace that time he'd turned the sign of the cross into an upthrust finger against his enemy, Roger Pierrot.

"Do you know what happens to little girls who commit sins of impurity?" Sister Hubertus hissed, towering over Marie, the six inch squared-off coif atop her head making her appear even taller, "They end up in Hell. Do you know what hell is like? It's eternal fire, burning day and night without cease."

"I-I don't want—"

"I-I-I," mocked the nun. "You'll have a small taste of what Hell feels like, and maybe that will stop you next time you're tempted to touch your dirty parts!"

Her words fell on Marie like cold, hard stones.

"But I got this itch, I was just tryin' ta—"

"An *itch!*" The nun's voice ascended to a screech; she sounded like a crow, outraged by an encroaching blue jay. "Oh, that's what you Indians call it when you get yourselves all worked up into debauchery, isn't it? I'll give you an itch, all right!" Her voice had become a gravelly growl. "Hold out your hands!"

THE EMPRESS OF IRELAND

Marie hastily thrust her hands behind her back. It was cowardly, it was not the Ojibwe way, which was to pretend indifference to pain in the enemy's presence, but she knew what was coming and she was crying now, gazing back over her shoulders at her classmates, hoping someone would come to her rescue.

She got only smirks and more of the *shame, shame* finger; her classmates were enjoying the show; it was their revenge, Marie guessed, for her being the smartest girl in the class, always knowing the right answer, her hand in the air.

Sister Hubertus whipped Marie's body around, jerked her across the top of the teacher's desk, and pinning Marie's arms, used her free hand to reach for the quart of kerosene kept handy to light the room's lanterns on dark days. Upending the bottle, she drizzled kerosene over Marie's palms, the chemical smell harsh in Marie's nostrils.

The room had gone silent, silent as it never was during the school day; there were always whispers, coughs, the scrape of muddy boots on the wooden floor, stifled giggles. Now no one even dared breathe, lest they miss something. All eyes held the victim in their merciless gazes. Even the *Shame, shame* had stopped.

"This, little heathen," hissed Sister Hubertus, taking a matchbox out of her top drawer and shaking out a wooden match, "is a preview of Hell. You must never forget how much it hurts."

She struck the match, dropped the flaming stick into Marie's palm.

"I do this only to save your immortal soul," the nun intoned as flames shot up, Marie's kerosene- drizzled hands turning into torches. She shrieked in agony, the pain so intense it ripped her out of her mind; she pounded her head against the blackboard; clawed at her hair, smelled her own frying flesh.

And now her hair was on fire! The silence in the room broke, her shocked classmates making a kind of *oohing* noise. Screaming, in flames, Marie fled, shot out into the hall, burst through the outside door, into the blessedly frigid air, flung herself into a snowbank, rolled in the powdery snow like an animal seeking a den.

The relief was instant, blessed beyond belief. She lay there in the snow, at the base of the school's hard brick walls, beneath the windows of the choir practice room, through which she must have been clearly visible, but the choir boys and girls were intent on rehearsing *Jesus Loves the Little Children*. She grew colder and colder. No one looked out the window at her; no one came for her. She was left outside, a filthy girl, an untouchable. Her blistered hands crept to her scalp, discovered that her hair had been burned to stubble except for a tuft at the back of her head.

She'd stayed in the snowbank the rest of the afternoon, occasionally eating a fistful of snow, until, stiff and nearly frozen, dimly aware of the shouts of children hurrying back to their dormitories, she had crept away, whimpering, found her way into the church, and crawled on hands and knees up to the statue of Mary. When she had wept herself dry, when the pain in her hands had subsided to a dull throb, she had heaved herself up onto a pew and fallen asleep there in the church. Only later had she learned that the nuns had never even searched for her.

Now, standing in the kitchen of the great ship, Marie touched the bald spot on her crown, where the skin, even after twenty-nine years, was purple and puckery to the touch, requiring careful combing to disguise it. The ship's doctor—a kind man named James Grayson—had once examined the scars on her head and hands and told Marie that the snow was what had saved her life, had prevented her from going into shock, had cooled off the burnt tissue so that her hands hadn't been permanently mangled.

THE EMPRESS OF IRELAND

She kissed the photos of her sons, heartsick at the thought that her precious boys might be enduring the kind of abuse she'd been subjected to. They'd been allowed to come home a few times since they'd been taken away, but each time the boys were less themselves.

Their lovely, shining black hair had been cut military short, and the deerskin clothing they'd worn when they'd been taken had been thrown out, replaced by stiff denim pants and ugly brown broadcloth shirts. Nimki had been renamed *Paul*; Noodin was now *Joseph*. They wouldn't answer to their Ojibwe names; they had started calling her *Mother* instead of *Nimamamama*. She felt she was losing them an inch at a time.

She had to get them away from that place before it destroyed everything about them that was good and kind and true; everything Ojibwe. She'd thought up various schemes—using a ladder to climb up to their dormitory window and stealing the boys away in the middle of the night, or snatching them off the street from the nearby town where they were sometimes allowed to go to buy candy if they had behaved *white* enough all week.

But everything had seemed too impractical, too open to risk. If Marie was caught, she would go to jail; she had no illusions about justice for an Ojibwe.

And then one day on Rue St. Pierre in Quebec she'd happened to pass a lawyer's office. *Jude Minkin*, the sign read. *Jude?* After years of Catholic indoctrination, Marie knew her saints: St. Jude was the patron saint of lost causes. And so she'd walked into the office and knocked on a door.

Jude Minkin turned out to be a ruddy-faced man with thick spectacles over bright blue eyes. He listened sympathetically to everything Marie told him. He said the way the native tribes of Canada had been treated was a humanitarian outrage, and it reminded him of the way his own people—Ukrainian Jews—had endured pogroms and murders and torture at the hands of

Christians in Ukraine, all sanctioned—even encouraged—by the government.

"There may be a way to get your boys back," he'd told Marie.

She'd stared at him, hope surging, but not wanting to be suckered, because she'd been lied to so many times. "What way is that?" she said flatly, disbelievingly.

"Have you ever heard of *Madawaska?*"

Marie frowned. Not an Ojibwe word—she thought it was Maliseet—but the languages were similar enough that she could hazard a guess. "*Land of Porcupines?*" she said dubiously.

Jude chuckled. "I don't know what it means. But it's a town near the southern tip of Quebec Province, where a stream forms the US-Canada border. It's in the American state of Maine. And look at this!" He pulled out a map and spread it across his desk. "It's only a few miles from your own village."

Marie bit her lip. *What was he getting at?*

Minkin smiled. "You see, we can retroactively establish that you and your sons lived at Madawaska. Then we can claim that your boys were taken from *there,* from American territory. The government of Canada had no right to forcibly remove American citizens from U.S. soil—it would be a case of kidnapping across international borders."

"But my people have always lived in Quebec Province," Marie objected. "This would be a lie!"

Minkin smiled. He looked excited, like a man gearing up for a race. "Of course it's a lie. If lawyers were a hundred percent honest, we'd lose all our business. It's a simple matter of getting the right papers and presenting them to a judge."

Not such a simple matter after all, Marie soon learned; it would cost a great deal of money to get the right deeds, affidavits, and property tax records, most of which would have to be done by an expert forger.

THE EMPRESS OF IRELAND

It would cost three hundred dollars—an incredible sum—more than the average person made in three years. Marie had sold everything she owned—her falling-apart house; her furniture, her husband's old shotgun—but still couldn't scrape together the money. She'd asked Hazlitt, her immediate boss, for an advance on her salary, but he'd flat out refused. *Against company policy*, he'd told her sternly.

So when Sean Corkoran, whom she disliked and distrusted, had slunk up to her on the day before the Empress was due to sail, offering Marie two hundred dollars to do one small favor, Marie had jumped at the offer. She had an inkling of what the little *zhingo* was up to, but she didn't care. The roll of bills he'd given her was not just paper—it was her beautiful boys' freedom, their future. She'd stuffed it into her apron pocket, planning to sneak off the ship, to hurry down to the lawyer's office, give him the money and tell him to start work *immediately* on obtaining those documents.

Just her luck, though—Hazlitt had caught her as she was sneaking off the ship and had marched her back on board.

She wished Hazlitt damnation in the boiling manure pits of Hell, and she hoped all the devils looked like Sister Hubertus.

Chapter 12

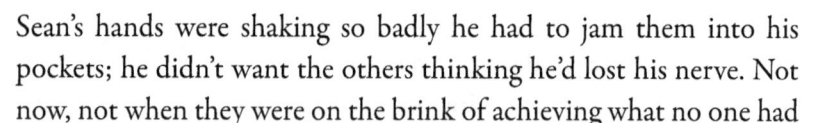

12:40 a.m.
Sean

Sean's hands were shaking so badly he had to jam them into his pockets; he didn't want the others thinking he'd lost his nerve. Not now, not when they were on the brink of achieving what no one had ever done—robbing the silver bullion on the *Empress of Ireland!*

"Here, *you* do it," he grunted at Murf, as though bestowing a favor, slapping the keys into Murf's palm. Albert Murphy, who worked as a tool and dye maker, had the steady hands of a craftsman. Carefully he inserted one of the keys into the left side of the padlock, a black steel rectangle nearly the size of a cash register, and turned it. The lock clicked, allowing Murf to pry up the shackle. Then he used the second key to unlock the padlock's right side. As soon as they were both popped, Sean yanked the shackles out of the heavy hasps bolted to the door. Half-expecting to hear sirens go off, holding his breath, Sean grasped the knob of the strong room's door. It turned; the door opened. *Opened!* This untouchable strongroom, this steel-plated, supposedly burglar-proof vault—was about to be his! Clutching his instrument case, Sean edged into the room, feeling as though he were stepping onto sacred ground.

Gorcey, Murf, and Moose trooped in behind, all of 'em twitchy with nerves, while Suds stayed out in the hall as a sentry, ready to signal if anyone came along. They must have found the Bakersfield guy by now; the alarm would be raised; the hunt would be on—they didn't have a second to spare! Hands shaking, Sean fumbled for nearly a minute before he finally found the cord for the light bulb and pulled it on.

"Cripes—there ain't no silver here!" Moose said, sounding like he'd been told there was no Santa. "Maybe we got the wrong room!"

"Course it's the right place, dumbass!" Sean growled, as the pallid yellow lightbulb revealed the room's disappointingly dull contents: none of the dazzling silver Sean had been picturing—just bundles of canvas-wrapped packets the size of bricks stacked on metal shelves, as ordinary as office supplies or boxes of Ajax janitor's soap.

He picked up a package at random and ripped off the canvas.

There! Beautiful as any jewel, a brick-sized bar of lustreless silver—heavier than he had expected, maybe ten pounds. Figure fourteen troy ounces to the pound—he'd done his homework—then what he was holding was nearly a hundred thousand dollars!

"*Mmmwwhuh!*" Gorcey, the dumb ape, having peeled the wrapper, was kissing the bar, "Come to Papa, you beautiful baby—"

Sean gave him a shot to the shoulder. "Stop screwin' around, jackass—get to work loading it."

Sean hadn't expected there'd be so many ingots—maybe a hundred, rough estimate. "Keep 'em in the wrappers," he ordered. "Just stick 'em in the cases as they are. And *hurry* for fuck's sake!"

Once again he checked his watch. The pickup launch should be setting out about now. He didn't trust the guy, but hadn't been able to find anyone else willing to pick up a cargo on the river at night. A ship the Empress's size, one seasoned sailor had explained to Sean, would have a draw powerful enough to suck in a smaller craft, maybe rip it to pieces with its enormous twin screw propellers. Only a boat with a gas-powered engine would be able to counteract the big ship's draw.

Finally an Eire do'Fein connection had found a *no-questions-asked* ex-con named Rene Boucher in a downriver town called Rimouski. He had a thirty-foot rig with one of those new outboard motors. The plan was for Boucher to anchor in Matane Bay the night of the twenty-eighth, watch for the giant ship to sail past, follow it from a couple miles back, then wait for Sean's signal—three flashes from a ship's lantern—before pulling up alongside the liner—a tricky maneuver under the best of circumstances; twice as difficult in the dark.

It was going to take pinpoint timing, and so much could go wrong Sean's gut had ached for the past two weeks—he thought maybe he was getting an ulcer.

Stealing the bullion would only be the first step, Sean had discovered; After that would come the complicated job of *selling* it. It was as useless as concrete blocks in its present form; you couldn't walk into a pub and slap a ten pound ingot onto the counter to pay for your drink.

The actual owners of the bullion—Canadian Trans-Global—CTG—would not want word to get around that the bullion had been stolen from under their noses—it would make them laughingstocks; it would send their insurance rates soaring; it would mean no company would ever again entrust them with a cargo. So the CTG would be motivated to keep it quiet; to pay a ransom that would ensure they got the bullion back.

After asking around in every bar and back alley in Quebec, Sean had finally caught wind of a guy who could grease the deal. It had meant traveling down into the States, crossing to Detroit, and ferreting out the man known in underworld circles as *The Banker,* a man who could negotiate a ransom with the CTG. He'd listened carefully as Sean had explained his plan, had demanded a huge down payment for himself, and then had explained that once they got hold of the bullion, they'd have to hide it in an easily-retrievable spot, somewhere along the river preferably, while the ransom was being negotiated. "Don't expect them to pay you face value," the Banker had warned. "They'll offer you a percentage. If you're lucky, you can walk away with a couple hundred grand."

"Oh, kee-ripes!" It was Gorcey, who'd just dropped an ingot on his foot.

"Shut up!" snarled Sean "You'll have every crewman on this tub down on us."

Satisfied that they all had their cases stuffed full, Sean banged on the door. Suds signaled back with the *all clear* and Sean cautiously opened the door. They moved out, single-file, Sean in the lead, his heart banging so fiercely he wondered whether a guy his age could have a heart attack, Gorcey next, limping, then Murf, and finally Moose, clutching two instrument cases in each hand—probably four hundred pounds dead weight; the guy was an ox.

Carrying their haul up the steep stairs of the B deck companionway was murder, and all of them were panting with the strain by the time they emerged onto the aft main deck, which, Sean saw to his dismay, was thronged with people. It was after midnight—why weren't these fools in bed?

"Oh, look, it's the *band!*" exclaimed a white-haired biddy, excitedly clapping her hands, trotting up to Sean with a simpering smile. "Will you fellers be playing another concert tonight?"

"Yes, ma'am, we surely will," Suds cut in, flashing a grin. "You be sure to come—and God bless you. God bless all o' youse, awright?"

"God *bless you?*" Sean hissed when she was out of sight. "You wanna get us all rumbled? Keep your trap shut. We don't want nobody noticing us."

Suds, who in Sean's opinion, did not treat him with the respect due to the leader of this expedition, scowled. "You can stuff it, big-shot! I was God-blessin' her like what a real Salvation Army guy would of done, or the old gal might've sniffed something funny."

Sean's knuckles whitened on the handle of his instrument case as he fought the urge to thump Suds—show him who was boss—but there wasn't time; they were just coming up to the freight elevator. It was used to move supplies between decks; he'd learned to operate it when he'd been a janitor and had grasped how it would be the fastest way to move the bullion from level to level. Even with their bulky instrument cases, they could all fit into the elevator at once. His crew stumbled in; he racked the crank to *Up* and pressed the motor's starter button. It caught, rumbled into gear. A juddering ride brought them to the top deck.

He cranked open the door and they all lumbered out, stepping onto the aft boat deck, then followed Sean as he led the way toward the starboard forward deck. He was just congratulating himself on how smoothly things were going when Hazlitt, the Chief Steward, appeared without warning from a doorway and shot them a hard-eyed look. Sean kept his head lowered, hoping Hazlitt wouldn't recognize him as an ex-janitor and demand to know why he was now prancing around in a Salvation Army uniform.

"Evenin' Captain," Gorcey called out. "God bless and keep you."

It was Gorcey-level stupid, but it happened to hit exactly the right note. "Evening," Hazlitt grunted, pleased to be mistaken for an officer. Snapping off a salute, he quickly strode away, probably scared one of 'em was about to shake a kettle at him, demanding a donation.

Sean was prickly with nervous sweat by the time they arrived on the starboard aft deck. Just ahead, solidly bolted to the deck, was the windlass, its long boom extending out over the railing. Unlike the giant cargo crane on the forward deck, used to load tons of coal, oil, water, and ballast, the windlass was a simple machine composed of a chain, a fifty gallon container, a hand crank and counterweights. It was used to load small cargo: provisions, cleaning supplies, bundles of life jackets and the like. It was too far aft to be visible to the watchmen on the bridge, but there was always the chance of a crewman taking a swing around the decks and poking his nose in. This was the most crucial part of the operation—the moment they were most likely to get caught.

"Unpack the bars," Sean ordered, his voice high-pitched with nerves. "Keep 'em in the wrappers, stow 'em in the bucket." As they set to work frenziedly packing the bullion into the windlass bucket, Sean hurried off to the midship locker where he'd stored the signal lantern. It had an oil-fueled wick set into a sturdy metal frame, with slotted shutters that could be opened or closed, enabling light to flash in short bursts. He'd arranged the signal—three short flashes—with Boucher, who'd assured him the light would be visible even ten miles upriver.

Boucher wasn't supposed to show up for another hour, but Sean knew if he had to wait any longer he'd go stark mad. Everything was ready; the lads ought to have the loot loaded—now all Sean had to do was send the signal.

Winching the cargo down to the boat was going to be tricky as hell, and then, Sean would have to climb down the side of the ship, using a rope ladder, into Boucher's launch. He'd learned how to scale a ship's ladder during his janitor's stint, forced to clamber down the ship's hull in order to wash the hundreds of porthole windows. Climbing down would be a piece o' cake for him, but he knew damn well none of the others could manage it. Besides, even in the dark, some sharp-eyed watchman would be sure to notice five men climbing down the side of the ship. So it had to be just Sean navigating that ladder, then boarding the launch and guiding the cargo into the boat as it was winched down.

The others would stay aboard the Empress until it got to Liverpool, then simply walk off the ship with the crowd of passengers before the theft was discovered. In Liverpool, they'd find a place to stay, then sit tight, wait.

Meanwhile, Boucher would haul Sean and the bullion upriver—to a cave in a cliffside Sean had scouted out a few weeks ago. Once the bullion was stashed away, Sean would contact the Banker to have him start working on the ransom, because by then CTG would have discovered the theft; the police would already be crawling over the whole liner.

The entire operation might take weeks, but when Sean finally had the ransom money, he'd send word to his crew through *Eire do 'Fein* that it was safe to come home.

It was a clever, well-considered plan—but it had nearly resulted in a mutiny.

"You get to play the big man, get the cash slapped into your hands, get to sleep in your own bed, while the rest of us are hiding away in some stinkin' foreign slum, living on beans?" It was Gorcey shooting his mouth off, but the others all chimed in with the same gripes, and to shut 'em up Sean had been forced to promise 'em a bigger whack of the profit. Which meant less for him, goddamn 'em.

Now, lighting the lantern's wick, worried that there wouldn't be enough oil to keep it going steady, Sean made his way back along the starboard deck toward the windlass, expecting to find the others waiting.

Only they weren't there.

The men, the windlass, the instrument cases—everything had vanished into a thick gray cloud.

Fog! A son of a bitching fog had dumped down! Sean let out a groan. Everything gone to hell because of a fluke he'd never factored into The Plan. Boucher would never come out in this pea soup. Even if he did, he might not be able to see the signal.

But sometimes fog lifted in just a couple hours—in which case they could still go ahead with the Plan. The fog might even work to their benefit . . camouflage what they were up to, swaddle them in a gray cloak as they hauled the bullion off the ship. *Maybe God had sent this fog to help Sean—*

"Oi—who gave you permission to take that lantern?"

Already on edge, Sean nearly leaped out of his skin as a figure materialized out of the murk.

It was that cocky little mutt Ludsnap, he saw, who apparently recognized Sean in that same instant, the two of them exchanging glares like clashing swords. He sensed the Scouser was itching to have a go at him as much as Sean wanted to pound *him*. They'd gotten into it a few times during Sean's janitorial days; Sean had discovered, to his surprise, that for a welterweight, the little bastard could pack a punch.

"I'll take that," Ludsnap growled, and before Sean could react, he'd jerked the lantern out of his hands. "Against regulations, in case you was paying attention in your mop-wielding days, Corko. No lights on deck—so some fool in a oncoming ship don't mistake your little gasolier there for range lights."

Sean clenched his jaw, itching to take a swing at Ludsnap. He shouldn't—not now, not with everything hanging by a thread. *Hell with it!* He couldn't resist—the little pillock needed to be taught a lesson. He loosened his shoulders, brought up his fists—

And jumped at the sudden jangle of bells and shouts from the bridge. His heart lurched violently. *They'd been discovered!*

Cursing Ludsnap, who was scuttling off with his lantern, Sean groped his way through the enveloping murk, stumbling toward where he thought the windlass must be, and then, his hearing amplified by his strained nerves, he caught the officers' voices up on the bridge.

His heart returned to normal with a sickening thud. *All that hoo-hah had nothing to do with him or the bullion.* Just something about lights sighted downriver.

Chapter 13

1:55 a.m.
Henry Kendall

The clang of a bell from the watchman in the crow's nest broke the silence of the wheelhouse. "Lights downriver, starboard," called the watchman, an eagle-eyed seaman named Carroll.

Kendall gave a start, realizing that he'd been on the point of dozing off standing up. He peered eastward into the dark night. Two pinpoints of light were climbing over the far horizon—the mast lights of a vessel.

"Eight miles, I'd estimate," said Jones, the First Officer, squinting out over the river.

"At our cruising speed, I'd give it about fifteen minutes." This from Moore, the Third Officer, chipper and wide-awake, in annoying contrast to Kendall, who felt dead on his feet.

"Her lights are dead in line, broad on our starboard, forty-five degrees off our bow, my best guess," Kendall said, reminding the younger man that *he* was the expert here.

"That means we'll cross diagonally across her path," Jones put in. "She's got right of way."

Sharples, the Quartermaster, made a dismissive *pffft*. "Plenty of time for us to cross her path and settle on our new course before we meet."

"Right you are," Kendall said, wide awake now, grateful for the chance to show off his seamanship. "Put the wheel over," he ordered Sharples. "Give us a heading of *North 73 east*."

The oncomer's mast lights were now about eleven degree to starboard off his own bow, Kendell saw. He scrutinized the other ship closely, until he was satisfied her lights indicated a starboard, green to green passing, a wide swath of river between them. It should be a purely routine—

It was at that moment, as he happened to swing his gaze to the left, that he noticed it. *Fog*. A great raft of it, roiling out from the western bank, an immense gray ghost that had materialized at the worst possible time and place—between the two ships, blocking their views of each other.

As the fog thickened into a sort of rolling murky swamp, the lights of the oncoming ship grew misty, leaving Kendall uncertain about the green-to-green passing. It had become far too chancy; he could not risk the ship; he had to bring her to a full stop. Reaching for the handle of the engine room telegraph, he cranked it to *Full Astern*, then yanked three times on the whistle cord, sending sharp blasts out toward the other ship—a signal understood by all seamen as meaning *We are going astern on our engines.*

An answering blast came from the other ship, but the fog warped the sound, making it seem to come from all directions at once. It had to be from the other ship, acknowledging the Empress's signal, Kendall reasoned; it was indicating that it meant to hold its course, that it would pass on a course parallel and starboard to the Empress.

Uneasy, he decided to see for himself. Slipping out of the wheelhouse, onto the right bridge wing, he stared into the fog. He couldn't remember ever being this jittery, even the night he'd been stalked by the insane killer aboard the *Isolde*. It was the fog. *Fog*, the bane of all seafarers—its coldness, its skin-slicking clamminess; the way it crept inside one's very bones. And as he stared into the fog, a nightmare materialized.

Sidelights! One red, one green, like the eyes of a monster, glaring through the murk—but it couldn't be—the ship should not be there in that spot; *could* not possibly be there, dead ahead—

And yet she *was* there, churning implacably along on a bearing that would bring her on a collision course with his ship.

John Carroll, high in the crow's nest, saw the huge black bulk of the oncoming ship—a heavily-built freighter with a chisel bow—loom up out of the fog, bearing down at a speed that whipped froth around her bow. "*Stop!*" he yelled, flinging up a hand—an instinctive human gesture, but as useless as trying to stop an oncoming locomotive.

Standing on the flying bridge, his heart pounding in his ears, Kendall groaned as he realized what was about to happen. All he could do now was try to swing the ship to lessen the impact. "Hard right over!" he shouted to Jones, hoping there was time to maneuver the liner over to starboard. Snatching up his speaking trumpet, he bellowed *"Go astern!"* at the other ship.

And then the freighter was upon them—its bow striking the Empress mid-ship with an ear-rending metal-on-metal shriek, sending sparks like lightning bugs sizzling up into the murky dark. Surprisingly, the impact was no harder than if the liner had nudged a piling while nosing into a berth—and that was terrible news, Kendall knew—it was the difference between a gut punch with a fist and an assassin's knife sliding between ribs. Their best hope now was to keep the stranger's bow wedged into the puncture it must have created, thus preventing river water from pouring into the Empress. If both ships stayed together, Kendall reasoned, he could beach his ship on the east bank.

THE EMPRESS OF IRELAND

He raised the trumpet to his mouth, but before he could utter a word the current had tugged at the freighter and she was slipping away, leaving his wounded ship at the mercy of the river.

Was he imagining it, or was the deck already tilting beneath his feet?

Chapter 14

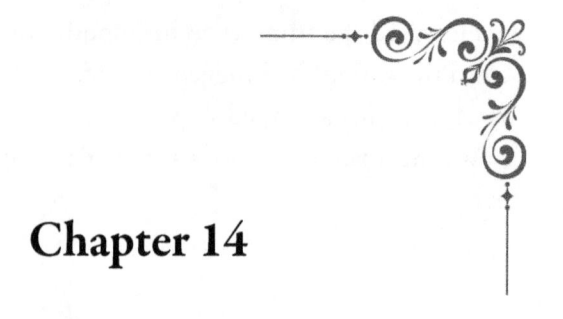

The Stordstad sliced into the Empress's unprotected side like a chisel into tin, cutting her open vertically from shelter deck to double bottom and penetrating many feet into her hull, cutting a hole below the waterline 25 feet deep and 14 feet wide.
   -Croall, James, *Fourteen Minutes,* Stein and Day, 1978

Louis never attempted to curb his cursing, drinking, whoring, or any of the thousand other sins the priests said you'd go to Hell for.

What did he have to fear? He lived in Hell already. It was a hundred forty degrees in the boiler room, a pulsing heat that scorched your throat and sucked sweat out of every pore in your body. He would have worked stripped to the waist if he could, but the furnaces were too treacherous. Shovel a half-ton of coal into Furnace number 4—the shovel itself weighed fifty pounds—and if you didn't watch how you stepped back, that Lucifer-sow of a Number 5 would give you a burn that would sear you to the bone. It was why Louis and the other stokers wore heavy denim coveralls, which afforded some degree of protection, though it made the men sweat ferociously.

Like the other trimmers in his crew, Louis was responsible for four boilers whose temperature must never be allowed to drop below two hundred twenty degrees. This meant frantically running from one furnace to another as though they were livestock bellowing to be fed. When he'd first signed on as a stoker, Louis had believed the job would require raw muscle and not much brain, but he'd quickly learned that the job required not just brute strength, but the delicate touch of a pastry chef. A trimmer had to spread the fresh coals evenly across the furnace gratings, and at the same time push the old ash into the ash pan, because ash acted as an insulator, bringing down the temperature of the boilers.

He had to watch the gauge above the furnace and keep the heat at a specific level so that it would *evenly* heat the water tubes in the boilers above the firebox. Too hot in one spot and the delicate tube would break. And there were hundreds of the little fuckers in a big boiler. Each leaking tube slowed down the ship; each cost time and money to replace.

When a trimmer had finished rotating between his boilers, he got a two minute respite during which he could stagger to the air pipe, cough the coal dust out of his lungs and drew in great breaths of cool sea air. Today, Louis sneaked in an extra minute to hurry to his locker and haul out his sketchpad.

He had to get the girl down before he forgot her details! The other stokers and trimmers thought he was sneaking peeks at dirty magazines on his brief breaks. If they knew about his drawings, they'd fall on him like wolves on a carcass: start calling him *Rembrandt,* scribble crude cartoons on his locker, and bedevil him mercilessly—which was why he must keep his drawings secret. Flipping the pad to a clean sheet, he used a wedge of coal—as close as he could get to charcoal—to begin a sketch, working in quick, sure strokes.

The neck first —the slender, lovely neck of the girl *Bridey*. He'd known the instant he'd seen her that he *must* draw her: the high, wide cheekbones, the beautiful eyes, the nose— too long by a centimeter, but it gave her face definition, character. He used the blunt side of the coal to smudge in the hollows of her cheek, and to rough in her hair.

Flipping through the pages of his sketchbook, he tried to view his work with a critical eye. Seagulls on a piling. Ludsnap's little cat—*how he'd itched for watercolors to paint that glowing orange fur!* Most of the sketches were of Marie Lavaliere, the cook. He could never quite capture the way her eyes slanted, but it was a joy drawing those cheeks—like apples beneath pie crust.

He had never dared show anyone his drawings, but he thought they might possibly be good enough to get him a chance at the Academy de Beaux Arts in Paris, though those high-brows would probably spit on him—a bull of a man whose ham-sized hands looked unfit to hold a paintbrush.

So his artwork would have to speak for itself—not just sketches, but paintings done during stretches of shore leave, using oil paints that cost more, ounce for ounce, than the finest cognac. Perhaps he'd find a professeur who would see raw talent, who'd speak up in his favor, who would . . .

The ship had stopped moving! Something wasn't right; you couldn't work on this ship as long as he had and not *feel* when something was off. Frantic voices came from the engine room adjoining the boiler room: the captain was ordering *Full Speed Astern*. What the devil was he doing? Louis didn't trust Kendall—he didn't know the St. Lawrence like Louis did; he was not *afraid* enough of it.

A shift to starboard brought a round of cursing from the stokers.

As Louis snatched up his shovel, heading for the coal bin, a monstrous screech assaulted his ears—metal murdering metal—and then the wall in front of him—*the wall, the ship's hull!* — splintered open with such force that rivets spat like machine gun bullets. A gargantuan black something burst through, like an ax blade splitting wood— a blade the size of a skyscraper—huge, *huge*, a monster that became the entire world —and Louis's reeling mind, refusing to accept what was happening—thought for a moment that the ship had struck a giant underwater rock—until he saw the steel, the precise, man-created lines—and realized that what he was seeing was a *hull*—the hull of a ship, and even as he thought that *This Could Not Possibly Be*, the monster surged forward, smashing the number 8 boiler, crushing the number 9 boiler—and now, above the monstrous grinding, the shriek of metal, the roar of escaping steam, came screams—the screams of crewmen being scalded by water the temperature of lava. Louis didn't understand what was happening, knew only that he must stop it— and his first, absurd thought was that he must *push* the monster back out.

Then the monster was suddenly gone, leaving a great, gaping hole, through which water burst as though from a breaking dam, a rush of water so powerful it tumbled him, arms flailing, mouth stretched in a howl, across the room, hurling him against the coal bunker, his back striking its hard edges, sending a shock wave of pain up his spine. He heaved himself to his feet just as another tidal wave of river water smashed through, surging across the room, gushing into the open maws of the furnaces, hitting the burning coals with a thunderous *whummpppf,* instantly creating clouds of boiling steam that mingled with the coal dust in the air to produce choking black smoke. Grignon, the crew chief, bellowed "*Sortez d'ici, maintenant!* Out, everyone *out*!"

A massive ear-splitting *boom*—Louis thought it must be Furnace 8, exploding. A grate flew through the air and struck a boiler, which cracked along its length, showering the room with boiling water and raining chunks of sizzling metal.

Around him vague forms moved in the murk, thumping into each other, uttering curses and cries of pain. Groping his way amid the sludgy smoke, struggling against a sucking tide already up to his waist, Louis stumbled over something he realized with a thrill of horror was a *body*. He found an arm, hauled on it, and lifted—but his chest seized up from the choking smoke and he bent over, coughing; it felt as though he was hacking up his lungs in slimy gobbets. When he could breathe again, he tried to find the man in the water, but he was gone. The smoke was thick as pudding, filled with burning cinders and clinkers. Worse than the smoke was his own disorientation—in a room whose every inch he had known by heart, Louis was lost.

His groping hand came down on burning hot metal. He screamed in agony—he'd touched a furnace! At least he knew where he was, though—the row of furnaces was on his right, which meant he'd gotten turned around, was heading in the wrong direction. The smoke thinned slightly, allowing Louis to get his bearings. To his relief he saw that the massive bulkhead doors had been left ajar—ordinarily a safety violation, but now the only route to an escape, because there was a ladder to the top deck on the other side.

But those doors were closing, swinging toward each other in jerky increments, and were now nearly touching, the gap between only the width of a hand.

Louis crammed himself into that gap, wriggling his shoulders, sucking in his big gut. *Make it through this door and he lived; fail to and he died.*

Chapter 15

2:07 a.m.

"Ludsnap!" roared Chief Steward Hazlitt. "Get over here!"

Snapper whipped around, cursing his bad luck. He'd been on his way to the lower deck to check on Charlie, see that he and the other boy weren't tearing around like lunatics, and now Hazlitt, who looked ready to spit nails, had caught him before he could duck out of sight.

"Go down to the ops room," Hazlitt rapped out. "Get the forward boiler room doors closed—*now!*"

"That ain't my post," Snapper protested.

Hazlitt slapped his face. "Do it, goddammit! Something's gone wrong—the ship's hit something—can't you feel the list?"

Furious at the slap, itching to punch back, Snapper discovered that he could indeed feel the list—maybe twenty degrees to starboard—in fact, he had to brace his hand against a wall to keep his balance.

Still holding the lantern he'd snatched off that scummy wanker Corkoran, Snapper made his way across the promenade deck. Passengers clogged the decks, most in pajamas, all of them frightened—although a few of the men wore anticipatory expressions: *something exciting was happening; they'd have a story to tell when they got back home.*

The further down Snapper went, the sharper the ship's list became—not only that, but the corridors down here were swirling with water! It had a strong tug, he discovered; he had to wade against it to get to the Operations Room, which was dark and filled with oily smoke; if he hadn't had his lantern he wouldn't have been able to see a thing.

His scalp prickled, and he felt a premonitory chill jag up his spine. Something else was wrong . . . It took him a moment; then it hit him—he was on the deck just above the engine room, *but couldn't hear the engines!* The huge expansion engines labored day and night, setting up a steady *thud-thud* that was the heartbeat of the ship

Now—no thud. *The engines were dead!* Snapper's own heartbeat, by contrast, was thumping away like a crazed thing; he had to fight down panic as he stumbled around in the dark room, choking on smoke, wading through water that sloshed about his shins. At last he found the key—a hollow-shafted tool the size of a hammer. He slogged over to the winding shaft, aware that the floor was tilting even more sharply now, and fit the key over the key stem like a boot fitting on over a foot. This notched the rack and pinion mechanism into gear on the doors one floor below, but the rest of the job was sheer muscle—it required turning a spoked steel wheel connected to the hinge shafts of the huge doors, which would close off the bulkheads to prevent their being flooded.

A case of closing the old barn doors after the nag was stolen, Snapper thought, struggling with the cumbersome mechanism, wincing as he felt a shoulder muscle tear. The entire ship's crew—seamen and stewards alike—had performed the practice drill to close the watertight doors just yesterday, managing to close all eleven bulkhead doors in three minutes flat. But now, in the dark, with water pounding in from some unknown source, and the ship listing heavily—so that in effect, he was pushing the door *uphill*—the flaws in the set-up were starkly revealed.

THE EMPRESS OF IRELAND

He swore through gritted teeth as he wrenched the wheel, cursing the cretin who'd invented this stink-dog of a system. Why hadn't the owners spent a few extra pounds on motorized controls—a simple button the captain could have hit to instantly close all bulkhead doors—instead of lavishing money on gold-edged dishes and potted palms for the ladies salon? Before this shit-storm ended, he was certain, people were going to die.

Chapter 16

2:08 A.M.
Bridey

Madame woke up moaning, sick and gaseous from champagne and red wine. "Get up!" she barked at Bridey, who'd just managed to drift off to sleep. "Help me to the bathroom."

Unlike the less-privileged in the lower class rooms, the first class suites had their own personal bathrooms, thus sparing Lavinia the necessity of sharing a common bathroom with the sort of people she would never have invited into her own house.

As Bridey groggily heaved herself off her narrow, lumpy cot at the foot of the big bed, Lavinia let out a squeal. "The carpet is damp!" she shrieked. "Not just damp—absolutely *soaking!*"

Lavinia was prone to wild exaggerations, but Bridey discovered that she was right about the floor. Not only was it wet, but in the glow of their night light, Bridey could see that more water was seeping in beneath the door—in fact, it was *gushing* in like a tide.

"Could be backed-up plumbing," suggested Bridey, as a vase toppled off the dresser and fell to the floor, making a dull *plooosh* on the soggy carpet— and now Bridey saw that the whole room was tilted to one side and the jars of cosmetics atop Madame's dresser were plunging off the edge like lemmings off a cliff. Bridey had to do a quick two-step to stay on her feet.

"This is absolutely *deplorable!*" Lavinia shrilled. "Bickerstaff shall hear of this, count on it! For what a room costs on this ship, one should not have to endure backed up plumbing! I intend to send off a telegraph first thing in the morning informing him—"

Someone pounded on the door.

Bridey opened it to find Ross, the steward who'd helped her maneuver an inebriated Lavinia back to the stateroom after dinner. He was holding something bulky and wore no trace of his earlier cheerfulness; in fact, his face was drawn and serious.

"I am *not dressed!*" Madame shrieked. "Close the door! I can't have a man seeing me in—

"Sorry, Mum, but it's urgent!" Ross said. "There's been an accident. The ship is listing—it may be going down." He thrust two life vests at Bridey. "Put these on, hurry out to the deck as quickly as possible. Don't stop to dress, don't take anything. Lifeboats are already being loaded."

"*Lifeboats!*" Bridey gasped.

"You need to hurry." Before she could ask more questions, he was gone; they could hear him running down the corridor, pounding on doors.

"This is *not* acceptable," Lavinia whined. "I intend to give Bickerstaff a detailed report on how rudely his stewards are—oh, don't just stand there, you imbecile—help me get dressed! My gray morning suit, I think. The black calfskin gloves, the duchess hat with the white plume—"

"But he said to get out right away," protested Bridey, and as more water surged into the room, swirling around her ankles and setting the cosmetic jars bobbing, she experienced a stark pang of fear. *Lifeboats! Could the ship really be going down?*

"I will not be hurried!" snapped Lavinia, fussing with her chin-firming strap. "Do you expect me to appear in public clothed in my *nightgown*? Find my stockings—and where did you hide my shoes, worthless girl—I don't know why I ever hired someone so—"

"Will you *hush*!" exploded Bridey, her temper frayed to the breaking point, her fear of Lavinia dwindling under the terror of a sinking ship. She shrugged into one of the vests without bothering to tie it, and thrust the other vest at Lavinia. "Here, put this on."

But the feckless woman just stood there, arms limp and helpless at her sides, still bleating about tattling to her precious Bickerstaff, until Bridey lost patience and forced the vest on over her head. It was bulky canvas inset with cork oblongs, the front and back tying together with laces. Bridey's hands shook as she fumbled to knot the ties, a task made trickier by the fact that Madame was putting all her efforts into trying to wriggle *out* of the thing. Pulling away from Bridey, she faced her reflection in the dresser mirror. "This thing is absolutely hideous! *Hideous*!" she shrieked. "See how it flattens my bosom—and adds absolute *pounds* to my waist! It's horrid, I refuse to be seen in—"

Bridey tugged sharply, tying the final knot. "Listen," she growled. "You can be a fat lady in a lifeboat—or a skinny corpse." Lavinia, who had lived her entire life as an overgrown baby, shielded from the rougher side of life, had no conception, as Bridey herself did, that things could go wrong very quickly. The *unthinkable* could happen in the beat of a heart: Bridey's own mother, wearing her best summer whites, had been marching in a suffragettes' parade, her face glowing with fervor for women's right to vote, when an automobile, driven by a drunk who'd hit the accelerator instead of the brake, had struck her, knocking her to the pavement, where she'd died moments later of head injuries.

Not taking precious time to fasten her own vest, Bridey seized a protesting Madame's arm and propelled her toward the door. As they stepped out into the hallway Bridey yelped in shock—the water was now knee deep, its current strong enough to make footing uncertain.

Even more frightening—the corridor was now slanted at such a steep angle walking was nearly impossible, burdened as she was with Madame, leaning heavily on her, gibbering in terror.

Suddenly Lavinia twisted around. "My sable!" she howled. "That coat cost four thousand pounds. I am not leaving without it!" Wrenching away, she floundered back into the stateroom, leaving Bridey fuming, all her instincts shouting at her to get out, to save herself.

Madame reappeared a minute later, somehow having managed to yank off the life jacket Bridey had so painstakingly fastened on her and donned instead, over her nightgown, a dark brown, high-collared fur coat, its hem made of dangling sable tails, giving the odd impression that the animals were crawling back up the garment, as though to nip the neck of the person who had poached their skins. She was clutching her overnight case—an expensive leather suitcase with brass fittings. Having carried it for Madame when they'd boarded the ship, Bridey knew it weighed at least forty pounds. "He said not to take anything!" she objected; at the moment she could have strangled this stupid woman.

"*I* don't intend to take it," Lavinia snarled "*You'll* carry it—it's what I pay you for! Go on, damn you, take it!" With surprising strength, she rammed the suitcase at Bridey, one of its hard corners jabbing Bridey's belly, making her gasp in pain. *What if it'd hurt her baby?*

It was a match to powder moment: all the rage and resentment she'd tamped down over the last two years suddenly erupting. Jaw set, teeth gritted, Bridey ripped the suitcase out of Lavinia's grip, swung it upward, and slammed it against the wall. Its locks sprang open; a cascade of cosmetics, toothbrushes, soap, shampoo, shoes, socks, slippers, and two dozen chocolate truffles spewed into the swirling water.

"Ooh, you horrid little snake—you'll pay for that!" Lavinia was so outraged the cords on her throat stood out like wires. "I'll have the police on you," she rasped. "I'll press charges, I'll—"

The overhead lightbulb buzzed, shot sparks, and abruptly died, leaving the corridor black as a coal mine, just as a fresh wave of water rolled in, sluicing along with such force that Bridey was nearly bowled over. Instinctively, she slammed her palms against the walls to steady herself, then, turning away from Madame, she began to forge a way through the rushing water, trying to recall the route she'd taken when Louis had walked her back to the room. If she just kept her hand against the wall on her right, she reasoned, she would soon reach the turnoff with the fancy lamp sconce that had reminded her of deer antlers.

Feeling as though she were in a bizarre, life-or-death game of blindman's buff, Bridey muddled along the corridor, hampered by her skirt, which was soaking up water like a sponge—water so cold it made her legs ache. *Here!* It was the antlered sconce—the passage branched left here, she was almost certain—and then there ought to be a staircase that led up to —

"*Bridget! Come back! Help me!*" Lavinia's terrified wail came from the far end of the corridor.

Lavinia Wilberforce was a horrible human being—self-centered, cruel, vain—and vindictive enough to follow through on her threat to have Bridey arrested for smashing her suitcase. *She didn't deserve saving*, Bridey thought savagely.

Still, she didn't deserve to be abandoned in the dark, left to drown.

Cursing her conscience, Bridey slogged back. Afterwards she didn't know how she'd done it—managed, in pitch blackness, through waist-high water, to get a terrified woman and herself up a tilted stairway and along a maze of corridors, but at last she and a hysterical Lavinia, still babbling about how she'd see to it that

THE EMPRESS OF IRELAND

Nathan Bickerstaff *heard about this*— stepped out onto the boat deck.

And into a scene of madness.

Frightened people milled about, frantically calling for lost family members, knocking into each other, shoving, falling down, shrieking in terror. It smelled of smoke and panic sweat and overflowing toilets. Crew members struggled to get to their lifeboat stations; terrified passengers pleaded with overwhelmed stewards for help carrying luggage. A bottleneck had formed behind a man who'd dragged an enormous steamer trunk up on deck and was shouting for someone to help him carry it. A grandmotherly woman in a cartwheel-sized hat tugged at a harassed seaman, insisting he help her carry a large cage inside which was a frightened, squawking parrot.

Bridey spotted Captain Kendall up on the bridge, shouting through a megaphone, but the uproar on the deck made it impossible to hear what he was saying.

Abruptly the ship listed sharply to the right. Amid panicked screams, dozens of people lost their footing and were tumbled across the deck, knocking others over in turn, creating a kind of human tidal wave and generating a stampede of frightened passengers trying to get out of the way, who in their panic, trampled those who'd fallen. The only passengers who were not panicking, Bridey saw, were the Salvation Army members, distinctive in their navy uniforms, many of them kneeling on the deck, loudly singing hymns or praying for deliverance—but only adding to the pandemonium.

"I want Elmer!" Madame squawked, clutching at Bridey with trembling hands. "I need my husband. Where *is* he? Why doesn't he come find me?"

"He was in the smoking room," Bridey said, sensing that Lavinia was teetering on the edge of hysterical collapse.

"Well, go fetch him," shrilled Lavinia. "He should be here. I need him!"

"I'll go look. Don't move from this spot," Bridey told her, pointing at the large, white, tuba-shaped thing jutting from the deck above them—some sort of ventilation device, she supposed.

She set out in search of Elmer, not because she cared about husband and wife being reunited—as far as she could tell, the Wilberforces despised each other—but because she didn't know how much longer she could put up with Lavinia without hauling off and smacking her.

She found Elmer on the port-side aft-deck, amid a cluster of men who'd evidently just spilled out of the smoking room. They were surrounding a crew member attempting to lower Lifeboat 4, while a steward yelled through cupped hands that the boat would not be launched until women and children had first been loaded.

The men, loud and disorderly, ignored the directive, turning on each other, elbowing and cursing, casting each other murderous looks, each determined to carve out a spot for himself in that boat.

There was Elmer! He'd buttonholed a steward and was raving to him how he was a close personal friend of the owner of this blasted ship, and if Elmer were not given top priority for evacuation, by God, he was going to sue the company and every sodding employee in it—

"Sure, you do that," responded the steward, giving Elmer a shove that sent him reeling backwards. Why, it was *Ross*, Bridey saw—the steward who'd warned her and Lavinia to get out of their cabin.

Rebounding from the shove, Elmer staggered into Bridey. He whipped around, fists upraised, ready to punch anyone trying to take his spot, before he belatedly recognized her. "Ah, the maid again," he snarled, his breath rancid with cigars and liquor. "Whaddaya want *now*?"

Bridey had to shout to be heard above the bellows of the other men, who were cannoning against each other, increasingly aggressive; one man was using his umbrella like a sword, stabbing at anyone who came near. "Can you come, please? Madame's frightened—she wants you to—"

"The hag can drown for all I care!" Elmer gave a cackling, lunatic laugh. "Ship's going down—matter of minutes. Here—I'll have this."

He took hold of the life vest she'd tossed over her shoulders and yanked it off her. "Every man for himself," he said, winking, as he pulled the vest onto himself and began shoving his way through the throng of tussling men—wealthy, influential men: politicians, business executives, clergymen, and the king of a small South Pacific island—all of whom believed their own lives were far more precious than those of anyone else on the ship, and to hell with *Women and children first*.

Chapter 17

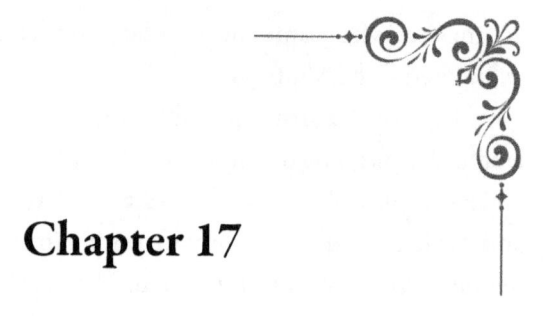

Charlie
 2:03 a.m.

What Tom dragged Charlie to see was, as far as the boys were concerned, the most wonderful thing on the ship—a *cricket pitch*, laid out along a covered corridor that ran parallel to the third class shelter deck. It had green coir matting instead of a lawn; it had a wicket and bats and balls and stumps and a starting bell, and lines marked off in white paint. Best of all, they had it all to themselves.

"I ain't never played cricket," Tom said. "Goofy name for a game, ain't it?" Snatching up a bat, he gave it an experimental swing. "These bats are weird!"

"You don't bat like hitting a baseball," explained Charlie, who played cricket with his mates at school and was known as a good bowler. His pa had shown him how to play and he'd loved it ever since. Once he found Pa in Liverpool, Charlie thought maybe Pa would take him to a professional cricket match, because the British had the best players in the world.

Tom, being American, couldn't get the hang of the game; he swung the bat so hard that the ball hit a light fixture and shattered it. They glanced around guiltily, sure that some angry steward was going to pop out and scold them, but nobody did—which was when Charlie noticed something odd.

"*Hey*, the floor's *crooked!*" he yelled, realizing that the entire pitch was slanting sharply to starboard.

They had fun running up and down the walls, doing somersaults, and sliding on their backsides as though on a playground slide. Giggling, giddy, they pretended to be crazy drunks unable to walk upright.

Their laughter died abruptly. Water was rushing into the corridor, seeming to be coming from everywhere at once, a gush of water so fierce it knocked down the wicket and tumbled the balls and bats away in its furious tide. Charlie was afraid he and Tom would be blamed for it—maybe it had something to do with hitting that light fixture— because adults always blamed kids when something got broken. "Let's get out of here," he whispered—always the best strategy, he'd found, when things started going wrong.

But moving through the water, which had suddenly become waist deep—-quickly stopped being fun; Charlie felt a small flutter of fear in his belly.

"Let's go back to the dorm," Tom said, forced to yell above the thunder of water. "We can climb up on the bunks, be out of this."

They made their way back the way they'd come, but it was hard work slogging through water heavy as mud. And *cold* —so horribly cold —their legs grew numb with the cold— in fact Charlie's entire body felt numb and he found that he was shivering violently. Charlie was a few yards behind Tom when a wave as high as the boys' chins surged through the corridor, knocking Tom off his feet. Charlie forced his legs to work, pushing against the surge, panting from the strain, his heart pounding painfully, all the happiness of a few minutes ago rinsed out of him, replaced by fear, because this was scary and serious and wrong and *why weren't there any adults around to help?* He stumbled over something beneath his feet, realized it was Tom— and grappled desperately until he finally got hold of an arm and hauled him out of the water, Tom gasping for air, his eyes wide, terrified. "I want to go find my ma," he quavered.

"Okay, but first we need to get to a higher deck," Charlie yelled, noticing that he could hear other sounds above the rush of water—screams, distant thuds, and a metallic screech that reminded him of the time a tornado had ripped off the tin roof of a neighbor's house. Just ahead he spotted the door they'd come through to get onto the cricket pitch —although that moment already seemed to be back in some other life, a life where nothing truly bad could happen to a kid. The door refused to budge, despite both boys throwing their shoulders against it—until Charlie realized that this, like most ship's doors, was on a track and slid open sideways. They fell through the door, discovering that they were in the girls' dorm, which also was flooded, and whose floor was tilted at the same dizzying angle as the hallway they'd just come through. Now Charlie could see where the water was coming from. Despite the rules against opening portholes, every single porthole along an entire wall had been opened, allowing the river to gush through in great cataracts, while terrified girls clambered up on their bunks to escape the flood.

"Hey! You gotta get out of here!" Charlie croaked, waving his arms, now noticing that there were a fair number of boys sprinkled in with the girls—little boys, no older than three or four years old—one of them was just wearing a pajama top and a *nappy! Where were the adults who were supposed to be in charge here?*

Well, it wasn't *his* job to do anything about them, Charlie told himself. *He* didn't want to be in charge of a bunch of blubbering, bed-wetting babies!

"Come on, let's get out of here," Tom urged.

There was nothing Charlie wanted more. Hands pressed against ears so he wouldn't have to hear the shrieks and cries, he let himself be dragged toward the door. "Which way do we go?" Tom's voice was high-pitched with fear.

"I think—" Something shoved Charlie in the butt; he pitched into the water, snorking water up his nose, coming up sputtering and furious, wanting to smack whoever—

It was a tiny blonde girl, he saw, eyes like saucers, tears drizzling down her face, and Charlie realized she hadn't shoved him; she'd lost her balance because a small boy had jumped up on her to get out of the water, and now it looked as though every kid in that room was trailing in his and Tom's wake, floundering through the water, mashing into each other like puppies in a basket—and all of 'em staring pleadingly at the older boys. Tom obviously felt no obligation to help the tykes; he was already in the corridor outside, chopping so rapidly through the water he was sending up a spray.

Not my responsibility. Turning his back, Charlie staggered toward the exit.

Behind him the shrieks and cries rose to an unbearable pitch. With the uncanny instinct of little kids, they knew that they were being abandoned, being left behind to fend for themselves.

An ache set up in his chest, centered over his rapidly-thumping heart and his lungs, which couldn't seem to suck in enough breath, until he sort of hurt all over— the sick feeling he always got when he'd done something wrong, accompanied by a nagging voice inside his head he didn't want to hear but couldn't block out.

"Oh, all *right,* then," Charlie growled, "I'll *do* it. But I'm *dumping* 'em first chance I get!"

Dredging fortitude out of his socks, he turned back, clapping his hands sharply to get the kids' attention.

Their small faces turned trustingly toward him—the closest thing to a grown-up they had at the moment, and then, to his amazement, they swarmed around him, tugging, grabbing, small arms raised in *lift me up* pleas.

"We gotta get outa here, okay?" Charlie yelled. "C'mon, *this* way."

Somehow he got them all herded out of the flooding dorm and into the corridor, which was slanted so steeply a lot of the little guys lost their footing and toppled into the water. Charlie lost track of the number of kids he had to haul upright, fighting a current that threatened to yank them out of his grip.

But he hadn't lost anyone yet! Something warm and heart-thumping fizzed through him. *Pride at his own bravery.* Maybe it ran in his blood. After all, he was the descendant of Alphonso Barrows, the great-grandfather who'd once been a slave on a plantation in the American South.

Mum had told him the story, which had been passed down in her family. Alphonso had run away from his cruel master, had been pursued by slave-catchers, fought his way through swamps, swum rivers, climbed mountains—until at last he'd crossed the border into Canada—where slave-catchers had no power.

He'd found his way to Quebec, to the small enclave of formerly-enslaved American Blacks who'd settled in the St. Roch area of the city. And he'd gotten married and had kids, and those kids had kids, and seventy years later Charlie had been born, a descendant of Alphonso.

When Charlie couldn't get to sleep at night, he sometimes told himself the story of Alphonso's escape the way Mum had told it to him; he liked to pretend that *he* was the seventeen-year-old boy fighting through the wilderness. He'd always wondered if he'd have been as brave if he'd been in Alphonso's place.

Well, now was his chance to find out. Of course Alphonso hadn't had a bunch of little squeakers raggle-taggling along behind *him*.

Glancing back over his shoulder, Charlie glimpsed something that chilled him to the bone: water was rising rapidly up the tilted corridor, coming on so fast it almost seemed to be pursuing the little ones.

"Hurry up!" Charlie screamed, but in that moment the ship gave a violent lurch to starboard, throwing him against the wall. When he scrambled to his feet, he saw Tom just ahead, at the base of a stairway.

Only the stairway was all crazy. It was as though a giant had picked up the ship and turned it sideways so that everything was upsy-downsy—the steps now reared up catty-wampus, the stairwell wall a slick, un-climbable slab. "There's no way to get up it," Tom moaned as Charlie reached him.

"*I* can climb that thing even if it's inside out!" Charlie boasted. It'd take a running start, though—and with all those little hands clutching at him, how was he supposed to—*No, wait!* There was a better way to go about it. "I'll boost you to the deck up there," he told Tom, "Then I'll lift the little goobers to you and you pull 'em up!"

It was not a bad plan, and might have worked—if at that moment, the overhead lights in the corridor hadn't flickered, crackled, and died, plunging everything into pitch blackness.

Chapter 18

Charlie 2:20 a.m.

Charlie grabbed Tom's shoulders, whipping him around so that the two boys were face to face, though it was so dark their faces were just blurs to each other. "Get up on me, Tom—I'm gonna boost you up the steps—"

He had to shout, because all around them terrified children were screaming for their mums. "When you make it up to the deck above us, run quick and find someone to help us—tell 'em there's little kids down here—"

"I don't care!" Tom blurted, sniffling. "I just want to go find Ma."

"Yeah, okay, but first find someone to help us—*ufff!*" Charlie grunted as Tom hoisted himself up, using Charlie as a kind of human ladder, his toes digging into Charlie's shoulders as he stood on them, trying to heave himself up the slick, sideways-tipped stairwell. Charlie clamped his hands around Tom's calves and thrust upwards, using every muscle he had, pushing from his gut, turning himself into a kind of human trampoline, powering Tom up, torqueing his body to compensate for the weird twist of the stairs, heaving, pushing—*and Tom was up,* belly-flopping onto the the floor above!

"*Go!*" Charlie yelled, just as small hands grabbed him from behind, pinning his knees, staggering him. It was a little kid, four or five years old, it sounded like—no way to tell whether it was a girl or boy. He bent and tried to pick the kid up, planning to hoist it up to Tom, but now a dozen more tykes swarmed around, clutching at him, bawling, screeching—and then the ship gave a huge lurch, tossing Charlie *on top of* a tyke who yelled in outrage—and just as he gained his feet, another surge rushed in, swirling the little ones around like socks in a washing machine. Water churned up to Charlie's neck, and suddenly all the terror he'd been holding at bay while he'd been heaving Tom up that cockeyed stairway slammed into him.

The freezing water, the shrieks of terrified toddlers, the tiny clawing hands, the cries of *"Momma!*—were all horrible enough, but it was the *dark* that was most frightening—like when the blankets got over your face while you were sleeping and you couldn't claw them off and you couldn't breathe, and in your nightmare you were crawling through a tunnel that suddenly was only an inch wide—that's what this darkness was like—a nightmare turned to horrible real life.

And then . . . a flicker. A pale flicker that dredged a Bible verse from Charlie's whirligigging brain, one he'd learned in Sunday school. *Then God said 'Let there be light' and there was light.*

Charlie had never known light could be such a wonderful thing.

"Oi, Charlie? you down there?" called a voice—a voice with that funny accent Charlie recognized as Snapper's. A moment later Snapper himself appeared at the top of the tilted companionway, holding a lantern, shining it down onto the upturned faces of the little ones, whose screams rose to such shrieks Charlie was sure his eardrums would bust.

"Oh, my bleedin' Judas!" breathed Snapper, whose first shameful impulse was to flee. Saving those tots weren't *his* job, after all. There had to be adults down there—anybody that wasn't *him*—to take charge. Someone trained to know what to do with thirty or forty terrified tykes

"Snapper! Do something—*hurry*!" Charlie yelled up, and Snapper wanted to tell him it was no good—he didn't know what to do either; he was practically still a kid himself, desperately wanting a grownup to tell him what to do.

"Is Tom up there?" Charlie called.

"Who?"

"Reilly—the American kid. He was going to go look for his ma—"

"Nobody here, mate."

"Throw me a rope and I can climb up," rasped Charlie, who sounded as though he was on his last legs.

"Ain't got a rope, mate—got my belt, though." Hastily Snapper set down the lantern he'd taken off that tosser Corkoran up on the top deck. Fumbling at his trousers, Snapper discovered he hadn't *worn* a belt today—what with Tabby running away, he hadn't took time to dress proper. Cursing his unpreparedness, he tried to move in two directions at once—back toward a locker that might hold some useful gear, and forward to reassure Charlie—and his stupid useless feet tangled their stupid selves and kicked over the lantern.

Kerosene splattered on the carpet—which was probably the only thing on this sinking monster that was dry—and the lantern's burning wick ignited the kerosene and suddenly the whole bloody rug was ablaze. The best thing he could do right now, Snapper thought, would be to drown his self and save the world from his own stupidity, because those poor kiddos what hadn't already drowned would now likely burn to death.

There was a fire hose around here someplace, though, Snapper recalled. The blaze, running along the rug as though in a race with itself, provided enough light for him to spot the hose a few yards away, pegged to the wall. Coiled up all shipshape, it was a length of tan canvas that looked more like a giant bandage than a fire hose. He'd had to learn how to operate the thing as part of his duties—-it was hooked up to a spigot in the wall and was designed to automatically inflate with the pressure of water when it was pulled out. Snapper yanked it off its hook, waited on an indrawn breath, and— *nothing!* Blasted thing just flopped there like a steam-rollered python. Likely all the water pressure had gone out when the electricity failed.

Close to a rope as you're gonna get, you thicko! The obvious solution practically punched him in the face. Hurtling back to the companionway, clutching the unspooling hose, Snapper attempted to stomp out the fire as he ran, succeeding only in setting his pants on fire.

"Charlie?" Snapper called down into the flooded companionway.

"I'm here! I smell smoke. Is there a—"

"Naw, nothing. Listen, I'm throwin' down a hose. Catch hold of it, and get as many of them pipsqueaks as you can to catch hold—"

"What? *I can't hear you*!" Snapper could just glimpse Charlie, wide-eyed, looking close to panic, surrounded by shrieking, terrified little kids.

"Gangway, Charlie—comin' down."

About to drop down to the lower deck, Snapper halted. *Bloody hell*—the hose had to be anchored to something, or he'd end up floating down there along with the nippers. Frantic, he looked around for something to attach it to—a ladder, a piece of heavy furniture, *something*— but he could hardly see in the thickening smoke, its heat scorching his eyeballs.

The ship lurched again, throwing Snapper against a wall—as though the great vessel was saying: *This is your final warning.*

There! The janitor's closet just down the hall—there'd be valves, pipes, all kinds of useful gear—maybe even life vests.

The closet was locked. *Locked, goddammit!* Snapper threw himself against the door, bruising his shoulder. Kicked it, cursed it in his worst Scouse, and damned to hell whoever it was that had decided the contents of janitors' closets were so valuable they had to be locked. He was pretty sure that kick had broken his foot.

Abruptly the door sprang open, knocking Snapper backward, as a man stumbled out of the closet—a well-dressed gent wearing a suit, and for a moment Snapper thought it was a passenger who'd accidentally been locked in and now was going to sue for everything the company was worth—and good luck with that, mate, because in a matter of seconds this ship was going to be worth no more than scrap iron.

" . . . attacked me," raved the man, who had an enormous lump on one side of his skull, a dangling rope around his wrist and a screwdriver in his hand. "When I came to . . . managed to free m' hands....jimmied the lock, only just now managed to—"

Belatedly, Snapper recognized him. "You're the Bakersfield!"

The man nodded grimly. "They stole the strong room key—"

"Forget it," Snapper cut in. "Worse things happening. Here, hang onto this." He thrust the fire hose into the man's hands. "Brace yourself in that doorway. When I tug, you start reeling the hose towards ya, wrap it around that standpipe there for extra support if—

"You ain't my boss, bub," growled the Bakersfield.

Snapper wanted to lock the arrogant prick back in the closet. "Ship's going down, arsehole! Just bloody *do* it!"

Snapper played out the hose as he scrambled back along the passageway, relieved to see that the fire was out, doused by water leaking from the ceiling—another ominous sign—might mean the deck above was flooded, about to give way.

Lowering himself gingerly down the tilted stairwell, clutching the hose while playing it out, moving backward like a mountain climber, Snapper plunked onto the lower deck—and found things worse than he'd anticipated. The water was up to his own waist here—water so icy it stung—and was up to the chins of most of the kids! Several small bodies, Snapper saw with horror, were floating face down!

His first impulse was to snatch up those cherubs, try breathing into their mouths the way the ship's doc had taught the stewards—*the kiss of life*—but while he was attempting *that*, some of the other squeakers might drown.

Right now he had to focus on saving the ones still alive. Maybe he could get the wee ducks to hang onto the hose while he hauled 'em up to the above deck, but they were screaming too loud to hear what he was saying.

It was Charlie who figured out what to do—he hauled himself up the hose hand over hand like he was doing the monkey bars on the playground, and then—*oh, that kid had mettle*— he anchored his ankles on something, stretched out full length on his belly, reached down like he was grubbing for carrots in a garden and began hoisting kids up, one after another.

Guided only by the grayish light of the dying fire, Snapper began pulling kids out of the water, their small faces ghostly in the dark. He heaved and shoved and manhandled them—some of them clinging to life by the flimsiest of breaths— up the companionway, into Charlie's waiting arms, and all the while terrified little ducks were grabbing at his legs, snatching at his arms, hindering his movements, but at last he thought he'd gotten every living child heaved up out of there.

It wrenched at him, to pull himself out, leaving so many small, drowned bodies bobbing in that slosh of icy, dark water.

Chapter 19

Bridey 2:25 a.m.

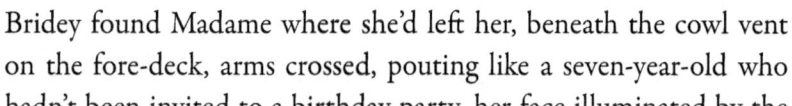

Bridey found Madame where she'd left her, beneath the cowl vent on the fore-deck, arms crossed, pouting like a seven-year-old who hadn't been invited to a birthday party, her face illuminated by the flickering lanterns stewards were stringing on a line between two bollards.

"Well, where *is* he?" Madame demanded as Bridey hurried up to her, out of breath from forcing her way through throngs of terrified people.

"He's not—he said you should —"

Go drown for all he cared? She had no intention of delivering Elmer's heartless message. "He said you should get in the first available lifeboat and he'd—he'd be along shortly," Bridey improvised, imagining that by now Elmer and his cowardly cronies had piled into that number 4 boat, had rowed themselves ashore, and were probably sitting at a fireplace in some hotel, passing around a bottle of whiskey and swapping lies about their own heroism.

"Well, what are you waiting for?" Lavinia shrilled. "Get over to a boat and *tell* them to save a seat for me. Tell them it's for a close relative of Bickerstaff. And get me a *first class* seat—I won't sit next to some third class riffraff!"

THE EMPRESS OF IRELAND

Reaching inside the sleeve of her sable coat, Lavinia pulled out the coat's attached store tag— the distinctive purple fleur-de-lis label of *Msr. Rondeau,* the most expensive furrier in Quebec. Around her, men and women, many bruised and bleeding, were in terror for their lives, desperate to get into a boat, *and Lavinia wanted people to know she was wearing an expensive coat!*

"Take it off," Bridey said. "It'll weigh you down." Having been the one responsible for hanging the sable in Madame's closet, Bridey knew the satin-lined garment, a fur designed to withstand the fierceness of Quebec's sub-zero winters, weighed as much as a medium-sized dog.

"Don't be an idiot. It's freezing out here," huffed Lavinia, giving Bridey a shove. "Go do your job—get me a place in a boat!"

With no idea how she was supposed to accomplish that task, Bridey began to make her way toward the nearest boat—but the ship suddenly heaved and lurched, sweeping her feet from beneath her, tumbling her against a tangle of deck chairs, turning the deck into a slippery slide. Disentangling herself from the chairs, managing to get a splinter in her palm, Bridey scrambled upright.

An enormous rumbling noise came from close by—it sounded like a freight train approaching. The Number 9 lifeboat, having torn loose from its davits, was thundering across the tilted deck, crushing anything in its path. A white-haired woman went down; an old man with a cane was sent flying like a ten-pin; the woman with the parrot cage was toppled as the heavy steel boat steamrollered across the deck. Almost too late, Bridey realized that the huge thing was coming directly at *her,* a lifeboat turned *deathboat.*

A memory flashed through her mind— her neighbor's St. Bernard, a big, friendly fella who always greeted her with a slobbery lick—who had one day suddenly turned savage, attacking a tiny girl who'd been skipping rope in the nearby yard.

The boat rumbled past Bridey, skidding the width of the deck, finally crashing into a group of women clustered against a railing, before it battered *through* the railing, taking the screaming women along like clumps of seaweed, and plunged into the river.

Bridey barely had time to register that horror before a clot of passengers whirled into her, carrying her along, her feet barely touching the deck, until they lurched up to the port rail, where crew members were struggling to free the 6-boat from its davits— but the ship was now listing so heavily that its hull was directly beneath the boat; the crew was fighting gravity as well as the weight of the boat, which swung out over the heads of the crew men.

Reserve Lavinia a seat? The notion was laughable.

Then she was caught up in another stampede as a mob jostled toward a boat on the starboard deck, where a crew was launching Lifeboat 3. It was already swung out above the river, close enough to the railing that people could step into it. Elbows flew; fists swung, and Bridey clamped her arms around her middle, desperate to protect the tiny being inside.

"Women and kids only!" bellowed a uniformed man, a steward named Gaade whom Bridey had seen handing out life vests earlier. Grudgingly, a few of the men gave way as Bridey tried to wriggle her way to the railing—but she was suddenly knocked to her knees as a group of men in scarlet uniforms muscled their way through the throng, using their suitcases as battering rams, forming a scrum that shoved back anyone who tried to move past them. One of their lot clambered over the railing and swung himself down into the empty boat.

It was *Butch Gorcey,* Bridey saw with a shock—Sean's mate, And—she'd have recognized that lanky form anywhere—*Sean himself,* muscling his way through the crowd.

The suitcases were actually musical instrument cases, Bridey saw, recalling that was part of Sean's scheme to transport the stolen bullion. *The ship was sinking, people might die, but Sean was still carrying out his plan!*

"Wait your turn!" roared Gaade, chesting up to Sean, flinging out his arms like a barrier.

Good for you, Gaade, Bridey thought, silently cheering, but in the next moment she caught sight of Moose McGill lunging toward the steward. Clutching something in his fist, Moose cocked back his arm and struck Gaade a hard blow to the head. Gaade pitched sideways and fell to the deck; now, with no one to stop them, Sean and his mates rushed the railing, threw their cases down into the boat, then jumped down themselves.

Shoving a path to the railing, Bridey leaned out over the boat. "*Sean!*" she screamed

Despite the witch's batter of mingled fog and smoke, Bridey could see Sean's head snap around, and for a moment their eyes caught. She held out a hand toward him—the man she loved, the father of her child.

He broke off their gaze, his eyes going distant, like someone tracking the figures in a ledger book, and Bridey could almost see the calculations ticking through his brain: *Time was racing away; time was everything.* The Heist hadn't gone as planned, but this had turned out to be much better—Sean and his crew would get away under the umbrella of the shipwreck; it would be assumed the bullion had gone down with the ship. But if they let Bridey into the boat, others would try to follow, and soon the boat would be overburdened—

I'm already in Sean's past, Bridey realized. *I've already gone down with the ship. Now there'll be no one holding him to a marriage he didn't want, no one forcing him to endure a squalling baby, nothing to keep him from becoming the hero he'd always fancied himself to be.*

Eyes blurring with tears, Bridey turned away—and stumbled over something—it was Gaade, prone on the deck, unconscious.

Kneeling beside him, she examined the horrible swelling over his left eye—a lump that could only have been caused by the blackjack she knew Moose always carried. Gaade moaned—a hopeful sign, Bridey thought—but he was in danger of being trampled by the panicked mob. He had to be moved to a safer spot—if there *was* one in this madhouse. Crouching behind him, Bridey caught him beneath his armpits, planning to drag him out of the flow of traffic—but just then a man came up alongside, nudged her aside, and began hauling the unconscious steward across the deck. It was James Grayson, Bridey saw—the ship's doctor Lavinia had schemed to be seated next to at dinner.

Grayson moved Gaade across the steeply-slanted deck to a sheltered niche between ventilation pipes. "Let's have a look," he said, kneeling beside the unconscious man.

Bridey was about to ask whether she should try to find ice for the swelling when a woman screamed. She looked up just in time to see a lifeboat loaded with passengers plummeting down from the deck directly above, the boat's pulleys squealing, its lines playing out jerkily, causing the boat to tilt sharply

To Bridey's horror, the boat abruptly pitched to near-vertical, passengers spilling out of it like discarded rag dolls—and then the out-of-control boat smashed down atop Lifeboat 3. *Sean's boat!*

Chapter 20

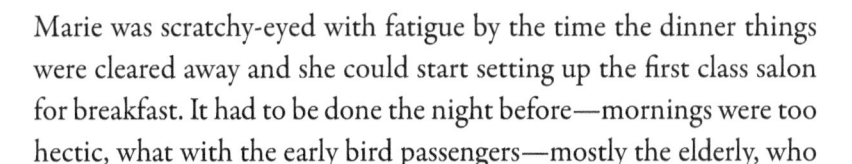

2:14 a.m.
Marie

Marie was scratchy-eyed with fatigue by the time the dinner things were cleared away and she could start setting up the first class salon for breakfast. It had to be done the night before—mornings were too hectic, what with the early bird passengers—mostly the elderly, who were up at dawn—demanding their coffee.

A plate fell off a nearby table. Just flipped off as though nudged by a ghostly hand, shattering on the hard tile floor. Marie swore, knowing she'd have to write a breakage report. Too many broken cups and plates and the comptroller would be poking his nose in, implying that maybe stuff wasn't really breaking; maybe the staff were selling Empress property on the black market.

More things began falling—coffee cups, saucers, cereal bowls, plates— a Niagara of falling crockery, and Marie, who'd been too busy to notice it earlier—now realized that the floor was tilted—in fact, it was slanted at such a steep angle she had to trudge *uphill* to get to the kitchen.

The ship was listing!

The first twinges of panic unfurled in her stomach. There'd been that *jolt*— about an hour ago, but she hadn't paid any attention to it at the time—and now there was a ruckus out on the deck—yells, screams, the sound of a frightened mob. Suddenly a siren wailed—a bloodcurdling shriek that was the signal for *All Hands to the Lifeboats*. What were they thinking, running a drill in the middle of the night, scaring the passengers half to death!

She'd just decided to find Hazlitt, who would know what was happening, when the ten foot tall glassware cabinet near the door shimmied, swayed, and then toppled to the floor, shattering a thousand dollar's worth of fine crystal, shards spraying outward in a lethal confetti. Lottie LaBeau, who'd been sweeping up the shattered remains of a teacup, shrieked in pain, holding up an arm peppered with cuts. Snatching up a tablecloth, Marie ran to her and pressed it to Lottie's arm, watching the white fabric turn bright red, and it wasn't just blood that made her queasy; it was the feeling that something was terribly wrong.

Denny O'Dwyer, one of the dishwashers, suddenly burst through the salon's doors, wild-eyed, shouting. "The whole feckin' ship is sinking! Get out—get to the boats afore they's all gone!"

Petey Bastion, who was mixing French toast batter, dropped a carton of eggs. The floor was now slanting at such a steep angle that a fruit basket atop a counter spilled it contents, bouncing oranges across the floor.

"I ain't stayin' here like a ninny, to be drowned in my shoes," screeched Mamie DuFarge, the Second Cook, throwing down her apron. Moving at an amazing speed for a woman of her bulk, Mamie fled—and that was the signal for the rest of the kitchen staff to abandon oranges and coffee pots and eggs, hopscotch around the broken glass, and dash for the door.

The qualm of unease Marie had felt earlier was now blooming into full-out panic. Could Denny be right? Could this vast machine, this vessel that had been her floating home for seven years actually be going down?

THE EMPRESS OF IRELAND

The overhead lights flickered and went out, plunging the room into darkness.

Chapter 21

Snapper

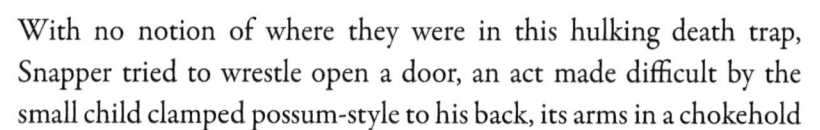

With no notion of where they were in this hulking death trap, Snapper tried to wrestle open a door, an act made difficult by the small child clamped possum-style to his back, its arms in a chokehold around his neck.

Finally wrenching the door open, Snapper stepped through, a swarm of children at his heels—he could hear their frightened squeals though it was too dark to see them. They'd been trudging along for hours, slogging along flooded gangways and crab-walking up companionways tilted like the interiors of fun-houses—and all in the pitch dark.

By Snapper's reckoning, they were somewhere amidships—maybe on the second level—possibly close to the promenade deck, and now he could hear other people out there—yells, curses, the blare of a siren. "*Oi!*" Snapper called, cupping his hands, "We need help here! I got a bunch of kids. Somebody—"

It was no good—his voice was worn to a scratch—the voice of a man who has been yelling encouragement and commands to frightened children for hours.

If they just had a bit of light, he could get his bearings, Snapper thought, groping feverishly through his pockets, hoping to find a dry match, knowing it was hopeless— his clothes were wet from knees to armpits.

Then, in a stroke of good luck—*long time no see, old chum*—Snapper pulled out a pack of Woodbines—squashed and flaking, but with a single, blessed wooden match tucked in among the cigs. Using his thumbnail—the kind of skill you picked up in pubs—he flicked the match. It caught, flared up in a stink of sulphur, allowing a brief, flickering image of pale, scared faces. There'd been a whole troop of little ones when they'd started out— but now he counted only nineteen heads—no telling what'd happened to the other poor little ducks. He'd made them hang onto the fire hose when they'd started their journey, but one by one the tykes had dropped their grips, until the hose had vanished under the water, never to resurface. Snapper had carried as many of the wee ducks as he could—piggyback or clamped to his chest or any old way they could latch on, as though he were a giant tyke-attracting magnet.

In the match's flare, Snapper saw that they were in the second class dining room, which still smelled faintly of tonight's supper, but which now resembled a saloon after a brawl—chairs and tables overturned, broken glass everywhere. The floor was slanted like the edge of a roof, and a wide, debris-strewn pond had formed between where they now stood and the salon doors opposite, which were the only exit from this room. How were his little ducks going to get across that pond, which was now swirling with water pouring in through the starboard portholes?

He'd have to carry 'em, making several trips back and forth, Snapper saw, groaning at the prospect; he'd already hauled this lot up four flights of stairs; his thighs shook with fatigue; his back muscles were screaming, and the foot he'd injured kicking that door was painfully throbbing.

As the match burned down, singeing Snapper's thumb, the room fell into blackness again—but not before an after-image had burned itself on his retinas —something that had registered on his eyeballs but not in his brain: there were portholes on *this* side of the room, just above the lower promenade deck. *Portholes no narrower than a small child's body!*

Snapper lurched toward that wall, the kid on his back tugging his ears, as though to steer him, another kid strangle-gripping his knees. Staggering in the dark, working from the memory of that single match-lit glimpse, he stretched his arms out, clawing the air until his hand struck a porthole. *Here was the latch!* Unhooking it, he swung it open from its hinged bottom; a clammy wraith of fog whiffling in, stinking of coal smoke. "*Oi, Charlie!*" Snapper called. "Think you can squeeze through this thing?"

Charlie was there in an instant, hoisting himself up, eeling through the narrow opening, and landing on the deck outside, trig as an acrobat.

"Here—take her." Snapper peeled off the little barnacle clamped to his back and passed her through the opening until her feet touched the deck and Charlie grabbed hold of her, steadying her. "*I got you, I got you, you're all right, I got you,*" Charlie chanted to the scared little girl.

A born big-brother, that lad, observed Snapper, as one by one, he hoisted the others through, and if he wasn't as gentle with the urchins as he wanted to be, it was only because he had an ominous sense of time running out. At last, when every duckie was through, Snapper stuck his head and right arm through the hole, whose diameter, he guessed, was about that of a dinner plate. Next, his shoulders, worming and squirming 'em, shredding his shirt, scraping his exposed skin. His upper half was out—and then came the awful moment when he stuck at the hips, half in and half out, like a big stupid radish that refused to be pulled out for someone's salad.

Charlie grabbed his armpits and yanked, and a tiny girl gripped Snapper's hair—and as he forced himself forward his trousers snagged on the latch, peeling down and puddling around his ankles, trapping his feet.

Stuck! Well, he couldn't stay here, trousers round his ankles like a man who'd died on the toilet, even if he had to leave a layer of skin behind. Twisting like a trout fighting a hook, he corkscrewed through the porthole, flopping onto a deck that was now slanted like a carnival tilt-a-whirl. As he lurched toward the others, he abruptly pitched to the deck, tripped up by the treacherous trousers, knotted at his ankles.

"Goddammitall to bloody fuckin' hell!" It blistered out of his mouth without any thought for his audience, bringing an eruption of gleeful snickers from his flock of ducklings, which intensified to high hilarity as Snapper hopped around one-legged, trying to pull his trousers off over his shoes—the which he hadn't took time to unlace. Just as he yanked the damn pants off, leaving himself with bare, goose-pimpled legs, and clad only in his knickers, Charlie pointed aft and called, "There's a boat!"

It was the 8-Boat on the port side, Snapper saw, but the crew trying to launch it was having a devil of a time, the ship now listing so severely that the boat leaned out over the men's heads. "We'll try the other deck," Snapper said, having to yell to be heard above the hubbub of frightened people too intent on saving their own necks to lend a hand with Snapper's little flock.

Hell with 'em. He'd managed without anyone else so far; he'd just keep on doing it. *"This way to the boat rides, ladies and gents!"* Snapper called, scooping up a tyke and leading his unruly mob along the *Alley*—which was what the crew called the narrow passage between the port and starboard sides of the ship. Small arms clamped around his waist, more hands clung to his elbow —and another pair of hands clutched at the elastic waist of his knickers, pulling them down, and the whole untidy, milling pack—some crying, some giggling hysterically at the sight of Snapper's skinny bare bum— tottered and wobbled toward the starboard deck.

Snapper's heart gave a sickening lurch as he took in the scene. Difficult to see in the foggy dark, but he could just make out that the ship was now canted so far to starboard that the three remaining boats, which the crew had somehow managed to free from their davits, didn't have to be lowered—the river was simply rising up to meet them. The Empress was on her beam ends now, water lapping at her decks, her starboard railing parallel to the water. He *had* to get these little ones off—and fast!

A screaming clot of people clustered around the number 12 lifeboat, which was being loaded with all the efficiency of a soccer riot. "Oi, hold up!" Snapper shouted, elbowing his way through. "Kids here—let 'em in the boat!"

The boat was already jammed like a tin of sardines, and those in it pretended not to hear Snapper's shout—they used their oars to push away from the ship's side, and suddenly the current had seized the boat, swirling it away upon the dark water, leaving those left behind to live or die aboard a ship sinking so rapidly its life span could be counted in minutes.

Chapter 22

Snapper 2:20 a.m.

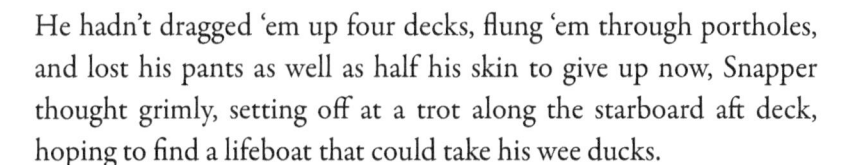

He hadn't dragged 'em up four decks, flung 'em through portholes, and lost his pants as well as half his skin to give up now, Snapper thought grimly, setting off at a trot along the starboard aft deck, hoping to find a lifeboat that could take his wee ducks.

He staggered, nearly losing his footing because the deck was canted at an angle only mountain goats could have negotiated, and now he had a new worry: that his ducklings might slide right through the railings and over the side. Their pitiful cries rang in his ears: *they were scared; they were hungry; they wanted a drink; they wanted their mums; they wanted to be carried; they had to do a poo,* and two of the boys were quarreling over a cricket ball one of them had found along the way.

Snapper didn't blame 'em for whinging. Come right down to it, he wanted *his* mum, too.

Stumbling against something, Snapper saw that the deck ahead was clogged with debris, blocking them from moving any further aft. Too dark to see what all the muck was, but Snapper thought he could make out a smashed dresser, trunks, suitcases, water drums, deck umbrellas, upended chairs—

And there, amidst this slumgullion, Snapper glimpsed something that made his heart leap—something with curved sides, something with a Number *1* stenciled on it in white paint.

"Who wants to dig for treasure?" Snapper called. His ducklings set in with ferocious glee, heaving and hauling and digging, though Snapper quickly realized this digging notion had been a mistake, because the whole rotten mess was studded with broken glass and jutting nails. He was just about to call off the excavation when Charlie lifted up a sodden mass of curtains to reveal the small boat Snapper had suspected lay beneath the litter— *the ship's tender!* This was the twelve foot dinghy used to ferry late-arriving passengers from shore to ship or for crewmen to run errands ashore. Evidently it had been knocked off its davits by that landslide of debris, shoved through a smashed railing, and now teetered just a few yards above the rapidly-rising river.

Heaving and hauling together, he and Charlie managed to get the dinghy launched, Snapper constantly glancing over his shoulder, fearing that half-crazed passengers would spot the boat and make a rush for it. Moving as quickly as he dared, Snapper piggy-backed the ducklings down into the boat, which, un-moored, rocked with every flurry of current.

"*No no no no no!*" screamed a tyke right in Snapper's ear. "*No boat! No boat!*" That got the others going—their shrill, terrified screams adding to the chaos. At last— all higgledy-piggledy, the way you'd corral a litter of wild badgers into a basket, Snapper and Charlie got the tykes tumbled into the dinghy, the operation conducted with the total opposite of *good and seamanlike order.*

Loaded beyond capacity, unbalanced, the dinghy wallowed in the water, rocking like a hobbyhorse. But at least the tub had oars—Snapper found them snugged against the burden boards. He passed two up to Charlie, who'd seated himself on a center thwart and quickly figured out how the oars fit into the rowlocks. Snapper took the stern thwart amid ducklings quarreling over who got to be next to him. There were no oar locks here; he just balanced his oars on the gunwales and poked them into the water on both sides, while trying to ride herd over the horde of small, unruly creatures who seemed determined to fall overboard.

"Don't know nothing about boats," Snapper called up to Charlie. "Closest I ever got to one was that time I took Rosie Dowling into the Tunnel of Love at Blackpoole Amusement Park."

"It can't be that hard to row a boat," Charlie called back, looking worried.

He was wrong though, as they both soon discovered. You had to use every muscle in your back and shoulders; you had to dig the oar in deep or you'd just be feathering the surface of the water—and you had to do it in unison with your rowing partner. Basically, you were moving the entire boat's weight with four slabs of wood, while fighting a current that had its own notions of where it wanted to take you, and riding herd on small humans bouncing around like jack rabbits.

Between him and Charlie, and with a silent prayer thrown up to St. Elmo, patron saint of sailors, they somehow managed to row a fair distance from the ship—maybe forty or fifty feet, Snapper guessed. Glancing back, he was shocked to see that hundreds of people were still aboard the sinking ship, standing on its hull as the water relentlessly crept up the sides, their figures silhouetted black against a macabre blue glow.

"Is that the Northern Lights?" Charlie asked.

"Could be," Snapper said, but that was a lie; he didn't want to say what it was in front of the little ducks. The light was coming from hundreds of life vests whose chemical flares had activated blue upon impact with the water—and most of those vests were on the corpses bobbing in the water all around.

The Empress's death throes were being lit by the dead.

Snapper strained his eyes, trying to make out Tommy among all those silhouetted people—Tom Ross, his dearest friend; they'd never had a chance to say goodbye to each other. No time to mourn just now, though—he forced his attention back to the task at hand.

"Put your back into it, Charlie," he urged. "She's going down soon—and we don't want to be near her when she does—she'll pull us down with her."

He was also worried about the ship's giant funnels, which, canted at a grotesque angle by the ship's list, appeared to have been wrenched loose from their moorings and were ominously wobbling. If those seventy-foot monsters went over, they'd smash every boat out here—and there were dozens within striking distance, Snapper noted.

A small child teetered on the edge of the right gunwale, about to topple into the water. Lunging forward, Snapper grabbed him and plopped him firmly on his lap.

Charlie gave a shout, and Snapper whipped around just in time to see what looked like an explosion aboard the ship—a flareup of fire accompanied by a muffled *boom*. The Empress rolled onto her starboard side, and began to disintegrate, anything loose thundering across its decks and shooting into the water—as dangerous as falling bombs to the lifeboats below, and as the debris hit the water it created a tidal wave that sent their own dinghy bucketing violently backwards, propelling it into the tangled remains of the toppled ship's mast—a mesh of cables and antennae wires, a lethal spider's web that ensnared the dinghy, leaving it unable to move forward or backward.

As the dinghy wallowed beneath the weight of the wreckage; the wet, cold, hungry kids whimpered, their teeth chattering with cold, their cries pitiable—but Snapper didn't know how to help them. He dug his oars in hard, trying to create enough momentum to propel them forward, but the ensnaring wires held them fast.

THE EMPRESS OF IRELAND

Charlie stood up, rocking the boat, and tried using his oar to jab at the largest cable hanging above them—but his standing up seemed to have been the signal for every other kid to jump up and lurch around the narrow space.

"Siddown," Snapper growled, yanking a small boy named Arno down onto a thwart. Arno responded by flinging the fiercely-fought over cricket ball in Snapper's face, chortling at Snapper's outraged expression—and then the laughter turned to sobs as the boy realized that his ball had bounced into the water and was now lost.

Snapper was utterly unsympathetic, but the small girl sitting next to Arno was softer-hearted; she patted the boy's back; then, to Snapper's surprise, began piping a song. "*En roulant, ma boule roulant, en roulant ma boule.*"

Another voice joined in, then another. Evidently this was a nursery song—some ditty all the kiddos knew. Snapper, with his meager French, thought *Boule* meant ball. Roll on, my ball—something like that?

" *Le fils du roi s'en va chassant,*" trilled someone, and the other ducks chimed in with the chorus: "*En roulant, ma boule—*" just as a huge, black *thing* thunked against the boat's sides. A hand clawed up over the gunwales, then a head and shoulder appeared —the *thing* was climbing into the boat.

Chapter 23

Bridey

She was struggling across the steeply-tilting deck, trying to get back to Lavinia, when the ship gave an enormous shudder, the floor shook beneath her feet, there was a reverberating *boom* like cannon fire and smoke roiled from the innards of the ship.

"Boilers must have exploded," Bridey heard one crewman call to another. She started toward him, hoping he could tell her what she ought to do—but the floor abruptly dropped from beneath her feet and she found herself tumbling down a deck that had turned into a vertical wall, screaming but unable to hear her own voice because her ears were still ringing from the explosion. She struck something—a railing?—and then she was falling, snatching at thin air—

And gasping in shock as her warm body was plunged into freezing water. Bridey had endured twenty-two Canadian winters but had never known cold like this —cold that pierced her bones, flayed every nerve in her body— cold so cold it burned, cold that was inside her, too, because she'd been screaming as she fell and now water filled her mouth and nose; pulsed against her eardrums.

This was death, Bridey knew, and it was terrible—it was her punishment for her wicked thoughts earlier. *You wanted to know what it would feel like to plunge into that water, foolish girl? It feels like death.*

It was there in the darkness with her—Death, merciless, mocking her own stupidity—*You thought Hell was fire? Hell is this cold for all eternity. Hell is knowing your own selfishness killed your baby.*

Not fair, not fair, not fair! I didn't mean it. I don't want to die. I want—

She struggled, kicked away Death, one thrashing foot finding something solid beneath; her toes just scraping it, bouncing her, shooting her body upward.

Face above surface. Gulps of air. *Breath— the most precious thing in the world!* For an uncomprehending moment Bridey thought she might have come up on the opposite side of the earth—all she could see was water, endless water; it must be an ocean, and it had *things* bobbing in it, the eerie scene lit by an unearthly blue glow that seemed to radiate from the water itself. She started to sink again; panicking, she grabbed onto the nearest object to hand—a chair leg! If she stretched her body out behind it, the thing might keep her up. She'd never learned how to swim, but she and her brother had sometimes paddled in the canal that ran in back of their street, using old auto inner tubes, so she understood the principles of buoyancy—some things kept you afloat; some things pulled you down.

Close by, a huge dark form thrashed toward Bridey, making odd squeals—a thing with black fur. *Bear* was her first horrified thought, because even in the water bears could be dangerous Then she spotted the pale, squinched-up face.

Not a bear—It was Madame, still swathed in the sable coat, and looking petulant, as though this entire disaster was something designed specifically to discomfort her. "Help me," she croaked—an order, not a plea, because she had recognized Bridey in that same astonished moment, and realized that here was a servant who must do her bidding. "Help me—I can't swim!"

She flung herself onto Bridey then, and it *was* rather like being attacked by a bear, the fur bristling against her face, the woman as hefty as a grizzly "Take off the coat!" Bridey yelled, above the noise of thumping waves, the screams from people nearby, and the thrum of her own heart in her ears.

Lavinia's teeth bared in a snarl, and Bridey braced for a rant: for being blamed for abandoning her, for all of this somehow being Bridey's fault—but at that moment Lavinia's chin sank below the water, her eyes went wide with panic, and gasping and spluttering, she flung out her arms and locked them around Bridey's neck, turning her servant's body into a sort of lifebuoy.

Using her! Bridey was a *thing,* as disposable as a paper napkin, and now Madame, whose vanity was going to be her own death, was risking Bridey's very life to save her own, because the coat had cost a great deal of money —whereas servants were as replaceable as broken crockery.

No! Bridey's response was the explosion of a pressure cooker; a *No* that blew out of her lungs, surged up her windpipe and emerged as a roar of rage—rage fueled by all the times Bridey had tiptoed around tantrums, had been scolded and slapped and cheated of wages—a *No* that broke Lavinia's deathlock, allowing Bridey to flounder out of her reach.

Some things buoyed you up, and some things weighed you down. Lavinia would always be that thing which dragged you down.

Flailing away from her, desperate to escape her clawing hands, Bridey bumped against something soft and bulky—a chair cushion! She shoved it toward the thrashing Lavinia, trying to force her to grab onto it, because it would keep her afloat if she only had the sense to use it!

Bridey cried out as something struck her head. Debris from the ship was plunking into the water, creating cross-currents that jerked the desperate swimmers bobbing in the water first one way, then another. Caught up in a surge, Bridey was wrenched away from Lavinia. She chopped through the water with herky-jerky movements, snorking water up her nose, coughing and gagging. Water splashed in her eyes, and it stung—the St. Lawrence being a tidal river, it was saturated with salt water. Her eyes burning, Bridey lost sight of Lavinia.

She'd lost her chair leg! Feeling herself sinking, she panicked, thrashing, yelling for help, swallowing water, sinking lower in the water with every jerky gyration, trying to recall how she'd seen people swim: you kind of jabbed your arms into the water while you scissored your legs—but her efforts to kick were hindered by the long skirt of her maid's uniform, which clung to her legs like a hobble-skirt.

Something the size of a suitcase bobbed past—a wicker picnic basket. *Catch it, quick!* Bridey lunged, flung herself atop it. Buoyed by the basket, Bridey found she was able to reach down to her skirt's waist buttons, to pry and jerk at them with fingers no more useful than frozen sausages. Finally giving up on unbuttoning, she simply ripped—*she'd never wear this thing again anyway.*

There! The blasted thing was off, drifting away, leaving her clad in the uniform top and knee-length under-drawers she'd worn to bed that night, not having been able to fit a nightgown into the paper bag Madame had given her to use as a suitcase.

Amazing how much easier it was to kick without the skirt hog-tying her, Bridey discovered, and for a few moments was able to fool herself that she was actually *swimming*. The thing was, though, that unless you kept on chopping your arms and kicking your legs, you started to sink! She kept chopping and kicking as long as she could, but soon felt her muscles painfully seizing up, refusing to do one more chop, one more kick.

She needed to rest. Rest would be utter bliss. And *sleep*! Strange as it was, she could have closed her eyes right then and there, let herself be rocked in the river's frigid embrace, and fallen into a deep, welcoming sleep. *Just let me rest!*

The baby! The thought jolted her back. Was the baby still alive? Could it feel the cold, curled up there in her womb? Had it felt the pain, the impact when she'd fallen off the ship; could it taste the water, raw and rank as a mud puddle, with an undertaste of fish?

Stop thinking of the baby as It. Marie had said it was a girl.

Her daughter. A tiny baby girl. What was she going to call her? *Julia—her mother's name?* But she'd never liked the name, though that made her feel guilty because she'd adored her mother. She wanted something unique for her child. A flower maybe—*Daisy? Poppy, Iris? Violet?*

No! She needed a stronger name for this child whose life was in danger even before she was born.

Something thunked against Bridey; she cried out in shock, saw that it was a large thing bobbing in the current. Debris? Something she could hoist herself onto and use as a raft? Then she saw the hand—a human hand, and it belonged to the body of a dead man, his eyes staring unseeingly upward at a sky studded with stars. Shuddering, Bridey pushed away from the corpse, lost track of her original direction, and gazed northward, just in time to see the Empress of Ireland, still lit by that eerie blue light, raise her lovely tail as her bow sank; and just a few seconds later the stern sank too, and the ship disappeared—as though it had never been. Like the tales her Irish gran used to tell about the fairy castles which turned to mist when humans blundered along. But now she spotted another ship approaching from downriver, all its lights blazing—was it a ship sent out to pick up survivors?

It was so far away, though. An ocean's length away; an impossibility for someone who could not swim, who was just flailing her arms and legs, swallowing water with each slopping wave, and so alone out here, surrounded by corpses, because she saw now that "her" dead man was not the only one—she was amid an entire watery orchard of floating dead people.

THE EMPRESS OF IRELAND

She would not be one of them! She would make it to that ship, and she would give birth to this baby growing in her, this little being who would not be some flowery plant, to be plucked and stuck in a vase and thrown out.

Her daughter would have a heroine name, like the girls in her favorite books. Like Anne of Green Gables, or Elnora in *Girl of the Limberlost,* the book she'd brought along to read that time Sean had taken her to Bai du Beauport, Quebec's lovely sand beach. She'd sat beneath an umbrella, reading, while Sean ran in and out of the water, but he'd gotten disgusted with her because she wasn't paying enough attention to his hijinks, and he'd yanked *Girl of the Limberlost* out of her hands and tossed it in the bay.

Everything Sean had done—forcing her to help in the robbery, slapping her, demeaning her, and—his final, unspeakable act—abandoning her to die while he rowed away with his mates—those were all horrible enough—yet it was the way he'd flung away her book, his disdain for something she loved—that Bridey now felt angriest about. There in a freezing river, a few quavery breaths away from drowning, she saw clearly that the man who'd said he loved her knew nothing at all about her. What Sean wanted was someone to serve him—a loyal little *Eire do 'Fein* wife, who'd wash his underwear and polish his bullets, and everything about her that made Bridey *herself*—her love of books, the poems she'd written—*poems a magazine had actually published!*—her yearning for college, her fierce desire to *make something of herself*, to avoid becoming just another boring Charlesbourg housewife—was something Sean would never even try to understand.

Besides—she was still mad because, thanks to Sean's drowning her book, she'd never find out the ending of *Girl of the Limberlost!*

Stroke! Ignore how your shoulders burn!

Kick, she ordered herself, but her legs were blocks of ice—they no longer seemed to connect to her body.

Kick, dammit! Kick for your baby!

Anne of Green Gables would not have given up. Anne would have considered the shipwreck a splendid adventure. Anne was a Canadian girl, like Bridey herself, all spunk and mischief. *Maybe she ought to call the baby Anne?*

She would do twenty strokes, Bridey decided. Twenty was a small enough number to be do-able. And when she reached twenty she would let herself rest. That would be her reward. To end the pain of trying.

Stroke.

She couldn't.

You must.

Her outthrust arm struck something hard. Wood.

A boat! A lifeboat, the lettering stenciled on its bow visible even in the dark: *EMPRESS OF IRELAND.*

She was rescued!

"I"m here," she croaked, suddenly terrified that the people in the boat might not see her, might simply row on while she sank beneath the waves . . .

Chapter 24

"*Help!*" Bridey whimpered, and when no one responded, she summoned the last of her strength, clawed at the gunwale, swung up a leg, heaved herself up and over, feeling, ridiculously, like a burglar climbing in a window—and fell into the boat.

It was empty, Bridey saw to her dismay, its bottom swimming in a foot of water. There weren't even oars, she discovered as she floundered in the well of the boat—just debris—broken boards, bits of metal. She retched up the river water she'd swallowed, sick with disappointment, not wanting to give up her fantasy: comforting hands, blankets, a thermos of hot coffee; people exclaiming over how brave she'd been—but there was no one, nothing, no help to be had—and all unprompted, the lines from *The Ancient Mariner* skittered across her mind: *Alone, alone, all, all alone, Alone on a wide, wide sea!*

She flung herself onto a cross-thwart in the center of the boat—a crude slat no wider than a ladder rung, but at least it raised her out of the frigid water sloshing around the boat's bottom. There must have been people in this boat— *what had happened to them?* Maybe they'd been knocked into the water by debris avalanching off the ship, Bridey reasoned, vowing to keep a sharp eye out in case there still might be survivors close by.

Her body spasmed in a great involuntary shudder. Oddly enough, she had felt warmer while she'd been *in* the water. Now, the night breeze against her wet, exposed skin felt like stabbing knives.

Whacking her numb hands against her arms, trying to rub circulation into her thighs, Bridey fought the torture of the piercing cold, setting her jaw to keep her teeth from chattering.

To make things worse, the boat bumped up against a chunk of debris and began spinning in circles, leaving Bridey dizzy and nauseous. After a short interval of to-ing and fro-ing, the boat got snatched up by the current and began to drift.

It was taking her downriver. Looking back over her shoulder, Bridey once again spotted what she thought were ship's lights, upriver. But the ship was so far away—they'd never see her in this tiny boat, and she was drifting farther and farther from that ship every second.

There'd be towns downriver, though, wouldn't there? She could just drift until the boat bumped up against a dock or something…

Just let herself drift. Wasn't that what she'd been doing all her life?

Getting engaged to Sean because she'd had a childhood crush on him. Because it was what girls did where she came from. You dated a fellow and then you got engaged and then you got married and had kids.

She'd wanted to go to teacher's college, but Mum and Pops said it was too expensive. She hadn't fought them on that; if she'd really been set on becoming a teacher she could have finagled a way to do it. She'd let her dreams of attending college slip away from her like a ship sailing in the opposite direction. Instead, she'd done what all her girlfriends were doing—gotten a low-paying job as a domestic.

Drifting. Aimless. She'd had the top grades in her high school class; her essays were so good they were sometimes read at school assemblies; her math test scores were the highest in the school's history—and what had she done with all those brains? *Two months after graduation she was bent over a washboard, scrubbing stains out of wealthy womens' tablecloths.*

THE EMPRESS OF IRELAND

Drifting. Planning to marry Sean because it would free her from the drudgery of working as a servant.

Lord, how she loathed herself!

Something in the lumpy stew sloshing around the boat's bottom bumped her knee. She picked it up: a jagged board with *LAND* emblazoned on it in fancy lettering.

She was about to toss it away when she noticed something else in that watery gumbo—something long and narrow. She snatched it up—a yard-long length of wood with a leather-covered handle and a flat blade. *A cricket bat!* Bridey had seen enough games—even played herself a little—to recognize what it was.

Reflex built out of old habit, Bridey hastily glanced around to make sure Billy hadn't seen her pick it up. Her brother always swatted her if she dared touch any of his sports gear.

But there was no one there, of course, no one to sneer at her as she leaned over the side of the boat and dug the bat into the water.

The boat sluggishly spun.

Oh, it was useless! The bat was too short to act as an oar!

Besides, you needed oars on both sides if you were attempting to row, didn't you?

Bridey snatched up the broken board. Bat on one side and board on the other, she stabbed at the water. *How her brother would jeer if he could see her now!* "To hell with you!" she screamed, using the bat to splash water on an imaginary Billy.

It seemed to her that now she had a bit more control over the boat, might be able to break free of the current relentlessly dragging the boat.

Wishing her arms were longer, wincing as her shoulder muscles screamed, Bridey set her makeshift paddles against the bullying current.

Never again would she let herself drift.

Chapter 25

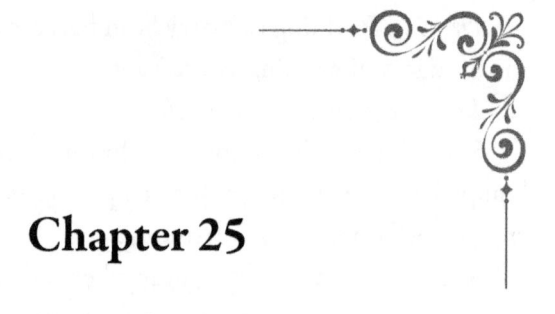

Louis had never learned to swim. He'd grown up in the Grigny area of Quebec, where the closest thing to public pools were the water-filled potholes on Scrabble Lane.

But there was also the quarry, outside the city an hour's walk away, an old cobalt quarry with steep sides, where runoff from snow pooled every spring. Swimming was forbidden there, but that only made it more alluring to Louis and his friends. Louis always stayed in the shallow end of the quarry, sneered at by his older brother Marcel, who, with his jackal-pack of friends climbed to the ledge forty feet above the pool and dived from there, laughing uproariously as they plunged.

One day Louis had climbed the back side of the ledge, crawled through the bushes until he was at the lip of the ledge, then gingerly stood up, staring down at the pool so far below, feeling sick to his stomach, shaking with vertigo. He was just backing away when Marcel came up behind and shoved him, sending Louis over the edge, "I'm teaching you to be a man!" Marcel shouted, chortling as Louis fell, shrieking in terror.

Louis had known he was going to die as the water came up at him and he plunged deep, deep, deep, swallowing water, flailing uselessly.

That same feeling of helplessness—of certainty he was going to die—of anger at his own body, which stubbornly refused to swim—settled over Louis now as he thrashed in the freezing water. He couldn't remember how he'd gotten into the river; his last memory was of burning his hand on the furnace. And now here he was about to freeze to death, his testicles drawing up tight into his body in reaction to the cold.

However he windmilled his arms and thrashed his feet, the river kept pulling him down, encumbered as he was by his work boots and his coverall, its pockets crammed with wrenches, screwdrivers, and all the other tools a trimmer always carried with him—but which had now become a ball and chain. Above him loomed the ship—enormous, dark, and with a great jagged hole torn into its starboard side by the outlaw ship.

Sick at heart, Louis watched as the Empress began to tear herself apart, her seventy foot tall mast teetering drunkenly before wrenching loose and pitching into the river, its wires and cables whipping wildly. And now her two massive funnels were swaying menacingly until—overcome by their own staggering weight, they simultaneously toppled, striking the water with the force of collapsing skyscrapers, the one on the right crushing a lifeboat beneath it, and creating a tidal wave whose surge hit the other boats dotting the river's surface, causing them to bob violently; one was swamped and capsized, spilling its passengers into a river jammed with wreckage and strewn with floating corpses.

Too late Louis realized his own danger. The giant ship was going down at the speed of a galloping horse, and as it sank it would suck everything down with it! *Swim, imbecile!*

Chopping through the water with all the grace of a moose mired in quicksand, fearing every second that he'd be pulled down, knowing he was going to die, Louis mumbled the *Acte de Contrition*—a prayer the nuns claimed might, at the last second, save you from Hell. Above his own mumblings, above the grinding of wreckage and the slap of current, Louis began hearing voices. *Sweet, high voices—the voices of pure beings, of angels*—which meant his death was near now, very near. He tried to angle his flailings in that direction, and now he could hear the singing again. It was in French, which would naturally be the language of angels. It was an old song, once sung by the voyageurs, and was being sung, he realized, by children!

There they were—in a boat close enough to swim to—but dangerously close to the sinking ship. It was the ship's dinghy, he now saw, tangled in wreckage, and it put him in mind of a dead orca he'd once seen, washed up on a beach, wrapped in squid tentacles, both squid and whale bleached of color, ugly in death. Lungs near bursting, arms about to fall off, Louis thumped up against the boat and with the last of his strength hoisted himself onto a gunnel.

"It's a giant!" squealed a frightened little voice, and he saw that the boat was filled with small children. *Close enough to angels—he'd always been sentimental about little ones.* "A monster!" wailed another child, and Louis realized what he must look like to them: big, bearded, huffing like an engine, a creature from the depths. "*Je ne suis pas un monstre, mes enfants,*" Louis rasped, adding in English, "I am no monster!"

"Oi—that you, Louie?" came a man's voice.

Louis recognized him —it was the steward called Snapper, the one who was always hanging around Marie. His voice was hoarse, the voice of a man tamping down his own fear to avoid panicking the little ones.

"Ship is sinking— get away! Quick, quick!" Louis croaked, in the most adequate English he could muster under the circumstances.

"Fraid our affairs is in a bit of a tangle here," Snapper said, jabbing an oar at a dangling wire.

Louis heaved himself into the boat, to cries of alarm from the children. "Be careful, Giant—you'll tip us over," a small girl squeaked.

Crouched in the dinghy's stern, trying not to squash small bodies, Louis fumbled through his pockets with numb fingers—and came up with a needle-nose pliers. He thrust it at Ludsnap, gestured at him to take the bow, hoping the man had enough seamanship to know how to balance a boat, then shooed aside a clump of children jumbled amidships, stood up on the center thwart, and delved into his pocket, fishing out the tin snippers whose weight had nearly dragged him to the bottom. He didn't ordinarily carry snips; it must have been God guiding him this morning to stick the things in his boiler suit.

The tangles of wires were cursedly heavy, the tin shears were rusty, and the wires, when they did cut, snapped loose with such ferocity he was terrified their whiplash would slash a child.

"I can help." It was a dark-skinned boy, older than the rest of the children, a boy who possessed a coolness that would have done credit to a grown man. Here was someone with a head on his young shoulders, Louis thought, thrusting his jackknife at the boy, who flicked open the blade, then shooed aside a cluster of children, stood up on the tiller bench, and began sawing away at a gnarl of tangled wires.

"Look!" one of the urchins cried. "The ship! The ship is going down!"

Louis risked a look over his shoulder. She was sinking all right, still lit by the eerie blue glow of the life vests on the drowned bodies. He stretched as high as he dared, chose a wire, crunched down on it with the snips, throwing his muscle into it. The wire parted, giving out a *twang* and slashing across his face as it whipped loose.

"That's done it,' cried Snapper, jubilant.

A high, sweet voice began singing. *"En roulant, ma boule, roulant. . . "*

Chapter 26

Marie Lavalliere

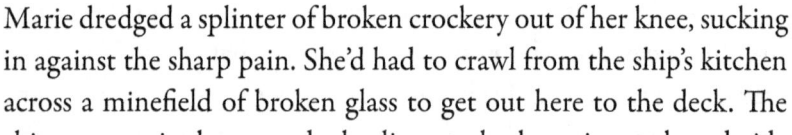

Marie dredged a splinter of broken crockery out of her knee, sucking in against the sharp pain. She'd had to crawl from the ship's kitchen across a minefield of broken glass to get out here to the deck. The ship was on its beam ends, heeling at the bow, its starboard side nearly submersed. This was the end, Marie knew; the Empress was going under and would take her with it unless she got out *now*.

She hauled herself up onto the aft starboard railing and straddled it, hunched like a jockey, finally managing to swing her legs over to the far side. Grasping the railing struts, she clung there, mere feet above the river, knowing she needed to let go before it was too late.

Yet she couldn't quite force herself to let go. This ship had been her home. Her cot had the imprint of her body on it; her kitchen bore the stamp of her own personality: its kitchen cupboards had her spices arranged in alphabetical order; she would never be able to replace the wondrous copper-bottomed skillet that sauteed as though it had a mind of its own . . .

Gripping the struts more firmly, Marie decided she would count to twenty and then—*ready or not*—let go. "Bezhig . . . niish . . . niswi . . . niiwin . . . naanan . . . n'godwaaswi . . . " Marie whispered.

On *n'godwaaswi* her hands lost their grip. She fell.

A shock of agony as her body plunged into the water, every nerve shrieking in protest. Around her, bodies bobbed limply, some face down in the water, drowned; others face up, appearing to have frozen in water cold enough to stop a beating heart.

It wouldn't stop *her* heart, Marie vowed. *Nothing* would stop her from returning to her boys. She'd learned to swim as a tiny child, taught by her mother, who'd called her *little frog*, but that had been in the sun-dappled waters of a gentle creek—nothing like this great brute of a river, with its patches of ice, its bullying current—a current so turbulent it ripped her apron off her body, and before she could snatch it back, the river whirled it away, pulled it beneath the waves. Marie groaned. *That apron had held the cash she needed to get her boys back!*

Then, upriver, she spotted lights. *There was a ship up there!* Marie set off swimming in that direction—fast and energetic at first, realizing she *must* get away from the dying liner, whose downward plunge would suck everything around it into its deadly vortex.

Her initial burst of energy soon fizzled out, though; her arms had become so numb with cold she could barely force them through the water, and she saw, to her dismay, that the ship she'd spotted earlier now seemed farther, as though it was moving away. "No," Marie called. "Come back! People are here!" The disappointment was so bitter it threw off her rhythm; she was no longer swimming, just thrashing in the water.

Wait, though! There, not so very far off, was an island! An island in the middle of the river, its tall pines silhouetted against a star-speckled sky.

Marie made toward it, planning how she would wait there, covering herself with boughs to stay warm until a rescue boat sailed close enough that she could swim to it.

But she didn't seem to be making any progress toward the island; her arms felt like stretched-out rubber bands; her legs were heavy as oak trunks. She thought of resting, of floating on her back for a while, and the temptation, the dire *need* to rest was so overwhelming she almost gave in to it.

Then she remembered something the ship's doctor had told her—it was a thing that happened to bodies exposed to cold too long—it had a Latin-sounding name she couldn't remember, but it meant that the insides of your body got so cold you could die. Once an elder from Marie's village—a woman—had lost her way in a blizzard, and even though she'd been wearing furs, she'd gotten so cold that when she was found she couldn't even work her throat to swallow the reviving tea she was offered. A short time later her heart had stopped.

Moving was life. Moving made your blood circulate to your heart: the doctor had explained it. *She would not stop moving.* Whatever it cost her, she would swim. She would stay alive; she would get her sons back.

It was hard to raise her head far enough out of the water to see, but it seemed to Marie that she was getting closer to the island. Was that the tang of pine she smelled, borne on the wind?

Just a few more yards . . .

And then—it was like a hammer blow to the heart—it threw off her rhythm so that she started to sink, inhaled water, and came up coughing and flailing—she saw that the island was not an island at all. It was an overturned lifeboat—one of the collapsibles— and the pine trees she'd seen were the silhouetted figures of women, standing atop the boat, holding oars upright, their shrieks sounding like quarreling seagulls.

With the tail-end of her strength, Marie lunged toward the boat, feeling cheated. She knew it wasn't the women's fault that they weren't the piney island she'd been picturing, but she was still irrationally angry with these helpless, foolish *boonoos— idiots—*so stupid they were *standing* atop a boat instead of trying to right it. She didn't recognize any crew members among this lot—they were all passengers; not a man among them. All the women had taken time to dress; most were wearing hats, whose feathers now drooped about their ears like sodden plumage.

No one extended a hand to help Marie up; it took her last ounce of strength to heave herself onto the boat's overturned bow. "Why ain't you *in* the boat?" she gasped.

"It tipped over," explained a woman with big front teeth whom Marie mentally named *Waboose*—Rabbit. "A crewman was rowing us, but then a big wave came and we were getting all soaked, so me and Minnie and Irma—we scooched to the other side of the boat and all of a sudden it tipped and we got thrown in the water, and Irma and Minnie and that crewman, they never . . . "

"*Beaucoup de femmes sont encore là-bas. je pense qu'ils sont noyés.*" It was Quebec French, from a woman whose teeth were chattering so badly she could barely speak. Still, Marie got the gist: several women and a crew member had drowned.

"Get off the boat, ladies—we can flip 'er back over," Marie said, astounded at their cow-like passivity. "Just slide into the water—if we all heave the boat together, we can push it back up."

Only Waboose and the Quebec woman—who gave her name as Mitzi— actually slid off the boat. The others, reluctant to leave a perch that was unstable but at least dry, clung to each other, refusing to move—until Marie reached out and yanked the ankle of the closest woman, who screamed as she was hauled into the water.

The others squawked bloody murder, but when they saw the grim-faced Marie coming for them, they jumped into the water like martyrs going to the stake.

Marie knew canoes and boats, but wasn't familiar with collapsible crafts. This one was shaped like an ordinary rowboat, but its sides were waterproof canvas stretched over wooden struts, the craft cleverly designed to fold up horizontally—collapse—when not in use.

Though it was built of canvas and lightweight wood, the collapsible was still a ponderous weight, and Marie got no help from the other women, who kept trying to crawl back atop the turned-turtle boat. Why couldn't the *boonoos* understand that they'd be better off *in* the boat? She'd have to take charge, Marie saw. There was a knack to getting people to work as a team—you had to make them feel they were capable, but you also had to let 'em know that if they didn't do their job, you'd give 'em grief.

"Everyone, get over on this side," Marie barked. Waboose and Mitzi scrambled over next to Marie, but the others just dithered around, bawling, getting in the way.

"On three," Marie ordered, "Lean on it, push, put all your weight on it. One, two..."

Marie was braced for what she knew would happen—the side of the boat would smack into them as it flipped—but she wasn't expecting the oar that came out of nowhere, cracking her in the face, an oar wielded like a club by a woman who was shrieking, "*Stupid, dirty Indian—you'll get us all killed!*" The attack was so unexpected Marie, caught off guard, fell backward into the water as the crazed woman swung the oar to smash her again.

An arm shot out in front of Marie, grabbing the oar, yanking it out of the crazy woman's grip. "Behave yourself, Edna!" she snapped. It was Waboose, Marie saw, the rabbity-faced woman whom she'd dismissed as of no consequence.

"We've got to go *under*, don't you see?" Waboose said urgently, clutching Marie's arm.

"What? *Oh!*" Marie saw what she meant. Why hadn't she thought of it herself? Taking in a lungful of air, Marie plunged headfirst into the water, diving beneath the upside-down boat. She surfaced into darkness, gratefully inhaling air. Something thumped into her and she let out a squeak of panic. "*C'e juste moi.*" Marie recognized the voice—Mitzi.

"Ah, *bon!*" Marie said, and it truly *was* bon having someone there alongside in the claustrophobic dark, someone smart enough to have brought an oar.

"*Ascenseur!*" Marie rapped out. "*Lift.*"

Impossible to see in the dark; they had to work by instinct and feel. Mitzi jammed the paddle blade against an upside-down thwart, but it was Marie whose back and shoulders assumed the burden, and as she strained, pushing from her guts, and furiously kicking her legs beneath the water, curses hissed from between her teeth, obscenities that would have had Sister Hubertus reaching for the kerosene, rage directed at the people who'd stolen her children, emptied her village, and treated the Ojibwe as less than human—and she still had plenty of anger left over for that one called Edna, who'd called her a dirty Indian and sucker-punched her with an oar.

"*Unnnnnnnnnnuhhhh!*" Marie gave a last push, anger lending her strength.

The boat rose up, heeled onto its gunwales, raining down all the objects that had puddled in its bottom—oars, billy cans, flares, and other gear, the craft's rough canvas sides scraping Marie's face as the collapsible teetered, swayed, decided which way it would jump—and then abruptly toppled, wanting to return to the position it had been designed for. It hit the water with an enormous squelchy thud, rocking violently as it sought equilibrium—but staying upright.

They'd done it! The women wasted no time in climbing into the collapsible, so heedless in their eagerness Marie feared they'd overturn the boat again. When at last everyone was in, Marie hoisted herself onboard, choosing to take the stern, where she could use an oar as a kind of crude rudder to steer.

She would try to move them toward the ship they'd spotted downriver. The current caught them up and swooped them along at a breathtaking clip.

"Do you think they'll have hot baths on that ship?" asked Waboose, sounding wistful. "I'd give everything I own for a hot bath."

Chapter 27

Henry Kendall

He'd abandoned the bridge—with the boilers gone there was no way to control the ship, anyway—and was helping his crew launch the lifeboats—a near impossible job on the port side, with the ship now listing so severely that the ship's hull, rather than the river, was directly beneath them, making the boats unlaunchable.

He was about to order the crew to switch over to the starboard boats when a blast assaulted his ears, a sound like the big guns being exercised on a warship. Air whistled from his lungs, and he was lifted so swiftly his feet flew out of his shoes; he found himself being catapulted through the air as though flung by a giant fist, his head scraping against an out-thrust pipe—and then he was hurtled into the river.

Afterwards, passengers would insist there'd been an explosion, but Kendall always believed it was simply air escaping as the Empress began her plunge to the bottom.

He could feel blood oozing from the cut on his forehead. Momentarily he was back in the South Indian Ocean, swimming for his life after the cargo hauler Jon VerDamn, loaded with spices, had gone down in a typhoon. Off to his right was Java, and the hulking remnant of Krakatoa, which had exploded just five years earlier, in '83. The sailor next to him in the water was bleeding from a wound, the flowing blood attracting sharks, their fins scything through the water as they circled, waiting to attack. Like most sailors, Kendall feared savaging by sharks above all other fates. Irrationally angry at the bleeding man, Kendall had grasped him by the hair and pulled him along in a sideways grip until they'd reached a life raft.

He knew there were no sharks in the St. Lawrence— the only good thing about this brute of a river. There was ice, though, chunks of it floating around, bumping against the corpses bobbing in the water. Dear God—dozens of them, poor sods, done in by drowning or the cold or both, and they were past any help he could give them.

"There's someone!" A voice from nearby—a voice he recognized, but could not quite place, lightheaded from blood loss as he was—and from despair: he was that most despised of men—a captain who'd lost his ship.

"It's the captain!" A voice in the darkness. Kendall winced. He'd been recognized. "Over there!" called another voice.

A boat, rowed with the expertise of experienced sailors, came abreast. Arms reached out, hauled him over the gunnels, landed him like a great, flopping carp in the well of the boat. "He's in bad shape," someone said. "Bleedin' all over the place. "We need to get him to one of them rescue ships."

"No." Kendall spat blood. "Row, goddammit—we're going to look for survivors."

He would take command. For one last time, he would command a vessel.

Chapter 28

Bridey

Without being aware of it, she'd slipped into a daze, her mind lost in a fuzzy nowhere halfway between asleep and awake while her body kept up the grueling task of rowing, her hands nearly frozen to the board and bat; she didn't know if she'd ever be able to unclench her fingers.

She came up out of the daze, heart pounding with terror at the great black cliff that had suddenly loomed up in front of her—and it seemed to be moving, churning toward her at a speed that created foam on the water. Angry at herself for being so inattentive, Bridey was startled when a deep, booming *brronnnk* issued from the thing—a ship's horn!

Now Bridey saw what she should have been alert to earlier—an enormous ship was heading toward her, about to ram her little boat!

Wait—they'd seen her! Bells rang, voices called, and a cone of light beamed down on her. The ship had slowed, angling so as to avoid hitting Bridey's craft. Craning her neck to look up, Bridey could just make out the ship's name: white letters against a black hull: *S.S. Storstad.*

"Sta pa Vi henter deg og tar deg ombord." a voice boomed through a megaphone in a language that was a garble to Bridey—*German, perhaps?*

A moment later the voice crackled out again—this time in heavily-accented English. "Stay there—we intend to bring you on to ship."

Stay there? What the devil else was she going to do—break out a full set of sails and scud away? Too exhausted to think—she *had* wanted to be rescued, after all, but she didn't know whether to trust this strange ship, Bridey dithered over what to do, clenching her bat and board like weapons, suddenly aware of how desperately she needed to pee.

Hands appeared on her port gunwale.

A moment later the head that belonged with the hands bobbed up, startling her so that she nearly lost her grip on her oars. *Where'd the blasted bugger come from anyway?* He must have swum over from the Storstad while she'd been turned the opposite way. In the dark the only features she could make out were his white eyeballs—and the yellow hair sticking untidily from beneath a seaman's beanie. His eyes flicked to the lettering on the side of the boat.

"Hello, Empress of Ireland," he said, flashing a smile, taking in every inch of the boat in one swift glance before he turned and yelled up at someone on the deck above, "*Det er bare en jente. Jeg kan ikke se andre!*"—which Bridey guessed meant he saw only one person in the boat.

"*Tillatelse til a ga ombord?*" he said, quirking an eyebrow at Bridey. "Permission to board?"

This struck Bridey as oddly formal, considering the circumstances; a laugh gurgled up, surprising her. Apparently considering this sufficient permission, the man hoisted himself over the gunwales, careful not to rock the small craft, and duck-walked his way to the center thwart, facing Bridey. "I am Aksel," he said "I shall row you to ship, you then shall go onto board." He looked around, puzzled. "*Hvor er arer?* Where oars is at?"

Bridey unclenched her hands from the board and the cricket bat and handed them over, feeling as though she were losing trusted friends. "*Rodde du bat med disse tingene?*" he exclaimed. "With this things you have rowed?"

He shook his head in disbelief. "Very well, I shall use. But it will make me a laughing-butt by my mates."

He set to, paddling with the crude oars much more efficiently than Bridey had managed, until he pulled her boat up alongside the *Storstad*. Something hurtled down from the deck above— an odd-looking device of wooden slats and rope. "Jacob's Ladder," Aksel informed Bridey.

It rose so steeply to the deck far above that it almost could have been the Biblical ladder from earth to heaven, Bridey thought. And her next thought was: *I am not setting foot on that thing!*

" I'm safer here in my boat!" she snapped at Aksel, jutting her chin.

"*Ikke vær redd jeg skal ta vare pa deg.* Have no fear—I shall much care take of you," coaxed Aksel, no slouch at reading a mulish woman.

Afterwards, Bridey wasn't quite sure how he'd gotten her up that ladder, because she kept her eyes squeezed shut from the moment the big blonde man slung her over his shoulder and began hauling them both up the ladder—she supposed he'd held onto the ladder with one hand and onto her with the other; she was only aware of being jostled and joggled, and of something hard-edged jabbing into her ribs, but she didn't dare complain for fear that it would throw off Aksel's rhythm and they'd both end up plunging into the water. She sensed they were high up now, and began hearing men's voices above, all speaking in the same language Aksel had used, though she made out the word "shipwreck."

"I will now give you unto Eric," Aksel said, "Do not feel fear." Eyes still tightly closed, Bridey felt herself being shifted, felt strong arms come up under her knees—*oh Lord, she only had on her knee-length bloomers!* Too curious to stay blind, Bridey opened her eyes to discover that another man, who looked like Aksel except for having a mustache like fluffy yellow yarn—had her cradled in his arms as though she were a big baby. More crew members were clustered around, all looking anxious. *"Er du skadet noe sted?"* a man asked, eyeing her in a worried manner, sounding as though he was asking whether she was injured.

"Se hva hun brukte til ro baten!" Aksel shouted, waving something in the air—and Bridey now understood what it was that'd been jabbing her during the ascent up the ladder—it was her cricket bat and LAND board! And Aksel was using them to pantomine rowing a boat, to roars of laughter from the crewmen.

The bat quickly passed from man to man, each exclaiming over it, and not one of them could resist taking a swing with it. Someone produced an orange, which became a cricket ball, and an impromptu scrimmage suddenly erupted on deck. It surprised Bridey to see that this lot—Scandinavians, she guessed, judging by their fair hair—knew cricket.

"Set me down!" she yelled, trying to wriggle out of Eric's grip, but he was too engrossed in the game to pay attention; she was shuddering with cold and had to pee something fierce.

"Hva i guds navn gjør dere idioter?" A woman's voice—angry—came from nearby.

This halted the cricketers; the bat and the orange disappeared in the blink of an eye, Bridey was abruptly set on her feet, and as a small, white-haired ball of fury stormed up to Eric, the others slunk away. *"Har du dritt for hjernen?"* she bellowed. *"Dumme menn! Gud frelse oss fra mennesker og deres dumhet!"*

Her bright blue eyes snapped; her cheeks flared red, and she cuffed Aksel on the back of his head as she scolded him. Bridey got the drift: They should have been tending to a woman just pulled from a lifeboat instead of horsing around.

Bridey felt something soft settle down around her shoulders—a blanket—wool, she guessed, judging by the warmth and weight. "You are from the shipwreck, ja?" the woman asked. 'Have you injury?"

Bridey shook her head, not sure if her frozen hands and feet counted as injuries.

"I am Sophie Anderson, wife of the captain," the woman said. "I speak some English. Please excuse how I pronounce. Now, my child, I shall take you to the *sykehus*—hospital—not fancy, but what we make-do, put together after the collision. We have many folk here from your ship."

Bridey stumbled after Mrs. Anderson, who led her down a set of stairs to a large room belowdecks—evidently the crew's mess hall—now converted into an emergency infirmary.

The crowds of bruised, battered people, the babble of voices, the moans—all were eerily reminiscent of the deck of the Empress in its last doomed moments.

The difference, though, was that here was order and organization. The most seriously-injured survivors, Bridey saw, were in cots in one area, while the less-seriously injured lay sprawled on blankets on the floor. A strong smell of rubbing alcohol, soap, and antiseptic permeated the room, overlaid by the cheering fragrance of brewing coffee from a nearby kitchen. A corner of the room had been partitioned off with hanging sheets, and as two crewmen carried in an injured child on a stretcher, Bridey saw, through the gap in the sheets, that the area had been turned into a surgery, and that the man bent over a makeshift operating table was Grayson, the Empress's doctor. So he'd survived!—a great stroke of fortune, his services being desperately needed.

"Alas, dear child, all cots gone," Mrs. Anderson fretted. "But I can—"

"No, no, it's all right," Bridey assured her, Only, I need . . is there a . . ."

"*Baderom, ja?*" Mrs. Anderson pointed toward a nearby door.

It was a men's toilet, Bridey discovered, with a row of urinals and a single stall. Locking herself into the stall, she hurriedly yanked down her drawers and released a flood, feeling enormous relief. But as she pulled up her underwear she saw something that made her gasp: *a blotch of blood.* Fear fluttered through her as she examined the spot more closely. As little as she knew about pregnancy, she was sure that bleeding wasn't a good sign. Did it mean she was losing the baby? *After everything her baby had been through, would it be surprising if it was in distress?*

There was only one person here who would know. Barefoot—her shoes lost somewhere in the river, Bridey left the restroom, padded across the *sykehus* floor, being careful not to step on anyone, and approached the partitioned-off area that marked the surgery. Yanking aside a sheet, she barged in.

Chapter 29

It was a cramped cubicle with a sheet-covered table serving as an operating platform. The strong smell of antiseptic barely camouflaged the rusty-nail odor of blood. His face drawn with fatigue, Dr. Grayson was bending over a small boy whose left shoulder had a raw-looking wound seeping blood.

"Press down with that bandage pad on the bleeding," barked the doctor, barely glancing at Bridey, only aware that there was suddenly another adult here, another pair of hands.

For the next two hours Bridey assisted, following the doctor's brusque commands. She threaded suturing needles, filled hot water bottles for the hypothermia patients, applied ice against swellings, taped over the splints he'd used on broken bones and even—though she nearly threw up while doing it—jabbed a syringe filled with an infection-fighting solution called *salvaran* into a woman's thigh.

During a brief interlude in the action, Bridey stole a sidelong look at the doctor. He looked to be in his mid-thirties, and had a broad, square-jawed face and brown eyes behind glasses with cracked lenses. Strands of wet hair clung to his forehead and his pajama top was still damp—evidence that he'd been in the river. Somewhere along the line he must have lost his trousers and been given a loaner pair; they were miles too large, held up with ship's twine strung through the belt loops.

Feeling her gaze, Grayson looked up from the cast-plaster he was mixing. "Guess I won't make this month's cover of *Gentlemen's Quarterly*," he said, grinning.

"Maybe with a more stylish belt," Bridey said with mock seriousness.

"You're that girl," he said, pointing at her with his plaster-mixing spoon. "The one who tried to move poor Gaade out of harm's way. Quite intrepid of you, considering what a war zone that deck had become."

"Do you know if Gaade—"

"No idea whether the poor chap made it. I was wakened when my room started flooding, ran up on deck still in my pajamas, and that's where I found you trying to drag Gaade. I rendered assistance to as many of the injured on that deck as I could, and then there was—some sort of explosion, I think. I was tossed into the water. Eventually a lifeboat picked me up and we spent the night rowing on the river, looking for survivors. It was around dawn when the Storstad took us aboard. How did you fare, Miss ... sorry, don't recall ...."

"Bridey Collins. And I think that same explosion blew *me* off, too."

"James Grayson. I'm sorry we have to meet under these circumstances."

Ask him about the spotting. At the very thought, a hot, prickling flush worked its way from her neck to her hairline. She *couldn't!*

"*God morgen,*" A crewman lifted the partition sheet and came in carrying a tray with mugs of coffee and buttery-looking cookies. He set it down on a shelf, took one look at the medical instruments and bloody bandages and exited hurriedly, a bit green in the face.

Dr. Grayson gulped his coffee as though it were life-saving elixir. Nose in mug, he gazed at Bridey. "I must say I'm impressed by how well you've assisted me this morning. Even most interns faint at their first sight of blood. I stand by my first impression of you as intrepid."

The doctor studied her as he chewed a cookie. "Are you up to another go-round, Miss Collins? This next lot won't be quite as bad off—they're the patients I initially evaluated but felt could wait while the most seriously injured were tended to. Now the second lot needs attending to, and I would appreciate the help of those competent hands of yours, if you're willing."

Bridey nodded, basking in the glow of his compliments.

"It should only be a couple of hours at most. We ought to be landing in Rimouski before long—it's a small town upriver where relief operations are underway, including a field hospital."

He gave Bridey a quick, assessing once-over. "You look a bit pale. Are you certain you're up to this? I never thought to ask whether *you* had been injured." The look he gave her was so kind and concerned it made her eyes prickle; she was afraid she was going to cry. Kept frantically busy assisting with patients, Bridey had momentarily forgotten her own problem—but now her worry slammed back into her. *The bleeding* . . .

Oh, the devil with it! "I'm going to have a baby," Bridey blurted, not daring to look at Grayson, fearing the shock and revulsion she'd surely see on his face, him knowing she was a *Miss* rather than a *Mrs.*

"*Are* you?" There was no condemnation in his face, she saw when she steeled herself to meet his gaze; he merely looked interested. "Shall I give you an exam?"

"*No!*" Let this man see her unclothed? "It's just that I—I noticed some—I'm not sure, but . . . flecks of— " She blushed furiously.

Grayson was having none of Bridey's whim-whams. He took her aside into a room that looked as though it was an officer's cabin and gave her a thorough once-over; he asked dozens of questions and listened carefully to her answers; *he examined the blood spots on her underwear!* He put his stethoscope to her abdomen and listened for the baby's heartbeat, and he did it all with such unembarrassed matter-of-factness it reminded Bridey of her yearly exams with old Dr. Boudreu, her family's GP. She almost expected to be handed a lollipop afterwards.

"I don't see any signs of a miscarriage," Grayson said, holding her wrist as he took her pulse. "It would not be surprising, considering the trauma you and your unborn child have been through, but I can assure you, having seen several women through their pregnancies, that babies are remarkably resilient little creatures. I believe yours is fine. He smiled at her, patted her hand. "Congratulations."

"Th-thank you." It was the first time anyone had found her pregnancy a thing to be celebrated, and it brought long-fought tears to Bridey's eyes. She wiped them with the wad of clean, crumpled bandages he handed her. "S—sorry," Bridey sniffled.

"Quite all right. Emotional ups and downs are common during the first few weeks of pregnancy. You must try to eat well. Drink plenty of whole milk. Eat fruit when you can find it. Rest with your feet up for an hour every day. Take walks. The unborn adore walks. It rocks them there in the uterus, you see."

"When..."

"Your due date? October or November, at a guess. I can give you a more definite answer when we return to Quebec. See me in my practice—I'm on Rue Delauney. Now, do you, are you ... *ummm*..." He took off his cracked glasses, rubbed them on the still-damp fabric of his pajama top. "Is there someone who'll be taking care of you? That is, do you... "

Have a husband—Bridey understood the question although he was too courteous to ask it. "I'm not ... Sean and I ... we planned to get m-married," Bridey stammered, unable to meet Grayson's gaze. "Only we had a ... he became ... he didn't want the—"

"See here, Miss Collins..." James Grayson put his glasses back on—she assumed they'd been cracked during the shipwreck. "I am well aware what brutes some men are. I am not convinced that the laceration on your cheek and the contusion under your eye were the results of the shipwreck. I have seen too many abused women in my practice to mistake what is clearly written on your face."

Bridey's hand flew to her cheek—a giveaway reflex.

"A man who uses his fists on a woman is no man," Grayson growled. "He is a despicable coward." He gripped her hands. "You have your child to think of now. If your husband-to-be has been physically violent to you, the chances are that he may also harm your child."

"I think he drowned," Bridey blurted out. "His lifeboat—I saw it go down."

"In that case, I do not know whether to offer sympathy or applause."

The boat's whistle blasted, and Bridey, feeling the ship's speed slackening, guessed they must be nearing Rimouski.

"Crewmen will be coming down soon to move the injured off the ship," Grayson said. "They'll be taken to the field hospital in the town, where I will be tending to them. You'll join me there, to assist?"

Bridey nodded. She set to work cleaning up the blood-stained bandages and the rest of the mess in the little surgery as stretcher-bearing Storstad crewmen swarmed into the *sykehaus* and under Grayson's directions began carrying out the injured, the doctor accompanying them, keeping a careful eye on the patients as they were carried up the ship's steep companionways.

The able-bodied survivors picked themselves up off the floor and began making their way to the top deck, and Bridey followed.

It had been quiet and dim in the infirmary, and in Bridey's mind it was somehow still nighttime, so it was a shock to emerge onto the top deck into bright sunlight, a stiff breeze off the river—and noise!

Apparently news of the tragedy had spread, because there were throngs of people clustered around the harbor, watching somberly as the *Storstad* nosed into the dock. A fleet of motorized ambulances stood waiting dockside, and men and women wearing Red Cross vests scurried about with medical supplies.

Jostled into the line of people waiting to disembark, Bridey distractedly looked about for her luggage—before recalling that all her meager possessions had gone down in the shipwreck

"Miss! *Miss Empress!*" Bridey turned at the sound of a familiar male voice. It was Aksel, shoving through the crowd like a human snowplow. "I bring your tings," he said, grinning, thrusting the LAND sign and cricket bat into her hands, before bending down and kissing her on the forehead.

Summoning up the *thank you* Mrs. Anderson had taught her, in the language she now knew was Norwegian, Bridey smiled and said, "*Tussen tak.*"

Chapter 30

Rimouski's schoolhouse was a vestige of the Victorian age—a three story monstrosity of grimy yellow brick, sharp gables, spindly chimneys, a bell tower above which flew Canada's flag, and a hazardous-looking fire escape zig-zagging down one wall. It was the largest building in town, serving as both secondary and elementary school, and was the only place capable of holding the vast throngs of humanity suddenly forced upon the small town. The Rimouski Relief Committee had designated it as a temporary shelter, its main floor to be used as a hospital, its schoolrooms becoming dormitories—one for men; one for women; one for children.

As it was situated on a bluff above the river, half a mile from the dock, too strenuous a walk for weakened shipwreck victims, a small fleet of horse-drawn wagons and motorized lorries had been commandeered to transport survivors to the school. Bridey, dockside, scrounging through a jumble of clothing townspeople had donated to the shipwreck victims, found a skirt that fit—and discovered that she'd missed the last buggy. *Well, then, she'd walk!* After all, Dr. Grayson had said walking was good for pregnant women.

But Bridey found that she couldn't lope along with her usual stride. After days on the water, solid ground felt strange beneath her feet; her legs insisting that they were still negotiating an uneven deck. Was this why sailors always walked with that rolling gait—was this what was meant by *sea legs?* The sun glared in her unshaded eyes;

the slope was steeper than she'd anticipated and she was hot and sweaty by the time she reached its summit.

The school loomed just ahead: big, four-square, and ugly. Spotting a line of stretcher-bearers moving injured people into the building through ground-level doors, Bridey simply followed them, anxious to get to Doctor Grayson, who'd be looking for her, wondering if she'd forgotten her promise to assist.

After the blistering heat, the school's cool interior was a relief. Bridey found the relief hospital in the school's basement, set up in what must ordinarily be the school's gymnasium. Its entrance was blocked by a long table, behind which sat men in military uniforms barking questions at the throngs queueing up to see a doctor—men who seemed to hold the power over who was allowed access to the hospital. Bridey, ordinarily a rule-follower, budged the line only because she knew Grayson must be in urgent need of her, and stepped up to the table.

"Well, what's wrong with *you?*" snarled an official wearing a flat-brimmed cavalry style hat that kept sliding down his bald forehead; his nametag identified him as Major Pym, Canadian National Guard. "You look plenty healthy to *me.* I suppose you're another of those penniless foreigners trying to winkle free medical care for some ailment you should have taken care of back in your god-forsaken country."

Foreigners? It wasn't the first time Bridey had encountered this attitude. Nasty rumors were being passed around —-that immigrants had sabotaged the ship; that Italian and Polish passengers in third class had sneaked into the staterooms of wealthy people to steal money and jewelry as the ship was sinking. *Ridiculous,* of course, but that didn't stop the rumors spreading.

The major's eyes raked cooly over Bridey, making her aware of what she must look like: her hair a damp, kink-ish mess from immersion in the river, her face sweat-streaked; her feet jammed sockless into the ill-fitting, scuffed shoes a Red Cross volunteer had thrust at her. The green wool skirt she'd pulled out of the jumble of donated clothing was wrinkled, had a lopsided hem, and smelled of mothballs.

"I'm not here to see a doctor!" Annoyed at the man's tone, Bridey squared up to him. "I'm here to assist with the injured people."

Major Pym prissed his mouth. "*Assist?* Are you a registered nurse?"

"No, but I—"

"Only accredited medical personnel are allowed to assist the physicians. They don't want a lot of silly women fainting all over the place, making nuisances of themselves."

He had an unusually high-pitched voice for a man, and that, combined with his oversized nostrils and fleshy jowls pouching around his collar, put Bridey in mind of Ollie, her aunt's Kate's high-strung pug dog.

"I wouldn't be in the way," Bridey argued." I've been assisting Dr. Grayson— we worked together on the *Storstad*— "

"*Worked together, eh?*"Payne stared at Bridey's chest. "I'll just bet."

Bridey's hand tingled with the urge to reach across the table and slap the smirk off this vile man's face. But she controlled her rage, calmly responding, "If you could just let him know Bridey is here—"

"*Bridey?*" It came out a sharp yip. "Planning a wedding night, are you?" His gaze, on her breasts, felt like dirty fingers. "You want me to interrupt one of them docs to tell him his dolly wants to see him?"

"I'm not his dolly." It grated out between clenched teeth: now *she* was the one growling. "Look, just check with Dr. Grayson—"

"Certainly not! Them docs is busy sawing off legs and stitching heads back onto necks and I don't know what-all. They ain't got time for trifling." Pym flicked his fingers as though chasing off flies. "Go on, now. You want to make yourself useful, march yourself off to the kitchen. Cook up some provender, scrub pots and pans, that kind of thing. Proper women's work."

"*Women's work!* I'd be much more useful—" *Never argue with an eejit,* her pa always said. And this Pym was the sort of idiot too puffed up with power to ever admit he was wrong, Bridey realized.

Her toe twinged painfully, reminding her of how long she'd been on her feet in tight, ill-fitting charity shoes. Not to be outdone, her empty belly grumbled.

Abruptly about-facing, Bridey stalked away, weaving through the crowd with only one firm goal in mind: a hot, sweet cup of tea. She went in search of the kitchen in the labyrinthine building, still seething with anger over how Pym had treated her—but she reserved some of her anger for Dr. Grayson. If he'd really wanted her help—*intrepid, he'd called her*— why hadn't he come out in the hall to find her, grease the skids a bit?

In this furious mood, toe throbbing, back still aching from her night of rowing, stomach twisting with hunger, Bridey stomped along the unfamiliar hallways, until, rounding a corner, she was accosted by a large, stubble-sprouting man who grabbed her arm and hissed in her ear, "Say, sis—ain't you one of them shipwreck survivors? I'm from the *Toronto Star*. I bet you got a good story to tell. Were you there when the collision happened? Folks is dying to know what really happened out there, we need first-hand accounts, so if you—"

Bridey found herself surrounded as more men surged forward, all cut from the same mold—brash, fast-talking, wearing cheap overcoats and gaudy bow ties—*they were reporters,* Bridey realized. Wrenching herself away from the first reporter, she scurried down an adjacent hallway, soon discovering that it was impossible to avoid reporters, who seemed to be everywhere, like ants at a picnic.

At last she stumbled across the school's lunchroom, only to discover that— judging from the dirty plates and glasses left out on tables, she'd just missed the mid-day meal. Her stomach grumbled; her toe twinged. She approached a sour-faced woman at a desk, jotting names and numbers into a ledger. "Excuse me," Bridey said. "Where could I get a cup of tea?"

"You wanted to eat, shoulda got here earlier," the woman snapped, barely looking up from her ledger. "We ain't running a restaurant here. You can help with the cleanup, though—kitchen's in there." She jerked a thumb toward a door.

Bridey pushed through the door, and in an instant her foul mood evaporated—because there was a tall woman standing at a counter, her back turned, pouring a kettle of steaming hot water into a tin washtub, and this could only be—

"*Marie!*"

Marie Lavalliere whipped around, her eyes widening as she saw who it was. "Bridey! *C'est incroyable!*" Marie enveloped her in a massive hug, and then they broke apart to regard each other. Marie was hollow-eyed and pale; she looked as though she ought to be spending a week in bed rather than tackling hundreds of unwashed dishes. Her damp hair was pulled back and pinned in a style that showed off her beautiful cheekbones—but also revealed the ugly bruise beneath her left eye.

"What happened?" Bridey asked, gently touching the bruise.

"Saved some ladies from drowning," Marie growled. "And for a reward got smacked with an oar."

"How in the world—"

"Never mind. How'd *you* get out?"

They spent the next hour exchanging stories while washing stacks of plates and mountains of pots and pans, only half-heartedly tending to the washing -up, because *catching up* was much more important than a bunch of cheap crockery.

Marie was just describing how she'd mistaken a cluster of women standing atop an overturned boat for an island when she suddenly let out a yelp, sprang to the stove, and yanked a pan out of the oven. "Coffee cake," she flung over her shoulder, but Bridey didn't need to be told—the fragrances of cinnamon, butter, and yeast told their own story.

Marie picked up a knife, sliced into the cake. "You look half-starved," she said. "You need to eat!" She aimed a look at Bridey's midsection, started to say something, probably to ask about her pregnancy— but at that moment the kitchen door swung open and a man burst into the room.

"*Birdbrain!* Been looking all over for ya!"

The room spun around Bridey. She prickled with heat; cold shivers ran through her, and she had to grab a table to steady herself. There in the doorway, looking far too solid to be a ghost, stood Sean Corkoran.

"*Sean?*" Bridey rasped. "I thought you—I saw your boat go down—"

He swaggered into the room, bringing with him a strong odor of cigarettes and sweat, strode to her side, pulled her against him. "Glad to see me, babycakes?"

The honest answer, Bridey realized was *No. No, she was not glad to see him; in fact her instant reaction had been horror.*

"How did you—how—" Bridey couldn't gather her thoughts enough to utter a coherent sentence.

"Got knocked into the water when that boat crashed down on us—but a Cork always bobs up, eh?" he said, eyeing Bridey as though she were something he was reclaiming from a *Lost and Found* box. "I swam around a while—you remember what a top-notch swimmer I am, right, Bird-brain?"

Still too shocked to speak, Bridey just stared at him, her heart thumping so hard it roared in her ears.

THE EMPRESS OF IRELAND

"Gorcey didn't make it, though." Sean tried to appear properly mournful, but his mouth twisted into a sneer. "You know what a fat slob he was—went down like a lead sinker. Murf and Suds didn't make it neither. I don't know about Moose—he ain't in the morgue anyways, I checked —he's probably sittin' in some bar, the lousy bum. I looked to make sure *you* wasn't in that morgue, too, Birdbrain," he added, his face softening; he even squeezed out a tear, and then ruined the treacly sentiment by adding, "Not that I was really worried. Pretty girl like you, some sap's always gonna help you out if you give 'im the wink."

"Is that what you told yourself, Sean? To absolve your conscience?" Bridey wrung her wet dishcloth so hard her knuckles turned white."You left me on a sinking ship! You abandoned me to save yourself! I came within an inch of drowning—"

"Keep your voice down, willya?" growled Sean, glancing nervously about, apparently worried that one of the prowling reporters might pop out of the woodwork. "You was outa your mind, Birdbrain—scared, hysterical—didn't know what you was seeing or hearing, in that dark and fog and all—"

Bridey shook her head. "I *saw* you, Sean. You were in that lifeboat. I know *you* saw me! But you turned your back.You rowed away, leaving me—"

"*Shut up,* you! Just shut your fucking mouth!" Sean's spittle flecked Bridey's face. She saw that he was about to lose control—the warning signs were there—the deep flush, the knotted jaw. His arm whipped back, ready to slap, but Marie lunged in front of Bridey, swinging a soup ladle against Sean's skull —a whack that sounded like a meat tenderizer pounding a tough steak. "Don't you set your hands to her," Marie snarled, raising the ladle again. "You pukin' coward—and you *know* you're a coward, don't you?"

Sean staggered back against a table, moaning and holding his head, and in that moment he looked so helpless, so boyish, so vulnerable—that Bridey's anger melted.

She found a clean washrag and went to him. "Sit down," she said, gently pushing him onto a stool. He had a lump on his scalp and a swollen earlobe which Bridey dabbed at gingerly. "That'll need ice."

"I'm sorry, Birdbr—Bridey," Sean whimpered. "I wasn't really going to hit you. I just got—" His voice trembled. "I been crazy with worry, scared you might have been—"

He snatched up her hands, clutched them in his own sweaty ones. "I'm just so thankful, so ....so glad you're okay," he whimpered.

"I'm glad you are too," Bridey said, and in that moment of mutual tenderness it was true.

He looked up at her, his eyes red. "Look, they're sending a ship to take everyone back to Quebec tomorrow. Me and you, we'll go back together. My folks was over the moon when I telegrammed 'em I was okay. They're throwing me a big celebration. Flannery's Bar is springing for a keg, and Ma's baking me a cake, decorated all fancy." He kissed her cheek. "Everybody'll be there—we can announce our engagement!"

He gazed expectantly at Bridey, obviously awaiting her cries of rapture.

She wavered, memories of the sweet times with Sean flooding back: the time he'd bought her a bouquet of roses, the time he'd rubbed her back for an hour when she'd sprained it carrying laundry; the night he'd first told her he loved her . . . and of course there were those blue eyes, black lashes, carved jaw—he was still the handsomest man she knew.

They could be happy together, couldn't they? Sean would finally get a decent-paying job, give up on all that *Eire do 'Fein* stuff; they'd have a little apartment, decorate it together; she'd have his tea waiting when he got home from work . . ..

THE EMPRESS OF IRELAND

Lies, lies, lies, lies! She was already starting to drift, to go with the current of other people's expectations. It had taken near-drowning for Bridey to accept the truth, but those hours in the water, when she'd fought the exhaustion of her body by thinking of names for her unborn daughter, had finally forced her to realize something: that marrying Sean would be cowardly and dishonest.

"When we get back, you can stay at my folks' house," Sean blathered, oblivious to the fact that Bridey had traveled leagues against the current, had faced down all the most cowardly parts of her own nature just during the few moments it had taken her to chip a fistful of ice out of the ice box.

"Ma won't mind you staying in the upstairs bedroom, next to *my* room." Sean said, winking. He got up, cut himself a large slice of Marie's coffee cake without bothering to serve anyone else, and crammed the cake into his mouth. "What with me and you's getting' married, it ain't like your reputation is gonna be sullied," he said, talking as he chewed. "Course once your belly starts to get big, folks will talk—you know how they count on their fingers—the old biddies always like a scandal, but if any of em says a thing, I'll—"

"Sean, there's no baby."

He stared at her, bewildered, the beginnings of anger flickering on his face. "Whaddaya mean, no baby? You lied to me? Tried to trick me?"

"I lost it, Sean. During the shipwreck—I had a miscarriage."

"There's—the baby's gone?" He wore an expression of male bafflement over the mysteries of the female body.

This was a crucial moment, and Bridey almost ruined it by laughing. "Yeah, Sean, no more baby. So you don't have to marry me."

"But . . . I *want to,* Bridey. Me and you—we been going together four years now. I got it all worked out—we'll live with my folks, save up for a flat . . .

Bridey turned her back on him, picked up a brush and began scrubbing a crusted frying pan. *Marriage*! *Was he serious?* Why this sudden enthusiasm for wedlock? It wasn't because he was wildly in love with her, Bridey knew. How could you be in love with someone you didn't know or understand, or even *want* to understand? He'd never even asked when her birthday was. He didn't know her favorite flower, or author—in fact he hated books! She suspected—her illusions about him having been washed away by the river— that Sean was feeling at loose ends. His bullion heist had gone askew, so he was not going to be the great benefactor of the Eire do`Fein he'd imagined. He had no job and was dependent on his parents for pocket money—but—*a wedding!* That had to be it! *Sean wanted a wedding*! The status of being a married man! The wedding feast, the booze, the toasts, the ribaldry, the excuse to get drunk—and best of all the *presents!* Gifts of money from the huge Corkoran clan. He'd have pockets stuffed with cash for a month or two; he'd act the big man in the saloon, buying rounds for his mates, while Bridey sat home with Sean's horrid mother.

"And we already done the sex thing—you know, what a husband and wife does in bed together," Sean said. "So we're as good as married—might as well go the whole hog, eh, Birdbrain?"

The platter Bridey was washing was slick in her fingers, about to slip out of her grip, but she didn't look at it; she wanted her eyes pointing into Sean's, wanted him to feel the sting of her contempt. "The *sex thing?* What you did to me in your uncle's attic was the worst thing I ever experienced!" She held his eyes. "You forced me, it hurt horribly, and I never intend to do it again!"

"You *will* do it, Birdbrain." His eyes were hard, cold. "It's your goddamn duty. It's what wives *do*. You gotta do it whether you like it or not, it's—it's a husband's *right*—the priests say not doing it is a *sin*!"

THE EMPRESS OF IRELAND

In the river that night, in water so cold it had nearly stopped her heart, with dead bodies bumping against her, Bridey had seen, as if watching a play, the course of a marriage to Sean. His passion, his loyalty, his love—it would all go to Eire do' Fein and to the barroom mates who made him feel important.

Sean would make no attempt to govern his temper—he would hit her; he would abuse her; he would blame her for his failures. Un-blinkered from her adolescent infatuation, she saw Sean for what he was: a dull-witted, incurious, lazy man who had to blame others so he didn't have to face his own shortcomings; his fits of violence erupted when he felt threatened; when he felt in fear of his weaknesses being exposed.

"I'll never let you near me again," Bridey flung at him. "I'd sooner go back and drown in that river than be your wife!"

His neck bloomed in hot red blotches, working their way up his jaw, his cheeks, his forehead, until his whole face was maroon—but it was his *hands* she kept her eyes on, so that when his right came up, palm open, to strike, she was ready, snatching up the big tin dishpan, holding it out in front of her like a shield, so his hand smacked against it, the metal making a ringing clang.

It must have hurt; he shook his hand in pain. "You *bitch!*" he grated out. He made a lightning move to grab her arm, intending, she guessed, to haul her somewhere where she'd be out of sight of other people, where he could punish her, beat her until he got the anger and humiliation out of his system.

No, you will not! Bridey came at him again with the dishpan, gripping its edges, moving so quickly Sean wasn't ready for it—pushing him backward with the big round pan, glorying in her own muscularity, her arms toughened by rowing against the ferocious current of the St. Lawrence—arms that had saved her life, arms now strong enough to shove his chest —*hard, hard*—setting her shoulders, her back, her very soul into it, because there were years of his cruelty to avenge. Soap suds flew, spattering across the walls and floor, and Sean, slipping on a soapy puddle, went down, skidding on his rump across the floor, thumping against a cabinet.

He looked up at her, shocked, disbelieving—as though his own fist had hauled back and round-housed him. He was panting, his mouth hung open, and a string of saliva dribbled down his chin.

"You know, I'm thinking I might just pop into Flannery's one night," Bridey said in matter of fact tones, keeping a grip on the dishpan, in case Sean launched a new attack. "That's where all your mates hang out, isn't it, getting drunk and telling stories about all the great old Irish heroes? I wonder if they'd care to hear the story of how the Great Sean Corkoran ran off in a boat to save his own hide, leaving the mother of his unborn child in a sinking ship? How'd your chums like *that* story, eh, Sean?"

"That's a real good story," Marie cut in, a wide, foxy grin on her face. "If any of those drunken plonkers doubts it, they can ask me. I was there, I saw the whole thing. I saw the great Corkoran run away!"

Sean scuttered to his feet and reeled from the room, leaving a string of filthy language in his wake like a stench.

"You weren't really there, were you?" whispered Bridey, who was beginning to shake all over; facing down Sean had taken everything in her, and she was left feeling sick and dizzy. "I didn't see you on that deck."

Marie shook her head, smiling. "Nah— but I believe it happened the way you said. Know what you ought to do? Go find a reporter—they're all over the place here—like wolf packs, wanting fresh meat, a new angle on the wreck. Imagine how they'd go to town on a guy who deserted his fiance, leaving her to drown!"

Bridey hesitated, a frayed filament of loyalty still holding her to Sean. "I don't know—that seems kind of cruel—"

"He deserves to be known as the piece of shit he is! Like that millionaire on the Titanic who got on a lifeboat disguised as a woman." She sliced into the cake, plopped a huge serving onto a plate and thrust it at Bridey. "You know who else would like to know about Corkoran? The Salvation Army people."

"Why—So they can save his rotten soul? I think it's too late."

"No, the Sallies are mad because stories are going around that men from their band shoved ahead of a crowd of women to get in a lifeboat."

Bridey shook her head. "That wasn't the Salvation Army—it was Sean's crew, in band uniforms so they could get away with—" She snapped her mouth shut. However angry she was with Sean, she wouldn't be a snitch.

"The bullion," Marie said. "It's okay—I already guessed most of it. Anyway, the Sallies have emerged as the real heroes— helping people get out of the ship, risking their own lives to help others. They lost a lot of their own folks, though—over a hundred Salvation Army members were drowned."

"Oh, Lord—that's horrible!"

"I know. Try not to think about it, alright?" Marie pulled a chair over. "Sit down, rest. Think peaceful thoughts. My grandmother used to say that babies can read their mama's thoughts, and when mama's sad, they're sad, too."

Bridey blinked. "You know?"

"That you lied about losing the baby? Course I knew. Your daughter is still there."

"I *had* to lie to him, Marie. Sean would be a terrible father. He gets angry when he thinks I'm not paying enough attention to him." She sniffled, wiped away tears with a dishtowel. "If he thought I was spending too much time on the baby, he might—oh God, he might take out his anger on *her*! That's why I told him I'd had a miscarriage—so he wouldn't have an excuse to insist we get married, give the baby his name and all that claptrap."

Marie smiled. "You did the right thing. You're already a good mother. You protected your child."

"But what do I do *now*?" Bridey said plaintively. "How do I raise a baby when I've got no place to live, no job, no money? I can't go home to my family like this—pregnant, unmarried, a scarlet woman. It's a small town—everyone would know."

Her hand crept to her midsection. "I don't know what to do. Unless—there are lots of people who want to adopt babies. Maybe I should—*Oh!*" She clutched her belly.

"What is it?" Marie said, alarmed. "You aren't—"

"I *felt* something! Inside! Like . . . like a little tapping. .... like I swallowed a fish and it's flipping around in there—"

"*Bridey!*" Marie's eyes widened; a smile lit her face. "That's your baby! It's called *quickening*."

"It's—this is *normal*?"

"She's telling you she's alive! She's moving and stretching and growing."

Bridey stood very still, pressing her hands against her abdomen, hoping to feel it again. For a moment she forgot to breathe, and then—there it was again: a faint sensation like the fluttering of butterfly wings—a tiny being saying, *"I exist!"* How could she ever have thought for one second of giving her up?

How was she going to feed and clothe and put a roof over this baby's head, though? She had no idea. But then, she hadn't known how to swim—and somehow she had swum; swum for her life, for her baby's life. And she'd rowed against the current.

But that would be her life from now on, Bridey finally understood. She was just going to have to keep on rowing against the current.

THE EMPRESS OF IRELAND

Chapter 31

Snapper

He'd been with his flock of ducklings from the moment they'd been hauled aboard the *Storstad* to the moment they walked off the ship, holding hands, in a hugger-mugger, bickering line down to Rimouski's dock. A middle-aged woman named Mrs. McCabe had taken charge of the refugees; Snapper was familiar with the type—overbearing, but with the sort of drill sergeant ruthlessness that got things done. She'd taken one look at Snapper and his struggle of ducklings before directing them to the town's school—now a temporary shelter for the shipwreck survivors. The children had been assigned a room whose desks had been replaced by cots and had a toilet just across the hall.

No sleep for him that first night. He was up a dozen times as his ducklings shrieked with nightmares. *"The dark! It's so dark! Mama, Mama! The water's coming to get me!"* He rubbed small backs, kissed small foreheads, changed soaking undies, rattled off nursery rhymes, sang nonsense songs, escorted sleepwalking kids to the toilet, fetched drinks, and sang that damn rolling ball song umpteen times—but he did it all ungrudgingly, knowing that he was the one constant in the lives of his ducks—the substitute papa who'd been with them through all the terrors of the last day and night. Well, him and Charlie, of course— the big brother all the ducks adored.

THE EMPRESS OF IRELAND

He awoke to the smell of coffee. Looking out over his sleeping ducks, Snapper wondered whether he could leave them long enough to go in search of a coffee—or if this was a civilized place—*tea*. He was just pulling on trousers—an ill-fitting pair Mrs. McCabe had scrounged up for him—when an unfamiliar woman burst into the room, waking half the kids, sobbing and calling "*Ronald! Ronald! I'm looking for my Ronald! Ronnie, are you here? It's Mama!*"

She ran to a cot, scooped a small boy into her arms, rocking him, crying over him, smothering him against her bosom, and scurrying out with the boy before Snapper even had a chance to say goodbye.

It was just the start. That whole morning distraught parents tramped through the kids' quarters, desperately searching for their lost children.

Snapper, his eyes burning from lack of sleep, and desperate for coffee, knew he ought to be happy for the kids reunited with their families. Yet every time one of his ducklings was taken away, a pang struck his heart. It was ridiculous, he knew. But they were *his* little lost ducks. *He'd* taken care of 'em, hadn't he? He'd kept 'em from drowning in that hellhole, *he'd* cheered 'em up and chivvied 'em along and near busted his back rowing 'em on that dinghy —and once they were on board the *Storstad* he'd made sure they were fed and bandaged and wrapped in warm blankets —and now, one by one, they were being taken away.

Bleedin' fool, he scolded himself. *What was you planning to do, take 'em home and adopt 'em? To a home you don't even got anymore—the ship that was your home now being at the bottom of the river?*

He reckoned he could leave the ducks long enough to mooch a cup of coffee. When he sneaked out into the hallway, Snapper was startled to discover that the corridors were shoulder-to-shoulder with people—-government officials, most of 'em, going by their suits and their air of self-importance—and officials always meant trouble, so best watch your step, boyo. Reporters swarmed around too, the damn vultures—and photographers, too, hauling their big boxy camera equipment around with 'em, getting in everyone's way.

One of 'em had stationed himself on the porch outside the school, and was aiming his camera down at the wharf, where a cargo ship was unloading a shipment of coffins. Even from this distance Snapper could see that a good many of those coffins were very small. *Children's coffins*, he realized, wishing he hadn't seen them, because each tiny coffin was a blow; each represented a duckling he hadn't been able to pull out of that terrrible dark water.

Snapper squeezed through the crowd to reach the lunchroom, where he gratefully accepted a mug of tea and a slice of toast and jam. He was just looking around the room, hoping to spot Charlie, when someone called "Oi—Ludsnap!"

A short man with a toothbrush mustache, wearing a badly-fitting suit, its shoulders speckled with dandruff, elbowed his way up to Snapper. "Ludsnap, ain't it— the one what saved all them nippers?"

Snapper instantly recognized the accent. "You're *Scouse*?"

"Jack Davies, *Liverpool Echo*. The which has paid for me to come over to this frost-accursed country to cover the shipwreck. Front page headlines in every paper in England. The States, too—and all of em's chasing the story, knifing each other to get first person accounts." He gave Snapper a friendly punch on the arm. "But you're going to spill to a fellow Scouser, am I right?"

Not trusting this bloke for a second, Snapper scowled. "How the hell did you even know who I was?"

Davies jerked an ink-stained thumb at a man leaning against a wall, puffing on a cigar. "That bloke over there pointed you out. Name is Harris, a Yank. Claims he was hired to guard the cargo on the liner, only some thugs sandbagged him and stuck him in a closet, then you hauled him out and made him help you fish a whole nursery school's worth of kiddies out of the drink. You carried those tykes up four decks and got 'em all on a boat."

Davies's eyes glinted. "This here's the hero story the public's been waiting for." Pulling out a notebook and pen, he gazed expectantly at Snapper. "So let's have it, mate."

Snapper glanced over at the man called Harris, who *did* look a trifle familiar, though he'd never gotten a good keek at the fellow down in that dark hallway. "There weren't no bloody heroics," Snapper growled. "Not on my part, anyhows. It was all down to Charlie—"

"Who's—"

"Charlie Barrows. Ten years old and twice the man me or you will ever be. He's the one ought to have his picture on the front page."

"A *kid!*" Davies screeched, nearly drooling on his notebook. "A *kid* saving other kids! They'll be running extra editions of the morning paper! And *my* byline!"

"Yeh, that's really great, sport. Just so you can sell papers," Snapper said scathingly, "all those poor sods won't have died for nothing."

Davies smirked. "You ain't gonna be on your high horse long, mate, not when you get a gander at what the *Echo* slaps in your palm for your story. This is *big,* man— maybe bigger than the Titanic! You know what the death toll stands at currently? A thousand people dead—six hundred of 'em's laid out in that temporary morgue in the church next door—and they figure eight hundred more never escaped—that ship sank so fast folks never knew what hit 'em—drowned in their beds or crushed to death when that freighter rammed the ship, their bodies still down in that cursed wreck at the bottom of the river."

He rubbed an ink-grimed finger over his mustache. "So where can I find this Charlie kid?"

Snapper regarded him through narrowed eyes. "You going to pay him?"

"He'd have to let us take his pic, but yeh, we'll pay."

Snapper found Charlie outside on the school's playground, looking out through the steel-link fence at the river below, where dozens of vessels were docked, including the battered *Storstad*, its chisel-like bow mangled.

"Awright, Charlie?" Snapper asked.

Charlie shrugged, looking totally unlike the wide-eyed, mischievous boy he'd been on the first day of the voyage—*yegods!*—could that have been just *two days ago?*—it felt like a century. He had a bruise on his jaw and a cut on his chin—probably from whipping wire when they'd cut the dinghy free. He wore a shirt so fresh from its wrappings there was still cardboard sticking out of the collar, and new trousers, presumably both shirt and pants a gift from the Rimouski clothing store which had donated its entire stock of merchandise to the bedraggled Empress survivors.

"There's a newspaper fellow wants to hear your story," Snapper said, nudging Charlie in the ribs. "I told him how you was the real hero of the whole thing, getting all them kids out safe and all. You want to talk to him?"

Charlie shrugged again. "Nah. Don't feel like . . . I ain't . . . "

Realizing that Charlie was struggling not to cry, Snapper stood there, feeling helpless, not knowing what to say, while Charlie struggled for control. At last he mumbled, "You know that church next door? It's Catholic and my family is Baptist, but Ma always says, any church is a good place for God to hear your prayers, so I . . . I went in there . . . "

Snapper's guts tightened. He guessed what was coming.

"Downstairs, the basement," Charlie whispered. "It's where they took all the bodies—the drowned people There's hundreds of 'em, Snapper. All lined up in rows. Rows and rows and rows. Their faces are covered by sheets, and people have to walk around in there, lifting the sheets to see if . . ."

He stopped, just stood staring out at the river, his eyes resting on the Storstad's crushed bow. "I found Tom," Charlie said, his voice cracking.

"Who?"

"Tom Reilly. That boy you—you said we had to go to bed, but Tom, me and him—we found this deck they turned into a cricket pitch, and we played for a while. Tom didn't know how you were supposed to hit the ball—he was used to baseball, and he hit the ball so hard it busted one of the lights, and then a minute later water started pouring in, and I thought maybe we broke something, that caused—"

"Rest easy, sailor," Snapper said. "A knocked-out bulb didn't sink that ship."

"The water kept getting higher. Me and Tom ran back to the dorm and I yelled at those kids to get out and some of 'em started following us and —we came to that stairs, but the ship was tipping over by then and the stairs were all crazy. So I—I sorta boosted Tom up the stairs to the deck above. I said he should go find help, but he said he wanted to go find his mum and sisters . . . "

He stared out onto the river, squinching his eyes against the glare on the water. "But then *you got* there and took charge, and Tom just—-I think he went off and got lost or something."

Charlie swiped his sleeve beneath his nose. "Tom's mum was down there in that dead bodies place, looking for him. They had the kids separate from the grownups, and there was . . . dozens and dozens of kids in there, Snapper! *Dead* kids, *drowned kids*!" His mum found Tom and started crying. Then I came over and I saw him. I saw his dead *body,* Snapper! He was all pale, kind of grayish white. And his eyes were open!"

"Oh, sweet Christ." Snapper gripped Charlie's shoulder.

"I thought . . . for a second I thought he was still alive, like, just knocked out or something, staring up at the ceiling, but he wasn't, Snapper, he was— he was so totally *still.* And he wasn't seeing *anything!"*

Desperately wanting to comfort him, Snapper was at a loss, afraid to say the wrong thing.

"How could that happen?" Charlie whispered. "Tom was so—-he was just alive a few hours ago—he played cricket with me. He was—how could he be dead so fast? How could that happen?"

*"*Donno, mate. Ain't bloody fair, is it?"

"It's because of that ship," Charlie growled, pointing toward the Storstad. "That stupid ship rammed us and killed all those people. I want to go down there and kill that ship. I want to blow it up with dynamite, I want—"

He started to cry, leaning against Snapper's shoulder. "How can he be dead, Snapper? What makes you dead?"

Snapper knew this wasn't really what Charlie was asking, but he gave it a shot anyway. "Water gets in your lungs. And you can't breathe, and that makes your heart stop."

"Why can't you come back? Jesus came back—he rose up out of the tomb."

"I know. But us humans ain't God, we don't come back. That's just how—that's just how things is. It's how our bodies are made. We die."

"I shouldn't have boosted Tom up there. I should have made him stay with me."

"He did what he wanted—went to find his family. Weren't your fault."

"Yeah, but . . . what if it *was?"*

"Say you'd stayed with Tom, helped him find his mum. You could have, you know—could have gone running off with him. But you chose different. You stayed down there and you helped save a lot of lives."

"But I *liked* Tom. We would have been friends. I didn't even *know* those other kids."

"You don't think they deserved saving?"

Charlie scowled. "I guess so."

"You know what I think?"

"What?" Charlie said dully.

"I think there's times when boys—even big chaps—need their mums."

It had taken a bit of detective work, as well as the help of one of the operators at the Rimouski wireless station to find the right person, but Snapper had managed to get off a telegram to a Mrs. Edward Barrows of Quebec, and arranged for her to come up this morning on the ship chartered for survivors' relatives. By now she ought to have arrived at the convent attached to St. Mary's, which had been turned into a sort of reunion center for the survivors and their families.

As it turned out, Mildred Barrows could not wait for Charlie to come to her; she came flying up the path, a Black woman in her thirties, wearing a hat with a jaunty plume, and flung her arms around Charlie, hugging him so tightly he was soon moaning that he couldn't breathe.

She was very pretty, and it was easy to see where Charlie had gotten his dark, dramatic eyes and wide smile. Never letting go of Charlie for a second, Mildred spent the next ten minutes repeatedly thanking Snapper for sending her the telegram..

"And thanks for keeping my boy safe," she added.

"It was the other way around," Snapper said. "Your son is the bravest bloke I know."

"Mum—I might be in the papers!" Charlie said, abruptly throwing off his gloom.

Snapper left Charlie and his mum to their reunion—which would probably include a scolding for Charlie's running away from home, if he'd read Mildred right.

Intending to head back to his ducks, Snapper suddenly halted, noticing a figure on the steps a few yards away, bent intently over a handful of papers rustling in the breeze.

No mistaking who it was; no one else was that big. "Mr. Giant," Snapper called.

Louis Perrault looked up, grinning. *"Bon jour, Reggie. Comment vont tes enfants?"*

"The kiddos? Not doing bad at all. What's that you're up to there?"

Louis tried to hide it, but not before Snapper had caught a glimpse. Done in soft pencil on paper he must have swiped from the school's art room, it was a sketch of Charlie and his mother. Somehow, in just a few strokes, he had managed to capture both mother and son: the physical resemblance between them, the mutual joy of their reunion.

" Didn't know you was an artist." Snapper said.

"*Artiste?*" Louis growled. "*Non.*"

"The hell you ain't. What else you got there?" Knowing he was pushing it— those big hands of Louis's looked like they could deliver a wallop—Snapper snatched the sloppy wad of papers. *Drawings!* He began flipping through them, marveling at the skill of the renderings: there was one of a freckly five-year-old he recognized as one of his ducklings—the one who'd kept singing the En *Roulant* song on the dinghy.

There was a sketch of a woman immediately recognizable as Marie Lavaliere, laughing and looking annoyed at the same time.

THE EMPRESS OF IRELAND

There was a sketch—obviously from memory—of a boat loaded with kids, tangled up in wreckage from the ship's mast.

There was Grayson, the ship's doctor, his eyes hollow with fatigue, wrapping a bandage around the ankle of an elderly woman.

There was an awkward looking gink he thought might be himself, judging by the cigarette dangling from the mouth.

Louis grabbed the drawings back, angrily crumpled them, and gobbed spit on them to show the depth of his contempt. "*Ils ne sont rien. Poubelle!*"

"No, they *ain't* trash!" growled Snapper, who had picked up a surprising command of French—and who also had surprisingly fast hands. He snatched the sketches out of Louis's fist.

Then—because he'd never lost his street cunning—he turned and ran. "Giving these to a fellow what works for a newspaper," he called over his shoulder. "Whole world needs to see these!"

JULIET ROSETTI

THE TORONTO DAILY STAR

June 15, 1914

Rub-a-dub-dub, 6 Men in a Tub

While many instances of courage and selflessness have been reported in the recent Empress of Ireland tragedy, reports have now surfaced of passengers behaving in a less than noble manner. According to crewmen, a group of men from the first class smoking lounge seized control of the #4 lifeboat, ignored the women and children waiting to board, commandeered the boat for their own use, rowed off, and were later picked up by a rescue ship.

These are the men who, having ignored the age-old dictum *Women and Children First,* now belong in the disaster's HALL OF SHAME:

~ *Quebec Businessman Elmer Wilberforce. Wife presumed drowned.*

~*Monsigneur Fulton Sheeran, Archbishop of Quebec Diocese*

~*Henry Lang, CEO 1st Northern Bank, wife drowned in stateroom*

~*Claude Thurston, Deputy Mayor of Quebec. Wife's body not found*

~*Quebec City Treasurer Alfred Davis. Wife presumed drowned.*

~*His Highness Viti Boromba of Tuvalu Island; both wives drowned*

Chapter 32

Snapper
 June 16, 1914

The Quebec Provincial Courthouse stood on a rise at the intersection of Rue du Tresor and Rue St. Louis, a massive five-story structure of pale cream stone in the Second Empire Style, crowned by a copper-topped clock tower. A thirty-foot tall doorway, arched like the entrance to a castle, added to the dramatic effect. Quebec Province's bright blue and white flag flew from the tower, whipping in the wind off the river.

The interior of the building was designed along the same grandiose lines, and as Snapper hurried across its marble floor, he expected to be stopped at any moment by an official demanding to know what the likes of him was doing in this place.

Eventually he found the courtroom, which bore a resemblance to the interior of a church: a wide center aisle ran between rows of benches; up front where the altar ought to be was a raised platform with an elaborate carved walnut backdrop and a statue of a blindfolded *Justice*, flanked by the Provincial and Canadian flags.

Canada being a dominion of England, the protocols of English law would be followed in this hearing. Seven magistrates sat at a long, polished table at center stage of the platform, and in the very center, solemn as God Himself, sat Justice John Charles Bigham,

Viscount Mersey. He had been the Commissioner of the Court of Enquiry into the *Titanic* disaster two years ago and was now being trotted out to preside over the inquiry into the *Empress of Ireland* shipwreck.

Snapper knew all this from reading the papers. The shipwreck of the Empress had been the lead story for the past three weeks, but now that the press had wrung all they could out of the sinking itself, they seemed determined to make headlines out of the court inquiry into the cause of the tragedy, with its possibilities for a dramatic courtroom battle between the two sides.

A London barrister named Butler Alkinwell was representing the Empress's owner, Canadian Trans-Global; Charles Sherman Haight, an American from New York, was there to lead the Storstad's team.

So many reporters and photographers thronged the courtroom that there was scarcely room for spectators. Snapper squeezed into a seat near the front, the section reserved for persons scheduled to testify. And he'd made damn sure he would be one of them.

Some fool had placed Kendall, the Empress's captain, and Captain Anderson of the Storstad, next to each other at the front table. Kendall looked the worse for wear, Snapper thought: pale, limping, and with a hacking cough. In the days since the wreck, Snapper had come across a good number of *Empress* crewman, and not one had a bad thing to say about the captain. Injured, thrown into the river, Kendall had been picked up by a lifeboat and had then taken charge, ordering the lifeboat's crew to row back and forth all night in the freezing cold, taking turns at the oars himself, and eventually pulling sixty people out of the water.

As for Captain Anderson, he had gone to enormous effort to aid the victims pulled aboard his ship, providing food, medical care—even brandy and whiskey—a gesture that had won the hearts of the Empress's crew.

What were Kendall and Anderson saying to each other up there at the table, Snapper wondered. The scuttlebutt was that Kendall, when hauled aboard the Storstad, had confronted Anderson, bellowing, "You have sunk my ship!"

"Nei, I did not. It was you, going too fast in the fog!" Anderson had bellowed back, and if it hadn't been for Anderson's wife getting between them, a fight might have broken out between the two captains right there on the deck. Might even see one here today; tensions were running high, and from the angry looks of the Norwegian lot, they didn't expect justice from an English court.

The hearing went on for hours, both Anderson and Kendall called to the stand, the Norwegian captain claiming that the Empress had changed course in the fog, sending the huge liner into the path of his collier, Kendall insisting that it was the freighter which had changed course, bringing the freighter on a bearing perpendicular to the Empress, which was why it had hit the liner directly midship.

All the Empress's officers were called up to testify, too, as well as all of the Storstad's officers. It wasn't until mid-afternoon that lesser mortals were called to the stand: stewards, cooks, regular seamen, boilermen—all were asked to give their account of what they had seen and heard that night.

"I will beg the court's indulgence to satisfy an old jurist's curiosity," Lord Mersey said, shortly after court stewards had come around with steaming mugs of tea for the eminences on the bench. "As many of you may know, I had the honor of presiding over the inquiry into the lamentable sinking of that great ocean-going vessel, the Titanic. One of those persons who testified—a Mr. Frank Rourke, was a boilerman on that unfortunate liner. Just recently I have learned that Mr. Rourke later became a stoker on the *Empress of Ireland*. A strange coincidence, is it not? And Mr. Rourke, against all odds, survived the sinking of both those vessels!"

A rare, wintry smile touched Mersey's face. "Since we are old acquaintances, and I have been told Mr. Rourke is here today, I would like to ask him the favor of coming up front to speak."

Frank Rourke? Snapper stifled a laugh. Rourke was a grizzled, bull-shouldered old Mick, a stoker in the Empress's boiler room. He walked with a limp because—so he claimed— he'd lost his toes to frostbite, bobbing in the ocean while the Titanic sank. Too bad the frostbite hadn't gotten his tongue instead, Snapper thought, because the old geezer never shut up—you couldn't go in the crew mess without hearing his booming voice spilling out his Titanic story. And God help you if the old fool got into the beer, because then he'd start singing, and nobody could get a night's sleep.

"Now, Frank" said Lord Mersey, looking down from his raised podium, "You survived two horrendous shipwrecks—and lived to tell the tale."

"Sure, that's the God's truth." Rourke had a freckle-spattered, weather-beaten face; his hands were as gnarled as tree roots. He appeared to be hanging on to sobriety by the flimsiest of threads.

"And where were you while the Empress was sinking?"

"Forty, fifty feet off, hangin' onto a spar for dear life."

"You saw the Empress go down?"

"'Deed I did. Thought she was going to drag me down with her."

"Out of curiosity," Mersey said, stroking his walrus mustache, "How would you compare the way the Empress sank with the way the Titanic sank?"

"Well, sir, I recall the Titanic went down real easy. Like a baby in a cradle." Rourke scratched his head. "But the Empress, now—she rolled over like a hog in a ditch!"

"Like a hog in a ditch," Mersey repeated, speaking over the wave of laughter rippling through the room. "I find your description quite . . . colorful, Mr. Rourke. Thank you—you're excused."

"Reginald Ludsnap," a bailiff called.

THE EMPRESS OF IRELAND

Started—he'd forgotten he was on the docket—Snapper got to his feet, strode up front, was sworn in and told to stand at the witness podium. Butler Alkinwell, the counselor for the ship's owners, started off the questioning.

"State your name, age, and address for the record, please."

"Reginald Ludsnap, Number 2 River Street, Quebec. Age twenty-seven."

He'd passed his twenty-seventh birthday in a tyke-filled dinghy on the St. Lawrence, but didn't think this bore mentioning.

"You were on duty on the *Empress of Ireland* on the night of May twenty-eighth?" Alkinwell squinted at a form he was holding. "The collision between the vessels indicates it happened at 1:55 A.M. Were you aware of the collision?"

"Felt a bump—didn't pay much attention at the time."

"Were you at any time in contact with Captain Kendall that night?"

"Might have spoken to 'im in passing."

"Did the captain strike you as . . . fully in charge of all his faculties?"

Snapper eyed him, trying to figure what he was angling at. "You mean, was he drinking or summat?"

"Just answer the question."

"Seemed all right to me." Snapper had taken a dislike to Alkinwell. He'd met a lot of his type during his stewarding days. The kind who snapped his fingers at waiters, who expected to have his every whim catered to, who expected lesser mortals to kiss his lordly arse. Good thing this wasn't a jury trial, because every working man in the jury box would have immediately wanted to take a swing at this arrogant tosser.

"Very well. Describe the events of the night, keeping in mind that what you observed may bear on discovering the contributing causes of the tragedy."

His high-handed manner grated on Snapper. "You want to know why all them folks died? You want to know where to fix blame?"

A part of him was cautioning him to shut up, but he was determined to speak his mind. "You can start with the damn watertight doors, all right? They're designed so that if one of the compartments floods, the door to the next compartment gotta be closed to keep water from flooding in. In point of fact, them doors are kept open most of the time so the crew and passengers can have free access to different areas of the ship."

"Oh, really?" Alkinwell raised an eyebrow, playing to Lord Mersey. "One hadn't realized you were an engineer, Mr. Ludsnap."

"Common knowledge," Snapper shot back. "Do you know how those watertight doors close?"

"Of course." Alkinwell sounded as bored as though he were being asked how a letter was mailed. "An officer on the bridge presses a button which—"

"No, he don't!" Snapper growled. "Some ships is like that—electronically wired— but the Empress was manual. We had eleven doors on that ship between the bulkheads, and a sailor or a steward was responsible for each door. If an emergency suddenly came, each fellow had to rush to his door to close it."

"I would like to dismiss this witness," Alkinwell said, scowling.

"Denied," intoned Lord Mersey.

"Obliged, your honor," Snapper said, nodding at the exalted personage above because it never hurt, in his experience, to show the nobs a little respect. "So like I was saying, to close the doors in an emergency, a crewman has to rush to his station. Then he's got to run and pull the key off its clips."

"Key?" Lord Mersey looked down at him. "You mean to say the doors were locked with ordinary keys?"

"No sir, it's a key about as long as your hand, and hollow. Now you grab your key—which wasn't easy that night, the lights flickering and then going dead, so you're in the dark, wading in water up to your shins, but you get to your station as best you can. You fit the key over the stem of the winding shaft, and that unlocks the whole mechanism, and then you take hold of the winding wheel— like the steering wheel on an automobile, only flush to the console. So then you turn the wheel counter-clockwise, and that swings the hinge shafts of the door that's one floor below, and the hinge closes the door."

Lord Mersey cleared his throat. "It does sound a bit … er … cumbersome."

"We did drills," Snapper said. "Us crew could get every watertight door on that ship closed in three minutes flat. Course that's under perfect conditions. Night of the collision we had to get them doors closed in the dark, with water rushing in, and if one door out of the eleven failed, that doorway stayed open to the rushing sea, and the compartment flooded, and then the water rushed into the next compartment, and so on, like a row of dominoes."

"This has nothing to do with the main focus of this inquiry," Alkinwell said peevishly. "You are wasting the court's time."

Prickly-hot, Snapper tugged his collar. "You said you're investigating why all them people died. Well I'm telling you why! Because the ones who designed the ship could have fixed it so's the doors had a motor connected electronically to the bridge, and all the Captain would have had to do was press a button. Instead they saved money by using the system that was old-fashioned even in Queen Victoria's day—"

"That is sheer speculation!" Alkinwell fumed. "no doubt obtained from drunken pub talk—"

"You know what else killed those people?" Snapper rolled right over him, his heart hammering, sweat spurting, and his voice going hoarse—but now might be the only chance he ever had to set the record straight. "Them lifeboats is what! And you don't have to take my word for it, because there's hundreds of people saw for theirselves. Why'd you want to go and put a two-ton lifeboat on a deck, huh? Them things turned into *death-boats*! Once the ship started listing, some of 'em broke loose and rolled across the deck like loose cannons! The number six lifeboat ripped loose from its davits and went thumping across the deck like a steamroller, smashed into a bunch of women clinging to the starboard railing. Crushed some to death, flung the others in the river."

Shrieks and gasps came from the crowd—this was a detail that hadn't been in the newspapers.

"And what about them portholes," Snapper blazed on. "Folks opened 'em to let in a breeze, but once the ship started to list. . . ninety-six portholes on that ship, and the river poured in like Niagara Falls."

A man in a loud plaid suit swiveled a camera on a stilt toward Snapper.

Poomph! The flash powder ignited, blinding him

Did this mean he'd have his picture in the paper?

As it turned out, yes. His photo was on the front page of the **Quebec Journal**, under a scorching headline: *Lifeboats Were Deathboats says Empress Steward.* And: *"Bulkhead Doors run on 'Victorian Age' system, Witness Claims.*

Chapter 33

Snapper discovered that he didn't at all enjoy seeing his own mug staring out at him from newspapers; he had no desire to be famous, having discovered at a young age that the less people knew about you the better off you were. At any rate, he had a more important matter on his mind just now—finding his lost Tabby.

Charlie Barrows, who'd eagerly offered to help, was waiting for Snapper at the agreed-upon spot: in front of Bugsy's Cafe on Fifth Street. And his mum was with him, the two of them sharing a helping of poutine, wrapped up in newspaper, while they waited.

"You're in the paper, Snapper!" Charlie yelled, holding up a gravy-smeared edition of the evening *Journal*.

"I could do without it," Snapper said, flabbergasted to see that in just the short time since he'd last seen him, Charlie had shot up two inches. No hug for dear old Snapper, either—Charlie gave him a manly handshake.

"Come on, I'll show you where I saw her," Charlie said, fidgeting with eagerness to launch the hunt for Snapper's runaway cat. Mildred, who appeared to have every intention of joining the expedition, had a lidded picnic basket slung over her arm—a woman of optimism as well as foresight, Snapper thought appreciatively.

The three of them set off on Harbor Drive, a paved street that ran alongside the river, bisected by a streetcar line and noisy with the growl of lorries and the booming horns of shipping traffic on the river. It was unrealistic to believe that a cat could have survived amid all these speeding vehicles, Snapper told himself, bracing for disappointment, telling himself how ridiculous it was to believe that he'd ever find his lost cat. He'd never be able to live with himself if he didn't at least give it a try, though.

They were close to the docks now, to the spot where Snapper had lost sight of Tabby. "It was that dark green building!" Charlie pointed to a dilapidated building with *Starkey Ship Outfitters* stenciled across the walls in faded letters. "I saw her sneaking in underneath. I tried to get her to come out, but she wouldn't. I'll show you!"

He dashed toward the building, tramped through a thicket of weeds, then got down on hands and knees and crawled toward the wood latticework skirting which hid the building's under-bay.

"Get out of there, Charlie—there could be rats," scolded Mildred. "And watch out for broken bottles, loose boards and—"

"*She's here! I can see her!* Snapper—your cat's in there!" Charlie's shout could probably have been heard as far away as the docks. "And she's got *kittens*!"

"Pipe down," Snapper cautioned. "Don't want to scare her, do we?"

Pushing through the weeds, he knelt beside Charlie, barely aware that his trouser knees were getting filthy, and peered into the dark space through a hole in the latticework, only to be greeted by a warning hiss. *Back off,* it warned. *It was her!* No mistaking that gingery sass! It was his Tabby, all right, and she was curled around a cluster of tiny fur balls. "*There* you are, old girl," Snapper croaked, tears unexpectedly welling. "Do you remember your Pops?"

She growled in response, protective of her squirming, squeaking kits.

"Got summat for you, Tabs." Digging into a pocket, he took out the chunks of haddock he'd bought from the fish market below his room—and had ordered cooked the way Tabby liked. A paw lashed out through the lattice as Tabby snagged the fish, dragging it through the hole and immediately tearing into it. No telling what she'd been living on—could she have learned to hunt mice, birds?

"I'm going in to get her out," Charlie said, flopping onto his belly.

"Half a tick," Snapper said. "This is her home now—she feels safe here."

"She cannot stay here," Mildred Barrows said firmly. "Laying on cold dirt, all sorts of nasty things prowling around—rats, skunks, snakes—just waiting to grab those babies. Now first thing we do is get them out of there, into this basket and after that we'll sort things out."

Lithe and limber as a cat himself, Charlie flopped onto his belly and squirmed through a hole in the skirting. "I'm in,"he whispered a moment later, although Snapper could have guessed that by Tabby's fierce hissing. "Mum—pass the basket through."

"Get the kittens in there first," Mildred said. "That way the mother will follow."

Moving slowly, so as not to alarm Tabby, Mildred pushed the basket through the jagged rent in the latticework. Charlie gently pushed the basket out a moment later, and now three mouse-sized forms writhed there; seconds later Tabby squeezed through the hole, jumped into the basket and reclaimed her babies, who greeted her with squeaky mewls.

The day was getting on toward dusk, but there was still enough light for Snapper to get a good look at Tabby. She was too thin, her ribs showing through her sides, but her nose and eyes were clear of the snot-like excrescences that indicated infection. She gazed up at Snapper with wide, golden eyes; he chose to read trust into them. "Remember me, don't you, old girl?" he cooed, gently fondling beneath her chin, the way she'd always liked. "But you didn't do half bad for yourself, did you? My heartiest congratulations on your bundles o' joy."

"These are very young kittens," Mildred said, stroking one of the tiny bodies. "Only a week or two old, I'd say. Their eyes are still squinched shut, and their ears are folded back, not perked like a cat yet."

There was just enough light to pick out the kittens' colors: one was gray with tiger-stripes; one was calico, and the smallest was a ginger—a miniature replica of its mother.

Snapper picked up the basket, and careful not to jostle the cats, walked home with Charlie and his mum, who lived in a two-story frame house in the Pike Hill district. He met Charlie's little brothers, who knew all about him from the yarns Charlie had spun about him. No sign of the missing Mr. Barrows, but the family didn't seem to be lacking for money—the payment Charlie had received from the Liverpool Echo, Mildred said, had been enough to pay their rent, food, and doctor bills for a year. Snapper set the basket down on the parlor floor and lifted the lid. Tabby hopped out and began a nervous exploration of the house; like most cats, distrusting new surroundings until she'd sniffed out every corner for dangers.

She seemed to like the spot Charlie fixed up for her on a rug close to the kitchen stove and thirstily lapped up the fresh water he put out for her, before digging enthusiastically into a chicken drumstick.

"So can they stay here?" Charlie pleaded, giving Snapper the big puppy eyes.

"It's a palace compared to what they'd have with me," said Snapper, who was living in a flat above a fish market, his room scarcely larger than a closet. He could barely afford to feed himself, let alone four cats.

"But it's not a permanent deal, all right?" Snapper added. "When I get back on my feet—when I get a decent place, Tabby comes back with me."

Charlie nodded solemnly. Mildred looked just as besotted with the kittens as Charlie, and Snapper knew it would be all right—this would be a good place for Tabby until such time as he could have her for keeps. She was already asleep, he saw, curled up on the rug, kittens at her side, kneading their tiny paws into her flanks to make the milk come.

It was full dark by the time Snapper left. Unfamiliar with Pike Hill's winding streets, he lost his way a couple of times and had to double back. Eventually he stumbled across his digs—Foster's Fish Market. Could have navigated his way by the smell, he reckoned—the place reeked to high heaven.

His was the upstairs flat, which was only accessible via an outside stairway. He was just stepping onto the stairs when a figure materialized from the alcove beneath the stairway, hoicked an arm around Snapper's neck, and jerked him backward. Acting on reflex, Snapper jabbed an elbow into a soft gut and was rewarded with an *oomph,* but the berk had a chum who emerged from the dark and introduced himself by pounding a rock into Snapper's face, and as he staggered from the blow, the first oik brought out something long and narrow he'd been holding at his side—*a hockey stick?*—and smashed it against Snapper's kneecaps. Screaming in pain, he crashed to the ground.

Chapter 34

The ground was the worst possible place to be under the circumstances, because here came a booted foot—direct delivery to the ribs. "Listen, you piece of trash," rumbled the first mug, who wore a seaman's beanie and spoke through a cloth wrapped around his lower face. "Our boss don't like you talking shit about his boat. Our boss wants us to learn you a lesson about keeping your mouth shut."

"Your boss," sneered Snapper, who had never learned the wisdom of not smarting off to the wrong people. "So you're one of Bickerstaff's arse-kissers?"

"*Shut up,* shut up, you little twit—" This was the second yob, who wore a derby hat with a ripped brim. He'd grabbed the hockey stick and was now emphasizing each word with a smash to Snapper's shins. "You show up at that courthouse tomorrow, you go telling lies to the papers, you're going to end up in the river with a fish stuffed down your snitching gob!"

As Beanie-guy's leg swung back for another kick, Snapper rolled, trying to evade the oversized, mud-caked boot, but here it came—square in the kidneys, and he was going to be peeing blood tonight for sure—

"Let's take 'im down to the wharf and dump 'im straightaways," growled Derby. "Anyone asks why he's in a barrow— it's our mate what's too drunk to walk—"

THE EMPRESS OF IRELAND

Somehow Snapper lurched to all fours— *God, the pain!*—then to his feet, and tried to run. His legs weren't taking orders, though—-and while he teetered there in an agonized crouch, Beanie Cap used the hockey stick like a lance, jabbing it against Snapper's side with such brutal force he was hurled into the dark space under the stairs— exactly where he didn't want to be, because it couldn't be seen from the street and held a rubbish bin of stinking fish guts. Teetering backwards, the back of his knees thudded against something and he fell—into *some sort of box?*—No, a wheelbarrow!

Spitting curses, Snapper tried to launch himself out of the barrow, but Derby Hat hurled himself onto his torso, kneeling with his whole weight on Snapper's midsection while Beanie rammed a rag into his mouth. "*Shipwreck hero disappears!*" he sing-songed as Snapper gagged and choked. "It'll be one of them whachacallits—a mystery!"

"Just shaddup, willya," snarled the other mutt. "Get the damn rope."

That was the moment the rubbish bin exploded.

The lid blew off, fish spewed everywhere in a stinking geyser of guts and blood—and the sound came an instant later—a sharp crack that could only be a gunshot.

A figure edged around the side of the stairs—a man holding a large pistol whose snubby barrel was pointed straight at Derby Hat's head.

"On the ground, both of ya's." The accent was American, and vaguely familiar, but Snapper's brain was in no shape to put name to voice. Prodded by the gun, the thugs flopped onto the fish-squelchy mud as the gunman brought something to his lips and blew—three piercing whistles. Snapper recognized it as a police emergency whistle, being well-familiar with the piping notes due to the many times he'd been forced to run from the police during his misspent

Liverpool boyhood; he knew exactly how quickly it could summon a whole squad of coppers.

An answering whistle came from nearby.

Snapper's attackers, who also appeared to grasp the significance of the whistles, scrambled to their feet and made a dash for it.

No, you don't, you lousy bastards!

Snapper snatched up the hockey stick and hooked Beanie's ankle, bringing him crashing to the ground as the gunman stopped Derby's flight by jabbing the gun into his gut. Suddenly coppers were swarming all over— Quebec City police officers, distinctive in their visored helmets and brass-buttoned uniforms, apparently delighted to slap cuffs onto the berks, and Snapper guessed that those two upstanding citizens were not unknown to local law enforcement.

The American fellow jammed his gun back into a holster—smart move, what with so many jittery rozzers around in a dark, crowded space— and flashed his own tin at the officers. "Benjamin Harris, Bakersfield Security Agency," he barked out—at least that was what Snapper thought he heard, because his ears were still ringing from that explosion and he was drifting in a fog of pain.

He was conscious enough to realize that he was being loaded into a horse-drawn ambulance, and then was being jounced and jolted over cobblestoned streets—an ordeal as likely to finish him off as a bullet. Before he could express his opinion of this mode of transport, the cursed hell-cart had halted, and he was being rolled onto a stretcher, much the way a fishmonger thumped a fresh halibut onto a scales.

He was hustled into a small room with a nose-stinging odor of medicine and dumped onto a high, leather-covered table. He didn't like the looks of all those sharp instruments set out there, but before he could work out how to do a bunk, a man in a white coat hurried into the room.

"Ah, Mr. Ludsnap. Another adventure, is it?" A familiar face—this one Snapper *could* put a name to: it was Jim Grayson, the doctor who'd saved countless lives in the aftermath of the shipwreck.

"No offense, but you smell like fish," Grayson said matter-of-factly, as he used a scissors to slice into Snapper's pants leg.

"I got my cat back," Snapper said, which totally didn't follow—maybe those oiks had cracked his skull.

Grayson chuckled. "Congratulations." He then proceeded to gave Snapper an all-over, painful examination—*his ribs—oh, God—it hurt to even breathe*—before delivering the news: his knee caps were badly bruised; his right shin bone was broken and would have to be set and put in a cast. Three of his ribs were fractured; his entire midsection would need binding with surgical tape.

"You'll have to stay here while you recover," Grayson said. "No more street brawling for a while."

"What the hell is *here*?" Snapper growled, in too much pain to be polite.

"Why, it's a hospital. St. Mary's," Grayson replied, looking as though he wanted to give Snapper's brain a thorough going-over.

Hospital! Better than the flat above the fish shop, Snapper thought. Still . . .

"Can't pay for it," he rasped. "Throw me back into the street." He was flat broke. He'd been scrounging around for a job ever since he'd gotten back to Quebec. He'd never sign onto a ship again, that was for damn sure—not that the CTG was likely to hire him again, now that he'd burned his bridges clear down to the waterline. He could tend bar, though, wait tables, work on the docks. *Right—he was just what a dock master wanted: a scrawny cripple.* Maybe he should go back to Liverpool, where he at least knew people, where his folks would put him up.

Nah, that'd mean a sea voyage, and Snapper never meant to set foot on a ship again. Besides, he had responsibilities here in Quebec: Tabby and her brood. Couldn't just go off and leave them.

"Don't worry about the fees," Grayson said. "This is a charity hospital, actually. He opened a closet and pulled out a pair of crutches. "You'll want these—to get to the toilet, that sort of thing. Give 'em a try."

Gingerly, Snapper eased himself off the table—a movement that sent shocks of pain through his ribs. Propping the crutches under his arms, he managed a couple of stumbling steps.

He was just getting the hang of the things when the door opened and the man with the gun came in. Only he wasn't holding a gun just now; he was clutching a bottle of cognac. "Thought you might be needing some pain relief," he said, grinning.

"You thought right." Snapper quirked an eyebrow at the doctor, who shrugged, which Snapper took as permission. He eased himself onto a chair, keeping his right leg thrust straight out in front, waiting as the doc found three glasses, and Harris splashed a finger of amber liquid into each glass.

"Cheers," Snapper said, when his glass was handed to him. "You're the Bakersfield bloke, ain't you? Second time you played a blinder, mate, first time being when you popped out of that closet on the ship. How'd you come to show up tonight, just as those noddys was mashing me?"

"Wasn't a coincidence," the Yank said. "I trailed you when you left the courthouse today—I saw you retrieve that cat, by the way. Look, I've worked on cases before where big corporations are involved. They have ways of dealing with witnesses they don't like." He tossed back his drink. "And they really don't like *you*, Ludsnap."

"Snapper."

"Got it. And it's Ben on my end, awright?"

He was in his late thirties, Snapper guessed: well-built and fit-looking; his hair neatly-trimmed; his eyes dark, alert—eyes that didn't miss much. There was something almost military in his bearing. He was a *type,* Snapper realized—the kind of take-charge fellow other men followed, a Shackleton and Scott kind of guy. Not bad, all in all, for a Yank.

Harris gave Snapper a look that told him he was being measured up at the same time he was taking the cut of the other man's jib. "I was in that courtroom today," Harris said, "and when you got up there and started in on how the watertight doors were operated like wind-up grandfather clocks, and how those monster boats rolled around crushing people—"

He gave a short, sharp laugh. "I almost swallowed my cigar! Those lawyers and all the big shots—they were there to assign blame for the collision, because there's *huge* insurance money at stake, depending on who's found liable. And then out of the blue you drop a giant monkey wrench into the proceedings, and suddenly it's not about who cut across whose path in that fog —it's about criminal negligence in the ship's design and operation."

Snapper scowled. "Hell, I didn't say anything any crewman on that ship hasn't said a million times. The crew's been complaining about those bulkhead doors for years. Same with the two-ton lifeboats."

"That's as may be, but yours was testimony under oath, not just some swabbie griping in a pub," cut in Dr. Grayson. "I don't think you realize how much weight your testimony carried today, Snapper. Let me tell you something." He looked down at his glass, as though debating whether to go on, and finally began to speak in a low, serious voice. "Most of the people who didn't survive that night didn't die by drowning or exposure to the cold. The majority of those I treated had broken bones, contusions, severe cuts... many of them died from their injuries. Most of those injuries happened during the ship's last few minutes, when the ship turned on its beam ends. Heavy equipment broke loose— the cargo winches, the ventilation ducts . . . and those lethal lifeboats of course. The ship itself became a killer."

Snapper nodded, remembering how he and his dinghy full of kids had been mired in the wreckage of the ship's antennae. If Louis hadn't shown up, they'd have been trapped there, dragged down as the ship sank.

"The company will never admit any of that," Harris said grimly. "That's why they want Snapper here to disappear. Like you say, Doc, he's a sworn witness—he's credible, he knew that ship top to bottom—and the papers have turned him into a hero, the guy who saved all those kids. People are going to pay attention. The CTG may end up with an enormous liability judgment against it. Wouldn't be surprised if there's class action lawsuits, too." He frowned. "If Quebec allows that sort of thing, you folks not being as lawyer-infested as the States."

Harris poured himself another drink. "I had a hunch the company might try something underhanded, maybe even try to bump you off. I thought you needed someone keeping an eye on you."

"Mate, you 'bout gave me a heart attack when you blasted that rubbish bin," Snapper said, giving a bark of laughter that nearly splintered his ribs. "What'd you use, a cannon?"

"Webley MkV—standard British service revolver. I generally carry a Colt—company policy—but it disappeared the night of the wreck."

"One o' my little ducklings didn't nick it off you, did they?"

Harris shook his head. "Some hood blackjacked me, stole my gun—it happened just before the ship sank."

"You were blackjacked?" Dr. Grayson stared at him, surprised. "So was Phillip Gaade, one of the stewards. It happened on the lower promenade, while the crew was launching a lifeboat. A rowdy lot was swarming around there, pushing ahead of everyone else—and when Gaade tried to stop them, one of them struck him on the head. I treated him there on the deck—he had a concussion and a nasty swelling consistent with being hit with a weapon like a blackjack."

"A lot of funny stuff was going on that night," Harris said. "Whoever coshed me took the key to the ship's strong-room."

"Bet they were after the bullion," Snapper said. "Know what I think? Them louts hijacking that lifeboat—they had the bullion with 'em, there on that deck."

"Then they never escaped with it," Grayson said grimly. "A boat on the upper deck slipped its davits and smashed down on it. Anyone who wasn't killed outright was flung into the water. I saw it happen."

"Then that's where the bullion is," Snapper said. "Bottom of the river."

"We can talk about this another time," Dr. Grayson cut in. "Right now I'm going to get you up to a hospital room, Reggie—see to it you get some rest. I'll have the kitchen send up a meal for you. What do you fancy?"

"Anything but fish."

Chapter 35

An officer from the Quebec City police showed up to question Snapper about the attack. His name was Robillard; he spoke English as well as Quebecois.

"Those thugs who assaulted you," he told Snapper, who was hobbling around his hospital room, experimenting with the crutches, "have admitted they were hired to intimidate you, to stop you from giving further testimony in the Empress inquiry. In fact, they were under orders to drown you, make it look accidental."

"Guess I can forget about getting my old job back with CTG, huh?" Snapper joked. "My prospects for career advancement is looking sort of dim."

Benjamin Harris was also a frequent visitor during the next week, usually bringing newspapers, cigars, and beer. He and Snapper talked mostly about the inquest, which was in its final week, due to wrap up soon.

"Got a proposition for you," Harris said one night, puffing on a cigar, sprawled out on a chair while Snapper, who'd had his broken leg set and put in a cast the previous day, hobbled around the room on crutches. "Thought I'd sound you out."

"Yeh? About what?"

"About what you're planning to do, now that no CTG liner is ever going to hire you again."

"Donno. Thought I might take up juggling. Chap on crutches juggling milk bottles—wouldn't that bring in the crowds?'

Harris grinned. "How'd you like to work for Bakersfield?"

"Don't know quite what it is you blokes get up to."

"We operate in the States mostly. Securities fraud, bodyguards for government officials, investigating threats to politicians—that kind of thing."

"Like beating up strikers?" said Snapper, whose dad had gone through a bloody dock strike back in 1901 during which the cargo companies had hired security agency thugs to assault union members.

"Nah, we don't do none o'that strikebreaker stuff—that's all the Pinkerton's dirty work. Bakersfield goes after bad guys, not some poor schmoe striking for a decent day's pay. You ever hear of the Letterbox Bomber in Philly? That was our guys who nabbed him."

Snapper rested on his crutches, interested but wary. "So you want a gimpy Scouser what don't even speak American?"

"You'd do just fine, buddy. You punch above your weight, you know that?"

"No clue what you just said, mate."

"You bat over 500. Not much scares you. You can think on your feet—like how you got those kids out of that sinking ship, scrounged up a boat, cut through that floating wreckage. You're not a big bruiser, but you do all right. I'd want you on my side in a pinch."

Harris started to laugh. "You think I didn't notice how you tripped up that thug with his own hockey stick? Pretty slick for a guy laid out flat, with half his bones broken."

He set a bottle of Molson's on Snapper's table. "You don't gotta give me an answer right away. Just think about it. And don't worry about the funny way you talk. Half the guys on our crews don't speak English—we got Serbs and Krauts and all sorts, gettin' outa Europe while the going's good—in case you didn't notice, a war's about to break out over there."

"Yeh, I'll have me a think about it," Snapper said. "But I ain't exactly a free man. I got dependents. Four of 'em in fact."

"Didn't know you were married, pal."

"I ain't, never fear. Only . . . do them New York apartments allow a bloke to have cats?"

Chapter 36

Bridey

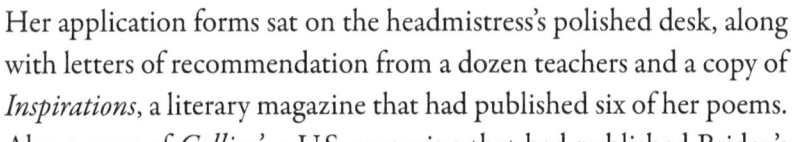

Her application forms sat on the headmistress's polished desk, along with letters of recommendation from a dozen teachers and a copy of *Inspirations*, a literary magazine that had published six of her poems. Also a copy of *Collier's* a U.S. magazine that had published Bridey's first person account of the Empress's sinking.

All in all, Bridey thought with pride, a nice little war chest of achievements.

So why was the Headmistress of the *Quebec Ecole Normale* staring at her belly instead of at her application forms?

Every applicant to *Ecole Normale*—the province's most reputable teacher training school, had to appear for a formal interview with the college's Headmistress, Bertha Wexmore, before being accepted.

Bridey had been in agonies over this all-too-crucial interview. She hadn't been able to afford new clothes; she was wearing the Rimouski skirt, clean and ironed but faded at the seams, and a jersey blouse borrowed from a roommate. She'd scraped her hair back into what she hoped was a demure, teacher-ish bun, but it had been windy on the streetcar here and strands were coming loose, as though birds had been pecking at her hair. Her hands smelled like tub-scouring powder; her chin had erupted in pimples overnight and somehow, she'd managed to acquire a stammer.

Mistress Wexmore, by contrast, was an exemplar of elegance. She was a tall, bosomy woman whose gray hair was parted squarely in the middle, pulled rigidly behind her ears and tucked into a crocheted pouf. She had flinty eyes behind wire-framed glasses and a small, downturned mouth. White lace frothed from the high collar of her lavender frock, centered with a cameo brooch.

She'd barely glanced at Bridey's portfolio, handling the papers with the tips of her fingers as though fearing contamination. Abruptly the headmistress rose, squezed out from behind her desk and walked over to the world globe that sat atop an ornate wrought iron pedestal. "I always like to show potential students one of the school's prized possessions," she said, in a voice that had the timbre of an un-oiled hinge. "This is an antique globe dating from 1850, a gift from Prince Leopold, the Duke of Albany, on the twenty-fifth anniversary of the school's founding. I keep it here to remind applicants of the prestigious reputation of the institution to which they aspire, a reputation burnished by its royal patronage."

For a royal, Duke Leopold had terrible taste, Bridey mused, studying the globe, which was done in dull grays and parchment colors and seemed to have left out the entire continent of Australia.

The headmistress gave Bridey an intense, head-to-toe scrutiny before returning to sit down at her desk. She was silent for a moment, staring pointedly at Bridey's midsection, then in the accusatory tones of a police inspector asking a suspect where she was the night of a murder, spat, "Young lady, are you *enceinte?*"

"Am I *pregnant?*" Bridey tried to infuse her voice with indignant denial, but a treacherous blush betrayed her. *Oh, Lord, why had she borrowed this figure-hugging blouse, instead of wearing her frowsy, forgiving old cardigan?*

"I think you *are!*" crowed the headmistress, shoving Bridey's forms back across her desk with such force that papers fluttered to the floor. Bridey bent to pick them up; when she came up again, it was to Mistress Wexmore's beady-eyed stare. "I don't know how you had the *gall,* in your *condition*, to apply to a program that exemplifies the highest moral standards in the province, when your very appearance trumpets your depravity!" Her mouth clamped into a hard, thin line.

"You won't *do,* Miss Collins, simply won't do at all. You are common and trashy and your request for entry to teacher training at my institution is hereby— " She snatched a stamp pad and stamper from a drawer, and with obvious relish, stamped **DENIED** in red ink across Bridey's beautifully hand-written application.

"But . .. I'm *married!* Bridey held up her left hand, whose third finger held the wedding ring Marie had lent her for purposes of respectability.

"Really?" Mistress's left eyebrow quirked upward. "Your transcript makes no mention of the fact."

"He's—we're—if you'd just let me—"

"No matter." Mistress Wexmore waved away Bridey's protestations. "Even if you *are* married, which I doubt, most school boards refuse to hire married women." There was something of Lavinia about this woman, Bridey thought—it was the way she obviously felt that *her* beliefs and expectations were the societal standard, not to be questioned by those of inferior station. "School boards, representing the norms for decency demanded by parents, eschew hiring married females as teachers."

"But that's ridiculous!" Bridey burst out.

Mistress Wexmore's mouth tightened. "Imagine the effect on adolescent children of having a woman with a protruberant belly standing in front of a classroom, inspiring pubescent boys with all sorts of impure thoughts, and raising questions in impressionable girls about matters not fit for discussion in respectable society!"

"So they don't hire married ladies because they might—they'll get—they'll have *kids*?" Bridey spluttered, disbelieving.

"That is not for one such as *you* to question. And I must say I find your attitude highly offensive!" Mistress Wexmore clutched the cameo at her throat. "I should like you to vacate my office immediately. Take your forms and—your little scribblings with you—they certainly won't find any place in *my* school's library."

Trembling all over, Bridey shoved her chair back, stood up, snatched up her papers —

Row against the current. Never drift.

She plumped back into the chair. "Well, you ought to read *this*," Bridey said, whacking the *Colliers* onto the desk. "It tells how I survived the sinking of the *Empress of Ireland*—I'm sure you've heard of it. Over a thousand people died. I nearly did, too, because I'd never learned to swim—but I swam anyway—I figured out how to do it and I *swam!* Then I found an empty lifeboat and it didn't have any oars, but I rowed with some boards. I didn't give up. I rowed and rowed and rowed and near broke my back but I didn't give up—- just kept on trying. I never gave up, I—"

"You have been told to leave—did you not hear?" The Headmistress's eyes were frostier; her nostrils were pinched, as though to avoid an odious smell.

"I bet there's lots of schools that would hire someone like me!" Bridey was back on her feet, breathing hard but determined to have her say. "There are folks who'd want their kids taught by a—a person who knows what it's like to struggle for what you want! You ought to at least give me a chance, Mistress Wexmore— let me take classes here, show you what I'm made of—I'm smart, and hard-working, and —"

An unladylike snort came from Miss Wexmore. "If word got around among the parents of my pupils that their innocent daughters were mingling with the sorts of trollops who breed illegitimate brats, why, the Board of Overseers would have my head on a platter! Now kindly remove yourself."

Mistress Wexmore yanked on a cord behind her desk. Distantly Bridey could hear a bell ring.

Send not to ask for whom the bell tolls. The Donne poem flickered across Bridey's mind. *It tolls for Thee. And it ain't good news.* Still determined to have her say, she leaned across the mistress's desk and stared directly into the cold eyes. "I'm asking you to reconsider. I know I've got what it takes to be a good teacher. If you could just give me the chance to—"

A hand fell on her shoulder. She looked up at a man in a denim uniform, who smelled as though he'd been varnishing furniture.

"Remove her from these premises, Scranton!" the headmistress ordered. "*Out. Out, out!* Out with the other rubbish!"

Scranton, whose bald pink head seemed to grow directly out of his shoulders without stopping along the way for a neck, grasped Bridey's upper arm and used it to steer her toward the office door.

Panic boiled up in Bride. This was Sean all over again! She was being manhandled, abused, humiliated . . .

No—She wouldn't allow it! She wrenched free, and when the man tried to grab her again, she shoved him. Hard. He hadn't been anticipating it; he staggered back against the globe, knocking it off its ornate perch. It rolled noisily across the floor and came to rest atop a floor grating, one of whose curlicued prongs poked a hole into Japan. "I'll see *myself* out," Bridey spat.

A minute later she was on the building's front steps, panting, heart hammering. Scranton had dogged her all the way down the stairway—as though he suspected she might try to pinch the ugly needlework samplers displayed on the walls or slide down the bannisters, displaying her underpants, shrieking in unholy glee.

In case she hadn't gotten the point, Scranton slammed the front door behind her and rammed home the bolt, a gesture clearly intended to convey: *Good riddance to bad rubbish!*

Still seething, Bridey stomped away from the building. The college, on a hill above the St. Lawrence River, was set amid a beautiful campus, its red-brick buildings handsome against the vibrant greenery of trees and shrubbery. For years Bridey had imagined herself as a student here, treading these flower-lined paths, mingling with other young women, maybe doing homework together, or being invited to someone's house for a taffy pull or a sledding party—

Oh, codswallop! Headmistress Wexmore had thrown ice water over that dream.

The back of her eyes prickled, and she thought she might start crying, but recalling what Marie had said about babies—*they react to your moods*—she took a deep breath, turned her back on the door that had been barred against her, walked briskly down the path and found the nearest streetcar stop. Rummaging through her purse, Bridey dredged up five pennies and used them to pay her streetcar fare. Her stop was four blocks from her boardinghouse, which meant walking the rest of the way—all uphill. The baby kicked the entire time.

Bridey was exhausted when she finally got home—if that's what you could call the narrow three-story house squeezed between a dental supply store and a veterinarian whose kennels rang with the yelps of dogs day and night.

All Bridey wanted was a cold glass of water and a ten minute nap, but before she could even set a foot on the stairway, Mrs. Krakowsky, her landlady, bore down on her "Bathtubs need clean, lazy girl," she shrilled. "You get to it now, you hear?"

Unable to afford rent, Bridey had negotiated a deal with Mrs. Krakowsky: she was to clean the house's six bathrooms in exchange for her room and board. Scouring tubs was harder with a bulky midsection, Bridey had discovered as her pregnancy advanced to what Dr. Grayson estimated was five months—and all the stooping and bending gave her a backache.

But she sang as she worked, not out of an excess of cheer, but because she believed the baby enjoyed being sung to. She supposed she should sing lullabies, but popular songs, she'd discovered, sent the baby into a flurry of kicks and somersaults.

"Casey would waltz with the strawberry blonde,
And the band played on,
He'd twirl round the floor with the girl he adored
And the band played onnn ..."

"Do you like that one, honey?" she asked her stomach. "Or would you rather hear *By the Light of the Silvery Moon?*"

Behind her, the bathroom door opened "Hold your shirt on, will you—I'll be done in just a minute," Bridey called irritably. That was the trouble with living in a house with nine women—someone was always needing the bathroom.

"What have they done to you, Bridey—turned you into Cinderella?" Marie Lavalliere stood in the doorway, looking ready to go to war with whoever had turned her friend into a bathtub-cleaning slavey. She pulled Bridey to her feet—no easy feat, considering that Marie was juggling a cardboard cake box, a large handbag, and a newspaper.

"You *sit!*" she ordered Bridey, pointing at the toilet seat. "You shouldn't be doing this kind of work in your condition. I'll finish the stinkin' tub!"

Bridey sat. Marie was a force of nature—not to be argued with. She was all energy and muscle; she had the tub sparkling in two minutes.

"Now let's go downstairs and eat cake," Marie said, holding up the cake box by its string.

The kitchen was a cheerless room, always dim because the building next door blocked sunlight, its only spot of color a dozen red tulips jammed into a jar.

"Go on, open it," Marie urged, setting the cake box on the table.

Bridey did, and discovered a triple-layer vanilla-frosted cake emblazoned *Congratulations!* in curly blue script. "It's to celebrate your getting into teacher's college," Marie said, slicing into the cake with a butter knife.

"I didn't get in, Marie," Bridey said in a strangled voice. "You should have saved your money."

"*Didn't get in*! With all those straight A's, those letters from teachers, those poems you got published—"

"The headmistress—Miss Wexmore—didn't even look at them. She just stared at my belly. I told her I was married, but she didn't believe me— she called me trashy and depraved and said a person of such low character would never—" Her tears were damming up behind her eyes, ready to flood, but to Bridey's surprise, a deep, bubbly laugh erupted instead.

"I behaved like exactly the kind of lowlife she accused me of being! I lost my temper and yelled and next thing I knew this janitor was dragging me out of her office. And I got scared because it reminded me of Sean and I kind of —I gave the guy a shove—but I pushed him harder than I thought, because he knocked over the old bat's globe and it rolled . . ." She was helpless in the grip of her own laughter. "It rolled across the floor, making this *wibbledy-wobbledy* noise—and it was a valuable antique given to her by Lord Von

Upsnoot or somebody— and I—well, that's the part where I said 'I'll show myself out,' and sort of galloped down the stairs."

Bridey was breathless, hiccupping with laughter but leaking tears, too, and shaking all over. "I feel a little drunk," she said.

Marie shoved a slice of cake at her. "Eat. You need sugar."

There were no forks, so Bridey used her hands to stuff cake in her mouth. *Trash, was she? Common, was she?* Fine! She'd live up to it then—she'd eat cake the way it was meant to be eaten, because it was really, really good cake! She chewed and spoke at the same time. "And that's the story of how I got kicked out of teacher's college before I was even enrolled!"

"You said you'd show *yourself* out?" said Marie, who had to stop eating because she was laughing so much.

"A touch of class, don't you think?" Bridey heaved a deep breath. "Sorta burned my bridges, didn't I? Oh, Marie— I had it all planned, how I'd earn my degree, get a decent paying teaching job so I could support my baby—I didn't want my little girl growing up thinking her mum was just the lady who scrubs the toilets."

"Here, take a look at this." Marie thrust the newspaper at Bridey, who stared at the front page story: *Verdict in Empress Inquiry Expected Friday*

"No, the second page," Marie said, flapping open the paper and pointing at the headline *Hotel de Cheverny to Open July 5th*, featuring a photo of a building that resembled a fairy tale castle. Bridey was familiar with the place, as all Quebecers were, because the hotel had been under construction for umpteen years. Finished at last, it was a seven-story building of terra cotta brick—an extravaganza of drum towers, cone-shaped roofs whose overlapped slate tiles resembled licorice pastilles, turrets and gables and carved corbels and oriel windows and weather vanes like upraised lances—and it all somehow managed to come together in magnificent harmony: a medieval chateau that seemed to have thrust itself up out of the russet sandstone of the promontory above the St. Lawrence.

"Do you know who owns that heap?" Marie asked.

"God?"

"Close. Nathan Bickerstaff."

"Bickerstaff! The owner of the *Empress*?"

"The very same." Marie gathered up their plates and carried them to the sink. "Every newspaper in the country is lambasting him, accusing him of cutting corners on the Empress, causing all those deaths. So now he's trying to redeem his reputation, opening up that big hotel a couple of years ahead of schedule—probably wants to shift public attention away from the shipwreck, get people talking about his fancy new hotel instead."

Bridey wiped frosting off her chin, finding it hard to dredge up sympathy for the problems of a millionaire.

"I know Bickerstaff," Marie said. "Did I ever tell you that? Him and his family used to travel on the Empress every summer, going over to England. And this one time I served him my chicken croquettes in cream sauce. He raved about 'em, Bridey! Raved like a madman, couldn't get enough. I had to make up a whole second batch just for him! He made me come out of the kitchen and shook my hand and said I ought to be awarded the *Order of the British Empire* ....oh, hell, Bridey, I admit it—I was flattered as all get-out. Then there was this time I fixed him beef tips with mushrooms, and he said it was better than what he got at the best restaurant in Paris."

Her face had turned a red that nearly outglowed the tulips. "Guess who he wants to be the head chef in the new hotel's restaurant?"

"Marie! *You?*"

"*Me!* Can you believe it! Working for more money than I ever saw in my life! Only first I had to agree to do this one thing every Sunday night."

"Oh, please, tell me it's not—"

Marie whacked her with the newspaper. "Not *that*, wiseapple! I got to fix him chicken croquettes. For the next ten years."

"Did you accept the job?"

"Nope." Marie chuckled. "I kept him dangling. It's good for rich old coots not to be toadied to all the time. I told him I couldn't do it because I was mourning my little boys, so cruelly ripped away from me. 'My mother's heart grieves for her lost sons,' I told him. 'The dishes I prepare would be too bitter with the salt of my tears.'"

Marie's eyes crinkled as she broke into a grin. "So Bickerstaff made a phone call. I don't know who it was to— the Prime Minister for all I know, because my boys are coming home. Well, not home exactly. Home is our village, Ashquasing. My boys are going to come live with me in the hotel. It's not what I always dreamed of, but it's the best I can do for the moment."

Marie held up a finger. "I made the old codger agree to another condition. I get to hire my own staff. And I want *you*, Bridey. You can do pastry, or salad, or be the soup chef, or decorate cakes, whatever you want. Look, I know this ain't what you wanted, hon—working in a kitchen instead of teaching kids. But you'll earn good money, and lodging's included so you'll have a place to live. In fact, you can tell that witch of a landlady where she can shove her scrub brush and walk out of here right this minute if you want!"

Bridey just stared at her, dazed.

"Threw too much at you all at once, didn't I?" Marie apologized. "You don't have to decide right away—take time to think it over."

When you're drowning and someone throws you a lifeline, Bridey thought, *you don't mull it over. You grab it. When you find a cricket bat in the bottom of a boat, you row with it.*

"Can we take the cake with us?" she asked.

Chapter 37

June 28, 1914

It took Lord Mersey over an hour to read the sixty-five typed pages of the Commission's final report.

"The main difference in the accounts told by the opposing parties," Mersey read, 'was the issue of whether the two ships were set to pass left to left or right to right. The question of which ship was to blame resolved itself to a simple issue: which ship had altered course in the fog? Having heard all the testimony, we concluded that it was the *Storstad*'s altered course that caused the collision.

In the case of the *Empress*, the court concludes that Captain Kendall was not wrong in stopping his ship, but would have been better advised to have given the oncoming ship a wider berth, so as to pass on a wider beam.

We do not conclude that his failure to give a wider berth contributed to the disaster; however we believe that his failure to have the watertight doors secured when there had been a warning of fog on the river was negligent."

There was a great clatter in the courtroom as reporters ran out, eager to send in their stories to scoop the competition.

Norwegian Collier blamed for Empress's Sinking, the headlines would read, mused Kendall, feeling a great deal of sympathy for

THE EMPRESS OF IRELAND

Captain Anderson. How easily it could have been the other way around: *Kendall's Course Change Caused collision* .

Anxious to avoid the jackal pack of reporters at the rear of the courtroom, Henry hastily sought another route out of the building

Whatever the verdict of the court, Henry knew he'd been tried in the court of public opinion. In most people's eyes he would be the man who was at least partly responsible for the deaths of all those people.

Negligent: the word burned in his brain.

He could bear that, Henry thought, keeping his head down, eyes averted, as he plowed through the clots of lawyers and law clerks.

What he couldn't bear was knowing that they weren't far off the mark:

Over and over again in the past few weeks he'd asked himself the same agonizing questions: why *had* he ordered his ship to go astern that night? Why hadn't he ordered the watertight doors closed earlier? Why, after the initial sighting of the other's ship's light, had he ordered a northeast heading? Why had he not been more prepared for fog?

The answers all came back to one simple thing: his own bad judgment.

After all those years at sea, after sailing square-riggers and steamers, after guiding ships through hurricanes and doldrums, after being promoted ahead of longer-serving officers—he had begun thinking of himself as exceptional—a commander who, unlike lesser men, could not make a mistake. And in his arrogance, he hadn't listened to wiser counsel, to men who knew the vagaries of the capricious St. Lawrence fogs.

What now? The Canadian Trans-Global would never give him a command again—nor should they—*those dozens of tiny coffins!*

White Star and Cunard wouldn't want him either, nor any of the big American lines.

He supposed he'd return to England, end up a figure of pity—an old sea captain telling tall tales in pubs for the cost of a pint.

Slipping out the courthouse's back door, he reconnoitered, then, satisfied that no reporters were about, he cut through an alley before turning onto a busy downtown street, eager to become an anonymous face in the crowd.

A newsboy was yelling up on the corner just ahead. It would be about the verdict, Henry thought, bracing to hear his own name mentioned, but to his surprise, it was something else entirely—something far more earth-shaking.

"*Archduke Shot to death by Assassin's Bullet! Murder, bloody murder!*" shouted the boy, waving the latest edition of the *Quebec Journal*. Henry recognized him—he was the kid who'd helped all those small children escape the shipwreck.

" Captain Kendall!" the boy rushed up to Henry. "Remember me? Charlie? Charlie Barrows?"

"Yes, of course I remember you," Henry gave him a friendly clap on the shoulder. "What's this you're bellowing about?"

"This King or Duke or somebody got killed," Charlie said, handing him a paper. "You can have a copy—no charge, Captain."

"Thank you." He looked Charlie over. A fine boy—smart and scrappy, one of the true heroes of the whole disaster. "You're in the newspaper business now?" Henry asked, smiling.

Charlie nodded, his eyes shining. "I get ten cents for every paper I sell. Helping out my family." He turned away for a moment to bellow into the stream of passing pedestrians: "*Franz Ferdinand Assassinated! Read All About it!*"

"You're a good son to help out your family, " Henry said, flipping a two dollar coin at the boy.

THE EMPRESS OF IRELAND

"They're saying this means war," Charlie said. "Do you think that's true?" "Will *we* get into it? Canada, I mean?"

"If England gets into it—and it will—then it means Canada must follow," Henry said grimly.

There was a stampede of buyers toward Charlie, and Henry slipped away.

War! He scanned the headline. Austria had already declared war on Serbia, and Russia supported Serbia, and Germany feared Russia—it was a fearsome tangle of alliances, but Henry had no doubt that by August all of Europe would be at war. The assassination was the fuse leading to the powder keg.

He had to leave for England immediately; he had to join up, before all the officers' commissions had been assigned.

His stomach sank as the horrible possibility occurred to him that today's verdict might mean he wouldn't be assigned a ship.

Well then, he'd enlist in the Army.

He wouldn't mind so very terribly if he was killed. It would be in service to his country; it would erase his stigma; he would die a hero.

He flapped through the paper until he found the table of ship's arrivals and departures. There! The *Alsatian* was sailing at four that afternoon. He could just make it if he hurried. He had nothing to pack; everything he'd owned—including the beautiful black opal—had gone down with the Empress.

Chapter 38

October 18, 1914

"I find it absolutely *scandalous* that a woman in your condition is out in public, much less climbing stepladders, displaying herself like a . . a mare in foal. It's indecent—I'm sure some would call it obscene. I shall lodge a complaint with the hotel manager!"

The dowager, who wasn't even a guest at the hotel, merely a busybody who'd been passing through the lobby on her way to the hotel's tea room, might as well have been Lavinia Wilberforce, risen from a watery grave and nattering about standards going downhill on the sinking ocean liner. There was a touch of Headmistress Wexmore here too—the eagerness to condemn any woman who dared set a toe outside society's rigid expectations.

Bridey finished thumb-tacking the last fold of the gauzy draperies to the ballroom's wall. Scattered with sequins, the fabric would create a dreamy background for the wedding ball to be held here this evening. Since the bride wanted an autumn theme, Bridey had spent the afternoon scouring the park near the hotel for boughs of bright maple leaves, which she'd arranged in vases all around the room.

Moving cautiously, clumsy in her near-ninth month of pregnancy, Bridey stepped down the ladder. If only she could dress the way men dressed! How practical to wear trousers and not have to worry about tripping on your own skirt hem. Or to wear painters' overalls of sturdy canvas, with pockets galore. She wore a navy hip-length jacket with a big, splashy bow just above her baby bulge, supposedly to divert the eye, and a dark colored skirt, the outfit designed to disguise her condition—as though pregnancy were a contagious disease.

Women were expected to hide away at home once their condition became obvious, but that was a luxury for the well-to-do. Working women had to go out and earn a living; housewives had to go out to do shopping, walk their children to school, hang laundry and do the hundreds of other chores that wealthy women like Mrs. Quivering Jowls here, the pearl-clutching old prune, had servants to take care of.

As the woman steamed off, no doubt to go make someone else's life miserable. Bridey began to gather up her supplies, glancing around the room, pleased at how pretty everything looked. She'd been at the Hotel de Cheverny for months now, but she still hadn't gotten over the thrill of working in such beautiful surroundings. The first thing one noticed when entering the building was the stunning curved double staircase—the centerpiece of the lobby, its steps veined white granite, its railing wrought iron in the newly-popular Art Deco style, gilded silver to pick up the silver marbling in the granite. The walls throughout the hotel's ground floor were vibrant teal, the drapes warm rose; the carpets lavish Aubussons in an intricate pattern of rose and peacock and silver.

Flowers were everywhere—on desks, on tables, in window nooks—oversized, extravagant displays of whatever flowers were in season: currently it was late autumn chrysanthemums sprigged with berries and acorns—the Cheverny was keeping every flower shop in the city afloat.

If you wanted to put a fine point on the matter, Bridey was kitchen staff—assigned to salads or potatoes or desserts or whatever

Marie needed on a particular day, but Monsieur Duquenne, the hotel manager, often pulled Bridey out for other duties: bedecking the ballroom or lobby for special occasions, or manning the front desk—and, having noted her precise penmanship, he'd sometimes put her to work copying accounts in the hotel's bookkeeping department.

Quite frequently now, Bridey had found herself doing more than merely copying numbers; she spied mistakes and corrected them; she found deposits that had not been made to the bank, bills that hadn't been paid— and along the way had discovered she had a real flair for accounting. Math had always come effortlessly to her: there was something about the logic of numbers that simply appealed to her; *she liked things to make sense!*

Monsieur Duquenne, by contrast, was absolutely hopeless at keeping the hotel's finances. He'd had the books in such a jumble last time he'd called on Bridey to rescue him, that it had taken a week to untangle the mess.

Never a dull moment in the Hotel de Cheverny:

One day Bridey might be in the kitchen, trying to produce a souffle that didn't collapse in the oven.

Another day it might be Duquenne's blasted bookkeeping.

Yet another day she might be talking to a giddy bride about the arrangements for her wedding reception.

Today, however, Bridey thought she might have overdone it a bit—all that tramping around scooping up leaves and all that traipsing up ladders—her back was aching something fierce. She knuckled her fists into the base of her spine, trying to massage away the ache, anxious to get back to work, because there was still so much to do for that infernal wedding. *The crystal!* She had to set the goblets out on the tables in the banquet room!

Stretching to reach the wine goblets, which—curse the things—were on the highest shelf, Bridey felt a small pop deep inside—followed by a gush down her thighs. *Pee? How embarrassing*—she'd hadn't wet her pants since she'd been a child...

Her belly contracted in a fierce cramp—and now it dawned on Bridey what was happening; Marie had explained it: the fluid surrounding the baby burst— and that was the onset of labor—*Oh, no, not now!* Not today, with so much to do for this wedding—and she had never finished sewing all the little things the baby would need; had kept putting it off, because the baby wasn't due until November...

"Babies don't care if you're ready for them or not," Marie had warned Bridey.

And Marie was right, as usual.

Another cramp racked through her—a cramp so painful it doubled her over; she sank to the floor, groaning. It was where Nimki found her when he came pelting into the ballroom a moment later, being chased by Noodin.

Marie's sons were nine years old now. They were very alike, but Noodin had wide-set eyes and wild hair; Nimki had Marie's slightly-slanted eyes and full face. True to his word, Nathan Bickerstaff, the owner of the hotel, had slashed through government red tape to free the boys from their boarding school and have them brought here to Quebec. They lived at the hotel, in a room next to Marie's, and from the moment they'd arrived had brought laughter, mischief, and gaiety to the place.

"Did you fall?" Nimki asked, bending over Bridey, frowning in concern.

"Get your mother," Bridey grated out, and was immensely relieved when Marie showed up a few moments later, solid and unflappable.

It was common now for women to have their babies in hospitals, but Bridey hadn't wanted her child born in a sterile hospital room, with its stern-faced nurse-nuns.

Her baby, she was determined, would be born in her own bed in her own little hexagonal turret room whose windows faced onto views of the river.

"You go fetch Dr. Grayson," Marie ordered Nimki and Noodin. The boys took off at a gallop, excited, and Marie helped Bridey up to her room, got her undressed and into bed.

The pains were coming hard and fast now; Bridey could barely get her breath in between.

"The doc can't come!" The twins burst into her room ten minutes later, shouting over each other. "He got called out to a 'mergency "

"At the army camp!"

"There was a big explosion!"

"The nurse said—"

"It might be *hours!*"

"All right," Marie said gruffly. "Now go do your chores. And stay out of this room!"

Bridey, whose kitchen co-workers had regaled her with stories of their labor and delivery ordeals, had secretly believed they'd exaggerated their travails—but now, as pain gripped her body in agonizing waves, she was amazed that any woman ever survived labor. Racked by pain, she was ashamed she'd ever doubted the stories. The pain of labor was not an exaggeration designed to elicit sympathy—it was a vicious monster!

"You'll get through this," Marie assured Bridey, kneeling alongside the bed, her voice calm, rallying.

"*No, I won't! I won't!*" Bridey gasped, thrashing from side to side in her bed. "I'm going to die! God damn Sean Corkoran for putting this thing in me!"

There were times during that interminable afternoon when Bridey, half out of her mind with pain, believed she was back in the river, swimming to keep her baby alive, knowing she had to move or she'd sink into that icy blackness.

And yet she wanted to stop trying, just wanted to give up, to let the river take her, because it would mean the end of her agony. Marie sat next to her, not complaining no matter how hard Bridey squeezed her hand during the pains.

The twins poked their heads into the room, demanding to know if the baby had come yet; Marie threw a pillow at them and ordered them to stay away.

The room darkened; it was night. Marie turned on the lamps but kept them dimmed—the bright light, she explained, would be too harsh on the baby's eyes.

Bridey sensed that someone else was in the room. Through a haze of pain, she looked up to see that Dr. Grayson had arrived.

Why, here they were, she and the doctor, on the deck of the sinking ship, and they had to help the poor unconscious man—she couldn't remember his name— couldn't remember anything in the midst of the all-consuming pain, and the ship was listing; they were going to be rolled off the ship; rolled into the freezing black water . . .

No, that wasn't right, either. She was in a small boat—and Marie's solid body was behind her, propping her up, ordering her to man the oars. *Where were her oars? There was the LAND sign, sitting atop her dresser. She gestured toward it, needing it.*

No—push! Someone was telling her to push. Well, that was stupid! You had to *pull* oars—you had to keep pulling on them because . . .

Her body took over, pushing, pushing . . . oh God, it hurt! She opened her mouth to scream, but she didn't have the breath for it, because her body was stretching, burning . . . she couldn't push any more. The ship was going down, everything was hopeless . . .

And in the middle of it, at the worst possible time, as the pain was reaching a crescendo, she felt something else. "Need the toilet," Bridey gasped.

"Nah, that's just the baby moving down," Marie said, "pressing on your whatchamacallit."

"Here's the head, Bridey," Grayson said in his deep, soothing voice. "Your baby's coming —only a few more seconds now... "

More pressure, more stretching, the doctor saying something about shoulders... and then, an odd sound, somewhere between a squeaking hinge and a kitten's mewl—the crotchety squawk of a new soul taking its first air into its lungs.

Bridey could see the infant now, between her legs, the umbilical cord still pulsing with her own blood, and then the doctor was taking the tiny thing in his big hands, and gently, gently, as though holding something sacred, he placed the baby on Bridey's chest. Her breasts were already leaking milk—her ducts had opened at the baby's first plaintive bleat, and Bridey pressed the small, wriggling wonder against her wildly beating heart...

She looked into her daughter's eyes. She'd been told that a newborn's eyes couldn't focus, but her baby stared back at her, she was certain of it—slightly cross-eyed, but *seeing,* seeing her mother.

No need for the name of a heroine from a book. Bridey had known for weeks that this tiny girl must be named for the kindest, bravest person Bridey had ever known.

"*Marie,*" she whispered, kissing the infant's small, round forehead. Her hair, slicked with birth fluids, was dark, her eyes deep blue, and it seemed incredible to Bridey that a newborn should have eyelashes, but she did—minuscule black feathers, resting on her round cheeks. And tiny, tiny nails on her miniature fingers. *Oh, she was perfect, perfect!*

"I know you don't want to part with her," Dr. Grayson said. "But I have to weigh her." Ever so gently, he took the baby from Bridey and placed her in a little brass pan lined with towels. He jiggered counterweights around and at last announced, "Six pounds one ounce."

THE EMPRESS OF IRELAND

"It felt like *sixty*," Bridey muttered—at which Marie gave a great whoop of laughter.

It was a night for laughing, a night for joy—and the joy banished all memories of the pain.

Chapter 39

She was really the loveliest baby, Bridey thought. All mothers believed their babies were beautiful, of course, but Marie truly was a lovely child by any standard. Delicate dark wisps of eyebrows, large round eyes, a beautiful little mouth—and Bridey's own chin.

Colic, though—that wasn't beautiful in the least. It started when Marie was a week old and went on for weeks, the infant in apparent pain, her face red, her fists clenched, her mouth stretched wide in a wail. Bridey spent hours and hours a night pacing her room with the baby on her shoulder. She sang to her. She rocked her. She rubbed her back. She gave her warm baths. She did everything but stand on her head, but still the baby screamed, and they were both going mad from lack of sleep.

"Colic is normal in a baby's first few weeks," Dr. Grayson assured a droopy-eyed Bridey as he stopped in for his weekly visit. "She seems to be healthy other than that; her eyesight and hearing are normal, she's gaining weight on schedule, and we know there's nothing wrong with her lungs."

One afternoon in late November as the hotel's staff was putting up holiday decorations, Dr. Grayson arrived for his usual visit and handed Bridey a blank birth certificate.

"You'll need to fill this out," he said. "Your child will need this for all sorts of official reasons throughout her lifetime."

THE EMPRESS OF IRELAND

He'd already filled in her time of birth: 7:54 p.m., October 18, 1914, and the Place: Hotel de Cheverny, Quebec, and scrawled his own name as the attending physician. Then:

Child's first name: *Marie*

Child's Mother: *Bridget Collins, age 23*

Child's Father:

Bridey had long ago decided that she would never acknowledge Sean Corkoran as her baby's father. But she wasn't going to condemn her child to illegitimacy by writing *Unknown* in that slot. Her best course, she believed, was to claim that her husband had been killed when the Empress sank. She'd obtained a copy of the Empress's death list from the newspaper office; she and Marie had spent hours going through the list, looking for a man of the right age, unmarried and hopefully unencumbered with a family who might one day show up asking questions.

The names on the list were mainly Europeans: from Poland, Russia, Czechoslovakia, Ukraine, Romania, Greece, Ireland—people who had been returning to their home countries, presumably for reunions with their families—families who would never see their loved ones again.

"Here's one," Marie says. "Ivan Bhrenkov, age 25.

"No," Bridey said firmly. "No Russians."

"Michael O'Connor, age 28, from Dublin."

"Too risky. The guy could be in *Eire do 'Fein* or one of those Irish things—word might leak back to Sean."

They'd gone through dozens more, and then Bridey had spotted a name she recognized. "*Thomas Ross!* I remember him—he was the steward who warned us to get to the life boats." She had only the vaguest impression of Thomas Ross—but thought she could remember his strong jaw and his kind eyes. Though she hadn't known him, she felt a small pang of grief for his loss nonetheless.

"Says on here he was twenty-nine," Marie said. "Hometown Stratford, Ontario. He probably died while he was trying to save people. Someday your little girl will be bragging about him."

"I'm not sure it's right, starting off her life with a lie, though."

Marie snorted. "You think it's better for her to grow up knowing her papa abandoned her mama on a sinking ship? You want her having a coward for a pop?"

Hearing it put that bluntly, Bridey knew she was making the right decision. An imaginary father was better than Sean Corkoran.

And so Thomas Ross's name went in the blank for *Father* on Marie's birth certificate. "Ross," Dr. Grayson said thoughtfully when Bridey handed him the filled-in certificate. "I remember him. Nice chap." And then he winked.

Noodin and Nimki were fascinated by the baby. Ordinarily rough and tumble, the boys were amazingly gentle with her; they learned how to support her head and neck when they cuddled her; they became expert diaper changers and champion burpers.

Then there was Louis Perrault, who could coax the colicy Marie to sleep when Bridey had given up. Something about being cradled to his big chest, being sung to in a hodge-podge of French and English soothed the baby girl to sleep. Louis now had his own studio, right next door to the hotel, although he practically lived in the hotel itself, taking his meals in the Cheverny's dining room, and when bored with his own company, mingling with the hotel's staff, always willing to lend a hand when there was furniture to be moved, heavy luggage to be hauled, a drunk needing evicting. The only thing he would not do was stoke the furnace.

The publication of his sketches of the Empress shipwreck, which had appeared in newspapers and magazines around the world, had made him famous. Consequently, his oil paintings were now in great demand; his original sketches of the shipwreck, made somehow more desirable by the spit and the crumple lines—considered evidence of his artistic temperament—were now on permanent display in Quebec's Musee d'Art. What had most delighted Louis, however, was being asked to teach drawing at the *Académie des beaux-arts de Québec*—he now had dozens of students, with more on a waiting list.

It amused Bridey to see that the man she'd first met when he'd escorted her back to her stateroom on the *Empress*—a man with a wild beard, unkempt hair, and coal-grimed hands, wearing a boiler suit, now had fully embraced the stereotype of an artist. His beard was beautifully barbered; he smelled of cologne, he wore clothes from the finest haberdasher in Quebec—and he topped off his shirts with colorful silk ascots.

Marie adored him; he was as close to a papa figure as she had ever known, but then all children gravitated to Louis; there was something about his size and strength that made them feel safe.

Bridey had worried that because her baby had the name Marie, there might be confusion over whether baby Marie or adult Marie was being referred to, but that problem was solved when Marie Lavalierre announced that hitherto she was to be called by her Ojibwe name—*Memengwa*.

"I don't want my sons forgetting who they are," she said, and made a point of speaking to them as frequently as possible in the Ojibwe tongue. Although she no longer worried about her boys being taken away, she disliked the fact that they were growing up in a white world rather than in her clan's village, where they would have learned the skills, heard the stories, and absorbed what it meant to be Ojibwe. She planned to take them back to Ashquasing every summer, where they could, at least for a few months, live as Ojibwe, know their relatives, learn to fish and hunt and hear the songs of their people sung around campfires.

As Marie spoke to her boys in Ojibwe, baby Marie picked up the language alongside of them. Her first word was *Gaygo*—because she'd heard Memengwa shout it at the twins so often. It meant *Stop that!*

Once Marie learned to walk—and then to run—she was impossible to rein in and was often a partner in crime with Nimki and Noodin. They turned the kitchen's dumb waiter into their own elevator; they slid down bannisters, they roller-skated in the third floor corridor; they built forts and castles out of the suitcases guests had left behind.

They also learned how to charm money out of guests by offering to carry bags or run errands. For a child, a grand hotel was a grand amusement park.

Chapter 40

March, 1919

Pierre Duquenne was the manager of the Hotel de Cheverny. A short man with a round belly and small feet, he had slicked-back hair pomaded to a gloss only equaled by the shine on his expensive shoes. His arched eyebrows and dark, expressive eyes gave him a soulful look somewhat offset by a jaunty whip of mustache that hinted at a bit of the rake. On nights when the ballroom was booked for a banquet or wedding, Duquenne appeared in tuxedo and black tie; on ordinary workdays he wore a superbly tailored gray morning suit with a silk cravat. He claimed to have an Achille's tendon injury—which had kept him from being conscripted into the military when the war broke out, and which forced him to use a polished mahogany cane to walk, but Bridey privately believed the cane was an affectation—a kind of accessory, to be twirled in a playful manner or threateningly brandished during heated arguments.

He was wildly popular with the hotel's guests, particularly the ladies, with whom he flirted shamelessly.

He spent his days at a podium in the hotel's lobby, at the foot of the sweeping double staircase, greeting guests as they entered the hotel—playing up to politicians, cabinet ministers, and minor members of royalty with such adroit flattery he was often mistaken for the French ambassador.

What Pierre Duquenne could not do, however, was run a hotel. He had no interest in the tedious day-to-day affairs of booking and billing, of seeing to it that the bedrooms had clean sheets, the bathrooms were cleaned, tablecloths laundered, the staff were doing their jobs.

But Pierre did have one outstanding gift: he could spot talent and ability, and he'd found it in the young woman who'd rescued his tangled bookkeeping time and again. He began to dump more and more of his unpalatable tasks on her.

So it was Bridey to whom the hotel housekeeper complained that the maids weren't cleaning the bathrooms properly; Bridey who bore the complaints from the hotel's restaurant when, during the war years, they could not obtain prime beef because of rationing; Bridey who saw the potential of the unused space on the first floor and had it converted into a gift shop; Bridey who knew what to do when the balky elevators refused to work.

She was now referred to as *Madame Ross, Hotel Directrice.*

She was given Duquenne's small office behind the front desk, while he took for his own purposes the royal suite on the second floor.

Bridey would have refused the job were it not for the fact that she was able to have Marie in the office with her, sitting at her own small desk beside Bridey's big desk, creating drawings with the paper and colored pencils Louis gave her or playing with her collection of stuffed animals—*never dolls*; Marie had adopted the boys' attitude: dolls were dumb.

Most days Marie ran off to play with Noodin and Nimki, often returning dirt-smudged and with torn clothing, but Bridey didn't mind; if kids were getting dirty, she felt, they were having fun.

THE EMPRESS OF IRELAND

From a fussy, colicy baby, Marie had turned into a sweet-tempered, cheerful child with an overabundance of curiosity and an endless store of "why" questions. Bridey had begun teaching her to read when she was three—a skill she'd picked up with surprising ease. When she wasn't with the twins she could often be found in one of the hotel's window nooks, engrossed in a book.

There came a time when other people's stories weren't enough for Marie: she started creating her own books. Blessed with a vivid imagination, she made up stories about kittens, puppies, butterflies—anything that struck her fancy, printing them on the backs of scrap paper, illustrating them with watercolors lent by Louis, and tying them into book form with yarn. Bridey treasured every creation.

At four and a half years old, Marie was pink-cheeked and blue-eyed, her face framed in soft dark brown curls. Hotel guests frequently commented on her prettiness, which vexed Bridey; She didn't want Marie to become spoiled, vain and self-conscious about her appearance.

Fortunately, Noodin and Nimki cared not a whit about her looks; they roughhoused with her as though she were another boy, and if she fussed about her clothing or hair they soon set her straight.

"Them two would take the mickey out of the Queen of England," Memengwa said of her boys, sighing in exasperation.

Memengwa often dragged Marie off to the kitchen to help with small jobs: peeling apples, rolling out little pie crusts, spreading frosting on cakes. Bridey gave Marie simple jobs in the hotel, too—dusting woodwork, folding towels and pillowcases, and anything else she thought a nearly-five-year-old could handle, because she wanted Marie to experience the good feeling of a job well done. Marie's favorite job was fetching the mail from the outside mailbox, which was built into the hotel's front wall, unlocking it with the little key Bridey had given her, scooping up the day's haul, and running it up to Bridey's desk.

On this raw March day with pebbly sleet falling, Marie came scurrying in, dumped the mail into Bridey's in-box, and excitedly announced, "There's a baby squirrel out on the sidewalk and he's lost his mum and he's scared—can I bring him in and feed him?"

"No, you may not," Bridey automatically responded, because Marie or the twins were always finding stray animals, begging to bring them inside and turn them into pets. Yesterday Noodin had brought in a young otter, which had gone tearing around the lobby, nipping at the hotel guests' heels.

Reaching absently for the top envelope in the bunch, Bridey noted that the return address was Charlesbourg; the letter was from Myrtle, her brother's wife.

Feeeling a frisson of apprehension that lifted the hairs on her neck, Bridey ripped open the envelope, scanned the letter.

Dear Bridget,

If you had troubled yourself to call home more frequently, you would know that your father has been in poor health. He is failing fast now, doctor says his heart is playing out. He may only have a week or two to live. If you want to say your goodbyes you had best come home soon. Myrtle

Chapter 41

"Mama, big bridge, *look!*"

Marie's nose was pressed to the window as the train clattered along the trestle above the Pine River. It was the first time Marie had been on a train and she loved everything about it—the huffing engine, the clacking wheels, the aisles of velvet seats, the wide windows with their views of fields and farms and herds of cows.

Pine River was only five miles from Charlesbourg, recalled Bridey—theirs would be the next stop! Jittery with nerves, she hauled their things down from the shelf—a small suitcase for Marie, a larger one for herself—and the picnic hamper Memengwa had packed with provisions enough for a journey across Canada—even though Charlesbourg was only two hours from Quebec.

Bridey had agonized over whether or not to bring Marie. Sean Corkoran still lived in Charlesbourg, and the possibility of running into him in such a small town had almost made her decide against taking Marie.

Still, this might be Marie's only chance to ever meet her own grandfather—and it would be wrong to deprive her of that chance, even though Bridey's father hadn't expressed any interest in meeting his grandchild; in fact he'd never even sent a note of congratulations when Marie had been born.

But after a great deal of soul-searching Bridey had decided that it was more important for Marie to have at least a faint recollection of her grandfather in years to come, and that the chance to meet him, however briefly, far outweighed the risk of encountering Sean.

Besides, she'd wanted Marie to experience the thrill of a train ride.

"*Charlesbourg!*" boomed the conductor.

"That's us," Bridey told Marie, and they joined the passengers queueing up in the aisle. The train jolted to a stop, the conductor opened the door, and the passengers swarmed out, Marie doing a hop-skip down the steps. The platform was wreathed in clouds of steam from the hissing engine, and the air reeked of coal smoke

Bridey found a hackney outside the station. The taxicabs in Quebec were almost all automobiles these days, but here in Charlesbourg, it was still mostly horse-pulled buggies. Half an hour later they pulled up at 710 Quince Street, at the house where Bridey had grown up—a rambling white two story clapboard.

The driver cheerfully helped Bridey haul their luggage, flashing a grin when she handed him a hefty tip. Unsure of the welcome she was likely to receive, Bridey thought of asking him to wait, but just then the front door opened and Myrtle came hurrying down the steps. She'd been Myrtle Fox when they'd been in school together—a name that suited her ginger hair and narrow chestnut eyes. Funny how things turned out, Bridey thought; her brother Billy had always had crushes on the class belles, the pretty girls who barely gave him a glance, but he'd ended up marrying plain-as-a-potato Myrtle.

"Why, knock me over with a feather!" Myrtle exclaimed. "Bridey! I had no *idea* you was coming. You should have—"

"I sent you a telegram," Bridey cut in. "The Western Union office confirmed it had been delivered to this address."

"Well, I never got no darn telegram." They stared at each other, Bridey certain Myrtle was lying, Myrtle brazening it out, playing the put-upon hostess inconvenienced by relatives so cloddish they showed up on her doorstep without warning. But the fact that her hair was carefully combed, that she'd put on a clean apron over a freshly-ironed blouse, and that she smelled like scented bath powder, gave the lie to her *I had no idea you was coming.*

"How is Pop?" Bridey asked.

"As well as can be—who's this, then?" Myrtle turned to Marie, pretending that she'd only just this moment noticed her.

"I'm Marie," Bridey's daughter piped. She had trouble with her *r's; it* came out Ma-wee. "Mawee Woss."

"Well, now, ain't you something?" Myrtle cooed, her voice all sugary. "And how old are you, honey?"

"Four years old, going on five," Marie said solemnly.

Inside, the house was barely changed from when Bridey had lived here, although the furniture looked shabbier and a faint smell of mildew lingered.

"I'll take you up to your pa, " Myrtle said.

"No need," said Bridey, an edge in her voice. "I haven't forgotten the way." A polite way of saying: *This used to be my home, before you and Billy muscled your way in.*

Showing off, Marie galloped up the stairs in front of Bridey, and at her mother's direction, turned into the first room on the right, the room that had always been Mum and Pop's bedroom.

Her father lay in the big double bed with the carved maple headboard and the peacock blue quilt Mum had bought at Hudson's Department Store years ago.

Albert Collins had always been a big man—he had the muscular build of the stevedore he'd been most of his life. Now he looked small and frail, flesh shrunken on bones, face tinged gray. Seeing Bridey, though, his face lit up.

"Bridey." It came out a rasp, barely above a whisper.

"Hello, Pop." She stooped beside the bed, kissed his forehead. He squirmed to raise himself on his pillow, though this obviously was an effort.

"You look more like your mum all the time," he wheezed.

"Thanks, Pop." She knew he'd loved her mother, Julia, and had always blamed himself for not having been there the day she'd been killed. Julia had asked him to come along with her to the suffragette march, but Albert, fearing the ridicule of his mates, had gone to the pub instead. And come home to the news that his wife had been killed by a drunk driver. "I could have pulled her aside if I'd been there," he'd told Bridey, sobbing. "I could have saved her." It had eaten away at him—knowing that he'd chosen the pub that day over his wife; it had driven him into depression, into drinking, into ignoring the fact that he still had a school-aged daughter who had needed a parent.

When Billy had married Myrtle, the couple had moved in here. Bridey disliked Myrtle, who'd returned the dislike in spades. Bridey grudgingly gave her credit, though—she *had* at least taken care of her dad after Bridey had left.

Albert's gaze went to Marie, who'd hidden behind Bridey and was now peeking around, her eyes wide as she gazed a little fearfully at the old man.

"Now who might this pretty little elf be?" Pop asked. His voice was a whisper; he struggled for breath; it whistled in his throat.

"Mawee," Marie fluted, her voice sweet and breathy.

Albert raised an eyebrow at Bridey. "Your daughter. Who's her pa, then?"

"His name was Thomas Ross, Pops," Bridey said, frowning, unsure how clear her dad's memory was; he seemed confused.

"Ross. That ain't Irish. I hope he's Catholic."

"He was English, Pop. We were married on board the ship. He died in the shipwreck. I wrote to you about it, remember?"

"I ... forget things a lot these days. She's a pretty thing, ain't she? Come give your . ... I guess I'm your grand-dad . . . give us a kiss, sweetheart."

Marie did, planting a tiny smack on the stubbly cheek. How long since someone had shaved him, Bridey wondered, vowing to prod Billy about it.

"Could ya see me to a cup of tea?" Pop croaked. "I get so thirsty. And Myrt—she's always so busy."

"Sure, Pop."

Guilt sank its fangs into her—it should be *her*, not her sister-in-law, looking after her father. Then her memory jarred loose and she remembered why she'd left in the first place. It had been those terrible years after Mum had died, when Bridey was just sixteen. Billy had married Myrtle a few months after Mum's death, and since they couldn't afford to rent a place, they'd simply moved into the family house. Myrtle had swooped in and taken over the cooking and housework, and open warfare had nearly broken out between the two women, Bridey keen to remind Myrtle that *she* was the daughter of the house, Myrtle firing back that Billy was bringing in a paycheck; Billy was paying for every bite Bridey ate. When the job with the Wilberforces had come along, Bridey had jumped at the chance to get away from Myrtle and Billy. In the years since, she'd been back only rarely; this place was no longer her home.

Leaving Marie in Pops's room, showing him how she could string the beads of the do-it-yourself bracelet she'd brought along, Bridey hurried downstairs to fetch the tea. She halted abruptly just outside the kitchen door at the sound of Myrtle's shrill, excited voice.

"The spitting image, I swear! The blue eyes, the hair, the nose—it's *him!*"

Bridey barged through the door, banged the teapot onto the stove, lit the burner, and found the tea cannister. Myrtle was on the wall phone, the trumpet-shaped receiver clamped to her ear. She darted a guilt-ridden glance at Bridey, turned her back, and mumbled into the mouthpiece. "Can't talk now, Trudy. Honestly,

I don't have a moment of privacy—what with people stopping by without warning, expecting to be waited on hand and foot..."

Trudy! A chill spiked up Bridey's spine.

Trudy was Sean's wife. Bridey's old friends, who kept her up on home town gossip, had tattled that Sean had married Trudy Keefe, who'd also been in Bridey's class at school. At the time—five years ago— the news had pleased her; she'd believed that a safely-married Sean would never bother her again.

But Myrtle and Trudy were apparently chummy, and she was almost certain that when Myrtle had said *spitting image* she'd meant *Sean's* spitting image. And it was all there in her daughter's face, the likeness, wasn't it?

What a mistake it had been bringing Marie here, Bridey thought, her heart thumping into a frenzied rhythm. Any second now Sean might show up on the doorstep, demanding to see the child she'd claimed to have miscarried.

Her father didn't have long to live—that much was obvious. She had a duty as a loving daughter, to see him through his last hours. But she was a mother now, too, and her first duty was to protect her daughter.

She poured the tea into a cup, hurried upstairs, set it by Pop's bedside.

"I have to go, Pops," she said. "I'm sorry."

But he was asleep, his chest gently rising and falling. She kissed his forehead, a raw ache in her throat, aware that this might be the last time she'd see her father, but her heartbreak was obliterated by her fear, by the overwhelming urge to flee.

The train left at five. They could still make it. Tired and cranky, Marie balked and whined; Bridey had to scoop her up and carry her, edging out through the side door, which opened onto the porch. Their suitcases were still sitting there—luckily, Myrtle had been too churlish to bring them inside—her nasty way of making Bridey feel unwelcome.

Suitcases in hand, she and Marie scuttled away as furtively as hotel guests skipping out on a bill.

Chapter 42

The minute Trudy set eyes on the little girl she knew Myrtle had been right. It *was* Sean's child. Hadn't her mother-in-law shown her dozens of photos of Sean as a small boy? Take away the girl's long curls and she was a dead ringer for Sean as he'd looked in a pony cart photo at age four.

She *was* a pretty child, no disputing that. Well-dressed too, in a pricey-looking red wool coat with a white tam-o'shanter hat and darling little white boots.

Arms outstretched for balance, the child was walking along the tops of the benches in the station's waiting room, making train noises and singing out "Mama, I'm going to Toronto! Mama, I'm going to Montreal, Mama, I'm going *alllll* the way to Nova Scotia—*wooo wooo wooooo!*"

And the woman was laughing! Perched atop a suitcase in an utterly unladylike manner, she was egging on the little brat, calling out the names of more cities. Trudy itched to yank the child off the bench. She'd *smack* the misbehavior out of her! She'd plunk the little imp down on a seat and make her sit prim and proper, hands folded in lap.

That child needed to be taught how to behave.

And Trudy knew exactly how to accomplish that. Hadn't she raised her three younger sisters when Ma had been sick all those years; hadn't she learned how to deal with bratty behavior?

Sometimes she'd used a hazel switch on her sisters; sometimes a belt, a carpet beater—whatever was to hand,

If all went to plan, she'd soon have the spoiled minx under her thumb, and then— *oh, then, just let her dare set a toe out of line!* There's be no more larking about in public places. No more fancy coats and boots either—they'd be sold off to a second hand shop *tout de suite!* Trudy would use the money to buy something nice for herself—Sean never gave her any spending money.

She'd rushed over to Myrtle's after the phone call today, eager to see for herself what Myrtle was prattling about, but it'd taken her a long time to powder her face and find her hat, and by the time she had arrived at Myrt's, it'd been too late.

"She done a flit," Myrtle said sourly. "Takes the brat and her luggage and trots off down the sidewalk, nose in the air. Aiming for the train station, I shouldn't wonder."

Mad with curiosity, Trudy had hailed a brougham and headed for the station. She'd never been here, never having had the need to travel outside of Charlesbourg. The well-dressed passengers lounging about the elegant, high-ceilinged waiting room or nibbling overpriced pastries in the little tea room made her feel countrified and uncouth.

She'd spotted Bridey and the child as soon as she'd walked in, what with the little girl being so noisy, jumping about, singing snatches of songs, making people nearby look at her and smile. *An attention-seeker, just like her mother!* Keeping low, Trudy skulked behind a luggage cart. Now she could spy on Bridey without the hussy even realizing she was here.

Peering through a gap, Trudy carefully noted every detail of Bridey's appearance. She was the same age as Trudy—nearly thirty—but could have passed for younger. She had wide, pretty eyes and a clear complexion—and she was wearing *lipstick,* the tart! Her hair was a rich shade of auburn, undoubtedly *dyed.* Tiny silver earrings sparkled in her ears, and she wore a pale gray traveling suit with an apricot blouse—chi-chi and expensive-looking.

Trudy eyed the little girl. The dark hair, the coloring— the resemblance to Sean practically slapped you in the face! Trudy knew that Sean had dated Bridey years ago; in fact Mrs. Corkoran still kept a photograph of Sean and Bridey together, taken on the Corkorans' front lawn. "They was engaged, you know, Bridey and my Sean," Mrs. Corkoran had said airily.

Engaged in what, Trudy thought, scowling at the little girl, who was skipping over to the water fountain. Bridey, who'd been in Trudy's grade at school, had struck her as the prissy, prudish sort—always with her nose stuck in a book, the kind of girl who wouldn't give a fella a good night kiss because it might smudge her reputation. But now Trudy saw that the goody-two-shoes image was a sham; all the while Bridey Collins had been putting out. She was a slut, a slattern, a strumpet, and she'd probably tricked Sean into getting her pregnant!

Myrtle had said the little girl was almost five. Add in nine months and she would have been conceived in 1913 or 1914, right around the time Bridey and Sean were still going out together.

It was so unfair! Here was Bridey Collins, who'd fornicated outside of marriage, and now was prancing around in her stylish city clothes, holding her head up like a decent woman, flaunting her bastard brat as though she was as good as anyone! And here was Myrtle, no baby after five years of marriage, people looking down on her, thinking the lack of kids was *her* fault. Well, they were wrong! It was *Sean* who didn't do his husbandly duty, who was out until all hours carousing with his bum friends, and when Myrtle complained he gave her a taste of his fists.

And now Myrtle understood why. He didn't desire his plain, hard-working wife, whose dowry had paid for the house they lived in, whose papa had given him a cushy job in the family's furniture business. And *why?* Because he was yearning after Bridey, the girl who'd let him do dirty things! There was a term for it, Trudy thought; her friend Clara had used that phrase in her divorce proceedings. *Alienation of affection, that was it!* Bridey had alienated her husband's affection, had deprived Trudy of her own chance to have children, the selfish bitch, swanning around showing off her tiny replica of Sean, the little girl who ought by rights to have been *her* child!

It was almost as though that trollop had *kidnapped* her child, Trudy thought, by now so worked up that she considered marching up to the policeman by the door and reporting a child-snatching.

"It was that woman over there!" she'd inform him. "I turned my back for just one second and she snuck off with my little girl!"

How different their marriage would be if she and Sean had a child! She had once broached the subject of adopting a baby; the idea had so upset him that he'd blackened her eye. But it would be different with a child of his own blood, Trudy reasoned. He'd be able to see himself in the little girl's face; he would be proud to show her off; and he would be grateful to Trudy for bringing about the reunion with a child lost to him for all those years. The little girl—Trudy was already planning to rename her—*Henrietta maybe, or Marigold*—would restore their marriage. Sean wouldn't spend as much time at the pub—no, he'd be too busy doing all those things doting papas did: teaching the child to roller-skate, to ride a pony, to sled down a hill, to build a snowman. And Trudy would make sure she was part of the fun. They'd go for Sunday walks together, the little girl between them, swinging on their hands. They'd go to Mass as a family; she could just imagine the admiring looks from parishioners as she and Sean walked into church with their daughter between them, all white-gloved and rosy-cheeked. But just let the minx start up with those tomboyish antics —oh *just let her try!* Once

Trudy locked her in a closet for a few days and fed her naught but bread and water, she'd learn to mend her ways!

"The five-ten train to Quebec City will be loading on Platform Three," a conductor bellowed into a megaphone as a rumble announced an approaching train.

Bridey Collins and the little girl popped off their bench and began making their way through the crowd toward Platform Three, Bridey struggling to carry two suitcases—hers and the girl's. Trudy followed, hanging back—but not too far back, because a plan was forming in her mind. Keeping a few feet behind, Trudy stalked her prey, keeping an eye on Bridey, noticing how slim she was—hardly anything to her at all! If she happened to be standing at the edge of the platform, it would just take a single hard push to send her over the edge, onto the tracks, as the locomotive roared down upon her.

In the crush and confusion no one would see who'd done it! She could snatch up the child, shove her way against the tide of passengers standing around gazing in horror at the bloody mess of flesh and bone beneath the lethal steel wheels—and be out of the station before anyone ever—

Trudy let out a cry of pain as her ankle turned—she'd stepped on an apple core carelessly thrown on the station floor! Pain shot up her leg, and she staggered against a pillar, clutching her leg, moaning.

"Madame?" A man in a derby hat, a well-dressed man with a toothbrush mustache and close-set eyes, stepped up to her and cupped her elbow, all solicitude. "Are you injured?"

"I . . . I don't really . . . I'm not . . . " *They were getting away!* She could just glimpse the girl's red coat as mother and daughter threaded their way through the crowd.

"I saw what happened," the man said, tipping his hat to reveal a receding hairline. "You stumbled over something on the floor. Terribly careless—criminally negligent on the part of the Northwest and Atlantic Railway, in fact! You could have been badly hurt! Perhaps you would like me to escort you to seek medical help?"

"No!" *She wanted to push him out of the way; she had to catch up with Bridey, she had to—*

But the damned pest was thrusting something into her hand.

"My card, Madam, if you should decide to pursue compensation. Maxfield Purbeck, attorney at law. My practice is on High Street here in town."

A lawyer! *The last thing in the world she needed to deal with right now was some small-time ambulance chaser!*

Disappointed by her lack of interest in sueing, the lawyer turned away, but Trudy barely noticed. The train was pulling out of the station, leaving clouds of steam in its wake. Would she really have gone through with it, Trudy wondered, coughing from the lingering coal smoke. Would she really have shoved that painted, powdered tart in front of an oncoming train, committed murder in order to possess a child who should have been hers in the first place?

She realized that she was still holding the lawyer's card. *High Street!* Why, that was on her way home! She must have been suffering from temporary insanity, thinking of murder and child-snatching when there were *much* cleverer ways of achieving her goals.

She hadn't liked Maxfield Purbeck. He'd seemed a bit of a sharpie—sly and opportunistic. But when it came down to it, wasn't that exactly the kind of person she needed?

Chapter 43

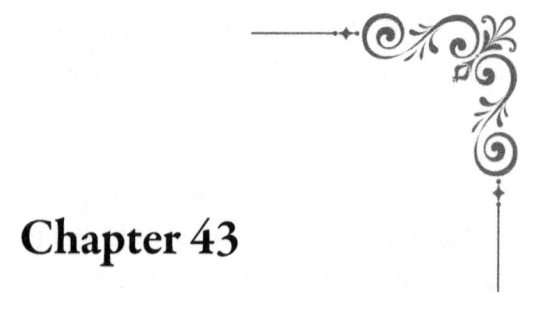

Quebec Arrondissement 3 Family Court

"Mr. Corkoran, is it true that you had carnal relations with Miss Collins?" asked the lawyer, directing his question to the man sitting in the witness chair.

"Oh, yeah, that's true for cert. Her was willing and I was primed and . . . the two of us was already engaged y'know, planning to be married, like. I'd already gave Bridey a ring what cost me two week's pay, a real nice emerald with diamond chips—I donno what she ever done with it, probably pawned it to buy herself stockings or hats or some such frippery. That gal had a streak of vanity pure through, always wanting attention for how she looked."

The last time Bridey had seen Sean Corkoran he'd been lathered in suds from the soapy dishpan she'd been beating him with.

Today, sitting in the witness chair in front of the judge, legs casually crossed, Sean was clean-shaven, his hair carefully parted, his nails trimmed. Wearing a dapper suit and sharply-pressed trousers, an expensive-looking watch hanging by a chain from a pocket, Sean was the epitome of the respectable citizen.

He'd always had the gift of blarney, but now, Bridey thought bitterly, he'd mastered the ability to take threads of truth and weave them into a tapestry of lies. Two weeks' wages for an engagement ring—*what a joke!* Sean didn't have a job back then; he couldn't have afforded a gumball machine ring!

Yet he'd managed, with a few well-chosen phrases, to portray Bridey as vain, shallow, and attention-seeking. Not to mention promiscuous.

"So I figured it was okay if the two of us went at it," Sean continued. "We was husband and wife in the eyes of the Lord, right? It would only be a couple months before we d had a priest say the words that made it all legal-like to go to bed together."

Sean's eyes flickered to Bridey's; his were cool and mocking. This was his revenge, she realized; his payback for the way she'd humiliated him when she'd told him she'd rather drown than marry him; now it would be *her* turn to be shamed, to be punished.

"When was this?" asked Maxfield Purbeck, a small, thin man with a narrow mustache, pomaded hair, and a bad case of denture breath. He was representing the Corkorans; it had been Purbeck who'd filed the petition for termination of Bridey's rights as a parent on the grounds that Sean Corkoran was the child's biological father.

The notification of legal proceedings had come out of the blue only a week ago, a thunderbolt in the form of an official-looking document ordering Bridey to appear in court on July ninth in regard to retaining custody of one Marie Collins, age five, her parental rights being challenged by a Mr. And Mrs. Sean Corkoran of Charlesbourg, Quebec Province.

Terrified at the thought of losing Marie, Bridey had gone into a tailspin. Ordinarily she was decisive and well-organized; as the manager of a huge hotel, she dealt with all kinds of problems on a daily basis, but she'd lost her footing; found herself unable to think straight, her sleep haunted by nightmares. She'd entertained wild thoughts of fleeing, taking Marie and lamming it down into the States.

What if she was caught, though? They'd throw her in jail and make Marie a ward of the court. Bridey would end up with a criminal record—and no judge would award custody of a child to a mother who'd been in jail. In the end, Bridey had decided that the only sensible thing to do was to show up at the custody hearing.

It was being held in a hearing room at the courthouse, in front of a judge, but it was not a trial in the strictest sense, simply an evidentiary hearing; at its culmination, the judge would issue a decree awarding legal custody of the disputed child.

"You must give exact dates," Purbeck now told Sean, "seeing as it determines the likelihood of paternity."

"Lemme see." Sean ran a hand over his jaw. His face was fuller, Bridey noted; he'd put on weight; he had the beginnings of a double chin, and his shirt stretched tight across a round belly; his fondness for beer had finally caught up with him. Bridey had heard through her old Charlesbourg girlfriends that Sean now worked for Trudy's father, who owned a furniture store and had bought his daughter and her husband the large house the couple now lived in.

"Middle of January, February—sometime in there," Sean said, tapping a finger against his chin. "I walked Birdbr—*Bridey*—home from a dance one night. She tells me alls her family is off at some shindig, so nobody's home and did I want to come up to her room?"

"Oh, you wretched *liar!*" Bridey erupted, jumping to her feet, nearly knocking over her chair. "That never happened and you know it!"

"Silence! Sit down, girl." The judge rapped his gavel. His name was Claudius Hurliburt; he was a family court judge who presided over most custody hearings in Quebec, and had a reputation for favoring fathers over mothers. A heavyset man in his fifties, he had a cobweb of hair across a bald pink dome and protuberant olive eyes behind steel-rimmed spectacles.

THE EMPRESS OF IRELAND

Her face flaming, knowing she hadn't done herself any favors with her outburst, Bridey plunked back down, fuming at the unfairness. Why was Sean being allowed to tell his outrageous lies; why was *she* the one told to shut up? She turned around to check on Marie, who was hunched at a table at the back of the courtroom, creating a crayon drawing. She hadn't wanted to bring Marie along, but the court order had stipulated that the child must be present. Only the threat of being jailed for failure to comply had made Bridey obey the order. Marie had been upset at first when she found she wouldn't be allowed to sit next to her mother, but the court matron had given her crayons and paper and she had settled down with them. Marie loved drawing, a talent nurtured by Louis Perrault, who often gave her squares of canvas, brushes and watercolors and encouraged her to paint. The thought that Marie might be ripped away from Louis, from Memengwa, from Nimki and Noodin, who were like her brothers—and from all the other hotel staff who were like family to her —was unbearable to contemplate. Bridey felt literally sick with dread, her stomach in turmoil, her head pounding with pain.

Bridey forced her attention back to the hearing room, where the loathsome Purbeck was asking Sean, "You then engaged in coitus with Miss Collins?"

Sean looked confused. "Engaged in *what*? You mean did we do the thing, did we f—yeah, we done it. I had her."

"Did you ejaculate in her... her womanly parts?" Purbeck asked.

"Uh... yeah."

A small, theatrical moan issued from Trudy, who flung an arm across her forehead like Mary Pickford in a moving picture, upon discovering that the villain has seized the family farm. Seated prominently near the front of the room, Trudy was squeezing every possible drop of drama out of the proceedings, and Bridey wanted nothing more than to march over and slap her face.

Because this was Trudy's doings, all of it. She and Myrtle had cooked this up together, Bridey was sure of it. Sean would never have done this on his own. It must have started with Bridey's visit back home in March.

Bridey hadn't missed how Trudy's gaze had fastened onto her daughter when she and Marie had walked into the hearing room earlier, had seen the greed and longing in Trudy's eyes, the hunger of the childless woman for a child. Of course it wasn't Trudy's fault she'd never had kids, but if she wanted a child so desperately there were plenty of orphans to adopt. *But no—she had fixed on having the child she believed Sean had fathered!*

They intended to use Marie as a prop, Bridey fumed; that was why Sean's lawyer had insisted Marie be brought to the hearing.

She knew that her daughter couldn't understand most of the adult talk in the room—in fact, she didn't even appear to be hearing it, engrossed as she was in her coloring, but Bridey hated that the words *ejaculate* and *coitius* had even been uttered in her child's presence.

"According to birth records obtained from the Registrar's Office," said Purbeck, with the air of a man who'd just fanned out a winning poker hand, "Bridey Collins was delivered of a female child on October 18th of 1914."

He pulled a calendar out of his briefcase and set it down in front of the judge. "As you can see, your honor, I marked off the months. October 18th is exactly nine months and three days after mid-January of that year. A normal pregnancy being nine months, this proves beyond a doubt that the child was fathered by Mr. Corkoran."

"It does not!" shouted Bridey, once again on her feet. "My child's father was Thomas Ross, a steward aboard the *Empress of Ireland*."

"Oh, *really?*" Purbeck turned to face Bridey, eyebrows hoisting up to his hairline. "This is the first I have heard of a supposed father. And were you and this .. umm ... Ross character ... legally wed?"

Bridey took a deep breath, hoping her face wouldn't give her away, because she was terrible at lying. "We were married aboard ship. Captain Kendall performed the ceremony."

Hurliburt's tufted eyebrows rose. "Do you have any proof of this? A marriage certificate, any sort of paperwork?"

"Everything was lost in the shipwreck," Bridey said, aware that a telltale flush was prickling from her neck upward. When she'd randomly chosen Thomas Ross as her supposed husband, the father of her baby, it had never occurred to her that someone might eventually demand proof that a marriage had ever taken place. "And my husband drowned in the shipwreck."

She exhaled sharply, trying to control her temper. "But his name is right there on the birth certificate—Thomas Ross!"

"She claims this husband died in the shipwreck," Purbeck sneered. "How tragic—and how very convenient! With no proof that Miss Collins was indeed wed to this person—the mythical Mr. Ross, then the child subsequently born would have been illegitimate, would it not? Yet here is Mr. Corkoran, a fine upstanding fellow, coming forward wanting to do the right thing, to claim the child as his own, thus sparing her the stigma of bastardry."

Bastardry! The word hung there in the air—a word that would cast a stain on her daughter's entire life.

How dare they?*How. Dare. They!* Just to hear that word uttered within earshot of her innocent child was an outrage! Shaking with anger, Bridey spat her words like hot nails. "Don't you *dare* call her that! My child *was* born of a wedded union!"

"We only have your word for it, Madame," rumbled Judge Hurliburt. "Unless you provide some form of documentation, the court has no recourse but to consider that the child Marie was born outside the bonds of lawful wedlock."

"Your honor, may I call the child up to testify?" asked Purbeck, whose every word virtually oozed oil.

"I will allow it, " Hurliburt said, once again showing blatant favoritism. "Matron, bring the child up here."

"*No—she can't!*" Bridey shouted. "She's too young, she doesn't understand what's happening, this is all very frightening for her—"

"You're out of order," growled Hurliburt "Sit down, madame."

Bridey sat, still seething with rage, wishing Memengwa was here, missing her solid presence. She had a way of staring at people out of flat black eyes, a way of projecting a threat without having to utter a single word. *My spooky medicine woman stare* she called it; Bridey had seen her reduce threatening drunks to drooling idiocy with that look. But Memengwa had taken the boys back to their home village, Ashquasing, for the summer and wouldn't be back for several weeks.

Now, prodded by the matron, Marie bounced up to the judge's desk. "I drew a horse," she informed Hurliburt, not in the least shy in the judge's presence. "A princess is riding him, see?"

The judge nodded, instantly falling under the spell of Marie's charm as most people did. That might work to her advantage, Bridey thought, but her optimism faded as Purbeck oiled his way up front, addressed the judge, and said "I should like to have Mr. Corkoran step up here if you please."

Bridey's stifled a groan, instantly grasping what Purbeck was up to. Sean heaved himself out of his chair and walked up to the front.

He wasn't alone, though. Trudy was stuck to him like a cocklebur. This was *her* game after all; hers was the hand on the chess pieces.

She elbowed Sean until he was standing right next to Marie, directly in front of the judge, making it impossible for him to miss the resemblance between the two: a casual observer would immediately have taken them for father and daughter.

"Well, hello there, Marie," Sean said, looking down at her, adopting a marshmallowy tone. "Do you know who I am?"

Bridey jumped to her feet, heart pounding. "Don't you *dare*—"

"Sit down," growled the judge, glaring at Bridey. "I'll have no female hysterics in here!"

"Don't be scared, honey—I'm your papa," Sean crooned, kneeling to bring himself eye to eye with the little girl. Marie gaped at him, confused, rocking on her heels as she always did when she was nervous. Bridey watched, chafing at her own helplessness, as Sean chucked Marie's chin. "You got a kiss for your daddy, sweetheart?"

"No!" blurted Marie, color blooming in her cheeks. "Don't wanna!" She backed away from Sean as he reached out to hug her. It was Marie at her most willful, and Bridey silently cheered her stubborn daughter, who always knew her own mind.

"It doesn't matter whether you want to or not!" Trudy scolded, shaking her finger in Marie's face. "When an adult tells you to do something, you do it, do you hear me, young lady?" She looked up at the judge, apparently believing she was impressing him. "There'll be none of that *I will* and *I won't* when she's our daughter, Judge—you may be sure of that!"

Seizing Marie's arms, Trudy yanked her toward Sean. "Go on now, you silly little goose, give your Papa a—"

"Get your hands off my daughter!" roared Bridey, shoving aside chairs to get to Marie, snatching her out of Trudy's grip, clasping her against her chest, feeling the little girl's body shaking with silent sobs.

"You see what she's like!" Trudy screeched, staggering backward in simulated fear, as though she'd been assaulted. "That woman is wild, unhinged, unfit to raise a child. The child needs a *normal* home, a Christian home, where she'll be taught good manners, where she'll be disciplined when she needs it, where—"

"Mrs. Corkoran, sit down!" thundered Hurliburt.

Trudy stomped back to her place, and Bridey sank into a chair, holding Marie on her lap, barely able to resist sticking out her tongue at Trudy. *Ha ha, you got busted too!*

Purbeck approached the judge. "My client does have an excellent point, sir. Setting aside the question of paternity, we have to consider the child's best interests. It stands to reason that she'll be better served by being raised in a traditional home, where there is a loving father to protect and guide her. Mr. Corkoran is a well-respected businessman in his community, a fine upstanding citizen, the sort of man a child can look up to. He and his wife own a beautiful house in the finest neighborhood of Charlesbourg and are able to provide a child every possible advantage."

"Don't wanna kiss that man," Marie blubbered, pressed against Bridey's chest, her body trembling.

"You won't have to, I promise," whispered Bridey, determined to keep her word even if it meant fleeing to the far corners of the globe.

"As for the feminine side," Purbeck pontificated, "a child needs a mother who is home all day, who can provide healthy meals, see to the child's moral values, nurse it when it is ill, and ...err....discipline it when it is recalcitrant. There could be no finer exemplar of such a mother than Mrs. Corkoran."

"On the other hand . . ." Purbeck swiveled his beady-eyed gaze to Bridey. "Miss Collins . . . "

"It's Ross. *Mrs.* Ross," Bridey snapped at him.

Purbeck snorted. "Ah, yes, wife to the fabled *Mister* Ross. Until proof is proferred that she was ever married, I shall refer to this woman as Miss Collins. Thus we have an unmarried woman, living in a hotel—hardly a wholesome environment for a young child. Rather than tending to the needs of her child—a woman's natural role—she is occupied with tasks throughout the day—I suppose she makes beds and cleans rooms, that sort of thing—while her child is left to fend for itself, exposed to all sorts of unsavory characters. I recently visited the hotel she makes her domicile—I suppose you could call it a bit of spying, *haha*— and witnessed the child Marie totally unattended, playing with children whose features clearly delineated them as wild Indians. If the child grows up consorting with savages, it will reflect badly on her; it may even stain her reputation for purity when she comes of marriageable age."

Rage swept Bridey; she understood in that moment how a person can actually commit murder in the throes of all-consuming fury. She wanted to throttle the stupid twit prattling about Marie's purity, and referring to those sweet, kind little boys as *savages*.

It was the Corkorans who were the savages, she thought, hands clenching into fists. It would be the most savage cruelty to rip a young child away from her home, from her mother, from Memengwa and Louis and everyone dear and familiar to her, to haul her away like a puppy picked out of a dog pound, to plop her down into a strange house with people who were strangers to her. Trudy, who'd just demonstrated her streak of meanness, would spank her and slap her and break her spirit; Sean would squash everything imaginative and creative out of her.

Never! In five minutes she and Marie could be on a train; it didn't matter where it was going, just away from any place the Corkorans could get their paws on Marie.

Her entire body trembling, Bridey stood, Marie in her arms, readying herself to make a dash for the door. She was half-turned, trying to control her shaking legs, when a man's voice rang out from the back of the room.

"'Scuse me, your honor."

The man who'd called out strode up to the front, paused just short of the judge's desk, and made a show of scanning the room. "Is there a Sean Corkoran present here?"

The judge stared at him, flummoxed. "Who are you, sir, and what do you mean barging into this—"

"Reginald Ludsnap, sir. I'm carrying out an order issued by the Seventh Arrondissement Criminal Court of Quebec to bring in a witness wanted for questioning, that witness's name being Sean Michael Corkoran."

Bridey gaped at him, dumfounded. *Snapper!* The last she'd heard he was working for some detective agency in the States, yet here, against all odds—he stood, unmistakably Snapper, though now tan and muscular, and the hair that'd always been cowlicks and scruff was expertly cut; his suit was superbly tailored and bore an official-looking badge on its lapel. Under the polish though, he had the same brash self-assurance, the same nerve, the same quirk of eyebrow indicating he found the world an absurd place.

"Do you mean to say you're arresting Mr. Corkoran?" harumphed Hurliburt, not finding any of this to his liking.

"Nah, he ain't under arrest, Judge, but this warrant here says he's to accompany me to the Seventh Arrondissement police headquarters for questioning."

Snapper thrust a sheaf of paperwork at Hurliburt, who adjusted his glasses and squinted at it. "*Wanted for Questioning?* I find this most irregular. Why didn't the criminal court authorities notify me prior to—I don't understand what this is in regards to."

"Mr. Corkoran has been named as a person of interest in the theft of two million dollars in silver bullion from the *S.S. Empress of Ireland* in 1914," Snapper said. "The theft still being under investigation, and certain facts having surfaced in the interim, the Quebec Provincial government has reopened their investigation into that theft. And Mr. Corkoran here is going to be helping the authorities in their investigation. Ain't you, Corko?"

Sean, who'd jumped to his feet upon Snapper's dramatic entrance, stared at him, his face alternating between flushed and pale, his mouth working but no sound emerging. He looked like a man out in public who'd suddenly realized he wasn't wearing trousers.

"So he ain't under arrest just now—they'd have had to send a copper for that—but since he's just going to be testifying, I'm to escort him across the street to Police Headquarters. Once his testimony is heard, the Commission in charge will decide whether charges will be levied. And *then* he'll most likely be arrested. Depends on a lot of things."

Snapper gave Sean a long, level look. "Course I can slap cuffs on him if he raises a ruckus, but, having a bad habit of eavesdropping, I believe I heard his lawyer describing him as—how'd he put it—*a law-abiding, upstanding citizen*? So we won't be needing cuffs just now."

He bowed to Hurliburt. "I see you've got business to transact with the prisoner, excuse me, *witness*, Judge, so I'll leave you to it and wait outside, trusting that your bailiff will notify me if the upstanding citizen tries any funny business."

Bridey didn't ask permission to be dismissed; she simply turned and walked out of the hearing room, still holding Marie tightly in her arms. Nobody tried to stop her; everyone was still too stunned by the bombshell that had just landed. Snapper was waiting outside the room, just as she'd known he would be, leaning against a wall, arms folded, lighting a cigarette.

Rushing to hug him, she managed to extinguish his cigarette and burn a hole in her sleeve. " I think you're about to save my life for the second time," Bridey said, laughing—the first laugh she'd been able to manage in days—and oh, how good it felt!

Snapper nodded his head toward the hearing room. "What the hell—'scuse me, that's no way to talk in front of a kiddy—but exactly what the halifax is going on in there? Why is that scum Corkoran anywhere near you?"

"Sean and his wife—they're trying to get custody of Marie. He's claiming to be Marie's father."

"*Him?*" Snapper exploded. "That spineless weakling who rowed off in a lifeboat, leaving you on a sinking ship?"

"Shh," Bridey cautioned. "You have a voice like a bullhorn, Snapper—they can *hear* you in there—"

"They bloody ought to hear it!" Snapper raised his voice to a near-bellow. "That judge ought to know how Sean Corkoran abandoned his sweetheart to die on a sinking ship, while he—stinking coward that he is—rowed off in the last lifeboat."

"Snapper, *shush !*"

"And now that gutless lily-liver thinks he's fit to raise a *kid?*"

A scowling bailiff came to the door, slammed it shut.

"If I spirit you away to get a coffee," Snapper said, "is that judge going to alert the Mounties to track you down?"

"It's a risk I'll take," Bridey said, her spirits rising, now daring to hope for the first time that things might come out in her favor.

In the basement coffee shop, Snapper bought an orange juice for Marie and teas for Bridey and himself.

"Snapper, how are you even *here?*" Bridey asked, stirring sugar into her tea. "I thought you were in the U.S. working for some security company."

"Yeh, I was. Only.. ." The tips of his ears flared red. "See, I met this gal in Montreal, name of Irene—she worked in a men's clothing store and I bought a tie from her. I asked her out and one thing led to another and pretty soon I'm popping the question and we go down to the Registry Office . . . and then. . . "

"One thing leading to yet another . . . " He flipped open his wallet, to a dog-eared photo of two boys, ages about two and three years old, both of them blonde; both with ears that stuck out. "That's John and that's Ned." Snapper couldn't keep the pride out of his voice.

"Oh, Snapper, they're adorable."

"No, they ain't. They're hellions."

"They look just like you."

"Yeh, more's the pity. Funny thing, Bridey. I never wanted kids, didn't want to be tied down, you know? But then, on the Empress, when all them—"

"Your wee ducks."

He grinned, very much the old Snapper. "Yeh. They done in my heart strings, knocked all the common sense out of my head, and next thing I know, I'm changing nappies for my own wee ducks. So, where was I? Oh, yeah, Bakersfield had me stationed in Chicago, but I didn't like being so far from my boys, didn't want 'em growing up hardly knowing me. So when the company opened a branch in Toronto, I tipped the right fella the wink, nabbed the job, packed up my Queenie—"

"Queenie?"

" Descendent of Tabby, my cat on the Empress. Once I got settled in, I heard the authorities has launched a big investigation into the whereabouts of the bullion cargo from the Empress—because they sent divers down to the wreck hunting for it and it was missing. I recalled the dodgy doings that night, like seeing Corkoran with a signal lantern . . . then there was that business about the fake Salvation Army fellas—so my boss pulls strings to get me on the crew investigating the bullion theft, and I get sent to Quebec."

He brushed cigarette ash off Bridey's sleeve. "I knew you were at that big fancy hotel because Louis and me keep in touch, so I stopped by there this morning and find your staff's all in a tizzy because some lowlifes are threatening to take your little princess away, and when I hear the bucket-of-muck in question is Corkoran, I figure to kill two birds with one stone— bring in Corkoran, who's the top person the investigators want to talk to, and at the same time scupper his chances of getting his mitts on your little duckie."

He paused to light a cigarette. "Know who it was that dimed out Corkoran? One of his old mate's brothers, name of Hank Gorcey, who always blamed Sean for not saving his brother Butch when their boat went down. So when word gets around the government is investigating what happened to the bullion, the brother offers up Corkoran on a silver platter." Snapper ground out his cigarette. "And that's how I came to walk into that hearing today. "C'mon, we better get back. Wouldn't want ol' Corko doing a bunk while my back's turned."

"Take your places," Hurliburt growled as Snapper, Bridey and Marie hurried back into the hearing room. "I am now ready to render my verdict."

Bridey was grateful for Snapper's bracing presence at her side, as her knees seemed about to give way. She hadn't expected the judge's decision so quickly!

She wasn't ready! Didn't want to hear it! Ought she grab Marie and run?

"Regarding custody of the child Marie Collins," Hurliburt said, his scowl blistering every adult in the room. "I believe that placement in a traditional home, with both mother and father, is the optimal circumstance for raising a child . . . "

A high, whining buzz had set up in Bridey's ears, and she could barely hear the judge's next words.

"However, certain . . . *factors* . . . have arisen which have required a re-evaluation of the situation. The fact that the presumptive father appears to be under suspicion for the committal of a felony, and may in fact face a period of incarceration, means that the child Marie would, in actual practice, be raised by a step-parent."

Tiny dots, like midges, danced across Bridey's vision, until they coalesced and she seemed to be looking out through a dark tunnel. The high-pitched buzz intensified.

The judge stared over the rims of his spectacles at Trudy Corkoran, whose face was now the color of used chewing gum. "A step-parent who has demonstrated very little affection for said child, while appearing to possess an unfortunate predilection for punishment."

He cleared his throat. "Therefore, my verdict is this: the Corkoran plea for custody is denied. Custody of the child shall remain with Bridget Collins. Or Ross, or whoever the dickens her name actually is."

It was nine at night by the time Bridey and Marie finally got back to the hotel. A fine drizzle was falling and Burt Skiffle, the night doorman, was kept busy running back and forth between arriving guests, shielding them from the rain with the hotel's oversized umbrella.

" I'll get the post, Mama," Marie said eagerly as they passed the hotel's exterior mailbox.

She dashed over to the box, inserted her key, which she proudly wore on a little chain around her neck— and dredged out the mail. It was damp and clumping together by the time they got inside. Bridey threw it on her desk, planning to deal with it in the morning, too wrung out to cope with it tonight, still feeling the effects of the weeks of anxiety over the hearing—a feeling akin to having a guillotine blade poised over her neck.

One of the damp envelopes caught Bridey's eye—good quality linen, official-looking. If this was more legal shenaningans concocted by Trudy ...

It wasn't though; it was an invitation, in beautifully engraved script.

You are hereby invited to be an honored guest at the ceremony marking the dedication of the monument to the victims of the Empress of Ireland tragedy at Rimouski, Quebec Province, on September 26th of this year.

Bridey recalled reading about it in the paper. There was going to be an enormous to-do, complete with government officials and ceremonies and all sorts of solemnities,, to mark the dedication of a memorial to the victims of the shipwreck.

There was a handwritten note at the bottom:

Your name being on a list of Empress survivors, I'm contacting you in regard to the event. A museum of shipwreck artifacts is scheduled to open the day of the dedication. If you happen to have any sort of memorabilia associated with the Empress, please consider donating them to the museum.

We expect a large contingent from Quebec City and have chartered a ship, the SS Champlain, to transport attendees to and from the ceremony. I hope to see you there. Sincerely, Mary (Mitzi) Barbeau

Empress Monument Committee

Chapter 44

September 26, 1921

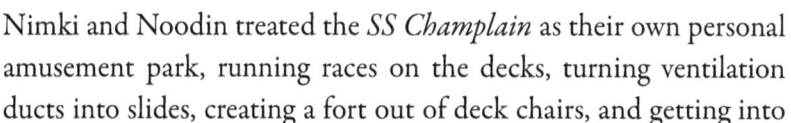

Nimki and Noodin treated the *SS Champlain* as their own personal amusement park, running races on the decks, turning ventilation ducts into slides, creating a fort out of deck chairs, and getting into so much mischief that one steward was heard muttering that keelhauling ought to be brought back as a punishment.

Watching them, grinning at their antics, Charlie Barrows guessed they were around ten or eleven years old—the same age he'd been when he'd stowed away on the *Empress,* hitching a ride to Liverpool in search of his missing dad. The American boy—Tom Reilly—would have been about the same age too, Charlie thought, recalling how he and Tom had played on the cricket pitch only minutes before the ship began to sink. He decided that he'd work that cricket game into the piece he planned to submit today—he'd been sent to cover the . dedication of the monument to the Empress shipwreck victims. As his byline had become more popular, Charlie had discovered that readers most responded to stories that veered into the personal, that made them laugh or tugged their heartstrings.

The thrill of reporting had never palled for Charlie, who had leapfrogged from selling the *Quebec Journal* on street corners to becoming a reporter for it.

As a newsboy, he'd read every word of every issue of the *Journal*. Other guys his age had boxers and hockey players as idols, but Charlie's heroes had always been the reporters who told the stories of the killer blizzards, the logging accidents, the whiskey barons getting rich on supplying booze to a U.S. dry under Prohibition, on crooked politicians, on lumber companies whose clear-cutting caused devastating mudslides... He'd begun to think that he might have the talent to write a slam-bang story himself, but the editors of a big city newspaper weren't about to give up precious page space to a kid who flogged papers on the street.

Then one day Charlie, whose hard life had taught him the wisdom of seizing a chance when the opportunity presented itself—had found himself in the right spot at the right time—at the scene of a dockside warehouse fire. He'd scribbled up a report on the spot, then run it over to the *Journal* offices. Panting and sweaty, he'd thrust his piece at the News Editor, who'd said he might possibly consider running it.

Seeing the story in print next day, with *his* byline, had been the thrill of Charlie's life. The Chief Editor had taken a liking to him, given him more chances at reporting, and had eventually made him a staff writer. It'd been six years now, and Charlie felt that he'd found the spot in life exactly right for him.

Making his way around the ship, occasionally forgetting that this wasn't the *Empress,* because the *Champlain* was configured so similarly, Charlie spotted faces he recognized on the crowded decks. He'd heard rumors that Captain Kendall would be attending the Rimouski ceremony, but thought it was unlikely; through his contacts, he'd learned that Kendall was living a peaceful life in England after serving in the war—and being acclaimed a hero for his actions in rescuing 600 refugees off the coast of Belgium, under enemy fire.

THE EMPRESS OF IRELAND

If only the war had lasted longer, Charlie thought, he'd have found a way to get over there. *Imagine the thrill of reporting from the front lines!*

He spotted a woman on the port aft deck, clutching a hat that was threatening to blow off in the wind. It was Bridey Collins, Charlie realized—now a few years older than she'd been the day she'd nearly jumped off the Empress, but still pretty. She was standing next to James Grayson, the doc all the newspapers had acclaimed as *The True Hero of the Tragedy.*

He and Bridey were deep in conversation. Ever curious, Charlie wondered what they were talking about. And why was Bridey holding an old board?

"I heard about the custody battle you endured," James Grayson said, snatching at Bridey's hat as it made another escape attempt "I'm sorry I wasn't there—I might have been able to help—but unfortunately both my parents had been ill with pneumonia and I had to return to Montreal to care for them. I understand the custody dispute was quite the battle royale?"

"I was terrified they were going to take Marie away. That horrible lawyer kept harping on about Marie being *illegitimate.* Because I had no proof that I'd been married." Bridey jammed her hat back on, still angry about the whole affair.

Grayson's eyes crinkled at the corners. "*Of course* you were married. On board the Empress, by Captain Kendall."

She threw him a sideways look. "You know very well Memengwa and I just cooked that up."

"I know nothing of the sort. Don't forget I was on that ship, too. In fact, I was at your wedding."

"What?" Bridey blinked, confused.

He took an envelope out of his breast pocket and handed it to her. "Be careful—it's the only copy, don't let the wind take it."

Bridey opened the envelope and pulled out a sheet of thick vellum paper, a masterpiece of scrollwork and flourishes and furbelows: *Certificate of Marriage* it read. It stated that Bridget Collins and Thomas J. Ross had been joined in matrimony on May 28th, 1914, by Captain Henry Kendall, whose signature was heretofore affixed, on board the *S.S. Empress of Ireland*, Province of Quebec, Canada.

"If anyone should ask, I was the best man," the doctor said, pointing to a signature under *Witnessed by*. "In fact, I particularly recall how beautiful the bride was. Louis Perrault was there too—see, there's his signature. As for Ross, I recall him being an all-right bloke. Last I saw of him that night he was heading down to third class, arms full of life vests, determined to get those poor devils out."

Bridey pointed to Henry Kendall's signature. "You forged it, right?"

"Not at all. I'm afraid a lot has been going on behind your back, Bridey—and it's all Memengwa's doing. Perhaps it's that sixth sense of hers, but she was convinced that sooner or later, you would once again be in a position where proof of your marriage would be needed. She's the one who went down to the City Registrar's office and obtained that certificate, which I then sent off to Kendall. It took weeks to get to him in England and be sent back—I feared it'd been lost."

Bridey shook her head in disbelief. "Captain Kendall actually signed the certificate? But he must know that he never performed—"

"I had to nudge old Henry a bit, remind him that in the chaos of that night, the trauma of being thrown into the water, his memory of performing a ceremony might have been . . .. umm . ...obscured."

Bridey rolled her eyes. "You, sir, are a bit of a confidence man."

Grayson chuckled. "Not the worst thing I've been called. But in this case a touch of the huckster came in handy."

Clasping the certificate to her breast, Bridey smiled a smile that on a bride would have been described as *radiant*. "Thank you, James. Thank you beyond all hope of expressing my gratitude, beyond—"

Before she could go on in this vein James Grayson simply leaned over and kissed her on the lips. "It's customary to kiss the bride, I believe?"

She looked up into his eyes, which were steady on hers, not wanting to admit, even to herself, how much she had enjoyed that kiss. "Why are we stopping?" she asked.

"*Stopping?*" He stared at her, confused, then wrapped his arm around her waist. "It's another kiss you're wanting?" he murmured in her ear. "Then I'll happily oblige."

"No, the ship!" Bridey said. "The ship is stopping."

Only a person who had survived a shipwreck could understand how a simple change of speed could cause a jolt of alarm. Bridey looked frantically around for Marie, who'd been there just a moment ago, but had somehow slipped away. "Marie!" she cried, panic edging her voice—then saw her daughter skipping toward her, her arms filled with flowers. "A lady gave them to me," Marie chirped. "We're supposed to throw them in the river."

The organizers of the memorial event, Bridey recalled, had provided masses of fresh red poppies, which since the war, had become the flower associated with remembering the dead.

Glancing out over the river, Bridey saw that the ship had drawn up alongside a tall buoy, rocking lazily in the current, the metal structure painted bright green—*for Ireland?* Lantern light flickered inside, a flame to mark the spot where the ship had gone down.

Clutching her poppies, Marie skipped over to the ship's railing. Much *too* close to it for Bridey's comfort.

One thing she'd learned since becoming a mother was that you never ceased being vigilant about your child, that even in deepest sleep, one ear was always cocked for your child's whimper. Danger was all around—speeding autos, runaway horses, the twins' reckless schemes—and now this flimsy looking railing—and Marie had toed up onto its lowest strut and was flinging poppies into the air, laughing as the breeze caught them and scattered them, the blossoms brilliant red-orange against the calm blue of sky, finally whiffling down to the water, to float upon the dark blue surface of the St. Lawrence.

At the moment they were standing, it occurred to Bridey, above the graves of a thousand people, lying deep in those frigid waters, many of them killed in the first brutal seconds of the collision, drowned before they even knew what was happening, their bodies now resting inside the hull of the great liner. "Was I on that ship?" Marie asked, flinging her last poppy over the side.

'Yes, you were, " Bridey said absently, gazing toward the Pointe au Pere lighthouse, remembering seeing that landmark the afternoon she'd stood at the Empress's railing, contemplating ending her life.

"I don't remember," Marie said plaintively.

"You weren't born yet," Bridey said. "You were still inside me."

"But I wanted to see the shipwreck!"

"You didn't see it," Bridey said, remembering the terror of those hours in the frigid river, struggling for her life, trying to protect the child inside her from the blows of floating debris, the buffeting from drowned bodies, "but you most certainly *felt* it."

Bridey wrapped her arms around her daughter, kissed the top of her head, recalling that other kiss just a few moments ago. She'd always thought of James Grayson as a dear friend, *but that kiss*—the way he'd gazed at her, his arm around her waist, the hopefulness in his voice at the prospect of another kiss—was it possible that she and James might move beyond friendship, into something—oh,

THE EMPRESS OF IRELAND

why was she lying to herself?—*this was a day for honesty, for coming to terms with the past*—why not admit to herself that she'd had a crush on James Grayson ever since they'd knelt together over the injured steward on the deck of the sinking Empress, and that James, who'd seen her at her absolute worst—in the agony of childbirth, and smeared with moose poop from that time she'd had to evict the straying moose from the Cheverny's lobby—somehow managed to find her attractive, seemed to value her opinion, and for a busy physician, spent a great deal of his time hanging around her desk at the hotel, engaging her in conversation. *And while she was owning up, why not admit that she spent far too much of her own time fantasizing about a future that might include marriage to James Grayson?*

Chapter 45

Rimouski, Canada, September 26, 1921

The monument was fifteen feet tall, a simple obelisk of shining, pale gray granite, its only decoration a wheat wreath sculpted into the stone. Below the wreath, etched into the stone, were the names of the victims, the print very fine because there were so many to fit in. The monument was set on a grassy swath overlooking the St. Lawrence, whose waters reflected its own wooded banks, ablaze with autumn color, a brilliant contrast to the somber grays and black of the mourners who sat in the open air rows of chairs facing the monument.

Canada's Prime Minister, Sir Robert Borden and a dozen other dignitaries sat in places of honor on the speaker's platform beneath the monument. Adeline McCabe—the Rimouski woman who'd overseen the care and feeding of the Empress survivors after the tragedy, served as Mistress of Ceremonies-a role she seemed born to. As people streamed into the glade looking for seats, the Rimouski High School band played a stirring version of *Land of Hope and Glory*.

Bridey and Marie picked their way through the audience, hunting for chairs. Bridey spotted a heavyset elderly man off to her right, his face hidden by the shadow of a fedora pulled down over his face.

THE EMPRESS OF IRELAND

It was Elmer Wilberforce! As she recognized him, he happened to look up, and must have recognized her in that same moment, because he quickly flapped open a newspaper and hid behind it.

Elmer had never recovered from the public scorn and ridicule of *6Men in a Tub*. Gay, easy-going Quebec didn't mind drunkenness, tolerated a man who had mistresses, and winked at politicians known to be on the take. It could not, however, abide cowardice, and a man who abandoned his wife to drown while he saved himself was met with contempt. Elmer had lost his business, gone bankrupt, and had been forced to sell the mansion on Rue St. Germaine, the house where Bridey had so miserably slaved away. Elmer's fellow lifeboaters had fared no better: the archbishop had been assigned to a prairie province; the others of the Six had been boo'd out of every pub they'd ever entered, and the Tuvalu Island king had been forced to leave the country.

Eager to weasel out of blame for himself, Wilberforce had showed up at the Hotel de Cheverny a few months after the shipwreck, cornered Bridey, and accused her, in vile language, of having abandoned her mistress. "You were responsible for taking care of her," he'd raged, spitting flecks of cigar tobacco. "You should have made sure she got into a boat—you were being paid to take care of her, weren't you? If I had known—"

"But you *did* know!" Bridey shouted. "She sent me to find you—have you pretended to forget that? You told me she could drown for all you cared, and then you yanked my life preserver off and took it for yourself!"

"That never—how *dare* you go around spreading lies!" Elmer huffed. "Probably sold your story to one of those scandal rags! There's libel laws, you know—I could sue you, I could make you regret—"

And that had been the point at which Louis Perrault had come up behind Elmer, grabbed him by the neck and marched him out of the hotel with a growled *"Sortez d'ici, lâche menteur!"*

Well, he *was* a cowardly liar—and Bridey had felt nothing but contempt for Elmer as Louis shoved him out the door. Seeing him now, though, she couldn't help feeling a bit sorry for the man, old and broken, his reputation in tatters, having to hide his face to avoid being recognized.

The assembled notables stood and gave their speeches, a priest sprinkled holy water over the monument, reporters crowded around, photographers took photos, St.Mary's Church choir sang *"They That Go Down to the Sea in Ships"* so movingly that nearly every person present was reduced to tears—and then the ceremony was over and people—many of them red-eyed and sobbing—straggled away. Once the crowd had cleared out Marie and Bridey— still clutching her jagged board—went up to get a closer look at the monument. *So many names, so many lost,* Bridey mused, resting her palm against the sun-warmed granite, tracing the etched lines beneath her fingers, the words of the Psalm sung by the choir now echoing in her mind. *"They that go down to the sea in ships, that do business in great waters; These see the works of the LORD, and his wonders in the deep."*

When she turned away, she found herself facing toward the town, looking up toward the sprawling old school building—it was just as hideous as she remembered it, but obviously back to serving as a school again. The front doors suddenly were flung open and children poured out, scampering onto a playground.

A woman—probably a teacher—emerged and made her way across the yard to a cluster of girls jumping rope. One of the little girls gave her a handle and she started twirling the rope, while a few of the other girls jumped, chanting a rhyme, their voices carrying on the breeze. *"Cinderella, dressed in yellow, went downstairs to kiss her fella ,by mistake, kissed a snake . . . "*

THE EMPRESS OF IRELAND

Bridey waited for the familiar clutch of the heart she experienced whenever she was near a school—a mixture of regret and sadness and self-disgust for not having pursued a teaching degree, the feeling that it should be *her* out there turning the jump rope; should be *her* explaining the fine points of grammar; should be *her* explaining fractions, should be her reading *The Wind in the Willows* aloud to the kids; it should be—

The feeling didn't come.

It was an outworn dream, Bridey realized— a vague version of some other self she was never meant to be, an old-fashioned notion of herself that had come to be replaced by the dazzling reality of who she now was: the mother of a happy, kind, creative daughter; the admired manager of the most elegant hotel in Quebec—a job that was like being a character in a cliffhanger novel whose end she couldn't guess—she had days that began with escorting minor royalty to their suites and ended with hauling drunks out of the building—not to mention that irksome moose that had somehow wandered into the lobby one night and which had to be shooed out by the Fire Department, but not before leaving its souvenirs on the floor and furniture.

Bridey winced as a splinter from her LAND board jabbed her finger. Her dear old lifesaving oar! That night on the St. Lawrence, rowing for her life, she had vowed not to drift, to chart her own path. Had she succeeded?

Why, yes she had! She had indeed, Bridey realized, her gaze skimming over the beautiful, dangerous river, her inner eye scanning the years that had passed since that night.

She *had* rowed against the current. She'd never felt the same passion for teaching as Louis had for his art, as Memengwa had for cooking. Becoming a teacher had only been a means to an end, after all, in a society where the only paying jobs for women were as teachers or nurses. Her goal had been to find a job that would support herself and her child. And she'd done it, hadn't she? She wasn't merely scraping by; she was earning a share of the hotel's profits that would allow her to send Marie to college someday. There'd be no snooty headmistresses stamping DENIED on *her* daughter's admission form!

"Ouchie!" Marie yelped. Lost in her memories, Bridey had accidentally bumped Marie with the board. "Sorry, honey," she said. "I can't wait to get this thing off my hands. If I can just figure out where the museum is."

"M-U-S-E-U-M," Marie spelled aloud, pointing to a building across a half-acre stretch of lawn. "Is that it, Mama?"

Bridey had been picturing a grand stone building like the public museum in Quebec, but the Rimouski Memorial Museum was a new-looking, two-story frame structure overlooking the harbor. "I think so. Well-spotted, Miss Eagle-eye!"

A crowd jostled around the entrance, and it took ten minutes before Bridey and Marie finally could get into the building. Bridey gasped as they walked into the first exhibit—a photo of the *Empress of Ireland* ocean liner so enlarged that it covered an entire wall, giving an impression that the ship itself was docked there. The background was the blue of the river, and the photo had been tinted so that the ship was shown in its original colors, from its coppery funnels to the flags flying from the mast. It almost seemed, Bridey thought, with a strange little jolt of her heart, as though you could walk across a gangplank and step on board the great liner.

"*Seven miles offshore from Rimouski lies the final resting spot of the ocean liner* Empress of Ireland." Marie read out loud from the sign beneath the photo. Now in second grade, she loved to show off her reading. "*The ship left Quebec on May 28th, 1914, bound for Liverpool, England. It was struck by the Norwegian freighter Storstad in a dense fog. The damage to the Empress was so great that its watertight compartments flooded and the ship began to list, sinking in only*

THE EMPRESS OF IRELAND

fourteen minutes, and resulting in the deaths of 1,136 persons. The exhibits displayed here are artifacts of the shipwreck."

They wandered around, Bridey hoping to find a museum volunteer she could hand her board over to, but the crowd was dense and slow-moving, and she didn't spot anyone who appeared to be in charge.

"Look at these funny things," Marie said, stopping in front of a display.

"Those are life vests," Bridey said, surveying the array of worn-looking canvas vests, each with *Empress of Ireland* stenciled across the back.

"*Death vests,* you mean. Them things was killers."

Bridey whipped around, recognizing the voice. "Snapper!" She'd seen him earlier, at the ceremony, and had been expecting that they'd run into him. "Why didn't we see you on the *Champlain*?"

"Business, luv. I was busy playing guard dog to all the bigwigs and politicians that was on that tub, in case some Bolshie had notions of taking pot shots. Now my shift is over, so I decided to wander over here, poke round the shipwreck bits, see if my old pay stub might have turned up."

"Why is this thing a killer?" asked Marie, pointing at the life vest.

The exhibit was marked *Do Not Touch,* but Snapper, ignoring the sign, hefted one of the vests. "Them cork inserts never worked proper—they hardened like cement. See this flap here? It weren't stitched down, so when a person wearing the thing hit the water, that flap flew up and punched 'em in the face. The vests were badly balanced too—some folks were flipped head down in the water. A lot of 'em had broken necks, killed by the thing what was supposed to save 'em."

"Guess I coulda kept that info to myself," Snapper said sheepishly, belatedly realizing that killer life vests were not an appropriate subject for a seven-year-old. "Let's move on—something ahead you'll want to see."

The next exhibit was an enlarged photograph of the *Empress's* crew: sixty or so men and women in stewards' uniforms posed on the ship's deck. Snapper pointed to a man in the second row. "There he is. Tom Ross. Best bloke I ever worked with. That's your pops, Marie. He could have gotten out on the first lifeboat, but his sense of duty was too strong—he went back down to help the ones trapped down there—gave his own life trying to save others."

His voice went a bit hoarse, and Bridey realized that Snapper—*tough, wiseguy, damn-your-eyes Snapper*—was close to tears.

"Never stopped loving you, Tommy," Snapper muttered, his voice so low that Bridey wasn't certain she'd actually heard him say it. His fingers traced across the face of the handsome, dark-haired man in the second row. It was a strong face, the face of a man who made decisions based on his conscience, a man, she now knew, who'd had the courage to love another man, and her heart ached for Snapper.

When Marie was closer to adulthood, Bridey thought, she might tell her the truth—that Thomas Ross hadn't actually been her father; that her own birth had come about because Sean Corcoran had once forced himself on Bridey.

Strange how things worked out, Bridey thought. Sean had only wanted to rob the bullion so he could pay for weapons for the Irish nationalists—but in the end, it hadn't been violence, but Irish wit and the ability to talk rings around their ancient enemies that had finally worn down the British.

Irish diplomacy is the ability to tell someone to go to hell in such a way that they look forward to the trip—one of Bridey's dad's old sayings—it made her smile now, thinking of it.

THE EMPRESS OF IRELAND

Just a few months ago representatives from Ireland and Great Britain had come together to peacefully create an Irish free state out of the counties of southern Ireland.

Sean's dreams of glory and heroism had never materialized, but at least the attempted robbery charges against him had been dropped for lack of evidence, and he hadn't gone to prison. And while the Irish free state was being born, Trudy had given birth to a son—which would, Bridey hoped, prevent the Corkorans from ever pursuing custody of Marie again.

Bridey, Marie, and Snapper walked around exploring more of the displays: one exhibit had a small wooden lifeboat—possibly the very one, Bridey thought, that had saved her life. There were other exhibits, neatly tagged and preserved for posterity: deck chairs and plates and cutlery from the dining room and suitcases and trousers and skirts and shoes—and although Bridey looked for it, there was no sign of the sable coat she'd once mistaken for a bear. Madame's body, sunk with the weight of the coat, had never been recovered. She rose up out of the depths only occasionally, to inhabit Bridey's nightmares.

"Mama, look!" Marie pointed to a display on the wall. It was poorly lit and Bridey didn't see what she was excited about until she tugged at the board Bridey had been hauling around. "It's going to fit!" Marie shrieked.

Now Bridey saw it—a wooden sign displayed on the wall—about five feet long, the words *EMPRESS OF IRE* lettered in emerald green. Whatever came after the IRE was gone—there was only a broken-off jag of board.

Bridey unclenched the board she'd been holding—the board with LAND written on it in ornate green letters, the board she'd used to clumsily chop a path against the current on that deadly night—so that she wouldn't drift out to sea.

"Allow me do the honors?" asked Snapper, and Bridey handed him the board. He lifted it, jimmying it sideways against the first board. After a bit of jiggling and jostling, the jagged ends of the LAND board slotted into the jagged ends of the IRE board as neatly as a piece fitting into a jigsaw.

EMPRESS OF IRELAND it now read.

"I recall this sign," Snapper said, standing back to look up at it. "It hung above the promenade deck, first thing you saw when you came aboard the ship."

A small crowd had gathered around as Snapper fit the board into place; they now began to clap. "*The Empress of Ireland*," Marie read out loud in her clear, sweet voice.

The crowd took it up. "*The Empress of Ireland, The Empress of Ireland.*" It rumbled through the group as a solemn chant; it sounded like an Irish toast, Bridey thought, imagining people in a pub raising their pints, bellowing "*To the Empress of Ireland!*" before downing their drinks.

"Outa way, comin' through."

A photographer loaded down with equipment muscled his way up to the front, framed a shot of the sign, and snapped the photo in an explosion of flash powder. It was that photo, rather than the one of the memorial monument, that appeared on the front page of a dozen Canadian newspapers next day, accompanied by an article under the now-familiar byline of Charles Barrows.

"What happened to your other oar—the cricket bat?" Snapper asked later, as he and Marie and Bridey were having fish and chips at a harborside cafe.

"Memengwa's twins found it one day and that was the last I ever saw of it," Bridey said, laughing.

Anxious to get back to the ship by its four o'clock departure time, they edged around the crowd at the front door, still waiting for tables, and left by what Snapper called the bill-skipper's delight—the rear door, finding themselves in a bin-lined, odorous alley.

"*Pew*! It stinks!" Marie exclaimed, yanking her collar up to her nose.

Something mewled from behind a crumpled cardboard box.

Marie ran to the box and reached into it. "Look!" She was holding a scrawny half-grown kitten. Wet, dirty, and shivering, it was giving full cry to its distress.

"Been living rough all right," said Snapper, as the kitten clawed its way up Marie's front and tried to nestle under her chin.

"He's hungry," Marie declared. "In fact I think he's starving! We've got to feed him!"

Beneath the grunge, the kitten was a beauty, its eyes round and aqua, its fur a melange of russet, caramel, black, and white. It reached up a paw and patted Marie's cheek, leaving a small, muddy imprint—in that moment marking Marie as its own and, Bridey suspected, capturing her heart forever.

"I want to keep him," Marie said. "I want to take him home and take care of him. Can I, Mama?"

Bridey automatically started to say no, then recalled that her child had just endured a day dedicated to mourning the dead, had learned about killer life vests, and had seen her drowned father staring out of a moment snapped in time.

Enough of death. The only possible answer was . . .

"All right," Bridey said, "but you'll have to keep him hidden—the ship might not allow animals on board."

"Tell you what, I'll tuck the kitten into my overcoat," Snapper said. "Nobody'll twig. By the way, this little charmer ain't a *he*. Look at that calico fur—calicoes are always girls."

Hurrying down to the dock, they joined the throngs of Quebec-bound passengers waiting to board.

No one noticed that one of the men trudging up the gangplank had a suspicious bulge in his overcoat; no one suspected that it was caused by a small cat, tucked against his chest, purring contently to the rhythm of Snapper's heartbeat.

Author's Note

I first came across the story of the *Empress* shipwreck years ago and fell under its spell. While the *Titanic* is famous world-wide, the *Empress*, which went down in circumstances equally dramatic and which resulted in nearly as devastating a loss of lives, is virtually unknown.

Why did this tragedy fade into obscurity? Perhaps it's because there were no Astors, no Guggenheims—no famous people to spark a media frenzy; the passengers were mostly European immigrants, ordinary people who'd made good lives in Canada and were returning home to relatives.

Then there was World War I. Only two months after the Empress sank, war broke out in Europe; soon battles and trench warfare eclipsed the story of the shipwreck.

The beautiful *Empress* sailed into a fog, and in a way, simply vanished from history. I've attempted to recreate that liner, to imagine its passengers, and to bring their stories back to life in a way only fiction can achieve.

THE EMPRESS OF IRELAND

Q. and A. with Juliet Rosetti:

*Q~ Did a cat really flee the ship before it sailed? A*ccording to existing accounts, this is true: the Empress's crew swore that the ship's cat ran from the deck just before the ship raised anchor. How could I resist putting that cat into the story?

Q ~ *Are the characters in the story based on real people?*

A~Most are fictional but the ship's officers are based on real people. Henry Kendall, the Captain, led an amazingly adventuresome life; the account of his nearly being murdered on the *Iolanthe*, of jumping ship, of sailing back to England on a leaking freighter—it sounds like the stuff of adventure novels, but it's all true—and I didn't even go into Kendall's capture of the murderous criminal Crippen.

Kendall was cleared of responsibility for the Empress shipwreck by the Inquiry Commission, but his career was under a cloud thenceforth. However, he redeemed his reputation by his courageous actions during World War I, rescuing 600 refugees sheltering at the British Consulate in Belgium as the Germans advanced. Captaining the *S.S. Montrose,* he worked out a plan to load the refugees into an old hulk, the *Montreal,* and have the working ship tow the older ship until all reached safety in England. He also survived an attack by a Kaiserliche marine submarine later in the war.

~Dr. James Grayson is based on the real-life Dr. James Grant, a recent medical school graduate who signed on as ship's doctor for the Empress. Escaping the ship moments before it sank, he was picked up by a lifeboat and taken to the Storstad, where he set up a makeshift infirmary and treated shock, lacerations, broken bones and hypothermia, all the while wearing his pajama top and pants held up by rope; there supposedly is a photo showing him in this garb, though, sadly, I didn't find it. He was considered by most survivors the "real hero" of the tragedy.

Q~Was there actually silver bullion aboard the ship?

A~Yes, the bullion, which today would be worth $20 billion, was being shipped to Europe by sea, considered to be the safest, most efficient way. The attempted robbery of the bullion is fiction; the bullion actually sank with the ship. There have been attempts to retrieve it, but the wreck lies 130 feet below the surface and diving is very difficult.

Q~*In your story, you have Memengwa mistaking an overturned boat for pine trees on an island. Is this based on factual accounts?*

One of the shipwreck survivors, a man, swam away from the ship, aiming for what he believed to be a piney island, only to discover that the "trees" were actually survivors atop a boat holding up oars.

Q~ *Are the killer lifeboats based on fact?*

A~Several lifeboats reportedly broke loose and rolled around decks. Witnesses reported seeing one of the boats slam into women clustered at a railing, taking them overboard, probably to their deaths.

Q~ *A cricket pitch on the ship—artistic liberty?*

A~ No, this is factual; there are photos taken of the ship's cricket pitch, located mid-ship on the second class shelter deck.

Q~ *Were Indigenous children really taken from their parents as described in the story?* ~A~ The parts of the story describing how indigenous children were wrenched from their families is, sadly, historically accurate. Many children were treated brutally; many died. According to some accounts, more than 150,000 indigenous children were taken from their families in communities across Canada and sent to what were called Residential schools. The same thing happened to many indigenous children in the United States.

Q~*Was there really a Hotel de Cheverny?*

A~Bridey's hotel is based on the Hotel du Frontenac, Quebec's most famous landmark. I had the good fortune to stay in that hotel during a holiday in Quebec and loved the place so much I resolved to put it into a story, though unfortunately, I had to disguise the name.

Translations: *Hva i Guds navn gjor dere idioter?* What in God's name are you idiots doing?

Dumme menn! Gud frelse oss fra mennesker og deres dumhet! (Stupid men! God save us from men and their stupidity!)

Har du dritt for hjernen?" (Do you have shit for brains?)

Sortez d'ici, lache menteur (Get out of here, you lying coward!)

Acknowledgements

Many thanks to James Croall, who wrote the excellent, informative *Fourteen Minutes: the Sinking of the Empress of Ireland*, which was my most valuable source when researching; I recommend it to anyone interested in learning more about the *Empress*.

Thanks to my O'Connell siblings who encouraged me throughout the writing of this book.

Also thanks to Tim Dantoin, who suggested the Irish independence theme, and Kathryn Cray, who generated the stowaway idea.

The Hotel D'Frontenac, above the St. Lawrence River

JULIET ROSETTI

Also by Juliet Rosetti

Kilts
Second Sight
You're Not Who They Say You Are
Night of the Burning Tents
Return to Sender
Cut
The Care & Feeding of Orphans and Strays
Second Sight
The Empress of Ireland

Watch for more at https://julietrosetti.net/.

About the Author

Juliet Rosetti is the author of several books of historical fiction, including *Second Sight,* the story of Yorkshire's famed Mother Shipton, as well as *The Escape Diaries,* a romantic suspense series, and several young adult historical fiction novels. She lives in Wisconsin. You can find her on Facebook and Blue Sky.

Read more at https://julietrosetti.net/.

www.ingramcontent.com/pod-product-compliance
Lightning Source LLC
LaVergne TN
LVHW011229160525
811381LV00007B/95